The

Widsters

Widowed Sisters
Discover Travel Therapy

BECKY ANDERSEN

ISBN (paperback) 978-1-7338535-0-7
ISBN (electronic) 978-1-7338535-1-4

Cover & Interior Design: Tru Publishing
www.trupublishing.com

Printed in the United States

Dedication

*To my husband, Dave, whose endless support
and love made this novel possible.*

Also by Becky Andersen

You've seen ads for online dating on television, in newspapers, and (naturally) on computer popups. The models are cute, handsome, young, or at least looking good for their age. But what REALLY happens when a computer semi-illiterate 60ish widow is prodded into this very 21st century form of dating? Anyone who has embraced the concept of online dating, no matter at what age, will find her adventures laugh-out-loud funny and charming.

Contents

Contents

Chapter 1

The Widsters

"You know, it really isn't so bad being a widow when you think about it."

I sometimes speak without thinking, never vice versa. And there are times when I think of something interesting that I feel I should share my thoughts. This morning as my sister, Tuney, and I were traveling, I thought about being a widow. And since for once I had someone to talk to besides myself, I voiced what I thought was a very interesting analysis of widowhood.

Tuney was driving and she shook her head slightly as if she wasn't sure she'd heard me correctly. She took her eyes off the road long enough to look at me in disbelief. Uh-oh!

"What did you say?" That question wasn't uttered politely.

Now I know she heard me the first time, but I played along. I raised my voice. "I said, it really isn't so bad being a widow. When you think about it, that is."

I halfway expected her to praise me for such a profound statement. Halfway, please note. We're sisters, she's the oldest, and evidently that makes me the annoying one. She narrowed her eyes and shot a look of disgust at me. But since that's

1

happened once or twice - times a million – during our lives together, it didn't bother me any.

"Uhhh! Why would you say that, Cardi?" she said irritably.

In her defense, just so you don't get me wrong (because I truly do adore my sis,) she'd been unusually short-tempered ever since her husband died over a year ago. I pointed that out to her once. Only once. Tuney got really defensive and told me I'd been just as irritable when my husband died a little over two years ago, so she could be, too. Huh! That surprised me. But after thinking about it, I realized she was probably right. Maybe all widows are that way. I'm not now. Maybe it's just that year of firsts. I don't like to think about that, mainly because it's all a blur.

Before I could explain why I'd thought about it not being bad to be a widow, Tuney slowed the car down and pulled off the road into the parking area of a small roadside park. Ye gads, what was so wrong with what I said? Out of the corner of my eye, I saw her fingers tighten around the steering wheel. I took a chance to turn my head towards her. I watched her shoulders heave as she willed herself to breathe evenly so that her blood pressure wouldn't spike the way it had been doing the past year. Her lips were curled under as she bit them, and she raised one eyebrow which meant I was going to be talked to as if I were a child. *Oh, great!* I think anyone who's the youngest in a family develops survival instincts. Mine kicked in. *I'm just going to act like I don't know she's ticked off,* I thought.

"Well, Tuney," I chirped, trying to fool her into thinking I was totally oblivious that I'd upset her. "I was just thinking and…" Rats! I glanced at her car clock and got distracted by the time. Distraction – It's happening more and more the older I get.

"Hey! Can we talk while you drive? We've only got 45 minutes until the bus leaves! You'd better get back on the road!"

I love Tuney to death, but I'd never let her know how much I look up to her. For as old as we are, we argue, quarrel and debate all the time, just as we did in childhood. On the other hand, I know in my heart my sister would give her life for me – and vice versa. We're there for each other when we need to be. I guess the non-verbal method is our way of showing sisterly love. Our dad always said we both had too much Irish in us. Nowadays, that would never be an excuse, but it was a great reason to use whenever we got in trouble fighting and bickering with each other.

I glanced back at her face and found my eyes locked with hers in a sister-to-sister stare-off. As I stared at my sister, confused as to what I'd said that tripped her trigger, I thought, *Where's Mom when I need her?*

Our Mom had a sixth sense if we were bickering. She'd magically appear before we got too out of control and would only have to say 'Stop it now' in a warning tone to make us both look up at her with all the innocence we could muster. *Us? Stop what?* But we never fooled Mom. She'd just follow up her order with The Look. That froze us, brought a smile to her face, and she'd leave. One of us usually followed her to tattle, while the other one found something else to focus on. The tattler (usually me) ended up being threatened with the loss of a privilege for snitching, given a cookie to sidetrack her, and peace would reign supreme.

Hmmm. Mom. *I'm gonna try it*, I thought.

I pictured our mother. "Stop it. Now!" I said in the same voice I used to break up fights when my own two kids bickered. I lowered my chin and gave Tuney The Look with the steeliest eyes I could muster. Dang it! It didn't faze her, except she frowned at me like I was crazy.

As we continued to stare, each too stubborn to quit, it flashed through my mind that we were going to be stuck with each other for a three day-two night "Get to Know Your State" tour. And I'm the one that booked the trip! The tour guide, Amy, is the daughter of a cousin of my late husband Kris, and she had been urging me for several months to take a trip with her. *Cardi, it'll be a blast*, she'd say. *Cardi, I love you and you'll have fun. Cardi, bring your sister – the tours usually have lots of people your age.* Like rubbing in the fact that AARP officially declared me a senior citizen almost ten years ago is going to make me want to ride with a bunch of other old people? No, thank you.

Shortly after Amy's last appeal, Tuney and I had lunch with some friends who'd been on a tour, and they loved it. So, out of curiosity – and realizing that life is way too short – I called Amy back and said yes. Tuney said no. However, I've had 64 years' experience talking my slightly older sister into doing what I want. She gave up when I pointed out that while we've lived in Iowa our whole lives, we've never been to the southeastern section before. But, she said, she and her late husband Tommy in fact had – when they took a trip to St. Louis, they'd driven I-80 to Des Moines, then caught Highway 163 to Highway 34, then caught Highway 27 – the Avenue of Saints, so she really didn't need to go back to that area.

Big whoop, I told her. I hid the fact that her ability to remember details worries me. Not that I worry about *her*, but it worries me that I don't remember things like that anymore. Who remembers the numbers of highways, anyway? And I'm younger than she is! But I kept telling Tuney that Kris and

Tommy would want us to go. Tuney gave in, partly, I'm sure, because she knew I wouldn't stop bringing up the subject, and partly because she agreed with me that Tommy would want her to go out and have fun.

She insisted on driving us to Des Moines to meet the bus. Nice of her, but she's not fooling me. This way, she has control over the radio. She picked me up fifteen minutes ago at 6 a.m. She looked tired, and I told her so. She told me she woke up way before the alarm went off, maybe subconsciously afraid that she'd either sleep through an alarm, or the clock alarm setting on her cell phone wouldn't work. In her 65 years, I've never known that to happen to her, but it didn't keep her from worrying.

I heaved a big sigh and finally quit staring at Tuney. I glanced at the clock again. We need to get going if we're going to catch the bus. I put down a deposit of $400 on the trip, and Tuney hadn't paid her half yet. I have no idea what annoyed her, but I'll be darned if I'm the first to apologize. I threw my hands up in the air in exasperation.

"Tuney, what is wrong with you? Why are you stopping?"

"Why do you think?" Tuney answered sarcastically.

I can be sarcastic, too. "I'm gonna guess you need a bathroom break already. After all, it's been a whole fifteen minutes since you've been on the road."

"Oh, come off it, Cardi!" Tuney's voice was raised in impatience.

I leaned back in my seat and blinked at Tuney.

"Well, what, then?" I sneered. Tuney just glared at me, then rolled her eyes, and sputtered,

"What do you mean 'WHAT?' What kind of comment was that? Good heavens, Cardi! Being a widow isn't so *bad?*"

She raised her hands in disbelief. "It's the most horrible thing in the world! I feel like life is over!" She threw herself back into her seat, crossed her arms and stared out the front windshield.

Whoa! My turn to express indignation. I heaved a big sigh. I planned this trip. I planned it not only for myself, but for Tuney as well. If Tuney was going to blow up when I was just hoping to exchange some dialogue, it was going to be a long trip. She didn't get what I was trying to say, obviously. I turned to my experience dealing with customers at the local bank. Smile. Stay calm. Try to explain. I took a deep breath. Communication, right? Kris always told me communication was the key to civilization.

"Tuney. Chill. I was trying to start a conversation, is all. I'm telling you to think about it. Being a widow is NOT the most horrible thing in the world!" I glanced at my sister, waited for a response, and getting none, decided to look straight ahead like Tuney was doing.

The silence that followed was punctuated by an annoyed sigh expelled from Tuney's nostrils. I snuck a peek sideways at my sister, then blew air out of my cheeks. She can be so obstinate sometimes.

I tried to placate her. Emphasize *tried*. "Wait a sec. Let's not start the trip out like this. Remember, I've been through everything you're going through…"

Tuney interrupted me with a groan of disgust, and spat out, "Don't start preaching to me that you're the expert on losing a husband, Cardamom! I don't want to hear it!" Her cheeks flushed with the heat of anger. She grabbed the steering wheel and squeezed it hard until her knuckles turned white.

I hate when anyone uses my full name. Almost as much as

Tuney hates when anyone uses hers. We both were given unusual names by our mother in an era when all our friends were lucky to have beautiful but more common names, like Deborah, or Tamara, or Susan, or Patricia. Because of Mom's favorite spice I am Cardamom Collins Cooper, 11 months younger in age and 13 months longer a widow than my sister. And I prefer to be called Cardi because the only time I'm called Cardamom is when someone's mad at me. Like right now. My sister Petunia "Tuney" Collins Thompson always wished Mom's favorite flower had been a rose. She certainly was acting a bit "thorny" now and was obviously mad at me. Well, tough, Tuney!

I folded my arms across my chest and glared over at her, but that didn't do any good. Tuney stared stonily ahead with her lower lip stuck out in a pout.

Geez! Were we going to act like little kids?

"Come on," I wheedled. "I'm not preaching! I'm trying to tell you something that I realized after Kris died…" I felt my throat closing and coughed. "You know. After being…alone." And to my horror I started to cry suddenly.

I dug my fists into my eyes. *Quit being a baby,* I told myself. Kris had been dead for two years. I decided a long time ago that I was sick of crying every time I thought of him, so I just don't cry anymore, or at least try my darnedest not to. And *now* I am? I growled, partially to clear my throat, partially because I was disgusted at myself and partially because sometimes Tuney makes me mad enough I'd just like to growl like an animal. I turned my head to look out the passenger side window and brushed aside some stupid tears that had somehow managed to evade my fists and trickle down my cheeks.

Tuney seemed bothered to hear my voice tremble because she reached over and touched my shoulder. I shrugged her off, but I knew I had her attention now. I took a deep breath.

"And besides, you're going to make us miss the bus, and I'm really looking forward to going. I booked this trip – for *us!*" My voice had a bit of a sorrowful whine to it. I always hated when my kids did that to me when they were little. But it usually worked. I am probably not the best parent I could have been. I would get mad at myself for caving into them and start to threaten time-out. Then Kris would step in and diffuse the situation. Good Pop-Bad Mom. It worked for us!

I felt Tuney staring at me for another moment. She dropped her face into her hands. I glanced at her and saw her tears forming, but was it because she and I were fighting after only a few minutes, or that I kind of lost it about Kris? Tuney squeezed her eyes shut tightly, wiped the few tears away that oozed out, and then straightened up.

"Oh, geez. Okay, Cardi. I'm sorry. This isn't like me to be so irritable."

I wanted to correct her, but survival instinct kicked in again and I kept my mouth shut.

"And I don't want to start the trip out like this, either. It's my fault," she continued as she glanced over at me just as I glanced her way.

We both looked away quickly, then after a moment both glanced at each other again. This time, though, we each started grinning reluctantly, then shook our heads simultaneously. I couldn't help it, but I giggled.

"Not to correct you or anything, but it is, too, like you to be irritable," I said with a grin. "Admit it. We're sisters and we must secretly love to squabble."

"Ope! I know," she sighed, surrendering to that fact. Then she chuckled. "Why do you make me so mad, then turn right around and make me laugh?" She batted my arm, half in jest and half because she wanted to punch me like she used to do when we were small. It was a gesture that was always tempered in love, I believe, because we really are close – although anyone who didn't know us well would never have guessed it the way we acted.

"Well, you do the same to me." I looked at her and debated for a second to keep quiet the rest of the trip, or not. Not. "I don't want to make you mad. I just want to have a meaningful conversation with you, and I am not trying to hurt you, or upset you, but if you'd just let me explain…"

She glanced over at me, and knowing my penchant for rambling, interrupted. "Okay, okay. Truce. So, go ahead and finish your thoughts - and explanations, if you have any - about why widowhood isn't so bad."

This time, I rolled my eyes. "Promise you'll listen and not get upset?"

"Nope. But I'm going to start driving again, so don't get me mad, okay?" Tuney – always the big sister. She started the car and got back on the highway with no problem.

I grinned. "I gave up years ago trying to not tick you off. It's never going to happen, especially not at the ages we are now!" I pointed my index finger in the air and made an imaginary chalk mark. "And that's one of the perks of being old – not caring what you say."

"We're not o…" Tuney started to protest but I cut her off.

"Yes, we are, and that's a whole 'nother conversation. But please let me get back to what I said earlier before I forget it!" Forgetfulness was one of my first fears after the shock of Kris's death wore off and I realized I was totally alone in my house. He wasn't going to be around for me when I forgot my phone, my reading glasses, where I put my book – just about everything that I knew I didn't have to bother myself with because I relied on him to keep track of *me*.

Tuney only grunted. I took that as an okay.

"First off, and I'm only saying this because I don't often get the chance to correct you," I glanced slyly at Tuney, who tightened her jaw as if to object, so I quickly added, "You're wrong that losing a husband is the worst thing that can happen. Think of your kids. And the grandkids."

Tuney pursed her lips and straightened up, then bit her lip.

I watched her smugly. "Right? I mean, I can't imagine losing a child or one of the littles. That's not the way it's supposed to be." I twisted over on one hip and earnestly faced her. "I know I'd rather *die* than to lose one of my kids or grandkids." I paused to see what Tuney would say.

Tuney nodded and looked over at me. "Okay. Point taken. I agree losing a child would be more horrible than losing a spouse. So, let's just say being a widow is the second worst thing that could happen."

"For us it would be anyway." I sat back in my seat and paused thoughtfully. I love to expound on things. "Just think of how many millions of women who ever lived in the world have lost spouses and had to find the strength to go on with life. We have to. Our kids are hurt – they just lost their dad. Our grandchildren have lost their grandpa. Although I suppose some people would think it might be even further down a list of things that are bad. But…"

"Cardi!" Tuney wailed. She is much more succinct than I. I think she was half afraid I would start ticking off the list of bad things and get totally off the subject. That has happened once. Or twice.

I grimaced. "Sorry! Okay, about the widow remark: I was just sitting here, and the thought popped into my head that you and I haven't had a trip alone together since college. And now here we are again. Two sisters on a road trip!" I waited for Tuney to express some sort of excitement over this thoughtful statement.

Tuney shook her head in disbelief. "That's it? Why didn't you just say, 'Hey, Tuney, you and I haven't had a road trip for years?' Don't you think that's how a *normal* conversation starts? I do!" Tuney looked back and forth between me and the road.

Ope! I could feel my face fall as I digested Tuney's suggestion for a moment. I shrugged unperturbed, and answered simply, "I guess so. But that's not how my thought process works."

"That's been apparent for years," replied Tuney drily. "Now let me concentrate on driving."

Chapter 2

Eau D'Ewww

I wriggled in my seat, heaved a few sighs, and flipped down the passenger side sun visor to check my makeup in the mirror. Makeup! Makeup was Tuney's and my shared love. Or shared bad habit, more likely. Ever since Mom allowed us to wear it when we were in high school, we've been addicted. We've gone through the various fads with makeup – white pearlized lipstick, barely nude lip gloss, deep red lipstick, liquid cat-eye liner with a wing at the corners, smoky eyes, blue shadow, pink shadow, false eyelashes, thick mascara, mineral foundation powder – and now, concealers for all the brown spots.

As we've aged, Tuney and I combined have probably spent thousands of dollars on anything that promised to erase wrinkles. I even tried Botox before my daughter's wedding. The needle hurt, and I'm afraid of needles. But I soon realized I'm more vain than fearful because once it wore off, I did it again for my 40th class reunion. I thought I looked young, and I felt young. Then I noticed my classmates looked at me funny. Now I just use a little eyeliner and mascara, just so everyone can tell I do have eyelashes. And I dot foundation on all the spots on my face. My main battle for beauty these days, though, is keeping the hairs off my chin and upper lip. I'm losing. I closed the visor mirror. It was too quiet in the car.

"Well, if you're not going to ask how my thought process works, I'll tell you!" I announced.

Tuney looked at me like I was totally daft and rolled her eyes again. I briefly wondered if she'd end this trip with her eyeballs permanently stuck toward the sky. "Where did that… Oh, man, Cardi! I thought that conversation was over. Okay. I give. Explain how your thought process works. Please. I'm dying to hear." She spoke in a tone as dry as the desert.

I rattled on. "You know how I talk off the top of my head. I was just thinking this was going to be a fun trip. And then I thought that it wouldn't be happening if we weren't widowed. And that made me feel sad. Then I thought 'I need to be more positive and find the good things in life,' and so…" I trailed off and shrugged. If Tuney doesn't get it, then I can't force her.

Tuney thought for a moment, then nodded. That encouraged me. Maybe she realized it could be a fun trip. I think she'd agreed to take it, not only because she wanted to get away, but because she thought I could use a break, too.

Grudgingly, she softened. "Okay. Well, thank you for finally dissecting your thought process and sharing it with me," she said sarcastically, but her glance at me came with a little grin, so I knew she wasn't totally irritated any more.

I shot her an equally wry look. Tuney winked at me, hesitated, then said softly, "Just keep in mind that I," she drew a big breath and corrected herself. "*we*'ve, both been through hell. And I know we're both going to survive. But I think my emotions are still a little more raw than yours." She paused, tapped her steering wheel with one hand as though she was giving herself a little pat. "Sometimes I feel like I'm in a nightmare. My life feels so abnormal now, you know?"

I knew all right and nodded. I leaned toward Tuney as far as my seatbelt would allow and managed to touch the top of my head against her shoulder. "It will get a little better. Just keep taking it day by day. That's what I still do," I murmured. I always thought that of us two, Tuney was the leader and I the follower, just by virtue of her being the slightly older one. But when I was thrust unwillingly into the role of first one of us to lose a spouse, I searched high and low for answers on how to continue life without half my heart. Tuney sometimes acted as though that made me an expert on the subject. I'm not. I don't want to be. I'm still searching. But after two years, not as often now.

Tuney reached her left hand across her chest and patted my head. "It's okay, little Widster. We'll make this a fun trip. And maybe it'll be more therapeutic than we both imagined."

I sat up and smiled at Tuney. "Widster? Did you just make that up? I like that term better than just plain widow. Seems more – oh, I don't know – *Familia!*"

"I'm sure others have used it and I must have heard it from somewhere. It's just a shortcut for widowed sister, I guess." Tuney shrugged, then smiled. "After all, our whole family has nicknames, don't we?"

We both chuckled and nodded. When we were little, I loved watching cartoons. It didn't take me long to start calling my older sister Looney Tuney. Tuney had to wait for years until we were in our twenties to find a nickname that was just as irritating to me as Looney Tuney was to her. But she got her revenge not long after I married Kris Cooper. Tuney started calling the new Mrs. Cooper "Cardi Cooper Party Pooper" just to get a rise out of me. It worked. You'd think as adults we'd be far beyond childish name calling. For some reason, we aren't.

Tuney looked at the clock on the car's dashboard. "Geesh! I'd better put the pedal to the metal. What time does the bus leave?"

I pulled the tour itinerary sheet out of my purse. "Oh, *now* you're worried! But don't be. We've got plenty of time. You picked me up twenty minutes early, remember? And even though you stopped back there, that still leaves us fifteen minutes of the extra twenty, and we're only about fifteen minutes from the pick-up point."

Tuney breathed a sigh of relief. "I hate cutting things close, though. I'll just keep it about five above the speed limit." She glanced at her speedometer. "Or six. I don't think I'd get pulled over if I was six miles an hour above the speed limit, would I?" Tuney had never gotten a ticket in her life.

"Don't ask me to condone breaking the law!" I held up my hands as if to push her suggestion away. It's called a speed *limit* for a reason. *You* speeding and breaking the law? Can I call your kids and tell?"

Tuney turned her face to me and stuck her tongue out. "Ha. Ha. Little Miss Perfect. I remember when you…"

For some reason I glanced at the road just in time to see an object of some kind lying right in the path of her tires. "Watch out!" I screeched.

Tuney whipped her head back to the road and my heart dropped in my chest. We both felt a *ka-thug* as the tires rolled over something.

"Holy schnikeys! What did I hit?" Tuney cried as she slowed the car down and pulled over to the side of the road. Frantically, she scanned her rear-view mirror, and I twisted in my seat and peered out the back window.

Before I could make out what had been run over, Tuney got her answer. A ghastly, clinging putrid smell filled the car.

"Ewww! Skunk!" we moaned in unison. We looked at each other with our noses wrinkled.

"Oh, no! Of all the animals to kill, I had to hit a skunk!" Tuney looked back in the rearview mirror and saw something black in the road. No other cars were around. She pulled back onto the highway. "Ewww, yuck! That's nasty! What do I do now?" she wailed. I knew she was probably thinking the same thing that I was. Our first instinct was to call our husbands and tell them. Even if they weren't around to do anything, just hearing their voices, and probably their laughter at our situation, would have helped.

I was still turned in my seat looking out the back window. "It was already road-kill. You just smushed it up pretty good, it looks like." I hate bad smells, so I pinched my nostrils closed. "Ugh. Maybe we need to get to a carwash before we pull up to the bus." Yeah! Maybe that's what Kris would have suggested.

Tuney put one hand over her nose and mouth. "You said we're fifteen minutes away from the bus? I can't drive for fifteen minutes with this stench, or I'll be sick. Is there a car wash nearby, do you suppose?"

I pulled out my phone and a wad of tissue that I stuffed against my nose. "I've got a travel app on this thing that if I can figure out how to use, I'll find where we are." I squinted at the phone for a moment. Then I dropped the tissues on my lap so I could reach down for my purse and pull my reading glasses out. When I wear my contacts, I really rely on my "cheaters."

"Ah, here! There's an exit in about a mile where there's a car wash!"

"Thanks," came Tuney's nasally reply. The disgusting odor was overwhelming and Tuney was holding her nose shut while keeping her hand covering her mouth. She looked over at my phone, frowned, and asked, "Is that a new phone?"

I brightened and although I'd smothered my nose and mouth against the tissues again, Tuney could tell by the crinkle of my eyes that I was smiling at her.

"Yes, it is. I love it!" Then I grimaced. "You know, Kris wouldn't give up his flip phone for anything, so I kept my old one, too. Just a month ago the battery died, and do you know what?"

"You bought a new I-phone," answered Tuney sarcastically.

I ignored her and chattered on. "When I took my flip to Verizon, they said they don't even make the batteries anymore!"

Tuney looked puzzled. "Aren't there new phones that are like a flip? Surely, they make batteries for those. Or couldn't you have found a replacement battery online somewhere?"

"Mmmm, maybe. I probably could have." I hesitated, looked ahead and then continued. Tuney was probably going to think I'm crazy. "But I talked to Kris, which is something I do all the time. I bet you talk to Tommy, too, don't you?" I glanced at Tuney and saw her raise her eyebrows and nod. Encouraged that Tuney hadn't disagreed with me, I continued. "And I told him, 'Kris, honey, if you were here, and your phone died before you did, and you had a chance to get a brand new phone that has all these neat apps like facetime so that we can see the kids since they've moved away,'" I paused to take a breath. "'Well, what would you say to that, Honey?'"

"He'd say 'Bull!'" and Tuney cast a wry look my way and then smirked.

That surprised me. Would Kris really say that? But then I thought about it and finally smiled back. "You're probably right! But you see, Tuney, stuff like this is another example of what I meant about widowhood not being so bad. Kris and I would have *argued* about a new phone if he were still here, and then one of us would have grumbled and been out of sorts for a while. This way, I know he's in heaven watching over me, and that if I ever do anything that he probably wouldn't approve of, I'd *feel* it!" I patted my phone. "I feel he's glad I got caught up with technology. Widowhood made me think about what I need to survive."

"And - you need an I-phone?"

"Absolutely!" I raised my beautiful new phone triumphantly.

"Oh, for Pete's sake! You're just crazy, Cardi!" Tuney waved the air in front of her nose and pointed to the exit ahead. "P-U! Watch for the car wash."

I merely looked at my phone and said, "In two blocks turn left, and it'll be there." I grinned. "And I may be Crazy Cardi, but that's better than being Looney Tuney!"

Tuney shot her right hand out and softly hit my shoulder. We both chuckled, and just like that, our sisterly tiff was over. As Tuney pulled into the carwash, I realized that just talking about Kris to someone else instead of just thinking about him made me feel good. Like he was still here. I need to ask Tuney if it would help her if I talked about Tommy more. I hope she thought about what I said. Other than running over the skunk, she was really enjoying driving. She'd always driven her own car around town, but whenever they went on a trip, Tommy always drove. If she was going to do as I suggested and look for positives in life instead of thinking life was over, she could count being able to drive whenever and wherever she wanted to as a "not so bad thing about being a widow."

Chapter 3

The Bus Trip Begins

Ten minutes later, we were back on the road, having put Tuney's car through the automatic car wash twice. And I volunteered to do the manual wash once in order to really power off the tires and hopefully remove anything "skunk." A slight skunky odor lingered in the car, but Tuney had stopped at a gas station and bought some air deodorizers. Tuney wasn't sure which smelled worse, the overpowering aroma of the deodorizers or the faint but clinging smell of the dead skunk. I thought they were both awful.

We reached our destination in Des Moines with a few minutes to spare, but we were still the last ones to arrive. The tour guide, Amy, and the bus driver, a man Amy introduced to us as Mr. Smith, hurried over to Tuney's car to help unload our suitcases. As soon as Tuney opened the hatch, the skunk smell wafted out. Tuney groaned and glanced at Amy.

"Can you guess why we're late?" Tuney asked. "I pureed some roadkill for the buzzards!"

Amy was tall with a super-smooth bob, hair that shone like it was polished mahogany, and a sprinkle of freckles across her nose. In spite of being younger than my daughter Heidi, she had a sense of calm and confidence, and the warmest brown eyes that crinkled with merriment. She chuckled at Tuney's comment and hugged both of us, using one arm. It was the best she could do as she held her nose.

"It's so good to see you both again. And you're not late, but I was just about to call you, Cardi, to see how close you were to getting here." She nodded toward the bus as the driver picked up both our suitcases and walked back to load them. "Go on in and find some seats. We're not full, but it's going to be a fun group."

"Do we smell to you?" I asked worriedly as the three of us followed the driver. All I could smell was that stinky odor and I worried it was clinging to me. I didn't want to be THAT person who reeked so badly no one wanted to sit with me.

Amy grimaced, and then said hesitantly, "Well, maybe just a bit, but probably just from sitting inside the car with the skunk smell. I'm sure it'll disappear quickly." She blinked, then offered, "You can sit in the back if you want."

The thought that I might smell like skunk the whole trip was more overwhelming than that awful odor. Then I remembered something.

"Ope!" I said and took off after the driver. "Oh, sir! Can you wait just one second!" I caught up to him and asked if I could open my bag.

He obligingly stopped, so I quickly pulled out some perfume I'd packed. For a second, I wondered why I'd even packed this. My Kris had always liked that scent on me, and for my last birthday when he was alive, he'd bought the perfume and matching hand lotion. I took a deep breath of the citrus-and-floral scent of it that I loved so much, and for a moment thought of the first time I'd sprayed some on my neck and wrists. Kris had promptly grabbed me, pretended the scent drove him wild, and kissed my neck.

I shook my head. *Positive thoughts!* Yes, that was a positive thought. I smiled for Kris, and sprayed the perfume in the air above, hoping it would settle in my hair and overwhelm the *eau d'odor* of the roadkill. *Well,* I thought, *Honey, I can't drive you wild anymore,* so *I may as well use this to drive something wild away.*

I looked up to see Tuney shaking her head as she and Amy got closer, watching what I was doing. "Oh, she's de-skunking herself with her favorite perfume!" I heard her tell Amy.

Amy laughed. "It looks like she told Mr. Smith to go ahead and load the bags, so I think she's keeping the perfume. Hope you don't run into any more skunks." I saw Tuney's shoulders sag. Amy immediately put her at ease by continuing, "Now no worries, Tuney. Please! You're here to relax and have a good time, and that's what I want for you. I have a feeling you're going to make some good friends on this trip. This group is a barrel of fun and laughs!" She came up next to me and smiled the way a mother does to a child she knows is planning a surprise attack on a sibling. I was holding my perfume as if it were a fire extinguisher, waiting for Tuney to get closer. No way was I sitting next to her if she smelled like skunk.

Tuney looked at Amy gratefully and nodded. "I wasn't sure I wanted to go on a trip at all, but we made it, even with the skunk, so I'm counting on the worse part being over. I'm truly looking forward to this, honey. You seem to be so patient."

"Atta girl!" Amy patted Tuney on the back. "I wouldn't be in this business if little things bothered me. And I have no need to be patient with either of you because you haven't done anything wrong!" She pushed Tuney gently toward me. "Better get your spritz, then hop on the bus. Our adventure is about to begin!"

Tuney chuckled. "Ah! 'Travel far enough, you meet yourself.' A quote that I always liked from a man named David Michell." She looked pensive for a moment, and I heard her say softly to Amy, "I think both Cardi and I need to find ourselves. After losing our husbands, we, or at least I for sure, don't feel like I know who I am anymore."

Amy patted her arm reassuringly. "Well, I love your quote, and I'm glad you two are here. I don't have a quote, but someone once reminded me that 'Travel broadens your horizons!' I hope your horizon becomes endless!" Tuney nodded and gave Amy another hug.

I came up behind Tuney and spritzed my perfume on her hair and clothes. Tuney coughed, glared at me, and then told Amy that we'd still better sit in the back until the perfume wore off. I just smirked at Amy. She gave me another hug, too, and I hopped on board the bus. As Tuney followed me, the rest of the travelers let out a cheer and started clapping. I was sure it was because they were anxious to get on the road and had been waiting for us. Tuney was self-conscious at first until she saw the smiling and friendly faces of everyone. I admit I ate it up, bowing and calling out good morning to everyone as we walked down the aisle. Tuney smiled at everyone, occasionally shrugging as she pointed at me. We finally found an empty row in the back of the bus.

"Take one side, and I'll take the other," I urged. "That way we can each have a window."

Tuney didn't argue. The bus seats were close together, but comfortable, and Tuney liked having her purse next to her so she wouldn't have to try to bend down to plug her phone into the outlet beneath her seat.

As soon as we were seated, the bus left the parking lot, only one minute behind scheduled take-off. Amy grabbed a microphone and quickly explained our timeline for the day. She told everyone that in about an hour and a half, we'd be stopping by the Amana Colonies to eat breakfast.

"Oh, good," whispered Tuney to me across the aisle. "I'm starved!"

"Me, too!" I answered in my normal voice. "And I want you to eat plenty on this trip. You've lost too much weight!"

Tuney nodded. "I know. That's what the kids keep telling me. But I can stand to lose even some more."

"We always can stand to lose a few pounds, Tune," I replied. "But you've lost too much." I smiled at Tuney. "Just enjoy. Here we go! Widsters on the road!" Now that we were on board, I felt like I was on a high school pep bus. But fifty years of bus improvement was a lot of change: instead of a rattling, dark old gas guzzler with a narrow aisle and hard plastic seats, this tour bus was downright grand. We could walk up and down the aisle, drink and eat whatever and whenever we wanted to, and even go to the bathroom. Buses sure had changed since the last time I rode one.

Amy finished up her instructions and then told the busload that she was going to walk down the aisle and have everyone introduce his or herself and tell the group something about themselves.

By the time she got back to Tuney and me, we had learned that there were six couples, three sets of sisters besides ourselves, a mother-daughter team, and the rest were friends, mostly women who were single by divorce or widowhood. Almost all were retired, half were on the bus trip for the first time in their lives, and they all seemed cheerful and ready for a good time.

Amy handed the microphone to me first. I glanced over at Tuney as she braced herself for whatever would pop out of my mouth.

"Wow!" I said. "I can tell this is going to be a fun trip!" I hadn't been able to see everyone in the front of the bus, so I stood up so everyone could see me. I thought that would be nice. "I'm Cardamom Cooper, but please-please-please call me Cardi. My mother loved baking and cardamom was her favorite spice, especially when she baked Scandinavian cookies every Christmas."

Some man toward the front of the bus hollered back, "So you're not Cardi B, huh?"

I had no idea what he meant by that, and I looked at Amy in confusion as I answered, "Uh, no. I guess you could call me Cardi C. The C is for cooper, and there's no B in my name."

Amy took the microphone for a second to explain. "Mort! I can't believe you're up to date on the latest in rapper stars!" She gave me a wink and continued, "For those of you like our Cardi here who are a bit confused by what one of my favorite prankster buddies, Mort, said, Cardi B is the name of a rapper who has won numerous awards for her music." She handed the microphone back to me.

I thanked her and said, "No, no relation, I'm afraid. I can recite some naughty limericks, but I'm definitely not a rapper."

"Cardi!" reprimanded Tuney. I heard Mort and some other men whistle and laugh.

I frowned at Tuney and waved a hand palm down as a signal to her to relax. Then I continued. "I'm retired from banking, have two children, four grandchildren, and I'm traveling with my sister Tuney. Her real name is Petunia because it's my mom's favorite flower. Good thing we weren't boys because our father would probably have named us after his favorite things, Jim Beam and Bud Weiser!"

As soon as those words left my lips, I regretted them. I sounded so unladylike. But the regret lasted only a second because the bus erupted in laughter. I could see why comedians do what they do. An appreciative audience is fun, I thought. Meanwhile, Tuney glared at me. I could tell she was feeling embarrassed and probably wondering what I'd say next. That, or worried that if her sister didn't shut up, there'd be nothing left for her to say. There was a soft murmur of ohs and ahs and lots of smiles bestowed on me. I smiled back and continued.

I drew a deep breath, lowered my voice, and spoke softly. "But like too many of you, way too many of you, I'm a widow. As a matter of fact, that's why I'm on this trip with Tuney," and I pointed the microphone across the aisle at Tuney.

"You see, we're both Widsters – that's the name my sister called us – widowed sisters. She lost her husband just a year ago." I pointed the microphone at Tuney, who reluctantly stuck her hand up and waved slightly.

My captive audience's murmur had now turned to one of sympathy and empathy. "And I told her we needed a fun trip for something different in our lives." Tuney grimaced when I held the microphone up and made air quotes with my fingers. "Just looking at all of you, and knowing how fun Amy is, because we're kind of cousins by marriage," I glanced over at Amy and Tuney and winked at Amy, "I know that you're going to be the best medicine for grief that we could ever possibly have."

Here the audience clapped and cheered. I nodded, smiled radiantly, and handed the microphone back to Amy, who handed it to Tuney. I plopped down in my seat.

Tuney started to speak, but both Amy and I urged her at the same time to stand up. Unenthusiastically, she complied.

She cleared her throat and started again. "Well, I don't know that there's much I can add to what Cardi said, except I'm a retired school teacher, have three children and five – no, now six! - grandkids " The tourists were quiet, but Tuney suddenly felt encouraged to talk by the way people looked at her and nodded. "I'm the older of us two sisters, by eleven months," a few chuckles interrupted her and caused her to smile, "which, I never thought of this before, but might possibly be because of Dad's favorite – Jim Beam!"

Some hoots, giggles and laughter broke out. Tuney was pleasantly surprised and looked over at me, thinking I'd be giggling, too. I wasn't laughing at all, but my jaw had dropped open and I felt my brow furrowing as I thought, *Gee whiz, Tuney can be an extrovert when she wants!*

"Well, anyway," Tuney said hastily as she looked toward the front of the bus with all the passengers. "I'm looking forward to seeing this part of Iowa that, I'm ashamed to admit, I've never really explored before. You all sound like a fun group to be with." She started to hand the microphone to Amy but brought it back to her mouth. "Ope! And in case you're wondering why Cardi and I are at the back of the bus like two little girls in time out, it's because I ran over a very pungent road-kill skunk on the way over this morning!"

A familiar chorus of "Ewww!" rang out, and Tuney grinned. "That's why we were late, and why you may have noticed our little perfume shower outside before we got on the bus. Hopefully we don't smell like skunk any more, and none of you will refuse to sit with us at meals!" She handed the microphone to Amy, sat down, and smiled as everyone clapped.

One of the two women who sat in front of her turned in her seat to talk to her. "That was wonderful. I can tell you two are sisters – or how did you say it? Widsters? You're going to be a ball to have around. I'm glad you're sitting with us four. I'm Bonnie, by the way, in case you didn't remember with all these other names floating about." She stuck her hand between the seats and Tuney shook it.

That began the start of what both Tuney and I thought later was the best part of the trip. We bonded immediately with the four women who sat in front of us. We talked to our bus mates as we headed east on the interstate. The two in front of me were Trudy and Belinda, while Bonnie's seat mate was Tammy. All four ladies were from the same town, loved the name Widster because they were all widowed, and like us Widsters were on their first bus trip. All six of us soon discovered we had a lot more in common. Grandkids, cooking, and being suddenly single were the topics we discussed. I had trouble at first remembering their names – darn memory! – so I announced that I was going to call them the 2Bs2Ts. They loved it.

Chapter 4

Death Vs. Divorce

I soon found out the 2Bs2Ts were good listeners, much to my delight and Tuney's chagrin.

"I told Tuney on the way over here that widowhood wasn't the worst thing in the world. I think if you have to lose a spouse, then we're the lucky ones," I announced. One of the women drew her breath in sharply, I think it was Tammy, and I remembered that during the microphone introductions, she had said she was recently widowed. The others sort of cocked their heads to one side as if waiting for an explanation for something they didn't understand.

"Cardi!" protested Tuney with her scarier version of The Look than mine was. She nodded toward Tammy. "There you go again. First you say widowhood isn't all bad, then you say we're lucky! You're absolutely crazy." She stared at me in exasperation, much the same way she stared at me the day I embarrassed her in front of a boy when I mentioned that Tuney got her first bra on her birthday. For some reason, Tuney had grown up and never out grown worrying about what others thought. Except me. Maybe because I was totally the opposite.

I looked apologetically at Tammy, but then merely shook

my head. "Hear me out, everyone." I scooted to the edge of my row so that I was next to the aisle and could talk to Tuney and the others more easily. "I know it sounds harsh. But what I mean when I say that is to think about all the other people we know who have lived through becoming single again. And losing a husband isn't just by death. I guess it must be what divorce is like, too, don't you think?"

Tuney frowned in thought, but the others murmured encouragingly, so I hurriedly continued. "I mean it's a death, kind of. A marriage between two people has ended. Ours happened to end in physical death." I looked thoughtfully at Tuney and thought of a good example. "Think about it. Death in the form of divorce happened to a lady we know, and it was horrible. Remember Mary Jo Casperson, Tuney?"

My sister's frown disappeared, her eyes rounded and it was obvious she knew where I was headed with this conversation. That she even understood me this time was a miracle, and a tiny smirk played at the corners of her mouth. Tuney drew her breath in and expelled it with a sudden knowing, "Oh. Yeah. Wait, you guys. I see where she's going." Trudy nodded her head in agreement while the others looked at me expectantly.

"I think I get you," said Trudy, looking at her friends. "My sister's divorced, and it is a death." Belinda patted her arm sympathetically as Trudy added, "And a shock!"

I nodded sagely and began my explanation. "This friend, Mary Jo, was always so happy talking about how great her husband Ed was taking her to Vegas, or the Caribbean, or over to Europe. And if he bought her flowers or jewelry, she actually posted a picture of them on Facebook with a little blurb about how thoughtful and loving her husband was."

"Really?" asked Tuney in amazement. "I was never Facebook friends with her, so I didn't know."

One of the 2Bs2Ts murmured, "I hate people like that," but followed it up with a chuckle.

"Oh, yeah," I assured. "Not that I was ever jealous, you understand. I showed Kris – my husband - one of her posts and threatened to take a photo of his dirty underwear lying on the floor. I was going to caption it 'My Husband has the Best Way of Making Me Feel Needed!'"

Everyone giggled, and then Trudy asked, "Well? Did that make him go out and buy you some flowers?"

"Are you kidding?" I snorted. "The next day there were more undies and socks on the floor. But with a new box of laundry detergent on top of them!" As Tuney and the others burst into laughter, I joined them. For a moment, as I talked about him, Kris was alive again in my mind. When I stopped laughing, I confessed, "I called him a son of a you-know-what, and we ended up making love like it was going out of style." I raised my eyes toward the ceiling and winked in case Kris was looking down at me.

Tuney's face contorted as the others gasped and giggled. "Oh, geez, Cardi. T.M.I! None of us need that much information!" But seeing me smiling happily, she smiled and reached over to squeeze my arm. I looked at her with surprise that she wasn't pinching me instead.

"Well, we don't mind hearing about it!" "I've forgotten what that's like!" "What a precious memory!" "Speak for yourself, Tuney!" chorused the 2Bs2Ts, along with more laughter.

I grinned and stuck my tongue out at Tuney. "Well, anyway, the point is I'd take a sense of humor over flowers and jewelry any day." I smiled at the memory of Kris, but then my thoughts returned to Mary Jo.

"Well, it appears that Ed had not only one, but TWO girlfriends on the side. Evidently whenever he bought one of them a gift or flowers, he either felt guilty enough that he bought the same thing for Mary Jo, or he did it to cover up his own sin." I hesitated for a second, wondering what Ed's fate in the afterlife was going to be. "Speaking of sin, may God forgive me, but when all this was made public, I felt…well, I guess you'd call it superior to Mary Jo. Because my hubby wasn't sleazy, you know? And I was so sorry for her. To think that Mary Jo caught him with one of those women – in their own bed – well, can you imagine?"

"Oh, man, he sounds like a jerk!" said Belinda. Her other friends harrumphed with disgust. All four wriggled in their seats trying to get more comfortable as they turned toward Tuney and me in suspense for more of the story. Tuney seemed fascinated with Mary Jo's tale so far. She'd been listening with her mouth gaping slightly open in surprise. She finally shut it, shook her head no, and said, "Ewww! I didn't know that. I can't imagine anything like that at all."

"Right!" I said triumphantly. "My point exactly. You and I would never have had anything like that happen because Kris and Tommy were the best men in the world."

Tuney nodded, a look of comprehension on her face. "Okay, gotcha now. You, me and women like Mary Jo are all without husbands, but you say we're lucky because our husbands never cheated on us."

Tuney looked surprised when I shook my head vehemently. "No! Not that. We're lucky because we can spend the rest of our lives bragging about our guys and remembering all the good times we had. That keeps them alive, don't you think?" The 2Bs2Ts and Tuney nodded in agreement. "Poor Mary Jo can't do that. She's been humiliated, shamed, and instead of whatever love she once had for him, she hates his guts now. He's dead to her and she's glad! She can't even stand to speak Ed's name. She's in my book club at the library and occasionally she'll remark that she'd give anything to have not caught 'Him with that Creature!'"

"Why would she say that?" asked Tuney curiously. "Would she rather be oblivious to him cheating on her?"

"No, I don't think that's it. I think it's that the memory of what she saw that day overshadows all the good ones she once had. See, she was supposed to have met some other friends at Martelli's – that's a restaurant in the town next to ours - for lunch that day. I guess Ed figured he had a couple of hours to have his own little 'nooner.' Anyway, one of Mary Jo's friends had bailed because of a sick child. The other one met Mary Jo but told her she only had half an hour because she'd forgotten a doctor's appointment, so they decided to just make another date to eat out. Mary Jo went home, heard noise upstairs, and … hmmm. The sight about scarred her eyeballs, she told the book club."

The women listening all tittered at that. Tuney looked more interested in what I was gossiping about than she had anything else I'd said in a long while. "Hey, what's the scoop? I never heard any details other than they had filed for divorce on the grounds of incompatibility."

I scoffed at that. "Incompatibility? Incompatibility is what happens when a night owl marries a morning person and they just can't coordinate. This was pure adultery, plus the other girlfriend got in on the picture when she heard about the first one. Guess she tried suing Ed for compensatory and general damages like pain and suffering, mental anguish and loss of consortium."

"No kidding? Consortium? Can she do that? They weren't married or living together, were they?" asked Tuney incredulously. "Man, how did I miss all this scandal?"

I shrugged. "You must not run in the same chatty circles that I do!" I licked my lips because they were getting dry from talking so much and stopped to grab a swig from the bottle of water Amy had provided in each seat. "But to answer your question, girlfriend number one – not the bimbo in bed, but the one who might have been innocent enough to believe Ed - claimed he'd lied to her about not being married, and swore he'd promised to marry her. She lived out East somewhere and Ed stayed with her whenever he had to fly there for business. And that was a lot! She said they'd been together for over six years! According to the private investigators Mary Jo hired for the divorce, GF One's neighbors all knew Ed as a neighbor AND assumed he was her husband."

"Ope!" Tuney's hand flew up to cover her mouth, and the 2Bs2Ts issued appropriate epithets.

Buoyed on by the reaction to this juicy story, I continued. "So yeah, probably not in Iowa could you sue for loss of consortium, but I guess out East you can."

Tuney shook her head slowly, digesting all this. "Wow! I don't know Mary Jo all that well, but I really feel sorry for her. And for the women Ed deceived, too. I had no idea all that had gone on. What a mess!" She tried to imagine what Mary Jo must have gone through.

I bobbed my head up and down, stuck my nose in the air and pronounced solemnly "It's like I said. If we had to lose our husbands, we're lucky it wasn't the same way Mary Jo did!"

"Wow!" was all Tuney said again. She rubbed her forehead. "Jeepers, Cardi. I never really thought about it, but you're totally right." She puckered her brow and said thoughtfully, "I almost feel guilty now that I think of the times I've heard about a friend getting divorced and just said 'Too bad' and not given it another thought. It's got to be devasting, especially if you don't even see it coming."

I nodded and opened my mouth to say something, but Tuney continued her thoughts out loud. "All the people who've stopped by to offer to help me, all the cards, phone calls, donations of food and money – I mean, if Tommy and I had gotten divorced, I doubt too many people would have done any of that, except maybe to find out what all the gory circumstances of our split were!"

I looked a little guilty, remembering how many times some of my friends called each other to see if anyone had any new "details" about poor Mary Jo. "I thought of that, too. Mary Jo's divorce was certainly scandalous, and I hope others' divorces are a bit more amicable. But whatever causes a split between couples, it certainly is an ending that I guess you can call a death. To one, if not to both partners."

Tuney was quiet for a moment, then said, "Well! Enough gossip." Everyone nodded, but then Tuney added, "Although I love hearing it, I admit!"

That was all the encouragement the 2Bs2Ts needed. Either we're all from scandalous and gossipy little towns, or human beings are pretty much all the same, but the 2Bs2Ts each had similar stories to tell. Tuney told me later she thought mine was the juiciest. I felt kind of bad then. I mean it wasn't like I wanted to win an award for talking about poor Mary Jo. I just wanted to make a point about losing a spouse, not to really spread old gossip. But I must admit, it was kind of fun to hear some of the stories the other ladies had.

Pretty soon, we were interrupted by Amy, announcing to the busload we'd be at our destination in a few minutes. Just in time – I was starving!

Chapter 5

Ox-Yoke Inn

I looked over the itinerary. "Mmmmm! Ox-Yoke Inn in Amana! I've heard about it. And I'm really hungry, too."

"Good thing," answered Trudy as she grabbed her purse. She reached for her makeup bag and opened her compact. "I've eaten there before, and they don't believe in skimping on portions!"

"And it's all delicious, homemade, good old-fashioned food," chimed in Tammy. "I've eaten there once a long time ago, but I don't think it's any different now than it was then."

"Sounds wonderful," answered Tuney. She checked her makeup, applied a bit more lipstick and smacked her lips. Satisfied she looked okay, she put everything back in her purse. I watched her, and when Tuney looked over at me, she smiled and gave a thumbs up. I felt relieved that Tuney was taking an interest in how she looked.

"Thanks, Sis," whispered Tuney across the aisle to me. "I'm glad you suggested this trip."

Phew! That made me happy. I just smiled and mouthed the words "Love you!"

The bus pulled into the passenger unloading zone in front of the Ox-Yoke. It took only minutes for us hungry tourists to depart in an orderly fashion, and soon Tuney and I found ourselves walking into a quaint and very busy restaurant. Since we were the last ones in, we found the place was almost full. (maybe being in the rear of the bus wasn't so great!)

"You from the bus?" asked a waitress when we hesitated, looking around for some extra seats. We both nodded. "You ladies just seat yourselves over here and I'll be with you in a sec," she said as she hurriedly placed two glasses of water and some menus for us on a nearby table only big enough for two. As we Widsters slid onto the seats, Tuney began to sniffle.

"My nose is running a bit," admitted Tuney as she swiped it with a tissue she'd pulled from her purse. "I wonder if that's from the skunk? Can you smell anything now, Cardi?"

"I think I smell bacon," I replied cheerfully. "My perfume must have cleared out the smells of the deodorizers and that stinky skunk!"

There were other smells that soon had me salivating. I inhaled deeply and filled my senses with the aroma of fresh-baked breads, mouth-watering ham, and citrus. Even the smell of grease from eggs and bacon frying topped off the delicious factor that I smelled. I swallowed the glass of water in a few gulps to try to control my hunger so I wouldn't order more than I could eat.

While we waited for a waitress, we looked around the restaurant. Every table was dressed with a blue-checkered tablecloth. Men in overalls and caps with farm equipment logos sat together at one big round table. They were laughing, eating, and drinking their morning coffee. Some tables were pushed together and filled with passengers from the bus. Some were occupied by elderly couples. There were even some business men and women, sipping coffee, but seeming out of place as they scrolled through their cell phones or texted in this old-fashioned homey area. Tuney watched them idly for a moment and wondered quietly aloud to me if they were doing business or texting a loved one. She and I both hoped it was the latter.

"This is a typical hometown, family-style restaurant, isn't it?" said Tuney brightly. "Did you see the posters for upcoming farm auctions on a bulletin board as we came in? Just like at home." She spotted a few plates being delivered to another table and pointed at them. "Look, Card! Look how gigantic that waffle is. And it's loaded with powdered sugar and maple syrup. Yum!"

"Sorry, sis, but I promised myself I'd try to cut back on my sugar intake these couple of days," I said. "I had to try on two pairs of capris because each one had somehow shrunk since the last time I wore them. I'm now wearing elastic-waist, stretchy knit, capris. I'm getting too fat!"

"I meant to tell you that you're a regular blimpo, Cardi," said Tuney mockingly as she looked me up and down. "Are you even up to 100 pounds yet? You're downright skinny!"

Tuney was being nice. Once upon a time 'skinny' would have applied to both of us. My favorite breakfast food, muffins, now sat atop my waist and spilled over. Thank heaven for tunic tops!

"I. Wish!" I smiled grimly and added, "No, I catch myself eating sweets just out of boredom now that Kris isn't around. I thought maybe I could break myself of doing that if I stayed away from them for a couple of days. And like I said earlier, *you're* the one who is too skinny."

Tuney was reading the menu and her eyes were drawn to items like French toast, cinnamon rolls and sausages. "Me, skinny? Never!" She put down her menu and leaned back against the booth seat. "You know, I try to watch my weight, too. And it's working. I'm seeing it increase every day!"

I chuckled as Tuney patted her stomach. "I know, I know! Maybe just at breakfast I'll give up some sugar. This road trip is going to have food opportunities like we won't get at home. I was looking at some of the brochures of places we're going to be near. Like fudge shops…" Tuney interjected a groan as I continued "…pie places, state's best cinnamon rolls, and I could go on and on."

"And those are just the sweets," added Tuney, licking her lips. "Dang it! You do know that since we're on a road trip, special rules apply, right? That means calories don't count," said Tuney. She dug in her purse and pulled out one of the brochures. "There are great places for steaks, tenderloins, here's one advertising fresh fried river catfish, tea rooms with cute little sandwiches and soups…"

I put a hand up in surrender. I think reaching 50 was the magic number where just thinking about food seemed to automatically add on the pounds. "Okay, okay!" I interrupted as Tuney eyed a plateful of bacon and omelets that the waitress was carrying to another table. She pointed out the plates to me, and I just sighed and grinned. "Okay. Assuming road trip rules mean we eat whatever we want, I agree to apply them. Just don't let me overdo the eating, all right?"

Tuney agreed. "If you don't let me overeat, either. I'll start a diet when I get home."

"I'm telling you, you don't need a diet! But I'll help you clean out your cupboards and fridge," I offered. "Especially the cookie jar." And I smiled innocently while Tuney snorted.

"You're too kind, Sis," said Tuney flatly, then winked at me. I grinned, too.

We were soon blissfully devouring the waitress's recommendation of "The Traveler" – two eggs cooked to order, two hickory smoked bacon slices, hash browns, an English muffin toasted, and homemade strawberry jam.

"Aww, why didn't we listen to each other about the overeating rule?" I sighed as I sat back after finishing my breakfast. "We should have split that plate. What a way to start the road trip!"

Tuney patted her stomach. "I don't usually eat breakfast anymore, and I'm stuffed. If we eat like this today and tomorrow, you'll have to roll me home. And gaining weight won't be doing my sore knees and hips any good."

Wearing down of cartilage and arthritis seemed to be one of the rusty spots in our golden ages. I twisted in my seat, trying to pop my back. I have a bad right hip that makes me sit more on my left side, and that seems to scrunch up my spine. If Kris were here, he'd rub it and…

"I agree," I said to get any thoughts of being without Kris out of my mind. I finished up my coffee. "Hey, do you need any anti-inflammatories before we get back on the bus? These do the trick for me, and I should be good the rest of the day, even if we sit the whole time." I dug in my purse, popped open a bottle of naproxen, and shook out a couple of tablets. I held the bottle up and asked, "Want some?"

Tuney nodded as she rolled her shoulders up and down. "Thanks. I'll take a couple of pills from you. I've got some in my suitcase, too, in case we run out." She downed the pain relievers with some water.

"I forgot to take some before we got on the road, and I can

really feel my hip!" I slid from my seat and stood up. It felt good to jiggle my hips a bit. I gazed idly around as I wobbled back and forth in place. One of the older farmers at the table next to our booth happened to look up, and grinned.

Tuney had also stood and suddenly poked me. When I looked at her in surprise, she rolled her eyes toward the men. I turned around, and seeing them all grinning at me by then, felt my cheeks redden, but I started laughing.

"Sorry!" I said to the men. I grimaced widely. "I hope that didn't ruin your breakfast."

"Not at all, ma'am," said one, and he even touched his cap with his hand as a tip of the hat. I surprised Tuney by taking a step toward the men and smiling at them. I heard her whisper urgently, "Cardi!"

One of the farmers noticed me putting my pills back into my purse as I approached. "We were just talking about getting older and what comes with that. If those little pills get rid of the hitch in your giddy-up, I'm gonna buy me some!" he said, while his friends chuckled. "Where are you ladies from?"

OMG, did I just hear a senior citizen pickup line? I thought. It struck me as funny, so I laughed out loud. Tuney, suddenly feeling protective of me, stood close. She stayed still, not sure if she should talk to these male strangers or not. If Tommy was with her, he'd have pulled up a chair and sat down with the men to visit, but she seemed to feel at ease. I had no qualms though, and before Tuney realized, I was talking to these strangers as if they were my best friends. The conversation was mostly one-sided because, as Tuney well knew, I could – and often would – talk a mile a minute. I talked about age-related physical complaints and recommended to the men to take naproxen because it helped me and Tuney relieve our aches and pains. Somehow from that topic, I shifted to describe our bus trip and the places we're going to see on this trip.

Tuney stood patiently next to me. She'd at least plastered a smile on her face, but she kept shifting from one leg to another as the minutes rolled by. Her eyes darted all around the restaurant as she searched for someone or something that she could use as an excuse to politely leave with me. Some of the bus passengers were making their way to the restrooms, others were finishing eating, and Amy and Mr. Smith, the bus driver, had disappeared.

When I mentioned that Tuney and I were "Widsters," one of the men said he had recently lost his wife. Soon both he and I were wiping away tears. I felt so sorry for him. I kept pulling tissues out of my purse, while the farmer kept using a big bandana to blow his nose. Tuney told me later, that she noticed other customers were looking aghast at the farmer every time he blew his nose. Honked was more like it, Tuney thought. Tuney feared the conversation could get long, personal, and wet, and decided it was time to leave. That opportunity came when I paused to pull another tissue out of my purse to wipe a tear away.

"Okay, I'm so sorry, but we really have to go," Tuney broke in as she simultaneously smiled at the men, gave me a look that urged her to leave, and pushed me along. "Our time is tight, and our bus is probably ready to go. So nice to talk to you all," even though she hadn't.

I glared at Tuney, patted the widower on his shoulder, and gave the other men a wave. Right as we walked out the door, I thought I should remind them about the naproxen. I called over my shoulder, "Oh, guys! Don't forget those blue pills. They really do help with stiffness."

Tuney had led the way out, but when she heard what I said, she froze, horrified. Turning to grab my arm, she stole a glance inside the restaurant, witnessed the men look at each other and then burst into a high cackling laughter.

"Oh, no, Cardi. You did NOT just say that!" she hissed at me.

I heard the laughter, too, and was puzzled for a moment. I started to retort "What?" to Tuney, then it dawned on me what I'd said. I felt my eyes widen in horror and my cheeks blaze red with embarrassment.

"Oh, geez, Tuney, let's get outta here!" I whispered furiously to Tuney. I hurried to the bus with one hand covering my eyes. If I couldn't see anyone, then maybe they couldn't see me.

As Tuney followed, her initial embarrassment over what I said gave way to hysterical laughter. Her face contorted as she tried to compose herself.

I almost ran to the back of the bus and slouched down in my seat. As soon as Tuney climbed in, I closed my eyes and ordered Tuney to tell the driver to start the bus. "Hurry! Start the stupid bus!"

"He can't until everyone's on, you goose!" said Tuney, enjoying seeing me squirm.

Just then the "2Bs2Ts," arrived and sat down.

"Sorry we couldn't sit together," Belinda began as she turned around to me. She stopped when she saw my face. "Oh, no, honey! What's the matter? Are you sick?"

I looked even more embarrassed. "Only sick of myself!"

The 2Bs2Ts immediately protested and urged me to tell them what was wrong. I just miserably shook my head.

"I'll tell you what happened," volunteered Tuney eagerly with a wicked grin.

I shot her a look. "Oh, you'd love that, wouldn't you?" The same mischievous smile she had when she was a child widened. "I most certainly would. It was the funniest thing in the world." Then adult Tuney appeared in her eyes, and she said a little more seriously, "But I won't if you really don't want me to, Cardi."

That immediately triggered Tammy, Bonnie, Trudy and Belinda to demand that one of us Widsters tell them. I grudgingly okayed Tuney to report how stupid her younger sister can be at times. As she disclosed how I had put my foot in my mouth, she made sure to embellish the situation a bit, and in no time, the back of the bus was howling with laughter. Even I started to laugh. I'd interject a few times so that everyone knew my thought process and why I said what I did. But by the time Tuney was finished, I was basking in the admiration our new friends seemed to have for the humor in Tuney's story.

"Feel better, now?" asked Tuney as she looked fondly at me from across the aisle.

I grinned crookedly at her. "Yes, I guess so. Do you?"

"Yup!" And Tuney settled back into the seat next to the window and looked out at the scenery. I could tell she felt a *lot* better. Guess it was worth making a fool of myself.

Still, my cheeks burned with embarrassment, I apologized once again. "Tuney, you know it's your fault. The one time when it would have been okay for you to either poke me or put your hand over my mouth, and you just stand there and let me prattle on!"

Bonnie turned to me and said with a grin, "Cardi, dear, don't be embarrassed. Keep in mind that at this age, we all tend to behave a little more...umm...unfiltered at times!"

Truer words have never been spoken!

Chapter 6

Tuney and Tommy

While both of us relaxed as we watched the August Iowa scenery flash by, I checked on Tuney every now and then to make sure she wasn't bored or anything. I wanted this trip to be a nice break for her. She turned her face sideways and leaned her head against the huge bus window to stare out the window. On the highway, the countryside ditches were filled with cattails, their long spiky green leaves already turning yellow at the base because of the summer's heat. The cattails were full and brown, with some bursting open a bit to let fluffy seeds loose.

With her forehead against the cool window of the air-conditioned bus, Tuney noticed the cattails, too, and pointed them out to me. She thought they looked like stuffing from a torn overfilled mattress. Every now and then clumps of sumac filled a side hill, and scatterings of shades of yellow from goldenrod and black-eyed Susan were augmented with purple loosestrife and periwinkle-blue chicory. Queen Anne's lace grew in vast areas, looking so much like piles of snowflakes on stems that Tuney mentioned to me that she was starting to think about winter. As they had so often since her Tommy died, her thoughts had turned to how she would get along without her husband of forty-four years. She shuddered to think she might have to learn how to start a snow-blower now that she was widowed. We'd both lucked out last year with a mild winter. Odds are in Iowa that we would get a lot more this time around.

Her remarks got me thinking about my beloved brother-in-law, Tommy. He was never Tom or Thomas to Tuney. She'd first met him in kindergarten, and in our small town, you were known by the name or nickname you grew up with. Tuney and Tommy Thompson – everyone she'd ever met had seemed to think their names were cute together. Maybe, I wondered, if Tuney'd ever gone by her full name Petunia, or a nickname of Pet, they would have been Petunia and Thomas Thompson, or Pet and Tom Thompson. No one would think that was cutesy, would they? Tuney and Tommy Thompson sounded like a circus act. Or a children's show.

Once Tuney admitted that as she aged, she'd become embarrassed when people gave them a quizzical smile after hearing their names together. Thank heaven, she told me, that they'd named the kids plain normal names that didn't begin with a T. She and Tommy had welcomed Joey (Joseph), Heidi, and Scott, and had been blessed when all three kids grew up, married and presented her and Tommy with grandchildren: Heather, Cybill, Jacob, Madison, Nolan and infant Jackson Thomas. I wondered if Tommy knew in heaven that Scott's wife Pam had announced she was pregnant with their second child two months after Tommy had died.

When Pam gave birth to JT, Tuney cried as she told me that the baby would never know his grandfather. There would never be a picture of Tommy holding his newest grandchild, or …At the memory of Tuney's anguish, I felt tears start to well up. *No! Snap out of it,* I told myself. *We just got through laughing our heads off. No more tears today.* Kris and I had two kids, Sammi (Samantha) and Kyle. Kris had gotten to be with all four of our grandkids, so I was lucky.

I glanced over at my sister and saw she had fallen asleep. But it looked like she was dreaming, too. Her mouth was slack, but it twitched into a little smile now and then. Tuney looked tired, I realized. Tired and old. There were shadows and bags under her normally bright eyes. Both of us had long ago decided we were going to embrace the wrinkles around our eyes and mouths as permanent laugh-lines. But I realized with a start that during the past two years I'd been grieving the sudden loss of Kris, Tuney had aged - and even more rapidly in the past year by grieving the loss of Tommy.

How fast life can change! Right before Kris had died, Tommy's annual checkup revealed he needed prostate surgery. In small-town Iowa, this meant a trip to either Des Moines or University of Iowa hospital in Iowa City. Even though it was almost three hours away, Tuney insisted that Tommy go to the U, not only because of their reputation for cancer treatment, but because both of their sons had attended the university. His surgery had gone well, and they returned home in just a few days. Kris and I had stopped by with some soup when Tommy got home. He'd been in great spirits while he and Kris laughed and joked together about male anatomy, even though he'd privately complained to Tuney that he hated having a catheter. She'd told him, she confided to me, that compared to giving birth, that was nothing, so he should 'quitcherbitchin!' We'd both laughed at that, but then Tuney had said sympathetically, "But I didn't point out that birth doesn't last the two weeks he has to wear that thing!"

Everything appeared to be fine. We all knew several men who'd had the surgery and recuperation had been rapid. Tuney had casually mentioned that the doctor said he'd let them know the results of the surgery within a day or two after Tommy had been released. They were expecting a standard phone call or text telling them the results were good and that he'd have a follow-up exam in three months. I remembered the day my doorbell rang and the surprise I felt when I opened the door to see my sister standing there. I'd known something was wrong immediately. She looked scared to death, and she was shaking violently. I looked for Tommy, but saw that she'd driven herself to my house, although I have no idea how she managed to do that in the condition she was in.

"Tuney, what is it? Is it Mom?" I had asked quickly and quietly, steeling myself for bad news. Mom was in her eighties, in a nursing home, and failing health-wise.

Tuney pushed past me and threw herself on my couch. "No. It's Tommy." She buried her head in her hands.

Thank goodness Kris had walked in then from the kitchen. Both he and I sat on either side of Tuney. I clutched Tuney's arm, while Kris had laid his arm protectively across her shoulder.

"What, Honey? Tell us. What's wrong?" Tuney listlessly told us that about a week before the operation, Tommy had complained that his back continually ached. He thought he'd pulled a muscle after he changed tires on his vehicle, she explained. Tommy's operation had gone smoothly but the doctor had wanted to run some more tests after he had noticed Tommy was coughing quite a bit.

"Both Tommy and I thought he'd just picked up a cold

virus or something at the hospital," explained Tuney as she stared at the floor. "The cancer evidently has already metastasized in his liver and his lungs."

I felt the air rush out of me. No! Not Tommy. He was only a few months older than Tuney. I looked over my sister's hunched form at Kris and our frightened eyes met. I felt tears well up as Kris looked like he was about to cry and just shook his head silently.

"Oh, Tuney," was all I could say. But Kris tried to sound upbeat, and I was grateful he was around. He wiped his eyes, then cupped her chin in one hand and raised her face until she looked at him.

"Hey, Tuney. Everything is going to be all right." He said that so firmly and assuredly, I believed him. She nodded tearfully at him. Quietly, he pulled Tuney to his chest and she began to sob as he patted her back and rocked her back and forth on the couch. He asked me to bring some water, and after a while, Tuney was able to sit up, wipe away her tears and take a drink. After she was composed, Kris began to talk. He told Tuney that Tommy was tough, that he knew Tommy could beat this, and that we'd do any and everything we could to help. He promised to take both Tuney and Tommy to the University for every appointment.

He and I talked that evening after Tuney left about how much we feared what was going to happen to Tommy and how Tuney's life might change. That night, I prayed to God to help them, and thanked God that my family was okay. Then the very next day, Kris went out to our garden and didn't come in. I found him after I'd hollered repeatedly for him to come in for lunch. The coroner told me Kris had died instantly. "Switch off," was how he answered me when I'd tremulously asked if Kris had suffered at all. My life was the one that changed. Upside-down. It had been over two years since I thanked God for anything else.

But it was then that I realized the importance and strength of a family. Tuney and Tommy came to *my* aid. I barely remembered anything about the funeral arrangements, the calls to other family members, the insurance, or having to buy a plot. Both Tuney and Tommy had found the strength to put their troubles aside and help not only me out with everything, but Sammi, Kyle and my grandchildren, too.

Once Kris was laid to rest, relatives had left, and I was alone, I spent a lot of time at Tuney and Tommy's. I insisted on driving them both to Iowa City for treatments because "Kris promised to do it, and since he can't..." Tuney would nod, and Tommy would kiss my cheek. Many times, I thought with relief that Tommy might be able to beat this horrible disease. For months both Tuney and I made Tommy's health – or lack of – our top priority. I made it through the anniversary of Kris's death by concentrating on my brother-in-law, and thought things just had to get better. A week later when I drove them to the hospital, Tommy was in a lot of pain. The doctor quietly and sadly talked to us about hospice.

Tommy lived for a little less than four weeks in hospice with Tuney at his side constantly. Tuney placed him at Loving Care Hospice about a half hour away from home. Tuney's kids and I took turns watching Tommy while Tuney would drive home, do laundry, pack some clean clothes and then rush back to his side. The end finally came peacefully for Tommy. His immediate family was with him when he took his last breath. I had been home asleep but woke up to my phone buzzing on the nightstand next to me. It was 5:30 in the morning.

I knew it was Tuney, and answered breathlessly, "Is he gone?" Tuney's voice was strained as she answered simply, "Yes," and hung up.

I burst into tears, crying as hard as I had when Kris died. I sobbed for myself as I relived hearing the paramedics and the police tell me there wasn't anything they could do for Kris. I sobbed for Tuney and her family as I tried to remember all that they were going to have to go through. And I sobbed because I'd loved Tommy as the brother I never had. He'd done a lot for me, I realized. His bravery as he faced his own inevitable death was given out of love. And so was my sister's. When Tommy was buried in the plot next to my Kris, sudden comprehension hit me hard. While caring for me in my deep shock, they'd bought Kris's and my plot, and must have bought their own at the same time - right after getting the devastating news about Tommy's cancer.

It was as I stood underneath the shower the morning Tommy died that I decided I was sick of tears. Kris had always tried to find the bright side of life. In his honor, I vowed to look for the positive. I'm not overly religious but I have always loved the words from the Book of Ecclesiastes - "a time to be born, a time to die, a time to heal and a time to laugh, a time to mourn and a time to dance." I figured I'd made the 'born' part, have mourned, am still healing, and not ready to die yet. But, by golly, that left laughing and dancing, and I decided that I could certainly choose to do that. Maybe not the dancing part – I needed a good hip and a partner for that. But certainly laughter was within my grasp. And already on this trip that had barely begun, Tuney and I had laughed. A lot. That had to be a good sign.

Amy stood up and announced that we were almost at our

next stop. Tuney slept through the announcement, so I slid over to her seat. I hated to wake her up – she had another tiny smile on her face. I hoped she was dreaming something funny. "Tuney?" I said softly. No sign of consciousness.

"Tune?" I touched her shoulder lightly. "Time to wake up."

"Hmm?"

"Tuney, we're almost at our next stop. Are you okay, or do you want to sleep some more?" I asked sympathetically.

Tuney's eyes widened and she sat straight up. She looked around in a daze, then got her bearings and stretched. "Mmmmm." She looked at me.

"Oh, Cardi! I was dreaming. Tommy and I were young again, and we were in that beautiful glen I told you was great for finding mushrooms. Remember? It's somewhere out in the country. I haven't been back since the time I was a teenager with Tommy. I don't know if I ever told you this, but that's the time I realized I loved him."

My heart sank. "Oh, Tune! I'm sorry I woke you."

She shook her head at my apology. "It's okay! I can sleep any time." She smiled at me and I thought that she looked much more refreshed than she had when she'd first fallen asleep. She rolled her shoulders, yawned again, and looked out the window.

I sat next to her silently for a moment, then asked, "Do you want to tell me about the dream? You look like it was a happy one."

She glanced at me, smiled, then turned to the window again. I thought she was going to just stare outdoors for a while, but then she began quietly talking, almost as if she was reading a book out loud. I leaned nearer to hear what she said.

"Tommy and I were just two teenagers mushroom hunting

morels near a bunch of trees, and we'd wandered quite a ways. We stepped out of the woods after following a path that animals, most likely deer, had made. The glen was so beautiful. It was bathed in a bright fresh gold from the spring sunshine. I couldn't believe where the path had led us. For a moment I stood still, smiling with so much delight at the scenery that my eyes were almost creased shut. The sun filtered through what few little leaves had popped out on the trees and dappled the green grass. I remember I turned my face upward to the sun and let it soak into my closed eyelids. But I didn't want to miss this enchanted fairyland of verdant newness, so I opened my eyes quickly. *This must be what Monet felt like when he started painting*, I thought. I was mesmerized by the colors in the glen . It was like they emerged as proof that winter was once again over. Every shade of green was displayed in almost myopic softness: moss tempered the rough bark of trees, new leaves unfurling in the sunshine were colors of lime, apple and emerald green. Those who were shadowed were a darker khaki or olive-green color. The variation of colors was delightful. Dotted among the greens were shades of blue, almost as if the sky had dripped its azure and cerulean colors to the ground. Patches of violets, bluebells with their pink bud casings, and some Sweet William among the trees added just the right accent colors. I breathed deeply and smelled the damp earth mingled with the wildflower's soft scents."

By now, my mouth had dropped open. Tuney's speech was not usually this eloquent. NEVER this poetic or descriptive! Tuney was a teacher and had taught school her entire adult life. For the past couple of decades, she'd taught in elementary school. But she'd always loved English, poetry and reading, and that love of words was pouring out her mouth. *I'm gonna have to look up what cerulean is,* I thought. Tuney leaned her head back against her seat, closed her eyes, and was silent for a moment. Then she opened her eyes. A little glint of tears appeared, but she grinned at me and continued.

"I glanced over at Tommy. He was standing near me and for the first time in the years I'd known him, I studied him curiously. He was certainly attractive and he was tall, which I liked. He was witty and fun to be with, too. For some reason, his height made me feel safe and secure, and this puzzled me. I considered myself independent, so why would I need to have those feelings? His back was to me so I could see his dark hair curled at the nape of his neck. There were golden glints on the top of his head from the sun. He turned to glance over at me, noticed me watching him, and grinned. A dimple on his right cheek deepened. I remember I caught my breath.

"Cardi, it was as though I were in an enchanted woods. Feelings I'd never felt before were awakening in me - just as the glen area was awakening with the spring weather. We'd been dating for a few months, off and on, and I realized that I'd taken him for granted all the years I'd known him. It was nice to know I had a date every Friday or Saturday night. But there in the glen, in the magic of spring, at only age 17, something else happened. Something deepened in me and instinctively I knew I loved this boy, and that we would marry."

I nodded, misty-eyed at the picture my sister's words painted. She reached over and patted my hand and turned toward me a bit.

"He walked over to me, grabbed my hand, and asked if I wanted to take a little hike in the woods – 'to keep looking for mushrooms,' he said. I nodded and smiled. I was half afraid to leave the moment I'd just experienced, and yet eager to be with him. But the magic I felt in the glen seemed to follow me with each step I took as we continued hiking.

"We found a big patch of morel mushrooms near a fallen log. After picking those and shoving them in a paper bag Tommy had brought, we sat on the log and talked. I'd always loved the topics he could talk about, and he seemed to enjoy my conversations, too. We started laughing at something he said, and I leaned over to hug him. Oh, Cardi! He took me by my shoulders, looked deep into my eyes, and then kissed me, hard and long. When he let me go, I leaned toward him and kissed him back. We both stared at each other and it was like we saw our future together. We smiled, and then sat contentedly with my head on his shoulder and his arm around me. After a bit, Tommy stood up, dug deep in a pocket of his jeans and pulled out a pocket knife. He walked to an area of the log where the bark had fallen off, leaving a smooth, clean surface. Quickly, but carefully, he carved both our initials in the log, encasing them in a crooked-shaped heart.

"We kissed again. And then again. When the sun had risen high enough that we knew we should listen to our stomachs and go eat, we walked together back through the glen to where the car was parked. I took one last look around me. The magic in this wooded area had been erased by the sun, but that didn't bother me. I could still feel it inside and knew I'd never forget this place or this moment. Tommy steered the car back on the trail a tractor made and we followed it to the country road. I knew I'd fallen in love and was loved in return. All I wanted to do now was to have the rest of my life start so I could always be with him on whatever road our journey took – forever."

As I watched her while she recounted the dream, I could see the effect it had on her. It was as though it washed her grief away. Her eyes sparkled, her cheeks blushed with a rosy pink, and a smile turned her face into sunshine. But as soon as her story was over, Tuney inhaled deeply and blew out her breath through parted lips. She looked out her window again.

"Oh, Tuney! That was a wonderful dream. How can you remember it so vividly?" I breathed.

She turned to me and I was startled to see how quickly her happiness faded. She said to me sadly, "That was no dream, Cardi. That's how Tommy and I fell in love."

Chapter 7

Amber

Amy had the microphone. "How many of you know about Amber?" she asked.

"What's she done now?" hollered one of the men in the middle of the bus. It was the guy who'd teased me about Cardi B. That set the crowd off in a fit of giggles and snickers. Amy put one hand on her hip and grinned.

"Very funny, Mort! You know, I have a special place for ornery people: in the back of the bus," she warned.

"Fine with me, as long as it's back with all those single ladies." came the mischievous reply. That was quickly followed by a cry of "Ow!" after his wife dug her elbow into his side.

"Uh-oh, girls," laughed Tammy as she turned to her friends and us. "Was Amy saying we have a reputation as trouble-makers already since we're in the back of the bus, too?"

Tuney laughed and chortled along with the others. I marveled how quickly she and I felt the comradery these women shared with her and me deepen. All six of us had only been together for a few hours, yet I felt as comfortable with them as if I'd known them for years.

"Shush," warned Bonnie. "I can't hear what Amy's saying."

"You haven't been able to hear for years – what difference is being quiet going to make?" teased Tammy. Bonnie gleefully nodded her head, stuck a finger in one ear and waggled it up and down as if it would clarify her hearing. We all giggled again, then turned our attention to the front of the bus.

Amy was explaining that this stop hadn't originally been on the itinerary, but after she'd heard about it a few days ago, she felt we needed to stop by.

"Amber is this tiny unincorporated town, but it has a huge claim to fame. It has the world's only hula hoop tree, called *Her Majesty!*"

We were driving on a county road, full of bumps and ruts. I glanced behind me out the back window, but could only see dust, dry and grey, billowing up as Mr. Smith drove on. Suddenly someone called out, "I see it!"

We Widsters craned our necks out into the aisle to look up front through the windshield. Sure enough, what appeared to be a dead tree was coming in to view. Instead of leaves, hundreds of plastic hula hoops hung from various branches like a rainbow of circular jewelry on a giant tree-shaped stand.

The bus was filled with vocalizations about it until Amy stood up with the microphone again as the bus pulled to the side of the road near the tree. "Just a reminder that we're about half an hour away from Dubuque. There, we'll stop at Fenelon Elevator, check in at Hotel Julien, visit the river museum, and have some free time for you to do what you want. And as a reminder," she paused and said with a grin, "we're very near a casino, so if for some reason you haven't paid me completely for this trip, see me before you go gamble!" Everyone laughed.

"Why would she let someone on who hasn't paid in full yet?" asked Bonnie. I had been about to ask the same thing.

Belinda snorted. "It's a joke, dingbat!" We Widsters and the others laughed. Glad I'd kept my mouth shut!

"Well, I didn't know. For sure, that is," grinned Bonnie good-naturedly.

Amy got everyone's attention again. "Right now, we have two options: one is that we can drive slowly past this tree and be in Dubuque by 1:00. The other option is to let you out to stretch your legs, get an up-close look at the tree, AND, if you want to, throw your own hula hoop on the tree!" She paused as everyone started talking again.

"But I don't have a hula hoop, you're saying, right?" she continued.

"RIGHT!" everyone replied in unison.

"I do!" she sang out. "Mr. Smith packed enough hula hoops for everyone and they're stored under the bus for those of you who want one. Plus I brought markers for everyone to write a saying, a wish, or just your name on the hoop before you throw it if you want to memorialize your trip to this one-of-a-kind stop! Any questions?"

Tuney and I looked at each other, and grinned. Then on a whim I raised my hand and Amy pointed at me. "Quiet everyone. One of the Widsters in the naughty part of the bus has a question."

Everyone turned as I stood up. I grimaced and called out, "I haven't hula-hooped for over fifty years. But I challenge anyone who wants to compete in a hula hoop contest to see who can get the most spins around. I'll buy the winner a malt at the next stop!"

Amy yelled "Woo-hoo!" Some people moaned, some clapped, and more than one called back to me, "You're on!" A male voice from somewhere in the front boomed out,

"Change the malt to a beer, and you're on!"

"I prefer malts!" I hollered back. I plopped back down in my seat as Tuney leaned across to me. Her face was concerned.

"Geesh, Cardi, why did you do that? I don't even remember how to hula hoop, do you?" whispered Tuney.

"No, I don't but I'm going to try," I said. Then I looked at her closely. "Tuney, are you worried how you'll look to others?"

"Maybe. I'm all for aesthetics, and me hula-hooping won't be pretty," Tuney replied drily.

"Quit it!" I ordered. "We're here to have fun. Haven't you ever heard of second childhood? And you don't have to play if you don't want!" I tried raising my eyebrow at her and added, "I think you're just worried I'll beat you."

She shrugged and muttered "No way," as we both stood to leave the bus. At least she followed me to the side of the bus where Mr. Smith was handing out yellow, red, blue, green and striped hula hoops to everyone. We joined the 2Bs2Ts and stood together, waiting to hear what was next from Amy. Tuney eyed some of the waistlines, especially of the men, and leaned over to Belinda.

"I know I don't have a waist anymore, but I think I have a better chance than some of those guys do to at least get one rotation around my waist," she smirked.

Belinda and Bonnie turned to look. Mort, the full-sized and good-natured heckler, had put his hula hoop up over his head and then tried to slide it down to his waist. Failing that, he tried stepping into it, but he could it only fit as far as the tops of his legs. He and the others gathered around him were laughing and cracking jokes. Mort hollered over to Amy that he needed a tractor tire innertube instead of the flimsy plastic he was in danger of cracking.

I pointed out to Tuney that at least someone was comfortable enough in his own skin to not worry about what others thought. Tuney looked narrowly at me, chewed her upper lip and was silent. But I saw her eyes darting around to all the people who were teasing Mort. He seemed to relish the wise-cracks and love the banter.

Others put their hoops around their waists and tried valiantly to get them to twirl. Mindful of the time, Amy called for the contest to begin.

"Since Cardi has a bet, I need her and anyone who wants to challenge over here," she announced.

"Wish me luck," I said to Tuney and the 2Bs2Ts. I held up my hoop around my waist and walked to where Amy and others were standing.

"We're right behind you, Cardi," said a voice behind me, "and we're wishing you only bad luck!"

"Yeah! I want a big, thick chocolate malt," came another voice.

I stopped, whirled around to see who was behind me, and almost caused the 2Bs2Ts to crash into me.

"Oh, no," I laughed. "You'd better not beat me too badly."

"Fat chance of that," huffed Bonnie. "I don't think I ever did this as a kid. I was a lot more supple then, and now…" and she stuck her tongue out at her hoop.

About eight contestants were spread out for the first round, and Amy hollered, "Ready, set, twirl!"

Contest on! I prayed the Aleve I took after breakfast was still working and began staring down at my hula hoop as it rotated around my painfully gyrating hips. One person didn't even make one rotation. I knew from groans and a few curses that some had started to lose their hoops, but I didn't dare look up. The count was at nine for me when suddenly Tuney bellowed loud enough for everyone to hear:

"Remember, Card, you got in trouble this morning by wiggling your hips like that!"

I gasped and straightened up, more surprised that she'd say that out loud than I was that she'd raise her voice so loudly. My hoop fell to the ground, and I hollered, "Dang it, Tuney!"

Fortunately for Tuney (so that I didn't blame her for losing), the last competitor other than me had lost her hoop at count eight. I did get a little revenge against her when one of the bus passengers asked me what Tuney meant. I made Tuney stand and tell everyone what had happened to me at the Ox Yoke Inn, thinking she'd hate repeating the story. But while she wrinkled her nose at me, she seemed happy to tell everyone, and even embellished it more than she had to the 2Bs2Ts earlier. A few people commented they'd seen me talking to the group, while one single lady spoke up and said, "I was jealous!" Everyone chuckled.

After she was finished, some people began their own contests. I urged Tuney to join in, but she refused. She was holding a hula hoop and twirled it around her wrist.

"I want to write something on this," she explained, "and it'll probably take all my strength to toss the hoop up in the tree, so I'm not wasting it on throwing my hips out of whack!"

"You're smart. I can feel my hips a bit. And my waist!" I rubbed and pinched the muffin tops gingerly. "Do you suppose I've lost any inches?"

Before Tuney could snort and give me another eyeball someone shouted to us to come back and watch the new competitors.

"Let's go watch," I said, grabbing Tuney's arm.

"No, you go," she insisted. "I want to think of something to write on this."

Tuney grabbed a magic marker from the pile Amy had laid out. When I looked back at her after one of the ladies lost her hoop on the second twirl, she had leaned against the bus and seemed to be thinking about what she wanted to write. The next time I looked for her, she had wandered over to the tree. She was watching people trying to throw their hoops onto the branches. It must have a been a huge tree at one time. It looked as though the trunk was burned once, and I wondered if it had been struck by lightning, or if someone had tried to burn it down.

Hoops of many different colors hung like giant gaudy bracelets on the "arms" of the tree. Tuney was smiling. The contest I'd initiated was over. No one beat my nine twirls, so I walked over to Tuney, carrying my hula hoop with me. She smiled when I gave her a high five and told her I'd won.

"That saved you some money, anyway, not having to buy a drink," she said. "Look, Cardi," and she pointed at all the hoops on the tree. "I remember the time when my granddaughter Heather was only four. She showed me and Tommy her "jooree." Both her little arms had plastic bracelets in different sizes from her wrists to above her elbows. Tommy had picked her up and told her she looked ravishing. He twirled her around in his arms, and she laughed and laughed. Then when he thought he'd better quit because he was getting dizzy, he sat her on his lap, and told her all the jewelry in the world would never be as coveted as she was to him." She paused and sighed, but I was glad to see she wasn't getting misty-eyed. I had finally learned, and hoped she had, that memories were fun and didn't hurt.

"I almost told Tommy that Heather couldn't possibly know the meaning of 'coveted.' But before I could, Heather just stared into her grandfather's eyes. Then she suddenly smiled, wrapped her small arms around Tommy's neck, and kissed his cheek. Tommy kissed her back, and then she hopped off his lap and went to play." Tuney placed her hand over her heart. "Oh, Cardi, you should have seen the look on Tommy's face. He watched Heather leave the room, he sighed, and then smiled at me and said, (and I'll never forget it) 'Ah, Tuney, isn't the circle of life wonderful?'"

I swallowed and gave her a hug. Here I was worried she'd cry at memories of Tommy, and I was the one getting misty-eyed.

"That's it!" she said suddenly and picked up her hula hoop.

"What's it?" I asked curiously.

Tuney ignore me and started writing on her hoop. In a moment, she showed me the carefully printed words on her hoop: *The circle of life IS wonderful, Tommy. No beginning. No end. Just one journey after the other. I'll catch up someday. Love forever, Tuney*

She stared at it for a moment, nodded as if satisfied with herself, then slowly walked nearer to the tree. It was no surprise that the lower branches had the most hoops on them. The upper branches were broken off, but somehow there were hula hoops almost three-fourths of the way up.

Tuney stood far enough away in the hope that she could toss the hoop and catch one of the upper branches. She held the hoop in both hands and planted a little kiss on it.

I played cheerleader. "C'mon, Tuney! Remember your softball pitching. You can do it!"

She looked over at me and waved. "Aw c'mon! You really

think I can remember back that far?" Tuney made a face at me but grinned, then threw the hoop as if it was a frisbee. A southerly breeze helped it soar a little higher than she thought it would. It hit the very highest branch and fell flat onto the branch below. Tuney caught her breath, expecting to watch it fall to the ground. We saw it teeter, then tip to one side and start to fall, but two smaller branches snagged it, and it rested securely hooked to the top of the tree.

I let out a yell. Some other passengers had watched Tuney throw it, and they cheered, startling her. She looked at them, and gave us all a thumbs up, smiling. "Well, Tommy, that was as high as I could get it, so hope it's close enough for you to read," I heard her murmur.

She looked at me and said, "Well, I can't twirl a hula hoop, but I didn't too bad a job throwing one!"

"No kidding," I said enviously. "Will you throw mine for me? I just wrote something to Kris."

Before she could answer, the sound of raucous laughter caused us to turn to see what was going on.

"Uh-oh," I grinned and pointed. "Look! It's the 2Bs2Ts." I squinted trying to see more clearly. "What on earth are they doing?"

"I have no idea, but whatever it is, they're cracking the crowd up. Look at Amy! She's bent over laughing!" replied Tuney. "Hurry up. Let's go see!" She grabbed my hoop from me and gave it a toss. It, too, went high, but not as high as Tuney's. However, it safely stuck on a branch with my little message to Kris: *I'm looking for the positives in life – and I'm positive we'll meet again, my love.* That was all I wanted.

We hurried over to the crowd. Belinda and Mort were surrounded by the rest of the tour group. Each one had a hula hoop around their neck. Trudy spied the Widsters and motioned us to come over.

"What's going on?" asked Tuney.

Just then the crowd screamed with laughter as Belinda swung her hoop around her neck and bent over a bit as she rotated her neck around and around to keep the hoop going. Everyone started counting. At seven, we could tell Belinda started to get dizzy and staggered a bit but managed to make one more circle for eight rotations. A few people closest to her grabbed her arms, and Belinda straightened up and grabbed her hoop before it fell over her body.

Trudy was laughing so hard she had tears in her eyes. "It's a hoop-off!" she explained. "Mort said he couldn't hula hoop the normal way but could beat anyone hula-hooping using his neck."

Tammy was next to Trudy and she was dabbing her eyes with a tissue. "Oh, goodness!" she exclaimed. "I haven't laughed this hard for years! You two missed the first couple of competitors."

Bonnie turned to us. "Oh, girls, this is hilarious. Mort's first challenger was that man over there," and she pointed at another man that I remembered was named Joe. His wife was holding his arm and laughing, too. "He got his hoop going, but had his mouth open, and his…" her face contorted as she tried to stifle the laughter that began to bubble "… his dentures…fell out!" And she went into another fit of laughter.

Darn it! I wished we hadn't missed that Kodak moment. But I noticed there were plenty of cameras and phones clutched in the hands of the onlookers. The bus trip would have plenty of photos to share, I was sure. Trudy grabbed Tuney's arm.

"Some other guys tried, too, but all they could do was spin

the hoop with their hand," she explained. "Mort just puts it on his neck and somehow he can get that thing going and, - what? How many times can he twirl it without stopping?" She turned to the others for an answer.

"Seven!" was the chorus.

"That's right," nodded Trudy. "And Belinda just beat that! And so now Mort has to get nine to beat Belinda or she wins!"

I started to ask just what it was she would win, but Mort suddenly held up his hand, grinning. The laughter and talking subsided as all eyes turned to him.

"Well, folks, as a gentleman," and he turned to his wife, who rolled her eyes and winked with a grin. "Why, Mary! I saw that, and I'm aghast and dismayed you'd make a face at me!" he teased. His wife Mary issued another eye roll, wink, and a loving smile at her rotund husband. He smiled back and continued.

"I may be considered a senior citizen, but I keep up with the times pretty much." Mort paused again because of the guffaws and snickers. He raised both hands in protest. "I know with all this MeToo Movement, I should treat the ladies with respect and dignity, but I'm not gonna do that."

He was interrupted again by not only his wife, but all the rest of the ladies who cried out in mock indignation. Mort was genuinely surprised.

"What? What did I say?"

Amy stepped in. "Why, Mort! You strike me as a guy who would always treat ladies with respect and dignity!"

Mort nodded, turning around to all the crowd. "Exactly. I'm a gentleman. And what I'm trying to tell you all is that while I would normally do what a gentleman does, which would be to let the very talented hoopster Belinda, here, win

– I'm not gonna do that because of the MeToo Movement."
He paused and looked smugly at Mary and Amy.

"Huh? That doesn't make sense." Tuney and I shook our heads, puzzled. The people on the bus were perplexed but half smiling with confused frowns on their faces.

"Uh, Mort," Tuney tentatively asked. He turned to look at her. "Just what do you think the MeToo Movement is about?"

"Why, equality!" he answered promptly. "You ladies deserve to be treated equally, just like anyone else. And that's what I'm gonna do! Just like I did to these other guys, I'm gonna beat the pants off Belinda – so to speak," Mort finished proudly.

Everyone burst into laughter, and a few people hollered in jest to Mary that she'd better teach Mort about current events and what they mean. It was Mort's turn to look confused. But Belinda walked up next to him and shushed the crowd.

"I know what he means," she responded. "And if he can beat the pants off me – figuratively, mind you – by getting his hoop to twirl around his neck nine times, then I will buy him a beer when we get to the Dubuque casino tonight!"

Mort cheered, as did everyone else. "Let the games begin!" he shouted. He placed his hoop around his neck, and I started chanting 'Mort, Mort, Mort, Mort.' Soon everyone else was good-naturedly intoning his name, too.

He bent over as far as his belly would allow him to and started twirling the hoop around his neck. "One, two, three," counted the crowd. Belinda had stepped back next to the us and was counting along with everyone else.

"Oh, Tuney, he's going to make it!" I breathed as he easily passed six rotations.

"No! Look! He's getting dizzy," pointed Tuney.

Sure enough, just like Belinda, Mort started to stagger. But before anyone could grab him, he grabbed his hoop and pulled it off his head as he headed toward a section of the crowd. He thrust his hoop in front of him as if it could help him regain his balance. Mary and Mr. Smith sprinted after him, but they were too late. As he plunged forward, the crowd parted, afraid of being knocked down, if not completely crushed, by the full-sized man. He made a last awkward attempt to use the hoop as a cane to right himself but ended up bending it as he fell headfirst.

A unanimous groan from the tourists filled the air, followed by a few screams and yells of concern and fright. Mort lay as flat as a man with a beer belly could lay. To our frightened eyes, it appeared he was not only on the ground, but suffering a seizure. His shoulders were shaking, and his head was moving from side to side. One of the bus passengers, a former nurse she had told everyone, pushed through the crowd, managed to lower herself to her knees and was bent over him.

Belinda had started crying, and so were some other women. Mary was next to Mort, frantically calling his name, and Mr. Smith was on his knees next to him patting Mort's back. The crowd moved closer, and we heard a few people murmuring prayers. The rest of us were as silent as a cat's paws on feathers. I started to shake as the memories of when Kris died flooded over me. I'd screamed his name over and over again, vainly trying to wake him up. I stood frozen next to Tuney, my eyes tightly shut, with her hand squeezing mine.

Suddenly, Mary cried out, "WHAT?" and slapped Mort's back hard. "You big JERK, you!" she hollered.

My eyes flew open. Everyone gasped, but their fright and confusion disappeared in astonishment as Mort rolled over, almost knocking over the nurse. He let out the biggest belly laugh Tuney and I had ever heard. Mort lay helpless on the ground, not because of any injury, but because he couldn't stop laughing. The relief that he was okay, plus the fact his laughter was infectious, soon had everyone but Mary joining in the merriment, too.

"Get up, you son of a bee!" ordered his enraged wife. Her very real fright that her husband had died was replaced by fury. Mr. Smith helped Mort sit up, and then a few other fellows helped pull him back to standing. He finally got control of himself and stood sheepishly looking at everyone around him. Mary glared at him, gave him a big hug, a kiss, and then punched him in the arm. It must have been hard, because he looked down at her shocked and grabbed his arm in pain. Tuney and I looked at each other and grimaced. We knew Mort wasn't going to get through the rest of the trip without the mother of all scoldings from his poor wife. I couldn't help but think I'd gladly change places with her to have Kris around to be mad at.

The realization of what everyone must have thought seemed to hit him harder than his wife. His face was a picture of shame and humiliation.

"I am SO sorry," he began. "It just struck me funny how that musta looked. An old fat man lurching around like a drunk with a kid's hula hoop." He started to chuckle again, caught the look on Mary's face, and faltered. "Well, let's just say that I was a big fan of The Three Stooges and Abbott and Costello when I was growing up. But I guess this is a lesson for me. I'll never try anything like this again."

He glanced over at Belinda, who was wiping the tears off her face with a tissue and looked sorrowfully at her. "I've frightened my beautiful wife, embarrassed myself, and from the looks of it, scared the daylights out of most of you. Belinda, I owe you a beer. Again, I'm so sorry.'"

Belinda glared at him for a moment, then winked at him and with a haughty tone replied, "If you think a simple beer is going to cut it, you're wrong, Mister! I'll let you order me a Coronarita!"

A few people clapped and cheered. Then Bonnie and the 2Ts whooped three cheers for Belinda and hugged her.

A very concerned Amy stepped over to the extremely chastised Mort. "Mort, you can tell how much people care about you. We're all just glad you're okay." She patted his arm, and he looked up at her with a hang-dog expression. I saw her peer sharply at him, then with a crooked grin she turned to the crowd. I had also seen him wink at her.

"Phew! Talk about highs and lows! But as the old saying goes, all's well that ends well." Amy rubbed her hands together. "If you haven't tossed a hoop on the tree, you've got five minutes to do so and get on the bus. The rest of you can go ahead and board. I don't know about others, but with all that laughter, I just about peed my pants. We need to get Dubuque and a bathroom – or else give me first dibs to use the restroom on the bus!"

Everyone started clapping, and all but a few boarded the bus. By the time everyone was back on board, we Widsters and the 2Bs2Ts had started visiting back and forth about what tiny towns, even unincorporated villages like Amber could offer. The couple who sat in the row in front of Trudy and Belinda had also joined the conversation.

"Have any of you ever ridden RAGBRAI?" asked Tuney. The couple, Doug and Barb, who had only recently moved to Iowa from Michigan to be closer to family, asked what a RAGBRAI was.

Kris and I had ridden on one, and so had Bonnie and Tammy with their late husbands. I stood up in the aisle between the Ts and B's row so the couple could hear Tuney and me better.

"It's a seven-day bicycle ride across the state that begins with everyone dipping their back tire in the Missouri River in the west. Each night the riders stay in a host town. Then the ride ends somewhere along the Mississippi River where they dip their front tire. RAGBRAI is an acronym for the Register's Annual Great Bike Ride Across Iowa."

"The Des Moines Register is a newspaper, and two of its columnists who liked to bike ride started it. It's the oldest, longest, and largest bike riding event in the U.S.," added Bonnie.

"In the world, actually," chimed in Tammy.

"Well, that doesn't surprise me. I still have the blisters from 1979 on my butt to prove it!" Bonnie said drily. She sat on one side of her hip and rubbed her hind end.

I explained how the route changes from year to year, and that small towns especially benefit from it.

"Why would that be?" asked Doug. He was so interested in our story that he was making notes on an old napkin he found.

Tuney leaned into the aisle from her seat. "There can be 10,000 people traveling through all the towns along whichever route there is," she explained. "Our little town has a population of only around 5,000 people and we hosted an overnight stay one year."

"Wow!" exclaimed Barb, duly impressed. "Wherever did you put all the people and bikes? And were there enough restaurants to feed them?"

"That's the big benefit the small towns get," I said. "This thing is planned a year in advance. Churches and other organizations can sell food. Most bikers have tents that are carried from one overnight stop to the next by large trucks and vans. And I'm always amazed about how many people from other countries participate. There are porta-potties and usually some sort of shower facility available if there's a school with a gymnasium."

"Which is a great place to stretch out in sleeping bags if the weather is bad," contributed Bonnie.

I went on to explain that the overnight cities need to have enough facilities for the bikers. Because some bikers prefer to stay in a bed each night, the towns also list people who are willing to house them. All the towns included in the ride can offer food, drinks and entertainment to the riders. That way, local churches and organizations who need a fundraiser can usually raise the amount of money they need.

Tammy and Bonnie supplied some stories of their own about their favorite food and unusual sights they saw during their week-long trek years ago. Tuney started thinking of how tiny little towns like Amber might benefit from such an event.

"Hey, you guys. We should notify the Register when we get back home to suggest they might want to check out Amber as a pass-through town, at least," she offered.

My eyebrows rose. "Oh, that's a great idea, Sis! The Hula Hoop Tree would be a great photo op, naturally. Amber could probably use some extra money. Wonder what else they could do to raise cash?"

All eight of us tourists put our heads together to come up with something. Before the bus reached the city of Dubuque, suggestions and ideas that had floated around included selling hula hoops, various games using hula hoops in the field by the Hula Hoop Tree, a contest to see who could throw the highest hoop on the tree ("Don't break my record, though," kidded Tuney), having hula grass skirts, leis and Hawaiian shirts on hand for a photo op beneath the tree, and selling amber jewelry. For food, they came up with grilled "Amber-gers" and fried veggie hoops (onion rings), "Amber-osia" drinks, and all sorts of Hawaiian foods.

"This was fun!" laughed Tuney. "I just don't know if there are enough people in that tiny town who could pull it off if RAGBRAI ever went through it."

"Oh, we Michiganites never underestimate the creativity of Iowans," declared Doug. "Our son-in-law is an Iowa native, and he and his family and friends are some of the nicest, most fun, and imaginative people I've ever met."

The conversation continued until Amy popped up in the front of the bus with her handy microphone to announce the next stop. The city of Dubuque on the Mississippi was near.

Tuney and I looked at each other and smiled.

"I'm glad we stopped there," said Tuney quietly. "I think Tommy would have enjoyed all the fun. And now his memory will always be on that tree. I hope, anyway, unless a big wind blows it down!"

"I'm just glad Amy kept bugging me to go on this trip," I confessed. "I never dreamed how much fun it would be to be able to talk and laugh so much with this many different people."

"Me, too," nodded Tuney solemnly. "Wonder what Dubuque will be like?"

Chapter 8

Into Dubuque

I'd been to Dubuque twice. Once through it on my way over to Chicago, and once through it on my way back home from Chicago. Shortly after Kris and I were married, we were invited to spend a weekend at one of his college friend's apartment and "do the town." I barely remembered that trip. I especially did not remember anything about Dubuque except crossing the bridge over the Mississippi.

I turned to the window and was surprised to see how the scenery had changed in the short time it took the bus to travel from tiny Amber to Dubuque. Not only had the traffic increased immensely, but the terrain had changed quite a bit. Steep and rolling hills were filled with oaks, birch, maples and pine trees. As the bus climbed up one hill, I saw that the blasting from construction of the highway years ago had exposed the underlying limestone and shale from the bluffs that were along the Mississippi River. If you had even the slightest imagination, you would think you were in the Colorado Rockies...well, maybe lots of imagination, but it did remind me of them. The bus drove along the top of the bluff and then began descending into the city.

Tuney was delighted to see the Mississippi and the huge bridge that spanned the river into Illinois and Wisconsin. I was, too, for that matter. The ol' Miss, Old Man River, the Big Muddy – no matter what you called it, was a wonderful, unique and very historical body of water. As the bus entered the city, I could see quite a few train tracks, boats and lots of older, beautiful homes.

"Oh, wow! Tuney, can you see this side? There are gorgeous old homes that are built on the top of the bluff. I can't imagine what a beautiful view they have!" I was pointing to the top of a big bluff that sat back from the river and overlooked a large part of the oldest section of Dubuque.

Tuney slid over to my side so she could see. She spotted something odd and when she pointed it out to all of us, the 2Bs2Ts got excited.

"What is that? It looks like train tracks going straight up the side," Tuney asked.

Belinda peered out her window. "Oh, that's the Fenelon Elevator," she gushed. "My late husband talked about going on it when he was young. And I think we're scheduled to go see it."

Tuney stared at the tracks and then pointed again. I saw what looked like a little box slowly descend from the top of the bluff. Halfway down, we saw a second little box meet the first one as it ascended and realized that there were two tracks. By now we could see that the tracks weren't straight up and down but at a rather steep incline.

Amy stood up in front and announced that the Fenelon Elevator would be our first stop. Belinda turned around and mouthed the words 'told you so!'

"We're stopping here for about an hour. For anyone who wants to ride the Fenelon Place Elevator, it's fun to ride and only costs $1.50 each way. Which adds up, in case you're mathematically challenged, to three whole dollars. You pay at the top." She scanned her phone and then read, "The Fenelon Place Elevator is described as the world's shortest, steepest scenic railway, 296 feet in length, elevating passengers 189 feet from Fourth Street to Fenelon Place where you will see a magnificent view of the historic Dubuque business district, the Mississippi River and three states."

Tuney saw someone in the front of the bus raise her hand and ask Amy a question. The back of the bus couldn't hear, and evidently it was a softly spoken question, because Amy nodded, then spoke into the microphone.

"I just got a good question. No, you do not have to ride the elevator! There are lots of interesting little shops and boutiques around here, plus some fabulous coffee shops. As a matter of fact, if you are going to ride the elevator, you may want to wander around down here first so that you're not waiting in line." She scanned the crowd, then asked, "Any more questions? No? Okay, then let's deboard by letting the back passengers off the bus first. We'll meet back here in one hour!"

"Yay!" I cried, scrambling to grab my purse and my phone. "Let's go Tuney. We can be first to the top and then head down and shop, okay?"

"Definitely!" Tuney grabbed her purse, we walked off the bus and hurried to the elevator car. It was built on a slant, with four rows of single seats and an aisle up the middle. Two seats in each row faced one another so that the passengers could look both uphill and downhill without having to twist or turn in their seats to see the views. There was a door with a window on the back that was closed for the climb upward. Tuney and I sat at the top section near the exit back door so we could watch the tracks and cable that would pull the car uphill. The 2Bs2Ts had followed us. After they climbed in, along with another couple, the car was full.

"We're ready," I called, looking for some sort of buzzer to press. "Why aren't we going?" Directly opposite of me, Tuney looked at me as if she were long-suffering. The look clearly was meant to say *just be patient!*

Tuney turned to face the hill. "That's the answer to your question," she pointed. "There's only one track, so we must have to wait."

"Huh? But there's not another track down here, so where would it go?"

The 2Bs2Ts also turned to look. "I thought there'd be two tracks," said Bonnie. "Didn't we see two cars going up and down when we drove into the city?"

"Yeah, I definitely saw that," I affirmed. I wondered if the other track ran a little further away from this one through the brush and trees that grew on the hillside.

The other couple riding with us were seated on the lowest level of seats. On the bus, they sat in front of Belinda and Trudy, so had visited with those two on the ride over. While we waited to begin our ascent, Trudy introduced them to me and Tuney as Larry and Sue. Larry smiled and pointed up the hill.

"I've ridden this years ago. Look uphill about half-way. This car and one coming downhill are each on one track. But see how it divides? That way the two cars pass each other on separate sections, then proceed up or down on the one track," he said.

Six heads nodded with knowing "ahs" as we Widsters and 2Bs2Ts spotted the divide Larry was talking about.

"It's really amazing to think this thing is over a hundred and thirty years old," he added. "And at that time, they had to have the technique just right so that the two cars counter-balanced one another." Suddenly, there was a clanging sound and the cable car began to move.

"Oh, geez, that scared me," I breathed, clutching at my heart. "Did Larry say this thing's over a hundred and thirty?" I looked dubiously at the metal tracks and the cable that I could see moving.

"Oh, look, everyone!" Tuney called out. "I see the other car is moving towards us!" We all looked up and out the back window, which was now the top window, to watch the approaching cable car.

The cable was heavily greased. When Tuney wrinkled her nose against the strong odor, I pointed out to her that it smelled better than the skunk. She agreed. The cable itself squeaked as if complaining about the weight it hauled. The sound of the iron wheels on the tracks and the groan of the wooden car as it swayed slightly on its ascent made me unconsciously tighten my neck and shoulders. I realized that both Tuney and I were leaning upward to "help" the car climb.

There were lots of vegetation on either side of the track. Grass scattered periodically with wildflowers and daylilies grew on the limestone rocks beneath the tracks. From the bottom of the hill to about halfway up were trees and bushes. I noticed stumps of those shrubs that had vainly tried to grow too close to the tracks and instead had been cut down to protect the elevator.

We got closer to the approaching car, then it veered to the

south the same time we veered to the north. The descending car wasn't quite full, but all the passengers in both elevators waved at each other. A few moments later, our car veered back to the south and was once again on one track upward.

We quickly arrived at an old white building featuring a sign that welcomed us. The car stopped and the back door next to Tuney and me automatically opened. As we exited, everybody started talking at once. There were two people standing outside a small window on the building, A woman inside the window was taking their money for the trip downhill. Tuney and I stood behind them, paid our three dollars each for a roundtrip ticket, and then walked over to a deck to enjoy the view.

The scene was spectacular. We Widsters could see some of our bus tour members standing far below and we watched as the cable car we'd passed on the way up now ascended full of people, while the one we'd ridden up on descended with passengers on their way back down. From our vantage point we could see a short street. It led to the bottom of the elevator hill and ran for blocks eastward before it stopped at a green area near the Mississippi River. The city stretched along the river. Most of its buildings were made of red or brown brick. Across the river were the tree-lined states of Wisconsin and Illinois. I snapped pictures of the view, then attempted a selfie of both Tuney and me.

"How old is Dubuque?" asked Tuney, wondering how its founders could build along, in and on top of the bluffs.

"I have no idea, but maybe Larry knows," I spotted Larry and Sue standing a few feet over and hollered to them. When they joined us, I told him, "We're christening you our history guru, whether you like it or not! What can you tell us about Dubuque?"

Sue grinned good-naturedly and remarked, "That's a lovely way to call him by what he really is – a know-it-all!"

Larry poked her gently in the ribs with his elbow and smiled down at her. I smiled at that but felt a pang of sorrow as I remembered Kris doing the same thing to me once or twice. I laughed as soon as Sue stuck her tongue out at her husband.

"Go ahead, dear," she urged. "I want to hear, too."

Larry cleared his throat and then began talking about how Dubuque was founded. A French-Canadian fur trader named Julien Dubuque came to the area in the 1780s. At that time, the Mesquakie, or Fox tribe, of Native Americans had settled here after leaving the Great Lakes region. Dubuque and the Mesquakie became friends, and the Mesquakie told him about the lead mines in the area, which he called the "Mines of Spain." The French Canadian and the Native Americans worked together to mine the lead found nearby because it was greatly in demand in Europe. Dubuque was the first European to settle in the state of Iowa, and he lived lavishly until his death when he was in his late forties.

I interrupted Larry. "Excuse me, but why were they called mines of Spain when Dubuque was French? Or why not Mines of Mesquakie – that has a nice ring to it, and they were the first to discover it."

"Good question," answered Larry. By now two more groups of the bus tour were crowded around them, some taking photos of the scenery and others avidly listening to Larry.

"I know you remember the Louisiana Purchase, right? The territory that is now Iowa was part of 'Louisiana' and therefore Spanish. The Spanish government even gave Julien Dubuque official control of the mines. He operated them, quite successfully, until his death. There's a monument to him just south of the city on a high bluff where he's buried."

Larry went on to explain that it didn't take long for the city of Dubuque to attract large numbers of immigrants who settled in the area. Fur trading, mining, button making from the fresh-water mussels, boat building, logging, mill working and meat-packing were just some of the jobs available to anyone who wanted to work. The Mississippi allowed these businesses to easily transport their goods.

"How on earth do you know all these things?" asked Tuney in admiration. "I taught school for forty years, and know some of Iowa history, but not this much with all the details you've given!"

Before Larry could answer, Sue laughed. "He's a retired professor of history from Iowa State University, so he'd better know a thing or two about it! Now, if only I could get him to learn to pick up his dirty clothes!"

"That must be a genetic male trait," Tuney laughed back. "My Tommy was the same way!"

I laughed, too. "We should take a vote among the ladies here." Some of the bus riders were getting back on one of the cable cars to descend, and we decided to ride down, too. "Hey! How many ladies have ever had trouble teaching their hubbies to pick up their dirty clothes? Raise your hands."

Almost all the women around us shot their arms up quickly. I looked pointedly at Larry while he and a few of the other men just shook their heads in good natured defeat. Tuney and I were still smiling as we grabbed the next cable car back to the bottom of the hill.

Once down on the street, we walked around looking at all the little shops. We saw our bus pull back near the elevator from where Mr. Smith had parked it several blocks away, We sauntered back and climbed aboard. After everyone appeared to be on, Amy counted heads and then hollered without her microphone to hang tight for about five minutes. Our hotel near the Mississippi River was the next stop.

Chapter 9

Checking In to Check It Out

The Hotel Julien was our next stop. We were scheduled to eat dinner in the hotel's fabulous restaurant and spend the night. Amy had already checked us in. When we entered the lobby, Tuney pointed at a sign.

"Cardi, won't this be fun? See? 'Modern Amenities with Historic Charm.' Wonder exactly how old and historic the Julien is."

"Actually," came the helpful voice of the clerk behind the counter, who couldn't help but overhear our excited – and obviously loud – chatter. "Several years ago, our new owner renovated the entire building. People still call us the Hotel Julien, but we've given Julien back his entire name. We are proud to say Welcome to the Hotel Julien Dubuque!"

We all moved a little closer to him, and he smiled widely at us. "Excuse me for boasting, but we have 133 guest rooms, a restaurant, the Riverboat Lounge, a spa, a pool, a fitness center, and large banquet facilities. There used to be 168 guest rooms, but they were small compared to more modern hotels. They were converted into 133 luxury rooms and suites. We also restored the lobby and grand ballroom, and you're all welcome to explore any of these facilities, as long as they're not in use, of course."

"How old is the hotel?" someone asked.

The clerk beamed. "Like so many buildings in Dubuque, we have quite a history. We can trace the beginnings of the hotel back to 1839." He received some 'wows,' 'ohs' and 'ahs' and encouraged, continued. "Right across the river in Illinois is the town of Galena. Abraham Lincoln stayed here in the 1850s, we believe, when he traveled to Galena to attend to some legal matters there. We're not positive, of course, because a fire in 1913 destroyed the hotel. But by 1915, it had been rebuilt."

I was looking at the beautiful dark woodwork in the grand lobby. Marble columns and gold wallpaper added an opulence that I wasn't used to seeing in hotels. *Probably,* I thought, *because Kris and I usually stayed in cheaper motels!* I poked Tuney in the ribs and whispered, "Can't you just see F. Scott Fitzgerald and Zelda here? It's so 'Gatsby,' isn't it?"

Tuney looked around and pointed out luxurious mirrors and chandeliers. "I can't wait to see our room," she murmured. I was so happy she was excited. I wanted to go ahead and find our room as soon as Amy passed out our keys, but a name mentioned by the hotel clerk, who was still reciting the hotel's history to other guests, caught my attention.

"Hotel Julien Dubuque has had some very interesting guests," he said. "Among them was Chicago mobster Al Capone. He liked our little town of Dubuque and supposedly when he had trouble in Chicago, he'd use the hotel - or as it was known during that period, the Julien Inn – as a hideout. Locals during that time talked about his underground garage in the area in order to hide his personal cars so he could remain unobtrusive while he was here."

Amy was listening intently and making some notes about the history, probably for future tours here, I thought.

"And we even have had Hollywood star Sylvester Stallone stay here during the filming of the movie F.I.S.T."

"Ooh," cooed Bonnie. "Which bedroom did he stay in? I want that!" The 2Bs2Ts giggled. "And the Widsters can have the room Capone stayed in," she added.

"Oh, thanks a lot," Tuney and I cried. The clerk started to apologize, but Tuney laughed and said, "You have to know that anything these people say is usually a joke!"

Just then Amy saw us and hurried over. "We're going to have a few more hours until all the rooms will be ready," she explained as the clerk nodded. "I suggest we walk over to the River Museum. I promise it's very interesting. The Casino is next door to that, too, in case anyone would prefer to try their luck. Lunch is on your own, and tonight we're eating here in the hotel restaurant at 6:30. Does that sound okay with everyone?"

We were thrilled to be on our own a bit more. Tuney and I took off for on the five-minute walk from the hotel to the museum. The five-minutes, combined with the heat and humidity near a river in Iowa in August, made it seem like five hours. In no time at all, I was dripping like an ice cube on a cookstove. I hate being sticky and sweaty, so naturally I grumbled all the way over and thought about turning back to the hotel's lounge. But as soon as we entered the museum, I was glad I hadn't.

I'd been expecting a musty old building by the river but was pleasantly surprised to find that the National Mississippi

River Museum and Aquarium was a beautiful compound built in 2003. And with deliciously cool air conditioning, I was relieved to discover. A walkabout outdoors led to an aviary, blacksmith, boat building exhibition, a wetlands area, a paddlewheel steamboat used to dredge the Mississippi and the oldest log cabin in the state – the Mathias Ham House.

As Tuney and I wandered inside around the main building, we were both enchanted with all the displays and exhibits that were not only kid-friendly, but fun and educational for adults, too. The museum wasn't just about the Mississippi River, but the ecology of waterways all over the world. The first river people, different methods of transportation, types of mammals, fish and birds found in or near water were just a few of the things that attracted our attention. There were statues and works of art, movies, posters and display cases to look at. We petted some stingrays that were swimming around a tank in the delta display. A flooded forest display had live wood and green-winged teal ducks. Species of fish one might find in the waters there, such as white bass, sauger, walleye and longnose gar were exhibited in a huge tank that mimicked the river water.

We examined flood tables, a conservation lab and watershed maps of the continents. When we'd been there an hour, I noticed people who were entering the building from the walkabout to the other areas that were available outdoors. They seemed enthusiastic and I decided I might as well visit these areas since we were here, despite the heat and humidity.

"You're crazy," Tuney said, when I told her where I was headed. At least she didn't call me Crazy Cardi. "You couldn't stand five minutes outdoors and that was over an hour ago," she pointed out. "It's quite a bit hotter now."

"Yeah, but…"

A chorus of "Hey, Widsters!" interrupted me. There were the 2Bs2Ts. They'd visited the hotel's lounge first, then evidently decided to explore the museum, too.

Tuney waved and smiled at them. "We were just debating whether or not to go back to the hotel, or to journey back out in the jungle heat to see the stuff outside."

Debating? Whatever!

"Well, it's three against one in favor of viewing the rest of the area," announced Belinda. "I'm the lone protester, but I just told the girls if we can find something icy and cold to drink, I'll go with them."

"We were just thinking the same thing," I said. "We should see all we can while we're here. Who knows when we'll be back." I looked pointedly at Tuney. She pointedly ignored me.

So, before anyone could change her mind, the six of us walked through the sliding doors, and…

"Oof!" The heat and humidity hit us as hard and as quickly as a cat on a mouse. In just the short time we'd been inside, the temperature must have risen one hundred degrees, and I gasped that fact out to the others.

"Suck it up, Buttercup. If the pioneers could handle it, we can, too," came the warning voice of my sweet-like-a-lemon sister. She was frantically waving a brochure around her face to try to make some sort of breeze. I'm proud to say that all six of us managed to make it to the paddlewheel boat - the William M. Black. By that time, we all decided it was the only thing we'd stop to see. Then we'd head back to the hotel or the casino and cool off until it was time for supper.

Once we'd walked aboard the moored boat, a little breeze sprang up over the river, and I was glad we'd decided to see this exhibit. At 277 feet long and 85 feet wide, it was huge. The Black had been built in 1934 as a dredge. Its huge side wheel was powered by steam. Walking on the main deck, we got to see the gigantic nuts, bolts, ropes, and pipes.

"How can this possibly float?" I asked in amazement. I stood with my mouth open looking at the huge smokestacks and the dredge pump engine. They were only part of the heavy metal that made up quite a bit of the structure of the boat, plus the paddle wheels weighed 32 tons each!

Tuney looked at the others and pointed at me. "She still can't figure out how airplanes fly, either," she said, mocking my habit of dreading to fly. I never could grasp the concept of physics needed to understand how tons of metal can soar in the air, but an ostrich can't.

"It's mechanical engineering, Honey, and I only know that because I have a grandson who wants to build airplanes!" chimed in Tammy.

I just shrugged. I don't mind not knowing *everything*. Sometimes it's neat to just feel awed by the magic of what a man or machine can do. "Well, *I'm* impressed," I said simply and ran my hand over a gigantic nut and bolt near the boilers.

When we'd finished exploring the main deck, we looked for an elevator to take us up another floor. The only way up, another tourist told us, was to climb the slender iron ladders found at the fore and aft part of the boat.

We looked at each other doubtfully, but then Bonnie said, "Well, if someone will push my aft so that I can keep going fore, I'm game!" We all giggled like little kids.

"And think of the pictures we can take from the top," I said. "There's the top level after this second deck, and the captain's office is up there."

"What?" asked someone.

Another tourist who had just climbed down one of the ladders, glanced at us, smiled, and with a half-apologetic wave of his hand, said, "It's called the pilot house. It's neat to see, so if you ladies can make it up, I'd go for it."

We looked at each other, then up the straight vertical ladder. I looked at Tuney, and she winced, but then bravely announced, "I think he just challenged us! I'll go first, girls. I'm afraid of heights, so if I can make it, you can, too."

She turned, slung her purse straps around her neck and began to climb slowly and carefully up the ladder. I was half-impressed, half-proud of my older sister because I knew she certainly was afraid of heights. The last time she'd been high in the sky was when we'd ridden a Ferris Wheel together. She'd been 21, and she screeched and screamed the entire time we were on it. It was the first and last time she ever rode one. From then on, any time someone asked her to go to an amusement park, she would adamantly declare herself deathly afraid of heights and then offer to ride the merry-go-round with whomever wanted to go with her.

"Did she say what we should do if she doesn't make it?" whispered Belinda, looking doubtfully up at Tuney's rear end.

"I heard that!" came the muffled voice of Tuney.

Belinda hunched her shoulders and snickered, as I whispered back, "She's got ears like radar!"

Tuney disappeared over the top of the ladder, and then leaned over the railing and called down, "Come on up! It was easy!"

It only a took a few minutes for the rest of us to gingerly climb up. The second deck had the crew's sleeping quarters, staterooms for the captain and engineers, kitchen, bathrooms and storerooms. I noticed Tuney stayed away from the edges of the deck, but she seemed to enjoy looking at everything. When we had finished our tour, we ended up by the last ladder to the top of the boat. Again, we all managed the climb. On top the third deck, or what I would call the roof, there was a small wooden structure with windows on all four sides. It was the pilothouse.

I walked closer to it. Another smaller ladder was against one side, so I climbed it. Almost to the top, I could look in the window. As soon as I did, I let out a shriek and almost fell backwards. As the others hurried toward me with shouts of concern, I was so frightened, I almost slid down the handrails instead of using the ladder steps. Once safely on the deck floor, I was surrounded by Tuney and the 2Bs2Ts asking what happened.

"Oh, for Pete's sake," I panted. The perspiration on my forehead wasn't caused only by the humidity. "I just got the bejeezus scared out of me!"

"You scared us, that's for sure," scolded Tuney. Her face was concerned. "Cardi, you came down those steps so fast, I thought you were falling."

"I'm sorry but blame it on that thing up there!" I pointed to the pilothouse.

"There's somebody up there?" whispered one of the others, as I was bent over to try to calm my breathing. "Who?"

I straightened up, feeling a bit calmer. I was tempted to see if anyone else would be as scared. I'd feel better about myself, I was sure, if I wasn't the only nervous old lady in the group.

"Not a who!" I said mysteriously. "A what!" and looked at all four.

Tuney started to look skeptical. But Tammy asked, "What? A spider?" doubting that I was serious.

"No. Not that kind of a what." I looked up at the pilot house, but from where we stood, we couldn't see inside. "Take a look for yourself!"

My friends and sister looked at each other. Tuney finally said, "C'mon, chickens. If there was anything scary there, someone would have warned us to be careful. I doubt there's anything bad."

"I'm not going up there again," I said, pretending to shiver. "Let's go home now!" I half-heartedly started back toward the ladder to the second deck, and Trudy followed me.

"C'mon back, Cardi! Tell them you're kidding! I can tell," said Tuney. She sounded so sure, that Trudy stopped and turned around.

I started laughing. "Dang it. She knows me too well," I admitted. Then I explained. "There's a dummy in the pilothouse. A real ugly one! I wasn't expecting to see anything that looked remotely human, so it really made me jump!"

Once assured there wasn't anything to worry about, naturally everyone started to climb up and peek inside. We even discovered a second ladder on the opposite side. Before too long, three sets of two women each would scale the ladders. Once on either side of the locked pilothouse, we took turns posing for pictures through the window next to the dummy. Hopefully, our photos looked like we each were standing next to the ship's pilot. When we were through with that, I stood on the deck and commented how neat it would be to have a dinner party on the roof where everyone could see all around.

"That would be wonderful," Tuney said, but then practicality set in. "But first, how would you get food up here? It'd be a little difficult carrying trays up the ladders." Oh! I hadn't thought of that.

"And secondly," she continued and started fanning herself with her brochure again, "it's hotter than blazes up here. I don't think too many people would want to get dressed up for a dinner in the heat and humidity. Let's get down and go to the hotel."

No one objected to her suggestion and dutifully we began our descent. We made it down very slowly from the ladders on the two decks. When we left the museum, the 2Bs2Ts tried to talk us into just crossing the street to the casino. They all loved to play slots, but by then, both Tuney and I were tired. I wanted nothing more than to take a long cool shower and shampoo my hair. It was frizzing on my neck and forehead and flattening everywhere else on my head.

"I think I'll go after I've had a shower and eaten supper. It'll be cooler by then, I hope!" I begged off the casino. Tuney agreed with me. We left the 2Bs2Ts with cries of good luck and Tuney and I dragged ourselves back to the hotel.

Chapter 10

Pennies and Slots

Once inside, we headed to the desk clerk to pick up our key. Amy was standing talking to him and when she spotted us, she smiled and waved.

"I've got everyone's key," she explained. She handed us two keycards. "Right after you left for the museum, the clerk found out our floor was ready for check-in, so the only ones who don't have their keys are Tammy, Bonnie, Trudy and Belinda."

"Call them the 2Bs2Ts – it's quicker!" I said.

Amy laughed. "Are they coming?"

I explained that they'd gone to the casino, so Amy decided to run up to her room for a minute to grab her computer. She was two doors down from us. She and Tuney walked up the staircase ahead of me. As my achy knees dutifully lifted my tired body up the stair after then, I noticed eye-level on one step something brown. and then said, There was a penny right in the middle of the stairway and I picked it up.

"Hey, look!" I called to Tuney and Amy. I held it up for them to see. "See a penny, pick it up and all the day you'll have good luck," I recited.

Tuney stopped long enough to glance at me, then harrumphed and turned back to continue climbing the stairs. "It's see a *pin* and pick it up," she corrected me over her shoulder. I shrugged. "Not when you're a banker," I explained. Amy giggled.

I stood for a moment longer and examined the penny. It was amazing that I'd even seen it because the penny was old and blended into the carpets black and brown pattern. I peered closely at it. On the back there were two sheaves of wheat.

"Ooh! A wheat penny," I muttered. They had only been made from the early 1900s to the mid-1950s which made them slightly rare, but still worth more than one cent now. Kris always enjoyed buying rolls of pennies from the bank when the kids were little and having them hunt through for wheat and Indian head pennies. I turned it over to the front to see what date was on it. 1950.

I started to call out to Tuney, but she and Amy had reached the top and were headed down the hall. I hurried after them. They had stopped for a moment in front of our room and I showed the penny to Tuney. She didn't appear to be impressed.

"Tuney, look at it. It's a 1950 wheat penny." I turned it over and over so she could see the wheat and the date. Tuney just glanced at it.

"So?" It annoyed me that she looked over at Amy and shook her head as if to indicate that I was pathetically boring.

"So that's the year Kris was born!" I kind of shrugged then. "I just thought it was kind of neat that I found the penny and then it was his birth year, is all."

Amy asked to see it and she confessed that she believed in "pennies from heaven" as a sign from lost loved ones. "My grampa always gave me a shiny penny when I was little," she explained. "Then after he died, I found a shiny new penny every day for a week. If it had been near my home or office, I probably wouldn't have thought anything about it. But I found them in different stores, and even in three different towns because I had to travel after his funeral!"

Tuney and I both said "Wow!" at the same time.

Then Tuney looked a little guilty. "Oh, Cardi! So you think maybe it's a sign from Kris. I'm sorry I seemed uninterested. That really is neat." She put one arm around my shoulder and gave me a little squeeze. "I'm just so tired all of a sudden, I wasn't paying much attention to you."

My annoyance faded. "Oh, that's okay. I want to think it's from Kris. But I hope he'd spend a little more than a penny on me!" I smiled down at the coin, and then carefully tucked it in my purse. *Just in case, Honey, it's really from you!*

Amy asked us about the museum, so we told her about it and thanked Amy for the events we'd already experienced. Tuney and I had our backs to the door of our room and Amy faced us. She didn't notice as a man walked past us, headed down the hall. But Tuney and I sure did.

"Oh, Amy, look at that guy!" whispered Tuney, pointing. Amy swiveled, and I squealed with delight. The man was dressed like a 1920s gangster, with spats, a black hat, black slacks and a pinstripe suit. I couldn't see the front of him, but I imagined he sported a silk handkerchief and a flower in his lapel. At the end of the hallway, he turned and disappeared into either a room or maybe another hallway. I couldn't tell.

Amy was thrilled. "Oh, my gosh! I've got to talk to the manager to see if he's an employee. I'm guessing they have people in different period costumes around here. Maybe they have Julien Dubuque, too. Wouldn't that be awesome to get them to pose with our tour group?" We agreed eagerly, then entered our room while Amy went to hers to grab her computer and then go back downstairs.

Tuney sat on the edge of her bed, then gingerly lay down on top of the cover. She groaned. "I'm just gonna lay here a minute. You take the first shower," she said. That was just fine with me. I couldn't wait to get out of the sweaty clothes and cool off. Plus, the soap from the hotel smelled good and I saw they had some sort of shampoo that I was eager to try.

I tossed her the remote control for the television before I went into the bathroom. "I'm going to wash and dry my hair," I said, "so give me 20 minutes." Tuney just waved a hand and closed her eyes.

The water was refreshing. When I exited the bathroom about 20 minutes later, I had scrubbed my face clean, reapplied my makeup, dried my hair into a nice straight pixie cut (I'd been told in my fifties that short hair on more "mature" women made us look younger) and just needed to get dressed.

"Your turn," I announced as I opened my suitcase to get a change of clothing. There was no answer. Tuney was sound asleep. I laid down after I got dressed, turned on the TV to *The Golden Girls*, and thought to myself that when the show was over, I'd wake up Tuney. What woke me up an hour and a half later was the sound of knocking on our door.

I sat up and looked over at Tuney's bed. It was empty. I didn't realize the hair dryer was going, so thought maybe Tuney had left and accidently locked herself out. When I opened the door, however, it was Amy. She saw my disheveled hair and sleep-confused look.

"Oh, Cardi, I'm so sorry," she began. "Did I wake you?"

"No. Oh, that's okay," I mumbled. "Where's Tuney?"

Just then our bathroom door opened and Tuney hurried out in her robe. "Here I am!" She looked at Amy. "Oh, Amy, we're late for supper, aren't we? I fell asleep as soon as Cardi went to use the shower. When I woke up, she was asleep, so I took my shower. We'll be down in five minutes!"

Amy laughed. "I bet you're both exhausted. I know I am, and I'm used to schedules like this. I called both of you, but when I didn't get an answer, thought I'd better come up to make sure you're alright. Do you want me to go ahead and order your dinner?" She told us our four options, so we each picked the chicken marsala, and she left.

I stretched and yawned. "Oh, I'm sorry, Tuney. I was going to let you sleep a half hour and then wake you. But I must have fallen asleep."

She laughed and said we'd obviously needed the sleep. "Jeepers," she added with a frown. "I feel like I've had more naps today than I did my entire childhood. Man, I'm getting old!"

I agreed with her that I was getting old, too. Then we both remembered Amy saying she'd tried to call us. Our phones were buried in our purses, though, so we quickly finished getting ready and rushed down to the hotel's restaurant. When we were seated, we found that we weren't the only ones who napped. Some of our fellow tourists all seemed a bit quieter than earlier. They were the ones who'd already checked out the casino. The rest of us had at least taken little naps, but no one had slept as much as Tuney and I had. We "nappers" decided that after dinner, we'd walk to the casino, play a few slot machines, and either have a drink there or come back to the hotel's lounge.

As a group of us was getting ready to leave the hotel, I

spotted Amy. "Hey!" I called out. "I just remembered Al Capone. Did you find out anything about that lookalike? Can we get pictures with him?"

Amy grimaced. "No, I'm sorry." She hesitated when we acted disappointed. "I'm afraid it would be impossible," she explained.

"Oh, why? Wasn't he an employee?" asked Tuney.

"No. He was a guest," Amy said. "A guest-guest." Before she could say anymore, another passenger walked up to her with a problem about the air conditioning in his room. I wanted to ask her what a guest-guest was, but since she was busy, we shrugged and then saw Bonnie talking to another passenger. I walked over to her to see how the casino had gone.

"I got five dollars!" she announced proudly.

"Profit?" I asked, impressed to learn someone had won something.

Bonnie's face fell, and she looked furtively around to see if the others were nearby. She opened her mouth to answer.

"No," came Belinda's voice as she walked up next to us. "Tell them how much you lost before you got the five dollars.

Bonnie bared her teeth in a mock smile. "Glad my hubby didn't live to hear about this," she said, "or he'd kill me!" She looked around. "I blew $150 before I got the five." She turned to Belinda. "And keep your big mouth shut about this, okay?" She poked Belinda good-naturedly.

Belinda just laughed. "What's it worth to you for me not to blab to everyone?" Bonnie just shook her head and grinned. She noticed Tuney and the other casino-bound tourists.

"Hey! Are you guys walking over there together?" Bonnie asked.

"Yeah, do you want to come?" I hoped they would. It would

be more laughs and I wanted to fill up on all that I could.

Belinda raised her eyebrows. "Bon-Bon," she drawled. "You don't want to lose any more money, do you?"

"Nooo," drawled Bonnie back at her. "But I'm not tired now, so I think I'm gonna go watch Cardi and Tuney for a bit." She looked at me, and what I thought was for Belinda's benefit, said to me seriously, "Don't let me gamble anymore, okay?"

"Oh, definitely," I assured. I looked at Belinda, and she gave a slight shake of her head and told me and Bonnie that she thought she, Trudy and Tammy were going to go to bed early. "Tammy doesn't want you to wake her up," Belinda warned. Bonnie put one finger over her lips and nodded silently.

As she turned to me, she winked. But after we all walked over to the casino, Bonnie kept her word. She watched us play – and lose. When I'd lost $20, I declared myself done. Tuney had won $50, and she cashed in her tokens. We'd spent about an hour playing and decided to wander around the casino to see what else was available. Bonnie told us there was a bowling alley. We also spotted some beautiful dining rooms in addition to some conference rooms and several food grills. Then Bonnie turned a corner and gasped.

"What?" Tuney and I cried out. Bonnie was staring ahead to the entrance of a theatre. A big billboard in front advertised that BAABA was going to be playing.

Bonnie clapped her hands. "I've absolutely GOT to see them!" she exclaimed. "I can't believe that well-known of a group would be here in Iowa!" She looked enraptured. She pulled her cell phone out of her purse. "I'm calling the girls," she announced. "They need to come over here to see this."

I looked at Tuney and saw she was as perplexed as I was.

When Bonnie didn't get an answer from the first number she called, she started searching for another. "I just tried Tammy. Maybe she's still with Belinda and Trudy," she explained.

"Wait, Bonnie," Tuney protested. "Who is BAABA? I can't ever recall them, can you, Cardi?"

No, I certainly couldn't and raised my hands in confusion to Bonnie. She put her phone down.

"Oh, Widsters!" she said as if we'd really let her down. "Everybody, and I mean absolutely everybody, has heard of BAABA!" She looked hopefully at us to see if that triggered our memory. We were still confused.

"You know. The group from Switzerland?" We shook our heads no.

"The 1970s?" No, we said.

"Meryl Streep was in the musical Mama Mia that they sang?"

Ooh! Instant recognition hit us, and Bonnie's face lit up. But then it was her turn to look puzzled when our reaction was anything but enthralled. Both Tuney and I shook our heads and burst out laughing. "Bonnie. What've you had to drink?" Tuney giggled.

Bonnie looked at us, totally perplexed. "What do you mean?" she asked.

"ABBA," I said emphatically. "A. B. B. A. *Not* the sound a lamb makes."

The way Bonnie's face changed almost put us into hysterics. She stood looking at each one of us with a dazed expression, then as she slowly realized what happened, her mouth slackened and eventually formed an "o" while she shut her eyes as if in pain. She even put one hand on her forehead and winced. When she opened her eyes, the absurdity about how she acted dawned on her and she started to laugh with us. So, there we were, three "mature" ladies with various shades of gray hair (or ash blonde, in my case) bent over laughing our heads off.

"I was waiting for you to say their top hit was "Mary Had a Little Lamb," I giggled.

"Oh! Or We're Poor Little Lambs, Who Have Gone Astray, Baa-Baa-Baa," sang Tuney.

"Wow, Bonnie, are you beginning to feel a little sheepish over the whole thing?" I contributed. Both Tuney and Bonnie groaned at that horrible pun. But then we all started laughing again.

Just then Bonnie's phone rang. It was Tammy, who'd left her phone to charge while she was next door with Belinda and Trudy. Bonnie told her the whole story and I could hear Tammy's peals of laughter.

"We're bringing her home, now," I shouted into Bonnie's phone. We were ready to leave and get back to the hotel. This had been one very long day.

Later, as Tuney and I crawled into our beds, she looked at me. "Promise me the itinerary isn't as busy tomorrow as it was today," she pleaded.

I just shook my head. "I'm not even going to look," I said as I rolled to my side. "I'm so tired, I could sleep for a week."

"Me, too," yawned Tuney. "G'nite, Cardi."

"G'nite," I murmured back. I think Tuney mumbled a thanks for booking the trip, but I barely heard her because as soon as I shut my eyes, I was out.

Chapter 11

Tuney's Meltdown

After breakfast at the hotel the next morning, the bus trip continued. In a few hours, we would arrive at Bonaparte, one of the "Villages of Van Buren County." As the bus climbed the hill that led southwest out of Dubuque, I was thrilled to see Tuney relaxed and talking with the others about the fun she'd had after only one day. Already, I thought, the laughter, the jokes, and the camaraderie with her fellow passengers was lifting the fog of grief that had silently enveloped her. Now if it would only mellow her big sister temperament!

As I gazed out the bus window, I realized I felt better, too. The beautiful scenery in this area of my home state delighted me. The limestone bluffs and the rolling hills weren't anything like the landscape near our town, and I was glad that I was finally seeing a part of Iowa I'd never seen before. *Kris would be glad for me*, I thought. *No, Kris IS glad for me!* A short distance south of Dubuque, my thoughts were interrupted.

"On the left side of the bus, we're coming up to a road that leads to Our Lady of the Mississippi Abbey," Amy announced. Naturally, every head in the rows in front of me swiveled to the left. All I could see were bluffs, trees, clouds and blue sky. "While we don't have time to stop to visit, if you ever get the chance to do that, it's well worth the trip. It's run by an order of nuns whose income comes from making the best candy in the world, in my opinion! Have any of you ever tasted their caramels?"

A few people nodded their heads, and I heard someone making smacking sounds as if the memory of the creamy treats triggered the taste buds all over again. Mort hollered up to Amy.

"Gotta question, Amy," he boomed. "Don't they make the caramels because they're Carmelite nuns?"

Tuney and I were puzzled as to why we heard a few snickers from some of the other tourists. I thought it was a legitimate question. Mort evidently had asked the question in all seriousness because he turned around, looked at those who were laughing, and mouthed in bewilderment, "What?"

Amy smiled. "Actually, no. Though that's what I used to think, too. Makes sense, doesn't it? Caramels from the Carmelites? But this order are the Trappistines." She blinked suddenly, grinned, and hastily added, "And I'll head you off at the pass, Mort – they do not make traps, either!"

Everyone laughed, especially Mort who had opened his mouth to make exactly that wisecrack. Amy waved at him and continued.

"What they do is welcome visitors and urge anyone who wants to join them in prayer, a retreat, or even to stay long-term to feel free to stop by. They have four small guest houses and a farm. The abbey overlooks a valley full of woods, with the Mississippi River in view."

"We should do that someday," Tuney said to me. She was serious.

"Really? You'd like to stay for a retreat?" I asked, genuinely surprised. I looked at Tuney with humorous suspicion. "Or do you mean to travel over here just for the candy, my sweet?" Tuney grinned. "The candy, of course," she replied. Then she turned solemn again. "But it might be nice to be on a retreat. You know. Just to get my mind straightened out." And she turned to look back out her window.

I slid over to Tuney's seat. Something about the way she said 'get my mind straightened out' sounded weird. "Are you okay, Tuney?" I asked.

She looked at me like *I* was crazy, and strangely, that comforted me, "Of course, I'm okay! What on earth prompted that?" she said loud enough the 2Bs2Ts turned around.

I hesitated. "Well, Tuney! You've always been the one with your mind 'straight.'" *That sounded brilliant, you idiot!* As much talking as I do, occasionally I just can't verbalize an emotion. I tried again to express my concern.

"I just can't imagine why you'd even consider going on a retreat. I think you're fine." I looked over at the 2Bs2Ts for reinforcement.

Bonnie nodded at us. "I think I know what Tuney means. Sometimes after a life-changing event, your mind is…uh…" she struggled to find the right words. "It's kind of like the old TV show, *The Twilight Zone*, you know?"

Both Tuney and I, along with Belinda, Tammy and Trudy, nodded.

"That's it, exactly," said Tuney eagerly. "Kinda like you're in your same house, watch the same tv shows, eat the same food, and talk to the same people. Yet for some reason, it's NOT the same!"

I nodded sadly. "It's like an alternate universe. Everything's the same, but something's wrong."

Trudy nodded, too. "Some*one* is missing."

We all fell silent as we absorbed Trudy's statement. Thoughts of Kris flashed through my mind, and despite trying to be positive, I suddenly felt I could cry. But then Tuney spoke up.

"It's not that I'm depressed or anything like that," she tried to explain. "It's just…oh, I don't know how religious you all are, but I've had so many questions that are unanswerable. It seems clinging to faith alone doesn't satisfy me. And I think…" She hesitated, confused or reluctant to say what was on her mind. In a moment, she drew a deep breath and said, "Okay, I'm just gonna say it…I'm so mad sometimes, and people tell me to just have faith. But the truth is, I don't think I believe in God anymore."

All of us were nodding, but sadly. I remembered two nights after Kris died I was screaming at God in the basement, daring Him to prove to me He really was real. It was because I couldn't wrap my mind around the fact that Kris, so full of life and energy, could suddenly cease to exist. I'd never told Tuney that.

"Oh, honey," said Belinda, her eyes full of sympathy and concern. "He understands. Get mad at God all you want. It's good to get it out of your system. I've been there. We all have."

The others and I nodded our heads, all the while staring at Tuney, who had bowed her head in misery. But she shook her head negatively at that. "I'd have to believe in a god to be mad at him, wouldn't I?"

"Tuney!" I said, bewildered. She'd never said anything like that before. How could she not believe in God? I remembered plenty of times, she'd utter thanks to God – when each of her children got married, when her grands were born, for beautiful skies, for rain and snow, for having wonderful parents and

tons of other things. I knew she believed because her thanks
to God had been a personal spoken word to Him. How many
times, I wondered, had both of us gotten down on our knees
in church and prayed sincerely, reverently and lovingly to Him
– to give thanks, to seek help, to just whisper something to
His ear that we couldn't to anyone else's?

As I stared in disbelief at her, Tuney looked at me, and then
addressed the others. "I know that sounds wicked. I'm a heathen
now, I guess. But one of the thoughts and memories that I've
had this past year has to do with something one of my little
students once said. I had totally forgotten about it, but now
it's been eating at me. Cardi knows this story. It's from many
years ago when I was teaching. After losing my husband, I've
thought about it a lot."

Everyone looked at me and I just shrugged my shoulders
and made a wild-eyed "I dunno" face. But as soon as Tuney
started talking, I remembered.

"I taught first grade, and once for show and tell, a little boy
– Tyler, I think his name was – brought a shiny new quarter
and showed everyone the gap where his front tooth had been.
Of course, he told everyone he'd felt the Tooth Fairy move his
pillow and take his tooth. Then, one of my other students had
to announce that there was no such thing as a tooth fairy!"

"Uh-oh!" "Oh, no!" and "Darn it!" came from the row in
front of us, and Tuney made a fake pout and nodded sadly.

"Oh, yes! And several of my little ones started crying, and
Tyler was all mad and upset. Some kids even pointed out their
permanent teeth to prove that they knew there was a tooth
fairy because they'd gotten money for their baby teeth. So, I
had an aide watch my class while I took Ryan, the little squealer,
into the hall."

Tuney shook her head and started wringing her hands. "He was so nervous, and he looked up at me with these deep brown puppy-dog eyes and kept blinking, trying not to cry. I think he thought he was really in trouble. I just told him: 'It's okay. We know you didn't mean to upset Tyler. It's just that it would be so nice of you to let the others have their fun with believing in the Tooth Fairy. You know, that's a grown-up secret!' He brightened up and grinned at the words 'grown-up,' and I winked at him.

"And that's when I made my mistake. I should have shut up, but my wink made me feel like he and I were co-conspirators. I kept talking and told him to remember when he returned to class not to tell them about Santa Claus and the Easter Bunny, too. Instantly Ryan's grin faded, and he looked so puzzled and asked why."

Again, Tuney's story drew some uh-ohs and oh nos. "Yup," she nodded grimly. "From the look on his face, I suddenly realized that while he didn't believe in the tooth fairy, he still believed in the others. I started stammering and tried to talk my way out, but this kid was smart enough to know better. I remember he opened his mouth in disbelief, and then said, 'You mean there's no such thing as Santa or the Easter Bunny?' Oh, girls, I was horrified and felt so guilty. And I was kinda scared I'd really get into trouble with his parents.

"I finally lied outright and said, 'No, of course there's Santa and an Easter Bunny. Who do you think comes to Grahams' Department Store every December? You've sat on Santa's lap before, haven't you?

"He thought for a minute, looked relieved, and nodded his head, and *I* thought I was going to be okay. But then the little dickens narrowed his eyes and looked so suspiciously at me I felt like I was in a police lineup.

'Yeah, but…' he said slowly as he started to put two and two together, 'last Christmas Mommy and Daddy looked at pictures of me sitting on Santa's lap when I was littler, and when we went to the store the next time to see him, Santa looked different.' He looked up at me, studied my face hard for a minute, then blurted out, 'Oh, Mrs. Thompson! There's NO such thing as Santa. There's no such thing as an Easter Bunny. And I suppose you're going to tell me next there's no such thing as God!' And he burst into tears."

I reached over to Tuney and patted her shoulder as the 2Bs2Ts all commiserated with her and started to reminisce about their own kids learning the BIG secret. But Tuney interrupted.

"You see, that's my point. We adults call it a "secret," but it's a lie, right? There is no such thing as a tiny little fairy who flies into kids' bedrooms at night, takes teeth and leaves money. There is no such thing as a rabbit who hides eggs and candy in people's houses or yards. And there's no such thing as a man who makes toys at one of the coldest spots on earth, flies with reindeer and magically enters peoples' homes and leaves presents for every girl and boy in the world." She paused, and then, painfully, asked, "So why is it then that we adults can't say there *is* no such thing as a god?"

A couple of gasps emanated from the row in front of us, but I was too fixated on Tuney's face to see who'd made them. Tuney had tears brimming in her eyes, but she had two red spots burning her cheeks. From past arguments and battles with her, I knew those marks meant her adrenaline had kicked in and she was getting angrier by the second.

"Are we just too afraid to be atheists because we don't want to believe that when we or our loved ones die, that's it? End of the line? Death is permanent? It's too depressing a concept for us to grasp, right? But is it any good to believe that some sort of entity created us, quote-unquote- *loves* us, and has promised us eternal life? Really? Think about this: We say God blesses us. But not all the time, right?"

Tuney could get mad easily. I knew that for a fact. But I'd never seen her work herself up or become so agitated. She was breathing rapidly, and her whole body was tense. She spoke swiftly, as if getting one thought out of her mind would make way for others to follow. She'd have been a great debater: It seemed she was bound and determined to convince us to at least become doubters, if not full-blown non-believers, in religion. Her tirade continued.

"Why else are innocent babies born sick? Parents with healthy babies shout to the world that God blessed them with a perfect child, but what do we hear from the parents of the sick or dead ones? Or when a tornado or hurricane wipes out a neighborhood, survivors tell the news media that God was watching over them. Fine. So – what about the neighbors right next door who got killed? He just decided to close His eyes? What about the constant wars in the world, even though each year, especially at Christmas, we pray our hearts out for peace on earth? And it's not just Christians' prayers but all religions all over the world who want peace. How's that working, huh?" She ended on a belligerent tone and ended up glaring at me.

An uncomfortable silence followed as we all stared at Tuney with our mouths open. My hands trembled. A deep-seated fear flooded my heart that Tuney was suddenly going to jump out of her seat, go running down the aisle and throw herself out of the bus. But she wasn't finished with us.

Tuney jumped on our shocked silence when we didn't answer any of her questions. "See? There is no answer. We make up something called having faith in God, our adult made-up "Santa." It's *all* made up, I tell you. It's a human thing because we're too dumb to understand that we're just like…like…like ANTS who are going to get stepped on occasionally - and there's not a fuckin' thing we can do about it! We're no better off than cavemen who believed lightning was caused by a god as punishment. And we go to church like a bunch of robots every week and keep praying because we're sooo superstitious about blaspheming this made-up entity who might punish us and send us to some made-up place called HELL for not believing in him. Well, I'm in hell right now. If God does exist, there's *nothing* worse that he could do to me."

That Tuney dropped the "f-bomb" stunned me almost as much as the rest of her outburst. To say I was shocked is an understatement. Tuney had worked herself into a frenzy, and I didn't know whether to throw a glass of water on her or run up to Amy to see if there was a doctor on board. Instead, I looked helplessly at the 2Bs2Ts before saying, "Tuney, we just talked yesterday about…"

"Shut up, Cardi, damnit! Let me finish!"

I reeled back. This was NOT my sister. My sister could get angry. That was a fact of life. But to hear her voice becoming shriller and almost desperate brought tears to my eyes and I began to panic. Something was majorly wrong.

She glared at me for interrupting her. As tears began to course down my face, she seemed surprised. Her mouth dropped open and her entire demeanor changed. The angry look in her eyes faded quickly. As if confused at my reaction, she looked away from me and cautiously regarded the 2Bs2Ts' expressions. They didn't appear quite as shocked as I was, but they were watching her with a mixture of concern, sadness, and sympathy. Whatever she saw in their faces seemed to drive away the rest of her anger. Tuney's shoulders sagged and in her face, I saw bewildered hurt. Like a child, she stuck her quivering lower lip out and pitifully, softly, wailed, "Why didn't God take me, too? I miss Tommy so much." She bent over and burst into tears.

"Oh, God! I'm sorry, I'm sorry, I'm so sorry."

I didn't know if she was praying to God or apologizing to us, but it didn't matter. I flung myself over her and hugged her as tightly as I could, crying like I had cried the morning Tommy died. Tammy left her seat and crowded in next to me, and she reached around and patted Tuney's back. I looked up to apologize to everyone but didn't need to when I saw tears in their eyes. They totally understood what was going on. After a few minutes of sobbing, Tuney straightened up and was immediately plied with wet wipes and tissues from the five of us.

Tuney hiccupped, swallowed hard, mopped her face, and then took a big deep breath. "Wow!" she muttered and sank back in her seat. We anxiously looked at her.

She regarded me, then the others, with a crooked smile. Then with a feeble attempt at humor, she quipped, "Okay. Does that answer your question about why I'm interested in a retreat?"

I clapped my hand over my mouth as a loud "HA!" burst from me. Then someone giggled. Tammy was still scrunched next to me, and she started laughing. Soon, all but Tuney were chortling, but at least she was still smiling.

As we quieted down, she put a hand on her forehead and shook her head. Then she murmured, "You guys are so wonderful. I have no idea where all that ranting and raving came from. But I have to tell you, I think I just got a boatload of grief off my chest." She patted her heart, and I noticed her cheeks started to flame up again, but this time it was like they did when she was embarrassed. It was more pinkish, softer than the horrible anger flames she'd exhibited a few minutes ago.

"You four," she nodded toward Tammy next to me and Bonnie, Trudy and Belinda who were crowded together now in the seat in front of us. "You must think I belong in an insane asylum, and I am so very, very sorry," she hung her head, dejected.

Tammy spoke up. "Tuney. You forget we're all widows, and I can't speak for the others, but I have had very similar thoughts about God and the...oh, I don't know what you'd call it... maybe the unfairness...of life."

Trudy spoke up. "Unfairness is a good word. Anyone who's lost a loved one is entitled to rant and rave. It's the only way to cope sometimes."

"Exactly right!" chimed in Bonnie. She reached over the seat to Tuney, and Tuney took her hand and held it. "Let me ask you something, Tuney. Have you had a giant meltdown like this before?"

"God, no!" said Tuney. "And I hope I never do again."

Bonnie nodded. "I ask because I have. Very violent, very angry and very, very tearful meltdowns – plural!" She looked over at Belinda, who leaned her head on Bonnie's shoulder. "I don't know if you know it, but I lost my Ken as a result of a motorcycle accident." Her friends nodded solemnly, as Tuney and I stared at her in shock. We both whispered we were so sorry.

"He didn't die right away," Bonnie went on stoically. She pursed her lips in thought. "You said something about being in hell. I've been there, too." She paused, as if debating how to continue talking to Tuney. "You see, Ken got hit on his motorcycle by a deer, of all things. You know – one of God's "gentle" creatures? Ken was always so careful when he rode his cycle. He rode it everywhere because he loved it so much. He always wore a very expensive and excellent helmet. I never worried about him when he rode. But I worried about other drivers. So I always prayed to God to keep him safe from anyone who was reckless around motorcycle drivers."

Her mouth formed a grim line. "I never once thought to ask God to keep him safe from some stupid animal."

I saw the pain in her eyes caused by recounting the time her husband was injured. She looked directly at Tuney, took a deep breath, and carried on with her story.

"According to the driver of the car behind Ken, this big deer just came up out of the ditch from nowhere. Ken went flying. Broke his neck, and he was paralyzed and in a coma with brain injuries. For fourteen months before he died."

I gasped, Tuney look horrified, and we both covered our mouths with our hands. Belinda quietly put her arm around Bonnie who smiled at the welcome sympathy.

"That was what? Eleven years ago?" she asked Belinda. Belinda nodded, and Bonnie continued. "When I relive it, it seems like only yesterday." She sighed. "So, he was relatively young in his late fifties. The doctors said he might come out of the coma, but he'd be a vegetable." Tears started to slowly trickle down her face. "Isn't that a horrible thing to say about a human being – that he could turn into a vegetable? I knew Ken wouldn't want to live like that, so I prayed to God every day to go ahead and take him. And every day, it seemed God ignored me. But He kept Ken's vitals strong – except for his brain functions."

She paused to wipe at her eyes with a tissue. We watched her silently and sorrowfully as she composed herself. "Eventually, I had to move him from the hospital to a nursing home that would take patients with injuries like his. It was four and a half hours away from home, so our kids couldn't always run over to see him as much as they wanted to. Medicare and insurance only helped so much.

"I owned my own floral shop. I wasn't around much to make an income. Without an income, I ended up having to sell it to pay for some of Ken's care. I slept in my car some nights when I was too tired to drive home after visiting him because I didn't have the money to spend on a motel. I didn't have his life insurance money because he wasn't dead."

Tuney's eyes had narrowed. "Oh, Bonnie. That is hell. Many times over. How'd you keep going?" She was crying, but her anger spots were back in her cheeks.

Bonnie reached through the seat and grabbed one of Tuney's hands. " I might have been in hell, but my poor Ken was in limbo. I think that was far worse than what I was going through."

"Oh, Bonnie," breathed Tuney. We were all silent for a moment. Tuney's anger had again faded but she looked puzzled. "But what are you saying? It sounds like of any of us, you should be the maddest at God. Or be a full-fledged atheist. I mean, God didn't answer any of your prayers. Isn't that what I was saying?"

I admit I was baffled, too, especially as to why Bonnie would tell that story after Tuney's outburst. But Bonnie just nodded at Tuney in agreement, wiped her eyes, sighed and smiled.

"At one point, I think if I could have come face to face with God, I'd have tried to beat Him to a pulp. I was that mad. That hateful. That much in need to find someone or something to blame. I even thought about learning how to hunt so I could wipe out the deer population." She shuddered, then looked deep into Tuney's eyes.. "But I'm happy to report that I'm past that, sweetie! And I'm not telling you this to try to one-up you in the grief department or to make you feel sorry for me. I just want to let you know that no matter how bad life gets, it *can* get better. I'm proof it will get better."

Tuney shook her head, perplexed. Bonnie tightened her grip on Tuney's hand.

"Don't you see? I didn't realize it at the time, but I'd been given a gift of being able to say a long goodbye to my darling husband. There were a few time, very few of course, but still times when I'd swear he could hear and understand me or the kids when we talked to him. And I went through hell, yes. But I also grieved so deeply that when Ken finally passed, I was relieved, even grateful that his horrible time was over. That was a gift. Life was waiting for me to move on. And I knew without a doubt that because Ken had suffered a long, drawn-out death just like God's son, Jesus Christ, he was in heaven immediately. I *knew* it, I tell you. In my heart. In my mind. And in my soul."

Bonnie paused to wipe her eyes again, and the rest of us followed suit. Then she squeezed Tuney's hand and shook it up and down a few times. "Life can be horrible and unfair. It can suck big time. But it goes on. And then, after a while, something happens, and you realize life can be sweet. It can be wonderful, and it *can* be worth living. You'll find that out some day. Sooner, I hope rather than later. One day, you wake up and you tell God that *you* forgive *Him*. And then you just feel better. But deep inside, you *know* He's already forgiven you for whatever you've said or thought or done. Or even better, you know He doesn't feel there was *anything* you ever did that needs to be forgiven."

She looked around at all of us, then back at Tuney. "I'm through now. Sorry for the epic saga. But maybe this bus is a great way to let go of some hurt that we're carrying. Anyway, Tuney, we're all here for you. Cuss up a storm and hate every-and-anything you want. But know that we've got your back, Widster!"

The others all chimed in, and I know Tuney felt the same kinship with these women that I did. I sniffed and wiped my eyes once more. I felt moved to embrace these four women who were so full of life. *Was life full of other people like them?* I wondered. I hoped so.

Chapter 12

Kris

As the bus trip continued, I was glad to see that while Tuney was a little quieter than the rest of us, she looked so much better. Maybe, I thought, a good *f'in'* rant and rave would do everybody some good. Get it out of our systems to allow tranquility to fill us up instead. I wondered if all widows went through the same emotions. I guess it would depend on how their loved one died.

I rested my head against the window. Compared to Bonnie's experience and Tuney's drawn-out wait watching Tommy battle cancer, I guessed that Kris and I could be called lucky. He didn't suffer.

Recollections of the shock of finding my own husband dead in the yard, a little over two years ago from a massive heart attack, flooded my mind. When I'd gone to the garden, I hadn't noticed him at first. When I finally saw him lying there, my first thought was that he'd decided to lay down to look up at the beautiful late spring cumulus clouds that were gently floating in the sky. He always loved to point out clouds and stars, maybe because as a banker he was usually inside dealing with figures and money. But then I noticed he was lying on some of the pepper plants he'd planted a few weeks earlier. The neighbors heard me screaming, and to this day I have no idea how they got me in the house, and who called 911. I had gotten through that horrible time thinking about all the fun times Kris and I had. When I remembered him alive, it was as if my life was normal for a few moments.

As I looked out the bus window, I thought about the almost forty years Kris and I had together. I wouldn't change a thing. After high school, I majored in business administration at The University of Iowa. In a small town, everyone knew who was doing what and where. It came as no surprise to me that the local banker called me when I was home on spring break before May graduation. One of the tellers was retiring in the summer, he explained. He knew of my major, so if I was looking for a job, he'd hold it for me. His daughter and I were in the same class in high school and since my parents had banked there their whole lives, I didn't even have to fill out a job application. So, after graduation, I moved back home to take a job at the local national bank.

A short time later, I finally got to use my degree when a position came up as financial analyst. I loved the job and loved seeing people at the bank. A year after I started at the bank, a new vice president by the name of Kris Cooper was hired. He'd been brought in to replace old Mr. Hennessey, who'd been VP for as long as I could remember. Kris was two years older than I, a fun-loving, handsome-looking man who was serious about banking – and me, I found out later!

We literally ran into each other while jogging soon after he had started at the bank, although Kris admitted some years later that he'd "stalked" me. For years after we were married, he would tell people that after he met me, he tried to find out everything about me that he could. I loved to jog, and unbeknownst to me, Mr. Cooper found out somehow where and when I jogged, which was usually early mornings and evenings. So, one morning, Kris started jogging in what he thought was a straight route where he would see me.

"I was afraid I'd been too slow and would miss her, so I picked up as much speed as I could," he recounted to whomever would listen. "Suddenly, BOOM!" He always slapped both of his hands together when he said that. His audience would unfailingly start or blink, but their grins egged him on and he'd continue. "For some reason that day, she'd changed her routine, jogged in from a side street and ran into me like a Mack truck against a wall! We each went flying backward."

I would always interrupt to protest then that he made it sound like I was the truck. "Say that *you* ran into *me* like a Mack truck!" But he'd just waggle his eyebrows and finish his story.

"I thought for sure I'd blown any chance I had with this gorgeous creature. She bounced off me, fell into a backward roll, and came up spitting fire!" He always cringed in mock fear at that point, and then would purse his lips in a pout. "And here I was, totally helpless, flat on my back with the wind knocked out of me!"

Through the years, I would interject my side of the story at that point. "Here I'd been, just minding my own business, and this...this..." and I'd point at my husband, "this Hulk whammed into me. I thought it was an attacker, but when I looked down at him, I thought he was dying. He looked like a fish out of water. He was trying to breathe and couldn't. I didn't know what to do!"

Inevitably, someone would ask with a wink and a grin, "Did you give him mouth to mouth?"

"No way! But I considered CPR by pushing my foot on his chest and blowing air down on him from where I stood!"

Everyone would start laughing, Kris the loudest. "When I finally got to where I could breathe, and she helped me up, she had the most horrified look on her face. I was her boss, you know, and I think she thought she was going to be fired."

I would nod. I *had* been horrified that the new bank vice president was hurt. But he had managed a weak smile, and as I helped him to his feet, he'd wheezed out, "Fancy running into you!"

It was then that I looked at him with new eyes. I've always loved people with a sense of humor. When he finally straightened up fully, he apologized profusely. He insisted he owed me a steak dinner. My first thought was I couldn't agree to eat with him because he was my boss. But as soon as I looked into his eyes, fully intending to reject his offer, I heard myself accepting. I had no idea why I did that, except that he was a hunk, and I liked him. I didn't want to jeopardize the job I loved, and I wasn't sure if there was a rule against dating anyone within a work place.

"Oh, but can we do that?" I asked shyly.

He looked puzzled. "Why not?"

"I mean, um…" and I remembered feeling my cheeks getting warm. "I mean, some people might think it's a …kind of like…um…a date?" I had no idea he was interested in me and had suddenly realized I was presuming it was a date. Maybe Mr. Cooper had only meant it as an apology.

He stood there grinning at me. "Miss Collins," he started. My heart sunk. He was going to say it wasn't really a date. I ducked my head in embarrassment.

"Miss Collins," he began again. "Have you looked around at the ages of the people who work in the bank?"

I looked up at him and shook my head, bewildered as to why he'd ask that.

"Well, since you haven't noticed, you and I are the only young, single people there. And as a vice president, I know there aren't any rules. Probably because no one ever had any need to make a rule like that." He winked at me and I grinned.

He took my elbow and began to slowly walk. As he looked down at me, his face suddenly changed, and he began to get embarrassed. He dropped his hand from my elbow and looked hard at me.

"Oh! But maybe you don't want to have dinner with me. I guess I should have found out if you're seeing someone already. And if so, that's fine. I don't want to overstep my authori…" he was interrupted by a quick kiss from me on his cheek.

"Okay, then," I called back over my shoulder as I took off jogging. "I'll talk to you later at work!" I thought I heard him start to whistle 'On the Street Where You Live,' from the movie *My Fair Lady*, and my heart soared. He was not only handsome, funny and kind, but a romantic as well! I almost started skipping.

"I even took some extra time to spritz on some perfume before work," I would tell Kris's listeners.

"And eighteen months after our jogging crash, I got to marry the most wonderful girl in the world," was how Kris always ended the story.

As the bus continued its journey south toward Bonaparte, I stared at the landscape that was fast changing from bluffs to flatter countryside. There were a few hills now and then. Whenever there was a river, there would be more trees. But the grass and fields looked dry. Sections of Iowa had a drought, and we were obviously driving through them.

I stretched in my seat, and then rested my head once again on the window. Oh, it was nice to remember my younger life. My "normal" life. Because of my sweet Kris, I proudly became Cardi Cooper. Our marriage produced our beloved daughter Sammi and our mischievous but fun-loving son Kyle. I took time off from working until both kids were in school. I really enjoyed being a stay-at-home mom for a while but was more than happy to get back to work.

Unfortunately, banking took a hit in the 1980s and lots of jobs were eliminated as people began using ATMs and later, online banking. Kris had gotten promoted to president of the bank, so I chose a part-time job that felt like it had been designed just for me: athletic shoe salesperson in a bigger city just 25 minutes from home. I loved the flexibility it gave me to stay home when one or both kids were sick. And any time I wanted off, without pay, of course, I had only to request it.

As the years passed, both kids married and started families. Sammi had Jason and Charlotte, and Kyle had Dylan and Lola. Both the kids and their families lived in Des Moines. I quit my part-time job and was able to see our two kids and the "grands" as often as I wanted before the little ones were in school. Now that they are older and in other activities, I don't see them as much anymore. Darn it!

All in all, life had been wonderful. Bonnie was right.

Chapter 13

Those Bickering Collins Girls

As I stared out the window, it occurred to me that maybe it wasn't just about Tuney taking this trip to start healing. I scooched over to Tuney's row. Tuney looked up in surprise.

"Are you okay?" we each said at the same time, then laughed. Then in chorus, "Yeah." And we giggled again.

Tuney patted my hand. "Jeepers, Cardi. You must have thought I was possessed by the devil, especially when I used the f-word!" She scrubbed at her mouth as if to get rid of that word. "I have never said that in my entire life!"

I stared at her with my mouth open. "Like heck you haven't!"

"Nope! Not the f-word," she protested emphatically.

"Tuney, you called me the f-word once in high school!" The 2Bs2Ts had turned around to listen and were delighted with our bickering. This time they could tell we were kidding.

Tuney frowned. "I did? I certainly don't remember that!"

"Uh, you certainly haven't forgotten the Home Ec Style Show, have you?"

The recollection visibly dawned on Tuney's face, She dropped her head, covered her mouth with her hand, and then she murmured "oh, no," from behind her hand. When she looked up, her eyes were crinkling with mirth at the thought. She and I started laughing.

"What? Tell us?" demanded one of the 2Ts.

"Well, I'm sure we'll both grow up some day. I hope," said Tuney with a wink at me. "You may have observed this, or not, but Cardi and I love each other infinitely. And even greater than that, we love to bicker with each other."

"Talk about fighting and acting childish!" I exclaimed. "This is so embarrassing, but whenever we're at one of our high school reunions, someone inevitably brings this up!"

When the 2Bs2Ts pressed us, Tuney began telling them about our lives growing up. It was as if she was transported back in time.

"I know when it comes to us fighting with each other, I'm as much at fault as Cardi is," she began.

"I have witnesses now – you all heard that!" I burst out, looking at each of the 2Bs2Ts and pointing at Tuney.

Tuney wrinkled her nose at me and continued. "I always figured it was normal. Childhood friends bicker or fight with their siblings. My own kids naturally fought with each other. But as our friends and family have all grown older, it seems everyone has mellowed and quit quarrelling, except us. I once thought maybe it's because we're too close in age."

Tuney paused to take a sip of water from a water bottle she'd brought. She gathered her thoughts then continued to tell the 2Bs2Ts all about us.

"Remember, we're only eleven months apart," said Tuney. "Before we were in school, our mother had even dressed us alike. For quite a while, people just referred to us as "the Collins *twins*. But when I was five and started kindergarten, Mom decided it was more fun to dress her girls differently. Dad agreed and pointed out that Cardamom could wear my hand-me-downs to save some money, too.

"Back then, both of us looked quite a bit alike, although Cardi was slightly taller and had a dimple. In high school her blonde hair had turned to what, at the time, was called "dishwater blonde.""

"I preferred to call it a dark ash blonde," I supplied.

Tuney closed one eye half-way as she looked at my hair, smirked, then continued. "I was more petite and had started coloring my hair with what the dye box called *Sun Kissed Californian* when I was thirteen. Yes, I know I'm vain!" Tuney admitted and then continued. "I was also the self-proclaimed boss over my younger sister. But we both grew up protecting each other from gossip or mean teasing."

I nodded in agreement, then inserted, "Yet, we could bicker back and forth bitterly sometimes. Once Mom even wondered aloud what life would be like if we'd been born boys and settled our disputes by wrestling."

Tuney made a mock shudder. "We both liked to joke around, and both had lots of friends in our small high school. We were football cheerleaders for four years. I was also a cheerleader for basketball boys' and girls' teams while Cardi was a wrestling cheerleader. I went out for softball in the springtime, while Cardi had been a high hurdler in track. And I guess I'd have to admit that we were both a bit stubborn."

"I'd have never guessed that," said Tammy sarcastically.

In the 1960s, Tuney reminded the listeners, girls took Home Economics for at least one year starting when they were juniors. Boys enrolled in Industrial Arts. In our small home town, it was an unwritten rule that each class would use the opposite sex's class as guinea pigs. It served several purposes, actually: the boys got free food, the girls' class housed a new kind of lamp from the shop each year, and more than one student over the years wished he or she could be in the other class, too. It sowed the seed of gender equality years before that became the norm. It also bonded the classmates.

The Home Ec class always appeared in the school's garage to watch the boys' year-end hands-on test of changing tires and sparkplugs. The boys in turn came en masse to watch the Home Ec Spring Style Show. There was no doubt that the junior and senior males enjoyed watching their female classmates strutting their stuff down the temporary platform runway through the gym floor. Mini-skirts were the rage, and there was more than one boy who hoped he could score a seat right next to the elevated platform where the girls walked.

"During my senior year, both of us were in the style show, modeling clothes we'd sewn during class projects. Cardi and I volunteered to sing a song about sisters as we modeled some A-line tent dresses with matching capes we'd each sewn. Ugh!" Tuney remarked remembering what the fashions were then. The others giggled. "Unfortunately, prior to the show we'd been bickering – no surprise - over Steven Winslow, the president of my senior class. He asked me if I had a date for the junior-senior prom. He didn't actually ask *me* out, was what Cardi kept insisting, because the next day, he'd complimented Cardi on breaking a record in a hurdle race she'd won the week before."

"Yeah! And Steve told me I deserved the biggest banana split money could buy! That sounded like a date to me!" I chimed in.

"He sounds kinda like a player to me," offered Bonnie. We giggled and Tuney continued.

"But, see, Steve hadn't actually said *HE'd* buy Cardi one," Tuney pointed out. "Both of us fumed at each other and schemed ways to get Steve to officially ask for a date. Each of us flirted with young Mr. Winslow so hard, he started getting catcalls from his buddies when they spotted Cardi or me headed towards him. Poor kid!" said Tuney remorsefully. I just scoffed.

"Anyway, by the time the modeling show rolled around, neither of us was speaking to the other. Tension between us was so high that the home economics teacher wished more than once that she had canceled our act. But the programs had already been run off on the mimeograph machine and I guess she knew we bickered with each other but always made up. The teacher crossed her fingers and hoped we'd settle our differences and put on a good show. I heard later that the teacher went home that night after the show wishing she'd gone ahead and canceled the entire thing."

I took over with my story to the delight of the 2Bs2Ts. "Both of us had taken dance classes and we thought we could add some modeling stances, a' la Twiggy and Jean Shrimpton, with some tap, ballet and jazz steps while we sang." I stopped and rolled my eyes. "Little did we know we were going to become a school legend: The night the Collins girls almost invented women's wrestling!"

Our listeners groaned, and some shook their heads, but they were all grinning.

Tuney then explained that our act was performed at the south end of the gym. The home economics teacher thought we'd made up and breathed a sigh of relief as the routine started out right on target. Until almost the end of the music, that is, when we both spotted Steve Winslow in the third row with a bunch of other boys.

"I stepped slightly in front of Cardi instead of standing next to her like we'd practiced. Cardi glared at me and bumped her hip into my side, then stepped completely in front of me so she could smile sweetly in the general direction of Steve and his buddies.

"The audience laughed and clapped momentarily while we kept alternately bumping each other, primping, elbowing – and still modeling our outfits. We were supposed to hold hands toward the end of the music and walk together down the attached runway. I dutifully picked up Cardi's hand and squeezed it hard."

"I thought she was going to break it," I said to the 2Bs2Ts, grimacing as I remembered how tough Tuney had been. "I know everyone heard me yell 'Ouch!' I pulled my hand violently from Tuney's grasp, then reached over and pinched her arm! Didn't even miss a beat to the music. Tuney took a step back and gave me a ferocious stare, then sneered at me. That did it! I reached out and slapped Tuney right in the face. Some of the audience thought it was part of the show and laughed, while some of our classmates who knew it wasn't in the act, gasped. I felt so horrible when I realized what I'd done. But then Tuney barreled into me, and we both fell in a heap of loose tent-dress material, with our capes all over the place." I shook my head sorrowfully and looked at Tuney. "Geez, every time I tell this story, I can't believe what we did!"

"I know," said Tuney, shamefaced. "Maybe it's fate's way of punishing us!" She grinned then continued. "Well, there we were. A high school junior and a high school senior rolling around, growling and muttering curses to each other..."

"And that's when you called me a mother rhymes-with-trucker, Tuney," I interrupted with a hint of triumph. The 2Bs2Ts snickered.

"Oh, yeah! That *was* when I did it. But only you heard it, so I'm not gonna count it," she said primly.

"Whatever!" I sat back, satisfied I'd made my point.

Tuney shrugged. "Well, then a few of the boys yelled "Cat fight!" and I heard the sound of scraping chairs and just knew it had to be our parents jumping to their feet. Mom said later she realized she'd gotten her wish about her daughters wrestling. She just stood looking at what had been two lovely young ladies, her pride and joy, now embarrassing themselves by this display."

"She was even madder than Dad was," I said to the 2Bs2Ts. They nodded empathetically, clearly siding with my mom.

"My forehead hit Cardi's teeth hard, and we both had tears in our eyes. We each said "ouch" and looked at each other at the same time, remember?" Tuney asked me, "And it was as if someone had doused a bucket of water on us. The fight was over. I think we both realized at the same time what just happened and we each scrambled to our feet. I know our eyes were as big as saucers, our cheeks burning with embarrassment and the audience looked absolutely stunned."

I patted Tuney's back. "But my big sis saved the day!"

"What'd you do?" asked Belinda breathlessly.

"I gave a big smile to the audience, turned to Cardi, hugged her tightly, and whispered frantically, 'Pretend this was the act!' Thank heaven she listened to me!"

"I know! I'm so glad I did, too. I turned to the audience and smiled, we held hands, raised them and bowed. The audience started laughing and clapping. We just looked at each other, hugged again (this time for real), kissed each other's cheek, and took another bow. Then with as much grace as we could, we exited the stage. We didn't get a chance to talk to each other before the rest of our classmates practically piled on us. They had questions and congratulations, and we just wanted to crawl home!"

Tuney laughed. "All I can remember is hearing 'That was SO boss!' 'FAB, you guys! Absolutely FAB!' And some even said they thought it was real for a second. Some others asked if that slap really hurt, which yes, it did, but I'd just say it was part of the act!"

"Oh, my gosh! You two sound like you were the hit of the night," said Trudy. "What happened after that?"

"Well, we hadn't fooled our parents or the teacher, so we were grounded and got Fs for the show," explained Tuney.

"Which just lowered our grades to C pluses, I think," I hastily added. "But the real punishment was that weekend and all the next week, and at reunions for years to come, the Collins sisters and our sister act was rehashed and debated. Some classmates deliberated as to whether anyone in the audience believed it had been real or fake. For some, the question of the hour was how on earth had we managed to wrestle that way without our undies showing." I giggled at the memory.

"But what happened with that Steve guy?" asked Tammy. "Did either of you ever date him?"

"No!" we both said in unison. Tuney clarified.

"It took us a week or two after the Home Ec show for it to sink in, but both of us realized Steve had just been trying to make conversation, not dates. The fact was he had never followed up with either one of us. Whether or not we'd succeeded in scaring away a possible suitor, we never found out. But I remember feeling about as low as a hog's chin on market day when I realized I'd made a fool out of myself for no reason! I don't even know where Steve ended up. Over the years he came to a few class reunions since he was class president. Then he stopped, and I haven't even thought to ask anyone whatever became of him."

Still reminiscing, I absently started to chew on my thumbnail, then added, "And being close sisters, we never officially apologized to each other. But life returned to normal as Tuney graduated and went to college at UNI, and I started preparing for my senior year."

"We didn't apologize ever, did we? Well, I'm sorry, Cardi!" said Tuney. She and I hugged, and I said I was sorry, too. The 2Bs2Ts clapped.

Tuney added perkily, "So, see? We love each other, but we've been conditioned to act this way, don't you think?"

There was silence, then "Uh, yeah," was the joint and very dry response from our fellow Widsters.

Chapter 14

Bonaparte

We'd been on the bus for several hours, and from my side of the bus I kept a watchful eye on Tuney. She seemed calm and relaxed, and every now and then, she'd scoot up to the edge of her seat to talk to Bonnie and Trudy for a while. But it was only after I leaned over to Belinda and Tammy as they sat in front of me and asked them if they thought Tuney was going to be okay, that I was able to relax.

"Cardi," whispered Belinda so that Tuney wouldn't hear. "I'd bet my bottom dollar she is perfectly fine now. I truly think she needed to unleash her grief and anger that's been stored up for over a year."

Tammy agreed. "I've been widowed almost as long, but my brother-in-law is a psychiatrist. And one of the first things he told me was that I needed to go through steps of grief, and one of them was anger."

That was interesting. I hadn't known that, but I vividly remembered being angry – more than once over the last two years. "Did he say how long it lasts, or if it happens more than once?" I asked Tammy curiously.

"No. He told me that basically they are just commonalities that anyone with any type of grief most likely will go through." She concentrated for a moment. "I can't remember all five, but I know the first stage is denial, then anger, and some others. But what Bob, my brother-in-law, said mental health experts really rely on are the symptoms of grief. We'll all lose someone, somewhere, somehow, someday. And there are so many different types of symptoms. He sent me some material and of course I talked a lot to him." She raised up one hand and began to count on her fingers. "But I specifically remember that humans suffer physically, emotionally, behaviorally and spiritually. We just witnessed a very normal reaction from Tuney that came from deep in her soul."

"I agree," said Belinda. "I lost my husband to cancer, too. He didn't do anything wrong in his life – ate well, exercised, didn't smoke, didn't drink, and he ends up with pancreatic cancer. I couldn't blame him, could I? Do you know who I ended up blaming?"

I was going to guess God, but Belinda wasn't waiting for any answers.

"And I think back now and can't believe my mindset at the time, but I blamed the Susan G. Komen Foundation!"

I was taken aback. I'd volunteered for that foundation after a cousin was diagnosed with breast cancer. "Belinda! Why on earth would you blame a cancer research organization?" I asked in surprise.

"Because at the time, I was mad that they seemed to be raising so much money for *breast* cancer and not sharing with other cancer research, like pancreatic cancer!" She shook her head. "I was totally irrational and angry. I needed to blame someone for Steve's death. Thank goodness, with time, we

learn to cope and most of us get our heads back on and realize…
mmm," and she gave a rather grim little grin, "…shit happens.
Sorry! But I guess that's why there are so many sad songs out
there. "Oh, Danny Boy," "Since You've Gone," and I don't
know how many others."

Belinda paused, and Tammy looked at me earnestly. "You
know, yesterday morning, you were talking about that friend
of yours - Mary Jo? The one who got divorced?"

I nodded, and she said, "None of us are immune to some
sort of tragedy in life, however small it may seem to others.
I'm approaching the year anniversary of my hubby's death,"
and I noticed her eyes started to tear up, but she smiled. "I
have longed for the first anniversary to arrive to prove to myself
that I survived a year. One year, I thought, and I'll have made
it through all the firsts and I'll be fine."

Belinda and I were nodding, mainly as encouragement for
Tammy to continue. She sniffed, lifted her eyeglasses to wipe
her eyes, and heaved a big sigh. "But having Belinda and
Bonnie and Trudy around me, I know there's no timeline, no
end date, nothing like that to mark the end of grief. And that's
because I have accepted that grief just can't be turned off and
forgotten." Then she smiled at Belinda and gave her arm a
little squeeze.

She turned back to me and said, "But we can have a fun
time trying, right?" The three of us burst into laughter, causing
Tuney, Bonnie and Trudy to look at us curiously.

"Okay, Sis. What're we missing over there?" asked Tuney.

Before I could answer, the ever-competent Amy announced
that we'd be stopping for lunch at a historic grist mill in the
tiny town of Bonaparte.

"This place is really cool," she explained. "They have great lunches, and we can wander around the area for a while after we eat."

"What a grist mill?" came a voice from the middle of the bus.

"Good question," said Amy into her microphone. "Did everyone hear that?"

Tuney and I were each sitting on the aisle seats. Tuney leaned over to me. "She sounds just like a teacher!"

I smirked. "You should know. But hush. I want to hear the answer."

Amy flashed a brochure in the air. "The question was, what is a grist mill. I've got a brochure here from the Bonaparte Retreat. That's the name of the restaurant. It's got a little history about their place."

She opened the brochure. "A grist mill grinds grain." She looked up and said, "Say that fast three times." Dutifully the bus passengers started saying 'a grist mill grinds grain' three times and soon everyone was laughing.

The 2Bs2Ts, Tuney and I all started giggling. I was struck by the ridiculousness of a bus load of senior citizens all babbling a silly sentence and snickering like they were little children. *But it feels good*, I thought and was glad.

Amy attempted to calm everyone down. "Okay, kiddos! Very good. But there's no prize for that." There were a few fake disappointed 'awwws.' She blew a kiss and continued. "Anyway, this mill was powered by water, and you can still see the big wheel on the back of the building. The town thrived because of the mill. People came to Bonaparte from miles around to have their grain ground into flour. Some wagons were pulled by horses and had to cross the river by ferry."

She glanced back at the brochure. "This tells how people

sometimes had to wait for days to get their flour, so Bonaparte hotels, taverns and stores really prospered. When we eat there, try to imagine looking at the river and seeing steamboats and paddle-wheelers heading to Des Moines or back to the Mississippi. This also mentions that Mormon pioneers from Nauvoo, Illinois who were headed to Utah stopped in Bonaparte. They even built several downtown buildings." She put the brochure away and looked at her passengers.

"I know a few of you have been in this part of Iowa before, but for those of you who haven't, there's so much history to soak up. It always amazes me to see what contribution our little state of Iowa adds to the history of the entire United States. Anyway, we should be there in about half an hour, so enjoy the pretty scenery along the way!"

Half an hour went by quickly. I had just started to doze off, when Amy announced we were entering Bonaparte. Like so many towns, little Bonaparte had been established next to a river – the Des Moines River - with one main street that ran along it. Extending from that, there were several streets that led inland. The bus drove slowly so everyone could see the old buildings that lined the streets. Main Street was paved, but I could easily imagine it to be dirt, with wagon wheel tracks and horses' hoofmarks. I wasn't surprised to see there were no yellow lines to delineate parking spaces. It looked like cars parked wherever they could find a space. Periodically along the streets were empty lots, some with some August flowers blooming, others with sun-parched dry grass. A rough gravel road in one space led to the rocks by the Des Moines River. I made a mental note to wander down there to watch the river water flow slowly by if we had time.

I alternated between looking out my window, then Tuney's.

I pointed out some buildings Tuney could see on her side and wondered out loud if there was an old historical bank.

"Maybe there never was one here in town," suggested Tuney. She was reading old signs fastened to the brick buildings.

I just looked at her. "Don't be silly, Tuney. I worked in a bank for years, and if there's one thing I know, it's that every town had its own little bank. If there was a post office, there was a bank. If there was a tavern, there was a bank. If there was a hotel, there was a bank. If there was…"

"Whoa! Okay, got it, got it," Tuney interrupted hurriedly. She looked out her window. Almost all the buildings seemed so old, one of them could have been a bank once.

I opened my phone to search the history of Bonaparte. I clicked on images and studied the screen carefully.

"Here!" I said triumphantly. "See?" I leaned across the aisle to show Tuney a picture of a large brick building on my phone.

As Tuney glanced at it, I spied a brick building down the block and pointed, "And there it is! It says here it was built around the time of the Mormon encampment. It was around 1881 or 82 that the building was a bank, then later through the years was a marble works, city library and town hall. Isn't that amazing?"

As the bus pulled slowly past the old bank, I took pictures of it. Limestone was used for the base, while reddish-brown brick was used to construct the rest of the building. The building was two stories high next to the street, but when I peered at the side of it, I saw a drop-off that revealed a walkout basement with windows. There were also windows on the ground level that looked to be in good shape, but windows on the second level were boarded up. After a few moments of snapping photos, I sat back in my seat with a sigh.

"Oh, man. I don't know why I just did that," I said to Tuney. "But I know Kris would have loved seeing this."

"That's why you did it," said Tuney, gently. Then she pointed. "Look at the false fronts on those stores, Cardi!"

Awnings hung from some of the stores, shading a few people from the hot August sun. The bus drove slowly by them, then turned off the main street onto some of the side streets.

Mr. Smith, the driver, spoke over the loudspeaker. "We're taking a mini-tour of the lovely town of Bonaparte," he announced. "Mainly because I need to make a detour to be able to park in front of the grist mill we just passed."

"Oh, my goodness!" I cried. "I didn't even notice it!" I peered out my window to look, but by then we were headed up a residential street. "Oh, Tuney! Look at the size of those homes!"

There were several beautiful old mansions. One was brick, the others had wooden siding, and they were all three stories tall. Large front porches with turrets, columns, and porch railings were evidently popular at the time they were built because they all sported them. Tuney noticed a narrow brick chimney on one.

"I wonder if we could tour these historic homes?" Tuney mused out loud.

I squinted at them, then shook my head. "It looks like they might be homes that are inhabited. Look at the laundry on the lines outside that white one." I pointed at a clothesline we could see from the side street, hung with adult-sized jeans, tops, children's shorts and some swimsuits.

Tuney smiled. "It always seems like really old homes are either B&Bs, museums or abandoned. It's nice to see one being used the way the original owner intended."

"Wow! This must have been quite the town in its day to have homes this size." I kept looking at both sides of the street as we looped through the tiny town's little residential area.

"I know. I love the history of these places. And I can't wait to see the restaurant. I hope they kept some of the historical structure in it," said Tuney. She turned to me. "Are you hungry? I sure am!"

That was such a normal statement from my sister that I almost clapped as I nodded back to her. Belinda and Tammy were right, I thought. Tuney seemed fine now.

Mr. Smith turned the bus back toward Bonaparte's Retreat on Main Street and parked in front of the restaurant. Everyone started to grab purses and cameras, while Amy announced that the back of the bus would be the part to unload first. We Widsters and the 2Bs2Ts cheered, and Tuney and I scooted to the front of the bus quickly.

After we exited the bus, with the ever-considerate help of Mr. Smith who made a show of being cavalier. Tuney muttered to me she secretly thought he was scared to death one of the elderly people in his care would trip and fall, so we both smirked as we stepped off the bus. We gazed for a moment at the huge brick mill-turned-restaurant.

From the street, it rose three stories, although a fourth story – probably an attic, I thought – could be seen from the side. The windows between each floor were quite a ways apart, indicating that the ceilings in each level were higher than a normal eight feet tall. The bus was parked directly in the front next to a covered porch which was elevated from the street. The entrance to the restaurant was at the top of the porch stairs. Tuney and I had to walk to the east end of the porch to climb the wooden steps.

"Look at the people coming out. They look pretty happy!" I noticed as we reached the bottom steps.

"And full," added Tuney. "That's a good sign!" We waited at the foot of the stairs as several couples were exiting the building, laughing and talking. The two men in the group were rubbing their bellies and one of the women was carrying two plastic cartons that Tuney assumed were leftovers.

"Mmmmm," I said happily as we stepped up on the sidewalk that ran past the building. "By the smell of it, I think this is going to be one of the highlights of the Widsters' trip to Van Buren County!"

One of the women who was carrying leftovers overheard me as she passed by. She smiled and waved her cartons enticingly toward us. "Be prepared for a gastric feast," she said.

We laughed, and Tuney good-naturedly berated her for torturing us with the delicious aroma. She grinned, and obligingly stuck the boxes behind her back.

"We don't live too far from here, so we eat here often. You'd think our stomachs would be stretched enough we could finish our plates, but we haven't been able to yet."

Her husband patted his ample stomach. "That's true. But I keep trying."

We Widsters chuckled and began to climb the stairs. One step up, Tuney stopped and turned to the couple. "Is there a specialty, or is everything good?"

"Well, I'd have to admit that everything is good. I've tried them all," said the man.

His wife chipped in. "They're known for their steak at supper. But for lunch, try the tenderloin, especially if you're hungry!"

"I didn't think I was that hungry until I smelled the food," said Tuney. She took another deep breath through her nostrils. I did, too, and could smell baked goods and other delicious, but unknown aromas.

The man grinned and called out, "Order pie for dessert when you order your lunch. Everything is made from scratch, so there are only so many pies a day. When they run out, you might be out of luck!"

I thanked them effusively "Because," I added, "I have ridden RAGBRAI and tasted every pie that's ever been on those routes. I live for pie!" I turned and headed past Tuney for the entrance to the restaurant.

Tuney shook her head and wasn't through talking. She pointed at me. "That's my sister. If she gets in first, she'll order, inhale the food and be ready to go before the rest of the bus even has a chance to sit down."

The couple laughed and wished us a good afternoon, and Tuney hurriedly followed me. I was waiting for her at the landing in front of the door. It was massive, made from heavy oak wood, solid metal hinges and a door knob, but with a small window that was too high for us to see through.

We waited for the 2Bs2Ts to join us, then I grabbed the door's handle and pushed it. It didn't move. I tried again. Still there was no movement.

I looked bewildered. "Do you suppose they're closing and locked it?"

Tuney looked at me like I'd lost my mind. "PULL it, Einstein! You usually push open a door from inside, so you'd pull it from the out." The 2Bs2Ts burst out laughing, while my cheeks reddened.

I rolled my eyes at Tuney. "I know that, boss! But look at this thing. The window's too high to let people on the other side know that we're here standing on the top step. What if someone were to come barreling out of here and knock us over?"

At that, I pulled with all my might and the heavy door flung open. We all gasped, and Tuney yelled out an "Ope!" A tiny and elderly lady, who had evidently just grasped the doorknob on the other side of the door, was pulled out by the force of my tug. Fortunately, Tuney's and my reactions were swift, and we caught the woman before she tumbled down the stairs.

Tuney grabbed the lady's arm as I began apologizing almost tearfully. Tuney also apologized to the little woman who was slightly taken aback but seemed to be trying to control a grin. She suddenly chuckled.

"Girls! Girls, I'm okay," she interrupted. "Here. Let's step inside for a second." And she turned back indoors, gently patting my hand and Tuney's and somehow shrugging us off her without offending anyone. The six of us crowded around a small bench inside and the woman sat down on it. Tuney turned to the 2Bs2Ts and told them to go on in and grab a table for six. With a worried glance at us Widsters and smiles at the lady, they hurried in before the rest of the bus could unload.

Tuney could tell I felt horrible. Hastily, she apologized again.

"This was all my fault. I teased my sister, here, for pushing at the door instead of pulling it open. And she had only tried to push it because she noticed there was no way to tell if anyone was coming in or out."

"Oh, Honey," smiled the elderly lady. Her tightly curled hair was light brown with a bit of grey showing at her temples.

She wore gold-rimmed glasses, slacks and a white shirt. She was also wearing what appeared to be a dark colored apron around her waist. She looked at the two of us.

"Please don't apologize! I've been coming in and out of that big ol' door for over 30 years. Longer because I was here when it was still a mill. And if you think this has never happened to me before, you're awfully naive." She straightened her tiny frame and held her hand out to me as she introduced herself. "There have been a few times when I almost tumbled into a pretty good-lookin' man's arms, so if there's anything to be upset by, it's that you're both ladies. I'm Marie, by the way, and I work as a waitress here."

What a great sense of humor she had! I threw back my head and laughed out loud. Marie looked like she was about 80 years old, but as she smiled at me, the laugh lines crinkled her eyes and made her look younger. Marie turned next to Tuney, who had dropped her mouth open, and pointed.

"Honey, you better shut your mouth. We try to keep the flies out of here, but if there's a loose one, it might head right inside there." Tuney snapped her mouth shut in embarrassment. "And we don't want to spoil your lunch," Marie added, grinning.

Tuney laughed. "I'm sorry. I was just dumbfounded when you said you're a waitress. You look..." and she hesitated, not wanting to further embarrass herself being rude, "... to be about our age, and we're both retired."

Marie's eyes twinkled. "You girls are sweet. I've lived in Bonaparte my whole life. It used to be well over a thousand people when I graduated from high school in the 1940s, and I've worked here in this town ever since. I work because I love being busy and I love seeing all my friends who stop by here every day. And meeting new people like you folks," she stated, smiling the entire time.

Tuney looked at her closely. "Did you say you graduated in the 1940s?" she asked curiously.

Marie grinned. "I can tell you're trying to do the math in your head," she whispered conspiratorially. "Yes, I'm in my 90s. My early 90s," she corrected primly. And gave us another grin.

My hands flew to my cheeks. "Oh, Marie! That's wonderful. How impressive of you to still be working."

Marie shook her head. "No. Not impressive, girls. Just lucky." Then she looked at her watch. "Well, I'd better get going on my break. I want to take a walk down the street and back. And you both better get inside and get your lunch before the pie's all gone."

"Thank you so much for talking to us, and again, I'm so sorry!" I said. We both gave Marie a gentle hug.

Tuney added, "It was amazing to meet you. And I'll keep my mouth closed until my lunch arrives."

I stepped to the door and slowly opened it in case anyone was outside. "You've got clear sailing, Marie," I announced. "Be careful coming back, though, in case we come rolling out stuffed like pigs and knock you over on this side!"

Marie laughed and slowly and carefully walked down the stairs. Some of the busload who saw me open the door stood at the bottom of the steps to wait for Marie. She smiled and threw waves at them like she was a queen. I stood at the top to make sure she was okay, but Marie was as sure-footed as a young girl and when she reached the bottom, she turned to look at us.

"Bye, now," was all she said as she waved at us. Tuney and I waved back.

Tuney watched her thoughtfully for a moment. "Do you

suppose she's widowed?" she asked. I started laughing, and poked Tuney in the arm.

"Good grief, girl! Whaddaya think? Odds are, yes. She said she's in her 90s and women outlive men usually. Why?"

Tuney blew out her breath. "Jeepers! I hope I'm that spry and smart when I'm her age!"

"Humph. That'd be a change," I teased.

Tuney tossed a slight grin my way and entered the vestibule. "She must be quite a character. She's got to have some secret for longevity and vitality. Maybe it's working for so long," mused Tuney. "I'd better rethink retirement."

"Or maybe it's *where* she works," I contributed. "If she's here a lot, she must eat their food, and maybe the food is even better than the ratings give it and it keeps you young!"

Chapter 15

Bonaparte Retreat

"Speaking of food…" said Tuney as she opened the door to the restaurant. I felt a comfortable little glow inside as we were welcomed to the Bonaparte Retreat by a smiling hostess.

"Hello, there! Are you from the bus? And are you familiar with our mill?" she asked.

"Thank you! Yes, to the bus, and familiar only from what we've read and from all the glowing reviews some of your customers outside have told us about," I said. The hostess turned from us to gather up some menus.

Tuney gazed at the interior. The first thing I noticed was how warm and hospitable the restaurant seemed. *It's like looking at a picture of Grandma's old place,* I thought. Tuney seemed thrilled and her eyes danced around the seating area, noting the exposed beams that held up the old mill's ceiling, the dark wooden floor with marks and grooves that probably came from old farm vehicle wheels, a vast array of antiques, and rocks on the window sills. The rocks got my attention. Some were rounded, some misshaped, but they all were kind of a grayish color, almost like chunks of cement.

"Tuney. Look at those ugly rocks at the windows. Do you suppose they're river rocks?"

Tuney turned, then shot me a knowing look. "You're making fun of our state rock."

"Huh?"

"Those are geodes, silly."

"No, they're not," I protested. "I've seen geodes, and they have crystals in them. And they're pretty."

"Wait'll we get closer to them. I can see they've been cracked open. That's when you see the beautiful hollows in them." Tuney absently patted my shoulder as if she was a teacher trying to mollify a child. I shrugged and looked around at the people in the restaurant.

Obviously, most of the clientele were regulars. The waitresses scurried about yet had time to chat with customers There were only a few young waitresses, but the majority were older, although not nearly as old as Marie. Clearly age was not a factor in any requirement for waiting tables, but the ladies all had things in common: boundless energy capped off with perpetual smiles.

Tuney saw the 2Bs2Ts were already seated, but at a table for four, since the only other tables for six or eight were taken. They were watching for us, and called out apologies, but we assured them it was okay. The hostess, who according to her nametag was Shirley, had picked up two menus and carried them over to a table that was next to a window. As we followed Shirley, she explained a little bit about the restaurant.

"A man named William Meek built this in 1878. Flour, oats and wheat were brought here from farms as far away as a hundred miles."

"Meek!" I said excitedly. When the hostess glanced at me quizzically, I hastened to add, "We're on our first road trip in years, and my sister and I love the history of Iowa. I read that the town used to be Meek's Mills. So, this is the original mill?

Shirley nodded and smiled. "It's quite historic. Hard to believe what some of the founding families must have gone through to establish this town. It's gone through floods and tornadoes, and of course economic crises."

"Oh, no," murmured Tuney. She looked up at the beamed ceiling and at the beautiful brick walls, and I wondered what they'd had to go through.

"But," Shirley added quickly, "you can't keep a good place down. I think Bonaparte and the entire county are all magical. I mean, just look at this mill! They don't make buildings like this anymore," Shirley glanced around. "I've been here twenty years, and I never tire of it."

"Really?" asked Tuney. "That's fascinating. When did it become a restaurant?"

Shirley paused to think and then answered, "1970. It had been abandoned for several years, and I'm not sure how long. But Rose and her husband Ben bought it in 1970, and she's been cooking here ever since!" She noticed some more people entering the restaurant. Shirley told us to be seated and said someone would be with us soon to take our orders, then left.

Tuney sat down on one side of the table next to the window. She picked up one of the ugly rocks I'd seen, then turned it toward me.

"Wow!" I said, impressed. The outer section of the rock was ugly, but inside were masses of white crystals. Next to my seat opposite of Tuney, I reached for another geode. This one had amethyst colored crystals. "These are beautiful!"

"Haven't you ever seen geodes before, Cardi?" Tuney asked, curious.

"I've seen samples on display at museums or rock shops, I think, but I've never actually held one."

"Hmm," she replied as she studied the rock. "The few years when I taught fourth grade, we examined geodes that I ordered from a catalogue. I'm not sure where they came from. Maybe right here! If it's our state rock, then there should be plenty of them, don't you think?"

I'd pulled out my phone and typed in *geodes in southeast Iowa*. I handed my phone to Tuney. "Look, Tuney. There's a Geode State Park east of here a ways."

She read about it, then returned my phone. She sighed. "I feel so stupid! I can't believe all the things I never knew about the state. I need to take my family on a road trip!" She smiled at me and then continued looking around.

I smiled back. I was relieved that she was enjoying the trip. The meltdown on the bus had scared me. But the sparkle in her eyes was back, she seemed genuinely intrigued by this historic mill, and I was so glad that she was enjoying the trip enough to want to take her kids and grandkids traveling.

"Hey, Sis. Look at the water wheel outside here," Tuney said pointing to a huge wooden wheel. "It has to be the original wheel to the mill, don't you think?"

"I wouldn't be surprised," I peered out the window, too. The mill's water wheel was nestled up near the building where we were sitting. "We have to go out and examine that thing before we leave here." I looked out toward the river. There was a pathway, an old flower bed and something else. "Hey, look at that old clock out there. I've never seen one like that before."

In the back yard of the mill/restaurant between the river

and the building stood a tall black pole. It almost looked like a street lamp. But instead of a light, there was a big white-faced clock. Tuney squinted her eyes and studied it further.

"Why, it doesn't have any hands, does it?" she asked. I leaned forward for a better look.

"I think you're right! It doesn't look like it has any hands at all," I said. I grabbed my phone to take a picture of it. After I'd snapped a couple of shots, I opened my gallery icon and pulled up a photo. Then using my fingers, I enlarged the photo. It wasn't the best picture, but we could tell for certain that Tuney was right. I wondered if it was going to be repaired.

Just then a waitress arrived with some water. She introduced herself as Karla and told us she'd be taking care of us.

"Here's your first job, then, Karla. Would you please tell us about that clock outside? Is it broken?" I asked pointing out the window.

Karla smiled. "Bonaparte's unofficial motto is 'Where Time Stands Still.' Times have certainly changed around here, but the peacefulness and sense of community is the same as it's always been. What better way to be reminded of that than to look at a clock that won't tell time?"

We looked at each other and smiled. "I love that," I said softly. "Shirley told us the whole county is magical, and time standing still would certainly fit into that picture!"

"Our guests always love the motto, too. After you eat, I suggest you walk around outside and look at the river. You'll understand why that's a perfect description of this entire area," urged Karla. "Now, have you ladies had a chance to look at the menu yet?"

We both ordered the tenderloins. "Those are customer favorites," smiled Karla.

"So, I've heard," said Tuney, with a twinkle. "I've also heard, straight from Marie's mouth, that we should order our dessert pie right away, too!"

"Oh, you met Marie," Karla cooed. We just love her to death! She's right, too. That was going to be my next question." She smiled. "What kind of pie would you like?"

Tuney ordered apple pie, but I hesitated. "I promised myself I wouldn't pig out on this trip," I explained.

Tuney looked at me sternly. "That's fine, but don't you dare think you're going to get a taste of MY pie, then!" She winked at the waitress.

"Oh, okay! If you're going to be selfish, Sis!" I glanced at the menu once more. The choices of sweet delights outweighed my resolve to diet. Again. "I might as well go for it, then. Pecan, please!"

Karla leaned down conspiratorially. "If I told you that these pies contain very little calories, would you believe me?" she whispered, looking slyly around.

We giggled like little kids. "Okay! If you say so!" I said merrily.

"If that's your story, I'm buying it," added Tuney. "I just won't check my bathroom scales when I get home!"

"Atta girl!" laughed Karla and left us to go place our order.

We spent the time before we got served looking around the restaurant. As soon as one of us pointed out a unique item, the other would spot something even more interesting. Everywhere something could be placed or fastened to was filled. There were antique cash registers, old signs, leather saddles, china, figurines, American flags, and even an old bar with a long mirror on it. Horseshoes were tacked onto some of the thick posts, carved wooden chickens and rocks were perched on some windowsills. Oil lamps, and photographs of people in uniform were scattered around some of the other furniture.

Before too long, Karla returned with our orders. The sandwiches' buns looked miniscule compared to the golden fried tenderloin patties that protruded from them. Our plates were heaped with not only the tenderloins, but crispy and salty French fries, a cup of Rose's homemade soup, a fresh garden vegetable salad, and pan-fried bread.

"Cardi," moaned Tuney, eyeing the huge amounts of food. "I think we'd better rethink your idea of how Marie stays so young-looking and healthy. By the looks of this food, the cholesterol level has to be life-threatening!"

I shrugged, bit into my tenderloin sandwich, closed my eyes in ecstasy, and smacked my lips in bliss. "This melts in my mouth. I'd work here every day, too, if I could."

Tuney bit into hers and moaned – a sure sign of agreement. "This is totally delicious. I'm so glad we came. Oh, my gosh, it's to die for!"

Both of us Widsters kept silent while we ate. At last, Tuney set her silverware down first and pushed her chair away from the table. "Uncle!" she groaned in defeat. "There's no way I can eat all this and have room for the pie! How are you doing?"

I signaled defeat, too. "I shouldn't have ordered dessert. I think my stomach's going to burst."

Tuney exhaled and signaled Karla, who stopped by the table. Before Tuney could say anything, Karla grinned. "Let me guess. Pies to go?" We just sighed contentedly and nodded with sheepish grins.

When she returned with our two pieces of pie boxed up, I thanked her. "This was all so delicious! Please thank the cook – she's fantastic."

Karla thanked us, and we gathered our purses and pies to take a walk outdoors. We could see our fellow bus passengers seated all over the restaurant and while a few were like us and getting ready to leave, most of the people were eating leisurely and visiting amongst themselves.

As we walked outside, being careful when we opened the door, Tuney drily commented. "Jeepers, I'm glad it's August and I'm not wearing Spanx!"

"Maybe because it's August and things expand in heat is why my waistband is so tight now," I stated. I pulled at the top of my capris and frowned. I thought the elastic was supposed to be more pliant.

"Can I borrow that excuse?" asked Tuney drily. "It doesn't make us sound like the gluttons we are!"

"I know!" I glanced around as we walked down the stairs. Just then someone behind us hollered at us to wait. The 2Bs2Ts joined us, moaning and groaning about how much they ate. Only Tammy didn't have a carry-out pie, and she explained it was because she hated pie.

"But I did clean up my plate, so I probably won't even want any supper," she said apologetically.

The others groaned. "I can't imagine eating any more today," said Trudy.

"But you know we will, darn it," moaned Belinda. She tried to suck in her stomach. And failed. Then she shrugged and admitted. "At least I'll eat the pie later. I must. It's calling my name already."

I chuckled. "I hear you. But my plan is to walk around here until everyone is ready to leave. Maybe I can burn off enough calories to take away the French fries at least."

"You mean ONE French fry," corrected Tuney. "I don't want to know how many calories we consumed. But I think supper is on our own tonight, so if we make a pact not to eat, I promise to stick to it."

Thinking the others would immediately agree with her, Tuney stood still with a smile on her face. She held her hand out palm down, waiting for the rest of us to slap ours one on top of the other. But there was only silence for a moment as the rest of us all looked at each other. Tuney's jaw dropped and she looked at us in amazement. "Oh, come on, you guys! Really? You think you can eat later?"

Tammy and I giggled as Belinda, Bonnie and Trudy nodded their heads vigorously.

"Tuney, I learned a long time ago to never say never!" declared Belinda.

"And supper is a while yet, so I'm sure we'll be hungry again by then," supplied Trudy hopefully.

"Besides it's easy to burn off calories." Bonnie announced breezily. " I once burned 2,000 calories in less than half an hour." She paused, and sure enough, Tuney pounced on that.

"What? No way!"

"Wa-ay!" was the reply.

"How?" asked Tuney, narrowing her eyes suspiciously.

"Easy! I didn't hear the 20-minute timer go off after I put two sheets of cookies in the oven."

Budda-bing, budda-boom. I didn't see that coming! I snorted and Tuney tried to swipe at Bonnie's arm. Bonnie danced away, giggling.

"Well, Cardi wants me to gain weight, and I think I've already accomplished that yesterday. But I guess we can just agree that calories don't exist on a vacation," Tuney announced amicably.

"Amen!" "I'll drink to that!" and a "Good!" came from some of us in answer.

Chapter 16

Where Time Stands Still

As soon as we walked outdoors and down the steps, we turned to the backyard. It was a park-like setting. The first thing the 2Bs2Ts did was walk over to look at the old millwheel. But Tuney and I made a beeline over to the clock. As soon as we reached it, Tuney turned to me with her finger on her lip.

"Hush a second. Just listen to the sounds from the river."

I could hear gentle gurgles, a slow swishing sound, and once a small splash and slap of the water as a fish rose to try to catch a bug. Other than the murmur of voices from people who were wandering around, they were the only sounds to break the silence.

"Don't you feel the quiet here?" Tuney asked me as I took a picture of her next to the clock. "It's like being in a Narnia-like setting."

I smiled at that. Teacher Tuney had always loved reading stories to her classes over the years, and the C.S. Lewis books were among those she treasured. But she'd told me once several years ago when the movie *The Lion, The Witch and the Wardrobe* was released, she thought the movie was better. I had been surprised because she was a staunch defender of the written word. "It's just that my imagination never picked up the special effects that moviemakers can do nowadays, and it was fascinating to watch," she had confessed.

She smiled back at me, then we walked away from the clock and sat on a nearby bench to relax. Her face was raised toward the sun, but behind the sunglasses she'd put on, I saw her eyes were watching some clouds. I looked sky-ward, too. A few dappled-grey balls of cotton-lookalikes were being torn apart into gossamer wisps by some invisible force miles above us. In a moment, the tendrils had evaporated into the ever-increasing blue sky. I sat next to Tuney and let my mind absorb the peace and quiet. Hearing the water in the background reminded me of the trip Kris and I took to Bermuda for our twenty-fifth anniversary.

I once told Kris that I knew I tended to be impulsive sometimes.

He laughed and said "Tended? Cardi, you are the most impulsive person I've ever met!"

I proved that while in Bermuda. I waded in a shallow area of a bay and saw a baby octopus. I was thrilled! I picked it up gently and caressed it. The tiny creature softly wrapped some of its arms around my own. I hollered at Kris to come see what I'd found. He took one look and screamed at me to put it down. I was shocked and embarrassed in front of other vacationers, and I did so immediately. He tried lecturing me about the dangers of picking up an animal I knew nothing about, but I refused to listen to him and had spoken angrily back at him, accusing him of being a "wuss."

It was the only time we'd ever gone to bed angry, each one sure he or she was right. Neither one of us slept well. I finally got up and quietly left the hotel room to go down for an early breakfast. While there, I struck up a conversation with the waiter and when he asked me if I was having fun, I mentioned how thrilled I'd been to hold the octopus. The shocked look on the waiter's face made me feel guilty about what I'd said to Kris. The waiter told me that while I'd probably been safe enough this time since it was a baby, I should never again try to pick one up.

"Some species can bite with their hard beaks and inject a paralyzing poison into your system," he'd said seriously. "People die from octopus bites."

I remembered feeling chastised and embarrassed a second time. I hurried and finished up my breakfast and returned to the hotel room. I quietly got undressed, put my pajamas back on and crept back into bed. Kris woke up as I did, and I cried in his arms that I was sorry I was so impetuous, and that he was right to have been concerned. We ended up making love, or having makeup sex, as Kris laughingly called it later. I told him I expected flowers since it was our anniversary, and by golly, he brought me bouquet later that afternoon.

At that point, I felt life couldn't get any better than that. I'd promised to try to curb my recklessness and never again touch an octopus. Kris had raised an eyebrow, said, "Just an octopus?" and grinned when I amended my promise to include "anything without your permission." I think he knew after 25 years with me that my spontaneity was not going to disappear.

"You know you terrify me sometimes," he'd chided me gently.

"How? What do you mean?" I'd asked, puzzled.

"Cardi, I love that you like to try different things, but, Honey, sometimes you try things without thinking of the consequences." He held up a finger to shush me as I opened my mouth to protest. "Such as paragliding that time in Puerto Vallarta when there was only one young guy on the boat towing you." He laid his finger against my lips as I started again to defend myself, and continued, "And the time we were in Aspen and you took it upon yourself to skip the ski lesson and went to the top of the mountain to ski down by yourself. And you marched right up to pet the bison when we were at Yellowstone. Each time you could have been badly injured, or even killed."

I remembered how terrified I'd been parasailing and skiing. However, I hadn't been with the buffalo, until I saw a sign later warning tourists not to pet them. "But I wasn't hurt!" I reminded him.

"Thank God for that. But the point is, Sweetheart, you are sometimes…" and he hesitated, not wanting to anger me again, then continued, "sometimes a bit reckless and impetuous." He bent over and kissed my neck. "And I don't ever want anything to happen to you."

"Hey! Whatcha thinkin' about?" Tuney asked. I hadn't realized I'd been smiling.

With a start, I looked over at her and smiled. "Oh, just Kris." I stood up from the bench and stretched and strolled over to the clock again. "I was thinking about some fun trips with him. You know – positive thoughts!"

Tuney walked over to me. "Well, it looked like they were definitely some happy thoughts of Kris," she said with a smile as she peered at me.

"Yup," I smiled back at her, and then touched the pole the clock was on. I was suddenly afraid I was going to start crying. Positive *thoughts* be damned. I'd rather have the real thing.

Tuney blew her cheeks out. "Let me take your picture,

Cardi. But watch out – that clock made me remember some good times with the old guy, so maybe there really is magic around here," she said brightly.

"The 'old guy?' Tuney Thompson, if Tommy was here, he'd slap your fanny for calling him that!" I teased.

She smiled. "I don't think I'd mind it a bit," she said softly. Then, she seemed to give herself a shake and said, "Positive thoughts, right?" I felt almost proud of her.

As Tuney walked over to the spot I had stood to take her picture, I looked up at the clock. "This is weird, but pleasantly so, don't you think?"

I smiled and tried to pose while Tuney fiddled with her phone camera.

"You're a regular Twiggy," declared Tuney, referring to the very thin British model of the 1960s that we'd both tried to emulate then. "At least a very old Twiggy! And a bit heavier Twiggy. Maybe more like a trunk than a twig."

"Tuney! Knock it off. Take the stupid picture already!" I stuck my tongue out at her right as I heard the camera click.

"Ope! Got it!" cried Tuney in delight. "Oh, boy, Facebook, here I come!"

"Oh, no! You wait a minute. Don't you dare post anything like that," I warned, trotting back over to where Tuney stood smirking. When I saw myself with my tongue out and my double chin more pronounced because of the way I'd pulled my neck in, I screeched at her.

"I'll pull every hair out of your head if you dare post that. Delete it! Now!"

Tuney just laughed. The 2Bs2Ts hurried over to us after hearing me shriek. But when they saw the picture Tuney had taken of me, they laughed, but insisted that I looked adorable.

I finally chose to believe them. Then they took turns posing by the clock, took a photo of us two Widsters together, and had Tuney take a photo of all four of them together.

By this time, most of the tour bus passengers were mingling outdoors. Some joined us, some wandered down to look at the river, and others were taking pictures of the millwheel. The 2Bs2Ts wanted to show us the millwheel before we had to leave on the bus, so we all walked back to it.

Though the Iowa summer heat had browned patches of grass, colorful holly-hocks that grew alongside the beautifully weathered brick of the old mill's side seemed to thrive with a vibrancy Tuney and I found enchanting. We all stopped next to the old mill wheel and stared upward.

It was at least two stories high, with wooden sections cut and planed to make the two sides of the wheel's circle shape. In between the two wheels were small wooden blades set evenly apart and fastened to each wheel. A huge metal hub had wooden spokes that were nailed onto the outer sides of each wheel. Tuney smiled as she stared at the wheel. It reminded her, she told me, of the time Tommy took one of the grandkids for a ride on a Ferris Wheel at the state fair.

"The one and only time," she remembered. "It had to have been about ten years ago. Tommy discovered when the Ferris Wheel stopped at the top that he'd developed a fear of heights he hadn't had in his youth."

We could all relate to that, "What happened to him?" asked Trudy curiously.

"Nothing, thank goodness. But he scrunched his eyes closed tightly and kept them closed the rest of the time. He made me swear I'd never let him ride it again!" Tuney chewed her bottom lip. "At least he finally quit teasing me about being afraid of heights. He could commiserate."

I looked at the wheel, then turned around to look at the river which was about 75 or 80 yards from them. "Think about it, girls. There had to be water right here where we're standing for this thing to operate. I know it's not a tremendous distance but look how far it is today from the river." I pointed to the river. The early afternoon sun's rays danced across the river current, making the brownish water look golden.

A slight breeze from the northwest lifted Tuney's hair and brought the smells of the restaurant to us all. She lifted her nose and breathed deeply. "I wonder what it was like before this was a restaurant, back when the mill was actually running."

"Probably pretty dusty, and I bet it smelled fishy, too, with the water so close," said Belinda as she looked above the giant wheel to the windows on the third level of the mill.

Tuney looked at her and blinked as she looked back to the river. "Well, you just blew my romantic vision of this thing," she declared. Belinda shrugged and grinned.

"Did anyone see the photo of the mill that was inside?" asked Bonnie. "I noticed it along with some other old photos. The entire river bank was filled with different buildings. It looks like Bonaparte was a busy and prosperous place at one time."

"Too bad we can't travel back in time to see what this place really looked like," said Tammy.

The others agreed solemnly, but before we could continue the conversation, Amy and Mr. Smith appeared around the corner. He walked on down to the river to notify the group down there it was time to go, and Amy gathered the group by the clock. The 2Bs2Ts, Tuney and I were the last to board. I stood on the stairs to the bus for one more look at the peaceful scenery. *Funny how many times I've been thinking of you,* I silently said to Kris.

Once on board the bus, Amy got everyone's attention. "I have another little stop to make if you don't mind," she announced.

"Only if it's something that won't make me dizzy," hollered Mort. He was rewarded with laughter from the rest of the passengers.

"Oh, I learned my lesson with you athletes!" retorted Amy. She continued through the tittering and chuckles of her tour group. "I happened to talk to Rose Hendricks, the owner of Bonaparte's Retreat. We're going to take a five-minute visit to see something near and dear to her heart." Then she sat down without any further comment, leaving the passengers to wonder what was next.

"Maybe it's a bakery filled top to bottom with pies," Trudy guessed. Bonnie guess maybe a special Bonaparte museum. But after just a few minutes, the bus turned down a gravel lane and I gasped.

Chapter 17

The Cemetery

"Oh, my goodness, is that a cemetery?" I heard another passenger ask. Tuney and I instantly scooted to the aisle seats and stared ahead. Then we looked at each other. Yes, we were going to a cemetery.

Bonnie turned around to them. "Is this a good idea, what with all these old people on board?"

"Watch it, toots, I'm older than you are," quipped Belinda. She winked at us and whispered out the side of her mouth, "But just by three months!"

Mr. Smith pulled over to the side of the road and Amy stood up again. "I know this isn't on the itinerary, but if anyone wants to get off the bus and take a closer look, you can. For anyone else look out the left window if you want to. I'm going to walk over there right now."

Mr. Smith opened the door and she hopped off. I saw the top of her head as she walked in front of the bus and headed a little way into the graveyard. Belinda and Trudy were in front of me, and they tried peering past Bonnie and Tammy, but couldn't see anything.

"I might as well go see," Belinda groaned as she stood up. "Every little step might be one less calorie gone from lunch!"

"Good idea!" said Tuney as she stood up to follow her. Trudy decided to get off, too.

"Tune. Hey! Look at that," I said from my seat next to the window. I squinted at the spot Amy had stopped. From a distance, it appeared to be a miniature house, made from granite.

"Could that be a child's grave?" I asked. "Oh, I hope not. But maybe she loved playing with dollhouses." I looked over at Tuney's empty seat and then spotted her in the aisle. "Hey! Wait for me. I want to go, too."

By then, everyone had decided to depart, so in a few minutes people were walking through the resting places of part of the Bonaparte citizenry. Tuney set off at a rapid pace up a slight incline toward Amy. I hurried next to her, afraid that being in a cemetery might make Tuney cry. Sometimes she did when we visited "the boys."

Tuney showed no sign of being tearful now. All around us were old grave stones, some slightly crooked where they'd settled in the earth, some with the markings hardly recognizable because of weatherization and moss. I paused once to read an old stone with only the first and last name barely visible. I traced my fingers over the name.

"Hey, c'mere, Tune! I can't tell the name, but I can kind of read the date. It's 1800s, both birth and death," I called out to Tuney, who stopped and walked back to where I was standing. I straightened up and looked sadly at Tuney. "Oh, it's a child!"

"There are so many children in old cemeteries," said Tuney looking around at the other old stones nearby. "I wonder what happened to this little one?" She caressed the top of the stone.

The 2Bs2Ts caught up to us and murmured sorrowfully at the child's grave. I squinted at the dates. "I can't make out the name, but it was only two when it died."

Bonnie leaned in closer to the weathered carving on the face of the marker. "February something, 1847 to something-something 1849." She stood up and frowned. "I wonder if this might have been a child of pioneers or maybe Mormons."

"Oh, that's right! We're near the Mormon Trail, aren't we?" I breathed. I stroked the top of the little marker. "Poor little one. Wonder if it died of a disease or was just too young to make a hard trek."

Trudy shrugged but touched the stone, as did Belinda and Tammy.

Tuney leaned closer to the gravestone. "I'd say probably a disease, like flu or pneumonia, or what was once called consumption – tuberculosis." She frowned for a moment. "I can't even imagine watching your child be sick and not being able to get a doctor or meds. We really are lucky we live in the time that we do now."

I nodded in agreement. "And if it was a pioneer who had to bury her child and then leave the area – I can't imagine how haunted you'd be by that!" I glanced at Tuney. "It's like I said – losing a child is worse than losing a husband. At least in my book!"

Everyone nodded solemnly in agreement.

Tuney stared at the little gravestone, then nodded slightly. "Yeah. I guess. I can begin to see why history equates pioneers as brave and 'sturdy' stock," she said, making air quotes when she said 'sturdy.'" She scratched her head. "I remember my world history because I loved how fascinating it was. And I know Europe had some immunizations in the 18th century.

There were some here in the US in the 1800s, but if I remember correctly, it wasn't until the early 20th century that medical science really took off."

She pushed up the short sleeve on her tee shirt. "Remember these vaccine marks, you guys? Back last century? Ha!" She had a smallpox vaccination scar on her right arm, barely noticeable after almost sixty years.

Automatically, the rest of us checked our own shoulder, then each other's. Tuney suddenly burst out laughing. "I can barely tell where mine is anymore," she said.

I grimaced, grabbed my reading glasses, and said, "I think I need a magnifying glass to find mine! We're just like these old gravestones. Getting worn down!"

"Ope! Except for the old-age spots. Geesh!" Tuney said, glancing at the rest of the group ahead of us. "Can you imagine what this looks like? A bunch of old ladies checkin' each other's arms out?

"Yeah, we're weird," chortled Belinda. "Any chance they'd think we were shooting up drugs?"

Tammy snorted. "Or looking for track marks!"

I frowned at a new mole I hadn't noticed before, then absently rubbed my hand hard over my arm as if to erase all the sunspots and skin abrasions that had accumulated over the years.

"No. Track marks are usually down lower on the arm by the elbow or wrist. At least, I think so," I added doubtfully.

Tuney looked at me critically. "Whatever. How would any of you even know that?" Belinda, Tammy and I only shrugged and grinned.

"Well, we'd better join Amy, or they'll all be ready to leave as soon as we get there," pointed out Trudy.

As we started toward Amy and the monument that had first attracted our attention, some of the passengers who'd been there for a few minutes began to leave and head back to the bus. I overheard bits and pieces of their conversations, such as 'awesome,' 'unbelievable,' and 'cost a fortune.'

As we drew closer, we saw the monument was no dollhouse, but a beautiful reddish granite headstone. Instead of the usual oval, square or pointed-top shape, this stone had a roof on the top where the deceased's name was etched. On one side, a three-dimensional small staircase ended at the top of a front porch that partially covered the face of the tombstone. On the stone, several little sections of bricks had been stamped into the granite, as well as windows with shutters.

"Wow! What is this?" I asked as Tuney walked around the stone.

"It's Bonaparte Retreat! Oh, my gosh, this is amazing!" exclaimed Tuney, pointing at the face of the stone with that name etched on it. "I love this!"

"Why would they have a replica of it here?" I asked, mystified.

"It's not a replica, you goose!"

Amy interjected. "It's an actual tombstone. Look at the top of the roof!" She placed her hand next to a plaque on the top.

"Oh, wow!" I said again, quickly read the inscription. "Oooh! So, this is Rose Hendricks' husband? The man who owned the restaurant?" I murmured.

"What a perfect way to pay homage to him!" Tuney gazed at the stone thoughtfully. "He must have really loved that place." Then mindful of her arthritic knees and helped by Amy, she knelt carefully down in front of the grave and touched the little stairs that ran up to the stone porch.

"Okay?" asked Amy. When Tuney nodded, Amy told us to take a few minutes, but then get back to the bus, and she left to join the other passengers.

"Have you ever seen anything like this?" Tuney asked me in wonderment. She examined the minute details. Posts on the front porch had been scored, and the scene was made even more personal with etchings of swags, a big water barrel and small windows. There was even a sign engraved above the porch that read "Bonaparte Retreat."

I knelt next to my sister and shook my head. "No, definitely not. There was nothing like this in what the mortuary showed me for markers when I bought Kris's and my stone. This is an amazing piece of what I would call art, wouldn't you? The Hendricks' must have loved this place a lot."

"And he must have been loved so much, too." murmured Tuney. She noted that the deceased had died several years ago. "You know, I haven't ordered a stone for Tommy yet. I wonder…" and she trailed off.

I broke into her thoughts. "Man! If his family got this monument for him, I wonder how lavish a funeral they had for him, don't you?" I studied the stone, then looked at Tuney.

Tuney blinked and looked at me. "Cardi!" she said testily. "I hope people never say that about Tommy's funeral! What a thing to say!"

"What? Don't sound like you've never wondered about funeral costs before! That's a normal question," I retorted, "Geesh. This is starting to sound like our conversation when we first started the trip!" I wanted to chew Tuney out for whatever bickering we'd done that she'd started, but I was aware the 2Bs2Ts were watching us. I saw Tammy whisper something to Bonnie, and then they all turned and started toward the bus.

"Hey, Widsters. We've seen enough. We're going back on board. You guys take your time," called Belinda over her shoulder.

I looked at Tuney and could tell she felt a wave of guilt wash over her. She shrugged, and half-way apologized "I'm not criticizing you, Card. I just…oh, I'm sorry. I don't why that irritated me. When you said that, I wondered if anyone had thought I'd been too cheap - or too lavish - on Tommy. I guess…well, I got defensive."

I reached over to touch Tuney's arm, full of remorse. "It's okay. You're right, though. That sounded pretty nosy of me. And no one thought that of you with Tommy's funeral." I sat back on my haunches. "Another episode of me and my big mouth, opened before I thought!"

Tuney grimaced. "Yes, and I know it's very easy to verbalize a thought before you actually think it out. Because I almost just said something to tick you off!"

"What?"

"In the interest of sisterly peace, never mind!"

I chuckled, then pulled my phone out to take a picture of the monument. "Well, this is certainly unique, that's for sure!" I stood up and then turned to Tuney. "But if you did something like this for Tommy, what would you do?"

Tuney didn't answer. She stared at the stone, then wondered out loud how hard it had been for this man's widow to decide what kind of memorial to her husband to buy. How long it had taken Mrs. Hendricks to come up with this? Had Mr. Hendricks even been in on the decision? Had he died suddenly like Kris? Or did they have time to say goodbye to each other like she and Tommy had? Tuney brushed her hand in front of her face as if to wave away the cobwebs of thoughts she had voiced.

I had no answers, but I don't think she wanted any. "Well, we gotta go. Mr. Smith is waving at us to come."

Tuney struggled to get to her feet, batting away my hand as I tried to help my sister. "Ugh! I hate getting old," she moaned.

"Well, quit being so stubborn and let me help you," I scolded. I struggled to get up, too, bent down and rubbed my knees. "I may have gotten up faster than you, but I hate getting older, too. It hurts!"

I watched Tuney doubtfully as she got on all fours, then lifted her rear-end up and straightened her legs. Once she was in what I thought could only be described as a camel-position, Tuney walked her hands back toward her feet until she could straighten up.

"Ahhh," Tuney breathed. "Finally!"

"Well, that was graceful," I commented cynically. Tuney looked at me sharply, then shrugged. I looked toward the bus. "Hey! Everyone on this side of the bus has their cameras out!"

Tuney whirled around to look, shoulders drawn up ready to hide her face. I broke into peals of laughter when she realized I was kidding.

"Cardi, you brat! Okay, you got me. But I hope for your sake no one did sneak a shot at me."

"He-he-he," I snickered. "You should have seen your face!" and I took off toward the bus, waving at Bonnie and Trudy who were peering out their window at us Widsters.

Tuney took one last look at the replica of Bonaparte Retreat, smiled wanly at it, and then hustled after me. I know she hadn't planned on thinking about headstones – had even shut her mind to the fact that she needed to get one for Tommy – but seeing the beauty and uniqueness of this stone seemed to get her to reconsider.

"Wonder what Tommy would think?" she asked me as we reached the bus steps. "Would he like something like that?" She sighed and boarded the bus. I knew in my heart that Tuney was wishing for the thousandth time that she could talk to her husband just once more. That's because I was wishing the same thing about Kris.

Chapter 18

Mason House

*I*t seemed like I just sat back down on the bus when it stopped again. And I wasn't too far wrong. The bus had arrived in the tiny and very artsy village of Bentonsport. It lay just a few miles west of Bonaparte where, the itinerary listed, we would have three hours to shop and relax. Afterwards, we'd head to nearby Keosauqua where we would spend the night in a magnificent historical hotel.

"Whew! That was quick," I commented to Tuney. "Here we are in Bentonsport. I've never heard of it."

Tuney looked out the window and saw the bus had parked in front of a large, two-story brick building. A sign in front identified it as Mason House Inn and Bed & Breakfast. She clapped her hands, no surprise to me.

"Card! Look at that," she said pointing the B&B. "I just love all the historical older places we're seeing, don't you?"

Mason House Inn sat on the north side of the street between it and the river. Both of us Widsters lived in older homes, and our hometown was full of houses well over a century old. Tuney had been involved in a historic renovation of an old home that had been converted into the town museum. Because she taught school, she'd been able to research not only the history of the type of building it was but found out some history of the families who'd lived in it, as well.

The inn was a beautiful brick house with what looked like three stories, and an addition to the east. To my surprise, a train caboose sat next to that. Tuney especially liked that the house looked symmetrical. The entry door from the south side had a wide white door, flanked by two windows. The second story had five windows, the middle one centered above the door.

The top floor was most likely an attic, I thought, where one window was centered above the second-floor middle window and perfectly aligned with the peak of the roof. A curved wedge-shaped window flanked each side of it. A small cat peered out of one of them.

"Oh, look at the kitty," I pointed. Tuney glanced to where I pointed, but she couldn't see anything. When I looked, the kitty had disappeared, probably to go back to prowl for mice, I thought.

"Is that caboose a gift shop, do you suppose?" Tuney asked. "Or is it one of the sleeping quarters?"

I pulled my phone out. "Hang on a sec. Googling!" and in a moment, announced, "Hey! It's rented out as sleeping quarters, but it also has a kitchenette in it." I gazed at the pretty yellow caboose, remembering the times I read "The Little Red Caboose," to my kids and thinking it would be fun to take pictures of this one to show my grandchildren. "Wish we could stay there," I said wistfully.

"Me, too," said Tuney. "But it needs to be red."

"Ope! I was just thinking about reading "The Little Red

Caboose" to my kids," I squealed, looking at Tuney in delighted surprise.

She nonchalantly shrugged, pointed to her head and said, "Great minds!"

"I'm in trouble if I start thinking like you," I retorted.

"Wrong! I would be the one in trouble if I thought like you!" and she grinned.

Before we could continue gently razzing each other, I noticed that Amy had risen from her seat and was answering questions. She finally took the microphone and everyone on the bus quieted.

"Well, here we are in one of the most interesting little towns in the state of Iowa," she began. "I have to apologize for one thing, though." She paused and shook her head. "Normally, we don't have too many glitches on a trip, but I got a call a bit ago from the hotel we booked in Keosauqua. We're supposed to stay overnight there tonight. But..." her pregnant pause had the entire bus silent as they wondered what her apology would be for. "We are going to have to stay here in Bentonsport for the night. The hotel had a pipe burst on the top floor. And it wasn't noticed until it had soaked through to the other floors!"

The bus hummed immediately with questions and comments from those who had ever suffered the same thing in their own home.

"Surely it didn't leak in every room there, did it? That's a big hotel," someone asked, loudly enough for everyone to hear.

"Good question," answered Amy patiently. "No, it didn't leak in every room. But they were having some renovations done in half the hotel. Those aren't finished. And now...well, now the other half is going to be renovated a few years sooner than planned, thanks to the water damage!"

More hands raised, and a few disappointed groans could be heard all the way back to our seats. Several questions were being asked at once. Amy rubbed her forehead but smiled. Watching her, I realized how little I knew about all the background planning and preparation it must take to make tour trips like this one work successfully. I wondered what Amy was going to do.

"Do you suppose we'll have to cut the trip short and maybe go home tonight?" I asked Tuney.

The 2Bs2Ts heard me. "I hope not!" Belinda answered. But then everyone was hushed again as Amy continued.

"Fortunately for us all, there are several B&Bs in Bentonsport who have enough rooms between them that we can all spend the night. Mason House here out front is one of them." A cry of hooray erupted from the bus and people started clapping. Amy looked relieved.

"Right now, I'm going to have you all get out and start shopping, walking, whatever you'd like to do. We'll meet back here at 5:00 and by then, I'll have you each checked in at the various inns. The bus will drop everyone off, except those of you at Mason House, and will pick you all up in the morning at 8:30 a.m. If anyone has any questions or concerns, you've all got my cell." She looked over the crowd, and not seeing any hands up, she smiled brightly. "Again, thank you all SO much for your cooperation, and you guys are the best group ever! Now go have fun! There are some unique shops around here."

As everyone clapped again and stood up to leave the bus, Tuney leaned over to me. "I love this Mason House, just from the outside. I don't even want to look at another B&B. Do you think it'd upset Amy's plans if we ask if we can stay here?"

"No, I don't think she'd mind. And I want to stay in the caboose, don't you?" I asked in a whisper so any other person who might want it wouldn't overhear. "I just Googled it and it's got great reviews."

Having agreed, we waited to leave the bus and were the last ones off. Tuney was relieved we could talk to Amy privately. Tuney asked Amy if she already had made assignments to the B&Bs.

Amy looked a little guilty and shook her head no. "I've never had this happen before. I was afraid if I told everyone they could pick where they wanted to stay, we'd end up spending hours driving back and forth between the B&Bs. It's just easier for me to assign the inns, don't you think?"

We immediately agreed. But either our agreement was too half-hearted, or Amy caught the guilty glances Tuney and I shot each other, because she lowered her voice and said slyly, "I don't suppose you two have any preferences you'd like to voice, do you?"

I tried to look innocent. That hasn't happened in over sixty years and didn't happen then. Tuney just grinned.

"Well, if it's all right with you, we'd kind of like to stay here at Mason House," offered Tuney.

I nodded and then pleaded, "And if it's possible, could we stay in the caboose? Please?"

Amy hesitated. "Well, you two can stay at Mason House – no problem. The thing is, the caboose sleeps four. And since there are several groups here with four members, I thought we'd better put one of them in there."

My face fell, and Amy apologized. "But, tell you what! Come with me to talk to Chuck and Joy, the owners. I know they give tours, and if you want to delay the start of your shopping, you might be able to look at all the rooms and take your pick – as long as it only sleeps two. Okay with that?"

We were thrilled with that chance and grateful for the sneak peek. We followed Amy dutifully to the front door of the Inn.

"Well, this certainly is an old home, and I think we'll both love looking at it if we get a chance," I remarked. It looked so welcoming and charming that I could hardly wait to see the inside.

We walked up the sidewalk to the Inn. Just as Amy raised her hand to knock, the door opened wide. I shrieked. A nice-looking gentleman stood there with an apologetic smile on his face, his eyes crinkled in amusement.

"Am I that scary-looking? C'mon in," and he stepped back out of the doorway.

I was mortified. Tuney shot me a look like I was a nuisance, and Amy started to giggle.

"I'm Chuck Hanson," said the man, extending his hand to Amy, then Tuney and me. "And no need to apologize or be embarrassed. If I don't make you scream every time you look at me, we're good!" And he chuckled.

Disarmed by his geniality, I followed Chuck, Amy and Tuney into the foyer. Amy introduced herself and then us. We turned to look at the now-crowded foyer and were immediately charmed.

Old photos of Bentonsport in its heyday lined the walls. The foyer held a staircase that looked like it was original to the house. The steps were worn, and the banister was slim. I peered up the stairwell and saw there was a landing with several doors around it. Those, I assumed, led to bedrooms.. I couldn't wait to explore to see what else there was.

Amy and Chuck began talking the logistics of getting at

least 15 people into rooms that weren't already rented. It was obvious that the chattering from the foyer carried throughout the house, because a smiling woman appeared at the top of the staircase and came down the stairs. In her arms she carried a block of quilting that she'd evidently been working on.

"Oh, there you are, Joy," said Chuck, beaming at her. "This is my wife, Joy, and these lovely ladies are…" He turned to Amy, and said, "I know I'm going to get your names all wrong."

I chimed in with a laugh. "I'm Cardi Cooper," and reached around my sister to shake Joy's hand.

Tuney turned to Joy with a smile, and said, "Hi, I'm Tuney Thompson."

"Tuney? Is that a nickname?" she said as she shook Tuney's hand. "I've never met a Tuney before!" Her eyes danced, and she had such a welcoming smile on her face that Tuney took no umbrage at her name being singled out.

"Petunia, as in the flower. My mom's favorite," said Tuney with an equally warm smile back. She beamed at Joy as if she'd known her for years.

"Petunias are my favorite, too," said Joy. Her voice was soft but warm and friendly. She patted the top of Tuney's hand before she let go. Tuney was surprised to see Joy study her face briefly. Joy saw her look at her and shook her head.

"Forgive me if I seem a little forward," she said apologetically, "but have you suffered a loss recently?"

Tuney drew in her breath. Before she could answer, Joy turned to me. "And you, too?"

I looked a little skeptically at her, then with a touch of suspicion answered, "Yes. But I imagine you get a lot of widows on bus tours, don't you?"

Chuck laughed, and Joy's smile broadened. "Yes, we certainly do. But not too many sisters," she said quietly.

I felt my eyes widen at that and looked at Amy. "Did you mention to them we were sisters?" I asked, surprised. "We don't look that much alike anymore!"

Amy shook her head no. Before she could say anything else, Joy interjected.

"I'm sorry. I should probably have started out by saying that I sometimes pick up vibes from people," she said.

"You mean you can read minds?" asked Tuney, warily.

I wondered if we'd better rethink staying here. Then I wondered if Joy knew I'd wondered that!

Joy laughed. "Oh, no! Nothing like reading minds."

"If she could," Chuck cut in, "I'd be in big trouble most of the time!" He smiled, and Joy looked at him, and with a theatrical widening of her eyes and lift of her brows gave a slow nod. I felt relieved and amused. These two were a cute couple.

Amy stepped forward. "Oh, Joy, that's so very interesting. Paranormal, energy and spiritual events fascinate me. Are you like a medium, or something?"

Joy looked at Amy and nodded. "Something like that," she replied. Then she looked at us Widsters. Both Tuney and I were staring with mouths slightly wide open. A look of concern swept her face. "Oh, please don't be bothered," she said comfortingly. She pointed to some brochures that were on a table in the foyer. "We don't hide the fact that this is a very special building. As you can see from these, Mason House Inn is haunted – and people love it!"

"Haunted?" cried Tuney and I at the same time. Sure enough, as I peered more closely at some of the brochures, I saw they advertised ghost walks, visits by paranormal experts and the history of Mason House."

"Oh, not every room. But yes, there are some that our friendly ghosts like to visit occasionally," replied Joy in a matter-of-fact manner.

Tuney uneasily turned to Amy.

"Uh, Amy," she wavered, and looked apologetically at Chuck and Joy, "no offense, please," she started.

"Of course not," interrupted Chuck, waving a hand, but also grinning

Tuney gave a slight smile and continued, "But staying in a haunted hotel or B&B wasn't on the itinerary."

"You certainly don't have to stay here," said Amy quickly and reassuringly. "And if you'd rather go on now and shop while I take a tour with Chuck, that's totally fine." She reached over to Tuney and gave her a little hug. "You know, we'll do whatever our guests want, and there's even a new motel about ten miles from here that we could house you in overnight."

"And we know that place and don't believe it's haunted at all," supplied Joy helpfully.

Tuney felt relieved. With what I hoped would be an unobtrusive gesture, I pulled out my phone and Googled 'haunted hotels in Iowa.' I quickly read through the list and suddenly giggled.

"Tuney! We were at Hotel Julien last night, and guess what?" I said, holding up my phone.

Amy obviously knew the answer because she was nodding her head yes and had a knowing grin on her face.

Tuney closed her eyes. "What?" she said apprehensively. "Don't tell me it's haunted." She opened her eyes and looked pleadingly at me.

"Says here it's one of the most haunted hotels in Iowa!" I said triumphantly. "And get this: it's rumored the ghost of a man seen in period attire *might even be Al Capone*!"

Tuney's jaw dropped open and she slowly turned to look at Amy. "You mean the guy we saw dressed up in the early 1900s suit was a ghost?" She shook her head in disbelief. "Nah! It had to be an employee, or a guest going to a party or something."

Amy just shook her head. "I saw him, too, girls, and I thought the same thing," she said. "Remember? I was going to ask the main desk if we could take a group shot with Al? Well, when I asked the clerk if their employees dressed up in period costume, he said no, but added that I must have seen 'Mr. Capone.' That's why I told you in Dubuque we couldn't pose with the guest because he was a ghost-guest."

"Ope! I thought you said 'guest-guest' and I was going to ask you what that was, but then you got busy with somebody else and I forgot," I exclaimed.

"Oh, holy moley!" was all Tuney could say. She looked at her arms and showed me the hair standing up because of the goose bumps she felt.

"Oh, no need to get upset," calmed Chuck. Neither he nor Joy seemed to be apprehensive at our alarm. "Mason House isn't haunted in the sense of scary movies, or spine-tingling Halloween tales," he explained. "Look at me! I never really believed there was any such thing as ghosts before we moved here. Now it's just like having some old family members pop in unexpectedly occasionally."

"That's right!" chimed in Joy. "It's more like Mason House Inn is such a neat place to stay, that we get 'guests' who just want to stay and visit."

Amy asked Joy some questions about the area, so Joy began showing her some of the brochures of other attractions in the area.

Tuney shuddered. I looked at her in surprise.

"Tuney! What's wrong with you? You love Halloween and getting scared. But I don't think Mason House is going to be scary at all!"

Tuney stared at the floor. There was a love/hate relationship with things scary that Tuney had had for years. Tommy used to tease her that he didn't understand why Halloween was her favorite holiday when she couldn't even watch Hitchcock's "Psycho" because it scared her. She knew who Freddie Kruger, Mike Meyer, Carrie, Blair Witch and all the old-time movie monsters were. But she had never actually seen any of the horror pictures that her friends watched. When she was in high school, she loved going to sponsored "haunted houses." They were usually make-shift decorated empty buildings or even people's garages that sprung up around Halloween time in order to raise money. A group of kids would go together, the girls screaming and laughing if something touched them, while the boys bravely acted like the journey through the horrors was no big deal – but they were as bunched up together as if they were in a football huddle, and occasionally one of them would yell in fright. Tuney always took her kids through so-called haunted houses but could never explain why she couldn't sit through a scary movie without having nightmares afterward.

"With the fund-raising haunted houses, maybe it's because I know it's all fake," she said to me years later when Halloween rolled around. She had refused to go to a movie about a demon doll called Chucky when I invited her. Tommy pointed out she loved haunted houses.

"If I ever saw a ghost or was in a horror situation for real, I'd probably die of fright right on the spot," she protested.

"But I know most of the people who are acting in these houses, and it's fun and for a good cause." Tommy had just sighed, grinned and left the room.

About a half hour later, Tuney told me afterwards, she had walked down the hallway to the kids' bedrooms to put their neatly folded clothes away that she'd just washed and dried. As she reached a corner to turn to Joey's bedroom, Tommy sprang out in front of her and yelled, "Boo!"

She'd screamed, flinging the clothes into the air, so scared that "I almost peed my pants," she'd told her friends later. Tommy laughed so hard he bent over. Tuney was furious, turned around, and stomped back to the living room. He'd peeked around the corner to see if she was still mad, and then walked on his knees towards her, apologizing the entire time.

"I folded the clothes and put them away," he said meekly when he reached her. "I'm so sorry, Tuney, but..." and the dimple in his cheek deepened as he tried not to grin. "you should have seen the look on your face! I thought your eyes would pop out!"

She could see the humor in it and was already thinking about what she could do to get back at him. But she didn't want to let him off the hook just yet. "I just got through telling you I'd die of fright, and there you go. You're mean, Tommy Thompson!" and she pouted a bit, but batted her eyes and gave him a half-grin.

He pulled himself up, and sat next to her, wrapping her in his arms. "I'm so sorry, Honey. That *was* mean. I'm really so, so sorry, Baby," and he nuzzled her neck, causing her to giggle because she was ticklish, and he knew it.

Remembering her story, I inexplicably felt like we had to stay here.

"Tune! Listen to me! Let's stay here. Maybe we'll be visited by Kris and Tommy," I whispered urgently.

Tuney looked startled, then concerned. "Oh, Cardi. You know I'd give anything to see Tommy again. I have prayed to God since he died that I could see him just once more – even if he was a ghost. But now I think of the boys as angels, not ghosts! And I don't want to meet strange ghouls."

I gave her a droll look. "And what's an angel? Have you ever seen one? Couldn't it be that our loved one's souls are just called by different names? Think about it. A spirit, a ghost, an angel – What's the diff? They're all disembodied personalities, right?" Then I pleaded "And if seeing angels or ghosts is even a possibility, wouldn't you take a chance that it could be Kris and Tommy? I would!"

"Of course, you idiot!" She wouldn't look me in the eye, though. I could tell she was debating with herself the pros and cons of staying in a haunted house.

I went on a campaign, pointing at Tuney and then at Joy and Chuck, who were now watching and listening to us with amused expressions. "Then here's a possible opportunity to have them be with us!" I pressed. "And like Joy said, we could pick a room that's ghost-free. Besides, you heard Joy and Chuck explain how friendly this place is. I can actually physically feel it, can't you?" I wasn't using that remark off-handedly. I felt warm and welcome here, as if I was home with Mom and Dad, or at Grandpa and Grandma's."

Tuney drew a deep breath and her eyes darted around the room. "Yeah. Okay, I feel it," she admitted. Joy nodded her head and smiled.

"And it's not a scary feeling, right?"

Again, Tuney looked around at everyone. "It's not a scary

feeling. Okay." Then under her breath I heard her say, "But it's still weird."

Joy smiled at our exchange. "You know, you two sisters remind me of me and my own sister. You have differing opinions, but deep down you're a lot alike."

"Except I'm the *classy* one," I said and dug my elbow gently into Tuney's shoulder.

Tuney lost her apprehensiveness at once. "Uh, excuse her, please, Joy. She meant to say she's the *sassy* one," said Tuney drily, rolling her eyes. *Nothing like sisterly disrespect to make things right.*

Amy and Joy laughed out loud, while Tuney battled a grin tugging at her own mouth.

I leaned toward Amy and barely whispered, "I was being nice and not saying she's the *smart-assy* one. Boom!" I drew back with a smug look on my face as Amy shot Tuney a look and giggled.

"I heard that, Cardi!"

I shrugged and dimpled at my sister.

Chapter 19

George

Tuney knew when to quit. "Okay. I might as well do *one* thing outside my comfort zone. Listen. How about we take a tour, and if there's a room that we like that's NOT haunted, we'll take it." She changed the subject immediately before I could voice my delight. "Joy, I'm a quilter and I peeked into this room over here," she turned and pointed to the room off the foyer. "I love that quilt! Is it antique?"

Chuck looked directly at Joy and said proudly, "She made that. And I think this is a good segue for the tour. Joy, why don't you start, and I can join you pretty soon." As Joy nodded, he excused himself to check on his vegetable garden.

Joy threaded her way through us three women, and said, "All right then. Let's start here in the west room."

It was like being on a kindergarten tour - we obediently walked single file into the quaint and charming room. But once inside, we split up to look more closely at the objects that filled it.

Joy stood in the middle of the bedroom. "We call this the Bentonsport Room. It was once a pub for men only," she said.

I tried to picture the room with a bar and tables, but thought it was tiny for a real pub. Joy noticed me frowning in concentration and quickly added. "It actually ran quite a way back through the house. As with a lot of the rooms, remodeling throughout the years has brought changes."

She turned to the bed in the corner that Tuney had seen. It had a huge wooden headboard. On the wall next to it was a smaller quilt that matched the blanket on the bed. "You asked about this quilt, Tuney. I have antique quilts, but in order to preserve them, I don't use them on the beds. I've made every quilt you'll see on the bedding."

Tuney was impressed and walked over to run her hands lovingly over the pattern. "This is absolutely gorgeous, Joy," she gushed. "You are one very talented quilter." She and Joy began to talk about different quilt patterns, while I wandered over to the opposite corner of the bedroom.

Two windows, one facing south to the river, and the other west toward the rest of town, had old-fashioned pull-down blinds and lacy-looking curtains pulled back on either side. The windows themselves were almost floor to ceiling. An antique dresser with an equally old basin and pitcher on one edge was next to one of the windows. A few old but sturdy-looking rocking chairs as well as other antiques were in the room. The walls were papered in a pastel pattern and about two dozen smaller framed photographs were scattered on them.

Amy was studying them. "Anything interesting, Amy?" I asked her as I came closer.

Amy pointed out a picture of the bridge across the street. Horses and wagons were on it. "Isn't it neat to see what some of these places looked like when the town was relatively young?" she asked.

I looked all around at the other pictures. "I can't believe the history just here in this house, let alone the entire town." And remembering Bonaparte, added, "Let alone this whole area of the state, for that matter!"

Amy sighed. "I really like this room. It reminds me of my Grandma's cottage." She turned to look at Joy.

"Why don't we go to the dining room where you'll have breakfast. I'll get Chuck to tell you all about our history in detail. Complete with our many guests," she added. She called to Chuck to come in from the garden and led us into the hallway where Chuck entered. "I'll get you all some refreshments. I've got coffee, iced tea or lemonade," announced Joy.

"And cookies," added Chuck, as Joy passed him to go to the kitchen. She patted his stomach as she passed him by. I almost laughed because that was something I used to do to Kris – and much like Chuck's, Kris's stomach was lean and firm.

The dining room was almost filled completely with a huge long table. A fireplace was on one wall. Near it hung a Civil War sword. Again, we were duly impressed by the antiques. Tuney asked if the furnishings were original to the house. Chuck explained that most of them were, but it had taken some detective work on their part to find some of them.

"You'll note that hutch over there," he said pointing to a tall hutch made of dark wood. Beautifully blue-glazed plates were housed in it. "That came by mule and wagon from out East and was an original piece of Mason House. One of the previous owners of the Inn took a lot of the original furnishings with him when he sold this place. Joy and I tracked down quite a few pieces and bought them back. The hutch was found in a barn, if you can believe it."

"You're kidding," I said turning in my seat at the table to look at the hutch behind me. "Who'd be silly enough to do that?"

"Well, I think the guy got sick after he retired from here, and my guess is that relatives just put stuff in storage, not knowing their real historical worth," explained Chuck. He waved an arm around the room. "This whole place is full of history. Besides being used first as a hotel, it was a stop on the Underground Railroad, a holding hospital for Civil War wounded – both Yankee and Rebel – and a sanitorium for tuberculosis patients. They don't make places like this anymore – or at least, they don't keep them standing for as long as this one has."

Amy, Tuney and I murmured noises of awe and appreciation for the house and its furnishings.

"Tell us about who built this house, please," asked Amy.

"That was one of the first things we researched when we moved here," said Joy as she brought in the drinks and cookies. "As people began to move westward, rivers like the Des Moines were an integral part of settlements. This was built by Mormon craftsmen on their way from Nauvoo, Illinois to Salt Lake City in 1846. The first owner, a man named William Robinson, ran it as a hotel. He called it Ashland House but owned it for only ten years. The next owners were the Masons, Lewis and Nancy. They were able to keep the home in their family for 99 years, if you can believe that!"

"Oh! I think I saw a picture of Nancy Mason out there in the entryway, didn't I?" asked Amy.

"Yes, we have several pictures of the Mason family. Lewis and Nancy renamed Ashland House the Phoenix Hotel. Locals just called it Mason House, though. If you checked our

Facebook page, you'll note that there's a cookie jar in every room. That tradition was started by Nancy herself so that her weary traveling guests could have something sugary to nourish themselves in between meals."

"Oh, that's such a sweet tradition!" murmured Tuney.

"PUN!" I said loudly.

Tuney jumped, then joined in the burst of laughter from everyone in the room. She rolled her eyes. "That was NOT intended, but thank you for pointing that out, Cardamom!"

"Sorry, I couldn't resist, Puh-tunia!"

Tuney's apprehension about ghosts must have totally disappeared because she looked relaxed. She loved history and was enjoying the friendliness the inn-keepers genuinely displayed. She grinned at the Hansons and said apologetically, "You two are a little younger than we are. But I'm afraid it seems sometimes we haven't grown up yet. We still call each other the names we went by as kids. Are you sure you can put up with some crazy baby boomers for a night if we end up staying here?"

Chuck held up his hands in mock surrender, and Joy smiled.

"Hey, Chuck, would you mind telling me how long you two have been the owners? Are you Iowa natives?" asked Amy.

Chuck sat back in his chair and smiled. "We bought this in 2001. I'm retired from the Air Force; Joy's dad was in the Air Force - so she's an Air Force brat - and we moved here from Ohio with our four kids." He chuckled. "When we told relatives we were moving to Iowa, they all asked if we would be growing the state crop – potatoes!"

We native Iowans laughed. "That's a very common misconception. That, and that we're the Buckeye State," volunteered Amy.

"Oh, that's funny," said Joy. "I wonder if folks back in Ohio hear out-of-staters call them the Hawkeye state!"

"My son has a T-shirt that says IOWA University, Idaho City, Ohio," I volunteered. "He wore it when he interned in New York because everyone out East kept getting the three states mixed up!"

"Oh, I've seen Kyle wear that," remembered Tuney. "Where'd he get it? It's hysterical!"

"Raygun," I answered. It was a favorite place of mine to shop for T-shirts for my kids, and now my grandkids.

"Hey!" said Amy, grinning. "Sorry, but we've gotten off the subject. I'm still curious. What made you decide you want to run a B&B, Chuck and Joy?"

Chuck grinned. "Like I said, we wanted a special place for our family that we could call our permanent home. Well, a friend had a friend who knew someone who wanted to sell a farm, and it was near here, so we decided to look at it as we traveled on vacation."

Joy took over the conversation. "And we ended up staying at Mason House for the night. It just happened it was for sale, so we bought it instead!" Her eyes softened. "We'd both moved so many times in our lives. This place – this home – just felt like it was meant for us."

Tuney sat quietly for a while, soaking in the conversations, and feeling strangely contented. When Joy mentioned her feelings about Mason House, she joined in the conversation.

"I know exactly what you mean, Joy," she said quietly. "Tommy and I lived for a number of years in our first home we bought after we were married. Do you remember that little dump?" she asked, turning to me with a smile. I grimaced, smiled back and nodded.

"Just out of boredom once, we went to an open house, mainly because we were nosy. It was almost immediate. As soon as I stepped inside, I wanted that house. I felt so completely at home, and so did Tommy. It was as if the house whispered 'There you are. I've been waiting for you. Come on home!'" She paused again, remembering how Tommy's eyes had lit up and how he'd pulled her aside to ask if she thought they should make an offer right away. "So, we bought it, right then and there. Crazy, isn't it?"

Joy had been studying Tuney while she spoke. Her blue eyes darkened sometimes when she narrowed them as Tuney spoke. Then in an instant, they'd widen to a lighter shade as she opened them. It was like watching time lapse on a blue flower that furled and unfurled its petals. I wondered what it was about Tuney that seemed to intrigue her. Joy and Chuck both shook their heads no in answer to Tuney's question.

"It's not crazy at all. I'd say you were very sensitive to your own feelings, and I dare say the house brought you much happiness, didn't it?" Joy asked.

Tuney nodded vigorously. "It was definitely meant to be. We had our babies there, made very precious memories there, and we've lived there for almost forty years." She didn't even realize she'd used "we" because thinking about her home brought only memories of Tommy and their three kids.

Joy looked at her curiously, then moved her chair a little closer to the table and looked across it to where Tuney sat. "If you don't mind me asking, do you feel like it's really become a sanctuary for you lately?"

Tuney's eyes widened, she furrowed her brow and shot a look over at me. "Uh, I'm not quite sure what you mean by a sanctuary? It's our home. I guess you could call it a sanctuary."

Joy nodded and smiled a reassuring smile, that deepened the laugh lines around her mouth. She must smile a lot, I thought. "I think that must have sounded like a strange question." She hesitated, then said, "I just have a feeling about you, that you feel, well, *protected* there so you're a bit more apt to be a homebody now more than normal."

Tuney dropped her head at the same time I gasped softly. That was something I had told her during the past several months, and one of the reasons Tuney had decided to go with me on this tour. She glanced up at me first, then Joy.

"Normal?" She gave a cynical chuckle, then confessed, "I'd like to get back to some semblance of normal. I had a major meltdown earlier on the bus today."

I was surprised she'd admitted it publicly. Joy reached over and patted Tuney's hand again. Tuney looked into her sympathetic eyes, startled, as Joy said, "God loves you, so don't feel bad if you got mad at Him."

Tuney and I both were – how do the British put it so precisely? – *gobsmacked*! Joy didn't seem disturbed by our utter astonishment and continued.

"I hope I didn't upset you. It's just that I'm sensitive to people's feelings. I've actually been called an empath before."

"Empath? I've heard that, but I'm afraid I don't really know what it means," said Tuney.

"It means someone who is very perceptive to others' energies, whether they're spiritual, physical or emotional." Joy looked at Chuck. "I guess it's one reason Mason House really spoke to us – and I do mean 'spoke!'" At that, she looked at an old grandfather's clock, and exclaimed, "Heavens, Chuck! I need to get going on supper tonight and I still have some quilting I want to get done."

I wanted to ask her what she meant by the house speaking to them, but before I could she rose from the table. "Excuse me, please, ladies. I'll leave you in Chuck's capable hands. He's practically a professional tour guide. He'll finish the tour, get you checked in, if you want" – she said pointedly at Tuney and me – "and answer any other questions about Mason House or Bentonsport you might have. I've got a houseful of kids and grandkids, plus a few of their pets to join our cats, all coming over at five. It's one of our kid's birthdays and they love stopping by for a celebration." She paused for a moment, looked at Tuney, smiled, and said gently but firmly, "I know you'll love staying here tonight. And you'll be okay." She then turned and started to leave toward the back of the house where we assumed the Hansons resided.

If there was any essence of the paranormal or even witchcraft in our minds, it vanished when Chuck hollered after Joy, "What kind of cake are you baking?" He winked at us. "Chocolate? It's my favorite!"

We very clearly heard the distant answer. "It's not YOUR birthday!"

Chuck turned to us with a sigh. "Never hurts to ask," he said, and clapped his hands together. "Let me show you the rooms so you can pick which one you want to be in. We have family-style rooms, rooms for doubles, or rooms for singles."

Tuney sat still, staring at the doorway Joy had left.

"You coming, Tuney?" I asked, rising to follow Chuck as he walked toward the stairway in the front.

Tuney looked up, a bit bewildered by Joy's empathy, but nodded as she stood up. "Joy's right. I'll be okay," and smiled reassuringly at Amy, who broke out in a big smile.

"I know you will, Tuney!"

We all filed up the stairs. The old staircase was worn in the middle from over a hundred years' worth of footsteps. I stared down at my feet as I climbed up and idly wondered how many kinds of shoes had trod upon the wood. Certainly, ladies' high-topped shoes, soldiers' boots and children's leather button shoes had been used. Then there were slippers, patent leather, rubber soled sneakers and sandals. Each step creaked with a slightly different whine, as if tired of holding the weight of so many humans for so many years. I felt my knees ache and grabbed the handrail. The wood was smooth and worn from the oil of many hands. It seemed to move slightly under my hands with every step I took, as if it was bracing for heavy pulls.

I was excited to see what was up here. At the top landing, there was another set of stairs that led to the third story. Chuck explained the third story housed their youngest daughter's bedroom and Joy's quilting room, so was closed to the public. Then he led us into the first of five bedrooms that were on the second floor.

"Ladies," announced Chuck, "here is the Maid of Iowa room. It's named for a Mormon steamboat that was built sometime in the 1840s, and believed to have been owned by Joseph Smith, the Mormon prophet in Nauvoo, Illinois. It brought Mormon converts from other countries up the Mississippi from New Orleans, and then was used to float passengers on some of the rivers in eastern Iowa, including right here at the Des Moines River."

We walked into the bedroom, admiring the pretty wallpaper, the variety of steamboat prints and paintings that were framed on the walls, and the full-sized fourposter bed that had another of Joy Hanson's beautiful quilts on it. Twin beds on the other side of the room had a matching quilt.

Chuck led us to the next bedroom, It featured a seven-foot tall sleigh bed carved from walnut. Tuney was the first to walk in, and she exclaimed in awe at the sight of it.

"Oh, my goodness, how beautiful! Cardi, forget about the caboose. Let's stay in this room. It's gorgeous."

Amy and I were standing next to a nine-foot tall mirror and I agreed with Tuney. The room was lovely. I gazed up at the mirror.

"And look at this mirror! Wow! I've never lived in a house with ceilings high enough you could put something like this in. And this room has a spectacular view and even this cute little foot warmer. It's got everything we could possibly need," I said.

"Sorry, girls! I'm not letting you take the room because it's a family room, and I'll need to house a bigger group than you two," said Amy. "Besides, it's August. You do NOT need a foot warmer."

"This is the Mason Suite," added Chuck. "You can tell families like to use it because of the two twin beds." The twin beds were in an adjoining room with an old trunk, a little vanity, some rocking chairs and a marble-topped dresser with a large mirror. All the woodwork was hand-carved, and the room was light and airy because of four windows.

Tuney stepped over to one of the windows and called out, "Oh, some of our travelers are going to be lucky for sure! This room has a great view of the river. It's gorgeous."

Chuck and Amy left the room to enter another one, and I grabbed Tuney's arm for a second before we followed.

"Do you suppose it's haunted, even if it's designed for families?" I whispered to Tuney.

She pursed her lips in thought, then said, "Probably not. And you know, I've been thinking. Maybe this empath thing

Joy has is just a special connection to brain waves or something. And if she's studied up on all the old residents here, her mind can make her think there are ghosts or something when it's just a tremendously high imagination."

"But…"

"Cardi! Hear me out. I'm gonna stay here tonight, and I don't even care what room, even if it has a reputation for being haunted. Because no matter what the reputation – or marketing ploy, if you'd rather call it that – the fact of the matter is, there are no such things as ghosts!"

She said that with conviction and I was totally surprised.

"Well, Tuney, I can't believe after all these years, you're finally saying something your whole family has tried to tell you forever!" I patted her back, and we started to walk toward the door to catch up to Chuck and Amy. Before we left Mason Suite, Tuney stopped and turned to me with a smile.

"I know, right? It makes me feel a little silly. I believe Joy has something we don't fully understand, but there aren't any ghosts. If there were, why do we just get scared by the at night? Because of the dark and leftover childish fears, is why." Teacher Tuney was on another role. She smiled at me. "And since I'm an adult, not a child, I don't…OW!"

Because she was standing next to me Tuney's sudden yell of pain was right in my ear. I immediately covered it with my hand as I drew back from Tuney in surprise. To my astonishment, Tuney was glaring at me.

"What? What happened?" I asked. I stuck one finger in my ear and waggled it up and down like I do on airplanes when my eardrum starts to pop.

Tuney put both hands on her hips. "Whaddaya mean 'what?' What'd you swat me for? That hurt! I'm agreeing with you about it not being haunted, for Pete's sake!" She rubbed her rear end.

"I didn't touch you!" I retorted. "For heaven's sake, how could I have hit your butt if you're facing me, Einstein?"

"How in the world should I know? I didn't dream it. It happened! I think …uh," Tuney's narrowed eyes suddenly rounded and got bigger as she stopped speaking. She and I stared at each other and then we quickly glanced around the room.

Tuney raised her voice slightly, but it squeaked as she asked, "Uh, Chuck? Could you come here a minute, please?" Suddenly she whirled around and put one hand on her lower back.

"What? What's wrong, Tuney?" I asked, alarmed as the color drained from my sister's face. Tuney clutched my arms with both hands. I could feel her shaking. I grabbed her arms above her elbows to steady her.

"Amy!" I called out, panicked. "Something's wrong with Tuney!"

"Is anyone behind me?" whispered Tuney. My mouth opened as I stared into Tuney's eyes and saw fear. Seeing her afraid made me feel apprehensive. I started to tremble a bit as I peered around her. Nothing. I felt a bit braver so I let go of her to investigate the Mason Suite. There was nothing out of the ordinary that I could see. I looked back at Tuney with concern and worry, and shook my head no.

"There has to be," Tuney whispered desperately. "I felt something!" She called Chuck's name again, only this time it was more like a screech, and I clutched Tuney's arms with my hands to support her in case she fainted. I'd never seen her face so white. I hollered for Amy as loud as I could. Tuney's grip was painful!

Chuck and Amy rushed out of the room next to Mason Suite. Upon seeing Tuney standing frozen as I clutched her shoulders, he surprised not only me and Tuney, but Amy. He only smiled.

"Let me guess," he said calmly. "You just got your bottom either pinched or slapped, right?"

Tuney moved her eyes slowly from where they'd been locked in terror on mine toward Chuck, and finally let her tense shoulders relax. She looked mystified.

"Ye-es," she said slowly. "What cause that? What was it?"

I heard Amy gasp and Tuney released her death-grip on me. The way Chuck was grinning defused the situation. I couldn't help but enjoy Tuney's confusion and embarrassment as she finally moved closer to Chuck and Amy and away from the Mason Suite.

Chuck and Amy started laughing. "It's not a what. It's a who. I wish I could formally introduce you to that little prankster, but he prefers to make himself known in a more up close and personal way," Chuck winked his eye at Tuney. "You've just met one of our ghosts!"

Tuney's mouth dropped open. "It's not really funny," protested Tuney. She was calmer now, but by the flash of her eyes I could tell her fear had fast changed to indignation. "Oh, thanks! I just convinced myself there were no such things so I could sleep in any room available. If you've got ghosts, what would possess them to touch me?" She involuntarily shuddered, but then raised her chin belligerently. I recognized that Tuney was preparing for battle, even if it was something she couldn't see.

"I'm sorry," apologized Chuck, but still with a smile. "If you're used to children, then maybe you can forgive poor George."

"Who is George?" I asked. "Was he born here? Is this his house?"

"Well, we're not sure of his real name, but some guests who have seen him describe him as a little boy in knickers about 12 years old, and he likes to tease and pull pranks on people. I don't imagine he has too many playmates to joke with."

"Oh," said Tuney, taken aback. She has always loved children. I just wasn't too sure how she'd think about an ethereal one. She looked around again. "Well, I am used to small children. I taught for years. But I guess I never thought a ghost retained its human traits that much. And a little child ghost doesn't seem so scary." She brushed off the back of her capris as if to brush away the touch of the slap and added. "Maybe." Then she took a big breath and said calmly, "Okay. I'm sorry I got scared, but I think – no, I know for sure now that I would rather have a non-haunted room if you have any." Then she drew herself up and with a spark in her eye that told me she was just fine, she said authoritatively, "And if George is listening, please let him know that I'm a former teacher. And if he *ever* pulls a prank on me like that again, I'll find a way to send him to time out!" And with that she stomped her foot and glared around the hallway.

"And she's just the type to do it, too, George!" I called out helpfully. I grinned at Tuney and was relieved when Tuney gave me a wink and muttered, "Darn right!"

Chuck grinned, too. "Hey, George!" he called out softly. "You heard the ladies. You need to behave, please, young man!" He paused as if listening. Tuney, Amy and I held our breath and listened, too. Nothing. Then Chuck shrugged and said, "Well, let's hope he heard and obeys!"

Tuney opened her mouth to say thanks and ask Chuck

about the child when there was a loud slamming sound. She yelped and I grabbed her arm.

"Jesus, Mary and Joseph! Sounds like he's mad!" cried Tuney, frightened again. She looked frantically around to see which door had slammed, but they were all open. Just then a voice from below hollered at them.

"Sorry, that was me!" came Joy's voice from the first floor. "My laundry basket caught on the handle and slammed the side door shut."

"Oh, thank God!" Tuney breathed as she let out a whoosh of air. She and I released our hold on each other as Tuney slapped her hand to her heart. "Is my heart still beating?" I started to chuckle, and Amy just shook her head and gave Tuney a hug.

"This is one for the books," said Amy. "Two ghosts in one trip – one a sighting and the other a 'feeling!'"

I had an idea. "Hey, Amy! I have a suggestion: put your orneriest passengers in that room. Maybe George can give them a run for their money!" I said drily.

"Mort might even scare George!" quipped Tuney. The color was coming back into her face, and now with Chuck nearby, it didn't seem so scary.

Chuck laughed but said if anyone ever felt like there was a ghost visitor that they didn't want to see, feel or hear, they could just politely tell them to please leave them alone.

"That's all you have to do?" asked Amy, scanning the hallway. "You have the ghosts well-trained then."

"That's all," stated Chuck. "Except for George. He's a bit ornery, but honestly, he's not vicious or mean. Just a kid!"

Tuney looked at me and mouthed the words *just a brat* before I raised my eyebrows at her and grinned. If she was able to half-way joke, then I knew she'd be okay.

Chuck finished up the tour by taking us to several more rooms, each with its own name. All were wallpapered and had beautiful antiques, Joy's quilts, and a cookie jar. There were several that Tuney and I would have loved to stay in, but they all held a minimum of three people. I was disappointed in not being able to stay in one of the beautiful rooms and started to talk to Amy about the other B&B in town.

"Hang on a second. Don't forget the first bedroom you saw off the foyer," reminded Chuck. "It's for two people. "The problem with it is it can be a bit noisy there at night when people come in and out. But our Wash House Room in the annex that's built next door is for two people. It's a king-sized bed and all reviews say it's extremely comfortable."

"Any ghosts?" asked Tuney cautiously.

"No, no ghosts outside the house itself," laughed Chuck. "Neither the annex nor the caboose is haunted."

"Sold!" I said, but Tuney wanted to look at it first.

The annex was attached to the inn. The wood used to construct the exterior of the building came from the 1858 Bonaparte Railroad Station, Chuck told us. Both Tuney and I were delighted to think that the station hadn't been demolished haphazardly and were glad the wood had been reclaimed and put to good use.

There were two suites in the annex: The Wash House Room and the General Store Room. The General Store Room had guests already in it, so Chuck opened the Wash House Room to show us. We were enchanted with the vintage clothes that hung on clotheslines draped on the walls in the Wash House Room. On one side of the bed was an almost primitive wooden washing machine used as a night stand. A couch, a desk and chair, and the king-sized bed, plus a shower in the bath room and air conditioning made for a cozy and comfortable room.

"Like I said – Sold!" I looked at Tuney for confirmation.

"Well, I haven't gotten pinched or slapped here, so I'm good!"

We both felt very comfortable in this room. While it was ground level, it still overlooked the Des Moines River, and seeing the clothes hanging on the wall reminded me of grandma and my mom hanging laundry out on the lines behind their homes. It was not only cozy in this room, but very relaxing.

Chuck wanted to show us the coveted caboose, but before he could, Joy called to him that some other guests needed to be checked in. Amy followed him to make her arrangements, but not before telling us to walk down the street to shop.

"You still have a couple of hours left before we meet up again," she said. "Mr. Smith will deliver the suitcases to the proper buildings, and then you can grab supper anywhere you want or do whatever."

Then as she left, she called over her shoulder, "By the way, I think I'm putting the 2Bs2Ts in the caboose. You two can hang out with them in the train if you want, later!"

"Oh, boy! Thanks, Amy!" we called back to her. What a sweetheart she was!

Tuney and I looked at each other. "Well, having those four nearby is going to be a blast," I said. "My cheeks hurt last night from laughing and talking so much yesterday."

"Me, too," said Tuney. "And I'm totally through with my meltdown earlier, so I hope they don't mind if I'm staying this close to them."

"I think being able to talk to other widows, especially ones who are this much fun, is good for both of us," I said with a quick squeeze on Tuney's arm.

She agreed, and grinned. "This will be fun – now that I'm

over my scare." She shuddered again. "I wonder if that really just happened. I mean, I don't believe in ghosts…"

"Yes, you do. Now, anyway!" I interrupted solemnly. "Tuney, the way you looked scared me more than George scared you. There had to be something or someone – an entity, if you will – that you could feel."

Tuney snorted. "It wasn't so much me feeling him, as HE was feeling ME! Weren't children from long ago more mature than they are now? I mean if he's 12, or rather, WAS 12, wouldn't he be pre-pubescent? Maybe he was a little pervert and he's been banished from heaven and has to haunt old ladies to get his kicks, and…"

"Tuney! Will you listen to yourself?" I started laughing. Tuney looked offended, then abashed.

"Oh, you're right!" She opened the door of the Wash House Room and she and I stepped outside into the sunshine. "Maybe he is just a child, and I should feel sorry for him." She paused and then shook her finger at me. "But I'll never read the children's book "Georgie the Ghost" to my grands again without thinking about my butt hurting!"

Chapter 20

Greef General Store

"Bentonsport," I read to Tuney from my itinerary I kept stuffed in my purse, "had been a thriving port of call on the Des Moines River with an estimated population of 1000 people once upon a time. Many of the buildings, built in the early to mid-1800s, are inhabited by the approximately 40 residents left. There are antique and craft shops, resident artisans such as potters, blacksmith, quilters, sculptors and more. The old truss bridge is now a pedestrian bridge and the former lock and dam has been transformed into a beautiful rose garden. Bentonsport is a picturesque village named one of the ten most beautiful towns in Iowa."

"Wow!" said Tuney, as she looked down the main street. "I can see why it's so beautiful. But I can't believe the population has dropped that low."

"I know," I commiserated. I stuffed the itinerary back in my purse, found my sunglasses and put them on against the bright August sun. "It's kind of sad, isn't it? I mean, think of the Mason House. It was once a pub and hotel, then a hospital. And now it's a B&B just full of old memories."

"And ghosts," added Tuney drily.

"But think of the new memories all the guests make," I said positively. "We weren't even officially checked in and look at the memory we've got of the place already!"

Tuney didn't say anything, but I grinned when she saw my sister rub her backside. I continued, "Well, anyway, let's go soak up some of the history around here."

"And fill our shopping bags with goodies," commented Tuney. "I feel the need for some shopping therapy!" She pointed down the road at a brick building. "Look! I see a bunch of people from the bus leaving that place. Let's go there."

What appeared to be an old-Western saloon seemed very popular. It was a large brick building with a board walk beneath a generous shady porch overhang. Baskets of flowers hung from the porch. A wine barrel with a checkerboard game on its top invited non-shoppers to sit a spell and play. An old-fashioned water pump was near the building next to the boardwalk. A wooden sign that read "Greef General Store" hung for all to see. A smaller sign read that the store was built in 1853, with the smaller west half of the store added in 1865. It was one of the largest general stores in Southeast Iowa.

"Think how old this is! It's over 150 years old!" Tuney exclaimed.

When we stepped up on the porch, I was fascinated with the windows that housed antique toys, glassware, and furniture. I could also see shelves full of beautiful handmade soaps, towels, some paintings and other items that I thought must be from local crafters.

"Let's go inside and see this stuff," I urged Tuney. We entered the store, delighted when a big bell attached to the top of the door rang. The first thing we saw was a sign listing all the businesses that Bentonsport had boasted during its heydays.

"Oh, my gosh! Look at all the different kinds of mills," I said as we stopped to read it.

The list was long. There was a paper mill, linseed oil mill, woolen mill, flour mill, four general stores, two hotels, three hardware stores, five churches, plow factory, stage line, wagon factory, shoe makers, bank, post office, cooper shop, tin shop, drug store, tailor, attorneys, insurance agents, and a newspaper.

"Look! You have a shop," said Tuney pointing at the listing of "cooper" shop.

My mouth formed an "o" and I frowned. "This sounds dumb, but what's a cooper shop? I never even thought about what our last name means!"

Tuney shook her head. "You know, I have no idea, either! I mean, a lot of names that end in "son" are obvious. Somewhere in history, there was a Thom who had a son." She frowned. "And I just assume that the spelling was changed through the years, but maybe Tommy's ancestor was really called Thomp!"

I giggled. "I guess since we're retired and single old ladies, we can be doing genealogy. Maybe we'll learn all sorts of things about names. Even our maiden name of Collins. What's a collins?"

"Google it. You're always Googling things. See what you can find out," urged Tuney. She was curious about our maiden name now.

"What does collins mean?" I said dictating the question on my phone. I snorted and looked up at Tuney with my nose wrinkled after I read what popped up. "That's no help. It talks about Tom Collins mix and drinks!"

"Maybe our ancestors were all alcoholics. That sounds good," Tuney smirked. Then she suggested, "Well, ask Google something like 'what is the origin of last name Collins.'" She leaned over to look at my phone.

"You know, you can do this on your own phone," I pointed out as I shrugged her away from getting too close to my face. "How come I always have to look stuff up?"

"Because you're the one who always wonders about things that no one has the answer to," replied Tuney evenly. Then she stuck her index finger on my phone screen. "There! What's it say?"

I read a definition. "This makes sense. It's British and Irish, a pat – ron - im – ick?" I tried sounding out the unfamiliar word.

"Patronymic means a name from a male ancestor. A matronymic name would be from a female ancestor," said Tuney, automatically.

I looked up at her and made a face. "Thank you, Teacher!" I continued to read, "A patronymic surname based on the name of Colin, so son of Colin, which is an English diminutive form of Nicholas." I looked up. "I didn't know there was any other form of Nicholas other than Nick, did you?" I didn't wait for Tuney to answer but kept reading. "It also can mean – and this is the Irish part – darling, a term of endearment applied to a whelp or young animal." I paused a second before it sunk in. "Darling for a whelp or young animal?"

Tuney was amazed. "Oh, for heaven's sake! Amazing what we can still learn, isn't it?"

"Hooray for Google," I answered smugly. "Who'da thunk it? Colin, or cuilein, darling – a term of endearment for young animals? Sounds pretty kinky, doesn't it? Yuck!"

"Cardi," remonstrated Tuney. She hid a grin. "Do you always have to find the naughty side of things?"

"Says the lady who just accused a 12 year-old-child of perversion," I cracked back.

"He's a ghost. And he's probably older than we are now, so he should know better," said Tuney primly. She pointed to my phone again. "Now look up cooper. Maybe there's someone with the first name of Coo or Coop. Hey! Do you suppose it just means a chicken cage!" She grimaced.

I rolled my eyes at Tuney but dutifully hunted for cooper. "Here it is! Oh, duh! This makes sense, too, as to why there would be a cooper shop in a town full of mills. A cooper is someone trained to make wooden barrels, buckets, troughs and so on. It says here the timber he uses is usually heated or steamed to make it pliable. And a cooper also makes wooden implements like rakes and wooden bladed shovels! This is neat. I'm gonna have to tell the kids!"

"Tell them Aunt Tuney said their name means chicken cage. I want to see their faces," teased Tuney. She looked around the store and spied something. "Hey, let's go over in this part. It's lined with shelves and cases full of antiques. It must be a museum."

We wandered through a few aisles, exclaiming over the old glassware and memorabilia from the various mills. Tuney looked up from some horse harnesses and in the next aisle saw something that made her smile. She excitedly called to me to come look at an antique doll.

"Cardi, do you remember Grandma Reynolds had a doll just like this?" she said pointing to an old china doll. "You used to love holding it and you'd try to sing it lullabies."

I bent over the case and studied the doll. "How old were we? I'm not sure I remember singing anything, but it does look kind of familiar." I looked at Tuney. "How on earth do you remember that?"

Tuney looked guilty. "We were four or five, I think. I was

jealous of you because Grandma always let you hold it first since you were the littlest and so cute, and..."

I interrupted. "YOU? Jealous of me? Ha! That's a laugh!"

Tuney was nonplussed. "Of course, I was jealous, you ninny." She shrugged her shoulders, cocked her head and smiled at me. "Why wouldn't I be? You were so darned cute and could get anything you wanted."

I glanced up at an antique mirror and turned my head from side to side. If I expected the image of cute little Cardi Collins to be there, I was wrong. The vision in the mirror was of an older mature woman, with wrinkles, dark spots too large to be counted as freckles anymore, and in need of a touch of lipstick. I heaved a big sigh. "I wish I still was!"

"You'll always be cute," said Tuney in a mock disgusted tone.

I just gave Tuney a look, then went back to studying the doll. "What happened to that doll? I don't remember ever seeing it when we were older."

"I dropped it," admitted Tuney with a big sigh of regret. "Shattered it into little pieces." She peered at the old doll again and sighed. "What I wouldn't give to have been able to buy this and give it to Grandma when she was alive as a surprise. Wouldn't she have loved that?"

"Why, Tuney, I didn't know that's what happened! How?"

"You fell asleep holding the doll when we were visiting at Grandma's. I thought I'd rescue the dolly because you were drooling all over her." Tuney paused, her eyes soft with reminiscing. "I was going to take her to Grandma and ask if I could have a tea party, but when I walked into the kitchen, I tripped on a buckle in the old linoleum."

I nodded and smiled as I remembered my grandmother's house.

"Anyway, I don't know how it happened, but the doll fell out of my hands and it must have been much more fragile than it looked. Like I said, it just smashed into a million pieces." Tuney touched the glass that separated her from the doll and began to look at the next case. "I remember crying. But I also remember Grandma picking me up and cuddling me and giving me a cookie." She paused again, grinned and said softly, "Funny. I feel like Grandma's right here next to us, don't you, Cardi?"

I looked startled. "Oh, that's so weird, Tuney. I do, too! I wish she really was!"

Tuney smiled, then sobered immediately. "Yeah, except I've had enough ghost stuff for a while." She shook her shoulders, pretending to shudder and said "Ewwwww!" Then she smiled again as she looked at the antique doll sitting dusty, but dutifully smiling in the glass case. "I haven't thought of her and that doll for a long time. Funny how seeing all this old stuff brings back memories."

I glanced at some doll-sized tea sets and said, "What I don't get is how some of this stuff is antique. I played with some of these things – like those roller skates over there – and I certainly don't consider myself an antique!"

"Me, either," said Tuney firmly. "Let's get out of here and see what else is around."

"Maybe there's something that'll make us feel young."

"You wish!"

"Or look young."

"*I* wish!" Tuney and I grinned at each other, shook our heads, and left.

Chapter 21

Iron and Lace

*D*own the street from the general store was an old weathered barn with a welcoming porch in front. It sat apart from the other buildings on the block, but had several cars parked in front, while other tourists walked in and out. A sign on the top front of the building read Iron and Lace.

Curious as to what that combination would look like, we entered. Inside were shelves and tables full of different colored pottery. There were bowls, plates, vases, statues and ornaments. All were beautifully glazed with shades of blue, green or brown. A handsome-looking white-haired man with a beard, mustache, and a very friendly face greeted us as we walked in.

"Welcome to Iron and Lace," he said. "My name's Bill. Is this your first time here?" He was seated behind the checkout counter. We greeted him in return.

I teased, "Can you tell we're first time tourists here?" Before he could reply, I exclaimed, "Oh, my gosh! Look, Tuney." I spied some iron candlesticks, along with some fireplace tools. I walked over to examine them more closely. "Do you make these?"

The proprietor walked around the counter and picked up one of the candlesticks. "I do indeed. Pretty good for an 80-year-old, don'tcha think?" he said proudly.

Tuney looked at him in amazement. "You are NOT eighty years old!" she said in disbelief.

I was in awe, too. "Jeepers! This area of the state must contain the fountain of youth. We met Marie in Bonaparte, and she's 90 and still working, too!"

Bill grinned, nodded and clapped his hands.

"I know Marie well," he said. "And there's no fountain of youth. We're just too busy and having too much fun to grow old! I've been a blacksmith for longer than I can remember!"

"He loves to tell people how old he is," came a voice from the loft above, "but he knows I'd kill him if he ever started telling people MY age!"

We whipped our heads around to see a lovely woman leaning over the railing of the loft, wagging her finger at Bill, but smiling. A stairway at one end had signs with arrows pointing upward and the words "More to See" printed on them.

Bill snickered. "That's my bride, Betty," he said proudly. "She's the one that makes all these beautiful pottery pieces."

"Don't tell me she's 80 years old, too!" I said, staring up at Betty, who grinned and shook her head with a definite NO at me.

Tuney picked up a small vase with the image of a Queen Anne's Lace flower. Like me, she'd assumed the "Lace" in the Iron and Lace referred to lace fabric. But she was delighted to see the "lace" in the store's name referred to the delicate white flowers that were so prevalent throughout Iowa's countryside. She held up the vase toward Betty.

"Queen Anne's Lace is my favorite flower! How on earth did you decide to make your pottery with them?"

Betty smiled, "Hang on! I'll be right down." By the time she reached the bottom, Tuney was coveting a Nativity set with the green glaze that she thought would look beautiful with her other Christmas decorations, and I had found five ornaments I wanted to give as gifts to some of my former co-workers. I still clutched the beautiful iron candlestick.

We introduced ourselves, and explained we were part of a bus tour. Betty and Bill started laughing. When Tuney and I looked questioningly at them, Bill explained.

"We love bus tours, and I especially love your group! Some were here about a half hour ago, and they bought so much iron that I wondered aloud if they'd have room on the bus. They told me once they filled the undercarriage, they'd start stuffing things overhead and could maybe pay the driver to leave half the passengers stranded so they'd have room! Ha-ha-ha!"

Tuney grimaced. "Mort! It has to be Mort and his buddies." She turned to Bill. "We've got some of the craziest but funniest people on board. One couple brought along two other couples and they are a scream. If it's who I think it is, he'll probably try to do that. He evidently does anything he wants." And she explained Mort's hula hoop fiasco. When she described him, Bill nodded.

"That's gotta be him. But I was exaggerating about how much he bought. It was just that his wife kept harping on him to quit buying so much. She bought her fair share, though."

"Bill," remonstrated Betty. "Wives don't 'harp!'"

Tuney and I burst out laughing at Bill's face when he answered meekly, "Yes, dear." He grinned and winked.

Betty smiled lovingly at him, then spoke to the Widsters. "You asked about the Queen Anne's Lace. You can lay your stuff here on the counter and then come with me if you want. I'll show you."

She motioned for us to follow her as she headed out the front door, holding a small vase that she picked up at the door. There, next to the street, grew wildflowers with lots of Queen Anne's Lace among them. Betty reached down and picked a small flower.

"I make sure to plant these here mainly for advertisement. But I also plant them in my garden at home," she explained. She pressed the front of the flower over the flower on the vase. "Just imagine this is green clay – that is to say, wet or dry clay that hasn't been fired yet."

Tuney and I crowded closer to her. "Oh, I thought maybe you painted these on," murmured Tuney.

"I actually tried that once. But it took a lot longer, So I came up with a method to embed the flower on the green pottery before the firing process. When it's in the kiln, the flower burns away, and I'm left with the beautiful imprint of these lacy little flowers." Betty turned and headed back inside.

Tuney walked next to her. "I've never seen anything like this. Do you teach classes?"

Betty nodded. "I do, but just a few times a year. I'm too busy with this shop to do more than that. And what I teach is Raku pottery."

"Ragu?" I asked, a few steps away.

Betty paused with a smile, studied me for a second and announced, "I like you! You're funny!" she said, nodding. Tuney burst into laughter as I grinned in embarrassment. I wasn't trying to be funny.

"R-a-K-u, Cardi," corrected Tuney.

I lifted my nose up haughtily. "I heard her. Did YOU hear her? I was being funny – like she said!"

Betty chuckled. "You ARE funny." Then she continued, "Raku is another form of pottery. As you can guess from the name, it's a Japanese method. We fire the pottery at a low temperature in the kiln, then it's moved to a closed container. That container has combustible materials like paper that ignite. And once it's done – voila! Beautiful colors and patterns are on the piece."

"Wow!" said Tuney. "I had no idea when we walked in here that we'd get such an education. You've fired me up to someday take lessons!"

Betty laughed, while I groaned. "Tuney! You made another pun! I can't believe it!"

Tuney waved her hand at me in dismissal. "I do mean that, Betty. I had fun taking my grandkids to one of those make it and bake it ceramic shops in Des Moines. It was fun, but the pieces were already made. The kids just had to paint whatever they wanted, then the store fires them in the kiln and we pick them up the next day. I never got to really know what all goes into pottery and ceramics."

"Well, then I'm doubly glad you ladies stopped in today," said Betty. "Please feel free to wander around, and if I can help you at all, just holler."

We shopped a while longer. The store was pleasant and cool with so many objects to look at, I knew we could stay here the entire afternoon. Unfortunately, I thought, the bus wouldn't be able to carry everything we wanted. Tuney and I both decided to call it quits about the same time.

As Bill wrapped our purchases, Tuney spied the 2Bs2Ts through the window. They were walking past the building and heading to what looked like an ice cream shop across the street. Tuney suggested we catch up with them and get something to eat. Bill overheard and offered to keep our packages behind his counter for a while. Thanking him, we hurried to catch up with the others.

Chapter 22

Sweet Creations

Standing by itself close to the old bridge and next to a large gazebo was a charming cottage, painted a sunny yellow with light blue gingerbread trim. A small front porch with a tiny roof, also with light blue gingerbread, added to the charm. A big sign on a post in the front yard read *Sweet Creations*. Under the name was also printed: *Fresh Homemade Fudge and Cookies, Sandwiches & Ice Cream and More.* A stone path led past the sign to stairs that welcomed visitors to come up and inside. The 2Bs2Ts were slowly walking up the path, and they turned when I hollered at them.

"Hey! Where've you two been?" asked Belinda when Tuney and I joined them.

I started to tell them, but Tuney interrupted them. "To the nether world, which I'll tell you once I get some sustenance in my system. Then we went to Greef's and finally Iron and Lace!"

"Nether world?" said Bonnie. "That doesn't sound like anything that was on the itinerary!"

I sidled up to her so Tuney couldn't hear and whispered, "Just wait! It was unbelievable – and spooky."

Bonnie raised her eyebrows, but then I glanced over at Tuney. Tuney was staring suspiciously at me, so I off-handedly remarked how hot it was, and then asked Trudy what she'd bought.

As all six of us walked up to the porch, Trudy commented on how cute the shop was.

"It looks like it could be in Hansel and Gretel, doesn't it?" added Tammy.

"Mmmmm! Smell the cookies?" asked Tuney, inhaling deeply. Then she sighed. "Why am I even close to this place. I'm still stuffed from lunch! Don't let me get anything except a diet pop!"

The others had been reading the signs that listed the kinds of fudge and ice cream that were available. They turned with guilty looks on their faces when Tuney spoke.

"Oh, darn," moaned Bonnie. "That's right! I wasn't going to eat anything else until supper."

"That's right, I forgot, too," groaned Tammy. Belinda and Trudy groaned along with them. They all hesitated on the porch, debating whether to turn around and go back shopping.

I pursed my lips. "Well, we've walked a bit, haven't we?"

Five heads snapped to attention and stared at me hopefully.

"And I think Amy said we're on our own for supper, right?"

Five heads nodded.

Belinda joined in. "That's right. So, we should probably at least just go inside and see what kind of sandwiches they serve. I mean if we have a *light* supper of sandwiches…"

"Yeah, yeah," agreed the chorus with vehement nods of various shades of grey-haired heads.

"So, we check out the food, and get some cold drinks because it's hot…" continued Belinda.

"And...?" said Tuney with a grin.

"And life is short – we're supposed to eat dessert first!!" I crowed.

"And there's no rule that says what time we have to eat dessert first," amended Belinda with her arms folded across her chest.

"Amen!" said I vehemently. I grabbed Tuney's hand and said, "Let's go, Sis."

This time, it was fudge, displayed prominently and abundantly, that greeted us. Cookies, salt water taffy, ice cream and other sweets were inviting us to try them. Tuney saw something Tommy had always loved and nudged me.

"Tammy, you don't like pie, you said. Do you like fudge?" I asked.

"No. I LOVE fudge," Tammy replied. She walked up to the counter. "And since I didn't order pie, I'm gonna be the first to order this stuff!"

"I feel almost obligated to buy a pound of maple nut fudge because it's Tommy's favorite. And that would be honoring him, don't you think?" Tuney whispered.

I shot a glance at her and dimpled, seeing that she was teasing. "Definitely, Tuney. You HAVE to honor Tommy, and let us honor him, too. Let me be the first to volunteer to help you eat it!" I peered closer to the case and said, "And I think I'd like to eat some of the peanut butter fudge, only as a way to honor the fact that my three kids were positively addicted to peanut butter when they were growing up!"

"Hey! I never thought of eating something as honoring someone," said Belinda. She pointed at a slab of chocolate creaminess. "Look, girls. I remember my grandma always made plain chocolate fudge so we wouldn't choke on walnuts. I'm getting some of that. For Grandma. Only because of my grandma!"

They all chuckled, and Tammy added. "I'm not going to be left out. Let's see what my husband would have liked..." and she looked at the samples. "Aha!" She raised her eyes to the ceiling, and said, "Hey, Paul, in honor of what a tiger you were in bed, I'm ordering some Tiger Fudge!"

We hooted with laughter and surprise, and several other customers snickered. Tammy blushed a bit, but then grinned. "Sorry!" she said aloud. Then to the others, she whispered, "Good heavens. I don't know what made me say that. Totally inappropriate."

The clerk at the counter overheard her, had seen Tammy speak toward the heavens, and evidently had put two and two together. She cut off a little slice of the tiger fudge and handed it to her. "Here, Honey, take a taste. I'm betting your husband would be honored to have this fudge named after him!" Tammy really turned red, but accepted the sample with laughter, tasted it, and nodded her head vehemently.

"Mmmmm! This is REALLY good! Okay, Tiger Fudge it is for me!"

We decided to buy fudge first, then ordered ice cold drinks. We exited to a patio that wrapped around the east and south sides of the store. The view overlooked the bridge and the gently flowing water of the Des Moines River. A friendly waitress wearing a nametag that identified her as Sue stopped by the table and asked us where we were from.

"Oh, we love you tourists!" she said when we described our Iowa bus tour. "And so many people don't even know about the Villages of Van Buren County."

"I know. I've been wondering why it took me so long to get here," declared Trudy. "But now that I know, I'm going to be coming back, either with you girls, or bring my daughters over here shopping!"

"I think that's great," said the waitress. "It's really such a pretty place." She pointed toward the bridge that they could see from and said, "If you haven't already, you should walk over the bridge to see Vernon."

"Who is Vernon?" asked Tuney, as she turned to look. She saw the pathway that inclined as it led to the entry of the bridge for pedestrian traffic across the Des Moines River

Sue laughed. "It's a what, and on the other side of the river. Vernon was first called South Bentonsport. It's abandoned now but there are a few old buildings still standing. The bridge was built in 1882 so that horses and buggies didn't have to take the ferry to cross the river. It's actually still one of the oldest and longest original bridges in the state of Iowa," she finished proudly.

We were intrigued. Belinda remarked that there seemed to be lots of people out and about today. The waitress smiled.

"You'll have to come back during festival time. We only have forty residents, but there are hundreds of people when we have our fall festival in October."

"Wow," remarked Bonnie. "Where do they stay?"

"Oh, there really are lots of places close by if our B&Bs here in town get filled up. And they do! People stay not only for the festival, but a lot stay to just spend some quiet time for a few days or even a week. Is your bus tour group staying here?"

"We were supposed to stay in Keosauqua, but they had a water problem. So we're splitting the group between two B&Bs. We're all staying at the Mason House Inn tonight," supplied Tuney spreading her arms to encompass the entire group.

"We are for sure?" asked Bonnie. Tuney forgot they hadn't officially heard yet, so she just nodded as the waitress continued speaking.

"Oh, you'll love it!" she said. "Joy and Chuck Hanson run it, and they can tell you so much more about Bentonsport and the Inn than I can. Where you're staying has nine rooms – make that eight rooms plus a caboose that Chuck converted into a suite. It's a real caboose that he got from Texas."

Trudy and Bonnie immediately brightened at that. "A real caboose? Oh, I hope we get that," Bonnie said, her eyes glowing. When I mouthed the words, "You got it," Belinda and Tammy clapped their hands.

As the waitress turned to go inside, Tuney wondered aloud to her friends, "I wonder what the difference is between Mason House and the other B&B?"

The waitress heard her and over her shoulder answered, "Mason House is haunted. You guys have a good time!"

There was silence for moment as the 2Bs2Ts sat still and looked at each other. "Wait. What did she say?" demanded Bonnie.

"She said 'you guys have a good time," replied Tuney.

"Right after she said our reservations are in a haunted house," I added with a grin.

Tuney glared at her. "Cardi," she growled.

"Well, you know all too well it is, Tuney! And it's not like it's a secret. The entry way in the Inn has tons of brochures on its ghosts. They're friendly," I protested. I turned to the others. "We can explain. It's what Tuney meant when she said the 'nether world' a bit ago."

"Haunted? No, that can't be right," said Tammy, shaking her head. "I'm not embarrassed to say this: I do not want to stay there!"

Tuney was exasperated. "Cardamom! Wait, you guys. First, where Cardi and I are staying, which is the Wash House Room, is not haunted or else I wouldn't be staying there either, and where…" she was interrupted.

"If we have to stay at Mason House, then I want the un-haunted room. I'll bunk with you in the – what'd you call it? Washing room?" Tammy asked.

Tuney held her hands up. "Chill, you guys. You're staying in the caboose because it holds four people. And it is NOT haunted. Just a few rooms inside the house are, supposedly. And they're all gorgeous, and most people never experience a, uh, an unexplained event."

"You mean a haunting?" asked Trudy, with a worried look on her face.

I giggled, and Bonnie turned to me. "What were you trying to tell me before we walked into this place? Something about Tuney?"

"Cardi Collins Cooper!" wailed Tuney irritably. Everyone turned to look at Tuney. She looked at each one in return, then rolled her eyes, gave up and said, "Okay, okay. I'll tell you." She sighed, "I got slapped on my butt supposedly by a 12-year-old!"

The 2Bs2Ts had each dropped their jaw. Belinda spoke first. "Oh, my goodness. Well, where was his mother?" she said indignantly.

"Probably in a cemetery somewhere," I murmured.

Belinda looked shocked. "You mean a 12-year-old GHOST did that to you?"

The 2Bs2Ts broke into gasps followed by chatter, and soon started questioning Tuney as to how she knew who it was, where it happened, and what she did. She couldn't help it, but she started laughing, and held up a hand to halt the questions and conversation.

"I'll tell you – just hold your horses. But the main thing is that when I went up those stairs to the second floor, I didn't believe in ghosts, but I was always afraid of them. I never went to horror movies or anything at all like that. Now that I've had my 'experience,' well, it doesn't seem so bad after all. I'm not nearly as frightened of what happened today as I was going to a Halloween party!"

"So, would you stay in that room?" asked Tammy, intrigued at the thought of knowing one very brave soul.

Tuney drew herself up, hesitated, and looked upward thoughtfully. The 2Bs2Ts were staring silently at her, waiting for her answer.

"Not on your life!" Tuney finally announced. Everyone laughed, and she began to tell how she and I came to be in the house with Amy. When she got to the part where George slapped her, I interjected.

"You should have seen her face," I chortled. "I swear her eyes were so wide and big that her eyeballs would have popped out if someone slapped her on the back of the head!"

"Thank you for that embellishment, Cardi," said Tuney in a tone that didn't imply gratefulness. She finished her story, and then sat back and listened to the conversation we other five were having about spirits, spooks, ghosts, goblins and the hereafter. Listening to some of the comments about being scared didn't seem to bother her. I noticed and wondered idly why. Just a little over an hour ago, she'd never been so frightened in her life.

Tuney suddenly slapped the table and sat up straight. The slap startled the others and they looked at Tuney in concern.

"Oh, sorry!" Tuney said quickly. "I didn't mean to do that." The others smiled tentatively at her. I was looking at her with curiosity. Tuney chuckled. "I just had an epiphany, I guess." She sat back in her chair again and explained, by ticking off on her fingers the points she wanted to make.

"I've been scared of 'scary things' my whole life. I guess because I never had anything really bad and truly scary happen to me before. I always closed my eyes and plugged my ears if I had to see some sort of ghost or ghoulish show on television. When I was young, I even held my breath if Dad happened to drive past a cemetery: I thought doing that would ward off any evil from the dead."

Someone made sympathetic clucking sounds, but Tuney's eyes were focused on the river and she didn't seem to notice us. She continued talking, but it was almost as if she were speaking out loud to herself.

"Today, I met a ghost. A ghost!" At that she glanced around at us and made a face in mock horror. "One of my most creepy, terrifying fears my whole entire life. And this was a real ghost. Not something on television or a Halloween-fun haunted house, or even a movie that I could tell myself wasn't really real. And here I am. I'm not hurt and I'm not scared. Not now, anyway," she amended hastily with a guilty look at me.

I giggled. She smiled broadly and then continued.

"So my epiphany is that for over a year now, I've actually been in the most frightening situation in my life and didn't even realize it. I've been scared out of my wits and saddened beyond anything I could imagine to be living life without my Tommy." She started to get misty-eyed but blinked rapidly and firmly continued. "But I have lived and will live for however long God lets me. And I've survived and faced death. I think that's pretty awesome. So in perspective, some naughty little invisible boy who pulled a prank on me is nothing to be afraid of. I've faced my worst fear and it wasn't little George." She smiled warmly at all of us. "As a matter of fact, we're all pretty awesome, aren't we?"

Someone clapped, three rose from their chairs to hug Tuney, and I felt more proud of my sister than I could ever remember.

"You know, Tuney," said Trudy thoughtfully after everyone had sat down again, "that was what I've felt since I lost my husband. I just couldn't put it into words." The others nodded in agreement.

"We're all in a horrible sisterhood, aren't we?" asked Tammy. She was mopping the tears from her eyes. "I'd give anything to have been able to trade places with my husband, but do you know what?"

"What?" sniffed Belinda, wiping her nose, as Tammy paused to take a breath.

"That was a rhetorical question," Tammy admonished Belinda with a grin, and got chuckles from the others. "I actually said that at my husband Paul's funeral to a cousin of mine – that I wanted to trade places with Paul - and one of my kids overheard me. She gave me the biggest hug and told me that if she had to lose one of her parents, she was glad it wasn't me because she knew Paul would have absolutely floundered, been lost, and probably died of a broken heart without me. She said, 'Mom, you're the strong one in the family.' I was so shocked. But after I thought about it weeks later, I was determined to prove her right!"

"Oh, Tammy," said Tuney, quietly. "I know what your daughter meant, and I think we probably all know that could very well be true. There must be a reason why under normal circumstances, males die first. I guess we females are the stronger of the species. Darn it all!"

Several of us started to get tears in our eyes again. Tuney and I reached in our purses for compacts. We looked at each other and smirked. We both used eyeliner and mascara, and we both had raccoon eyes, not only from a few tears, but from the sweaty heat.

"Ope!" said Tuney as she used a compact mirror to see what damage had been done. "No more tears, girls!! Is there a restroom we can use here to repair the damage?" She and I excused ourselves, found the ladies room, and took turns using the sink to wash off our faces. Tuney almost didn't reapply her makeup, but then told me since there really were ghosts and Tommy might someday make an appearance, she'd better stay in the habit of trying to fight off old-age. "Even though I'm losing," she muttered as she tried to draw the eyeliner through the crepey skin of her lids.

"I'm with you on that!"

As she dabbed under her eyes, she asked me, "How old do you think I'll be before I ever feel I'm not naked without makeup?"

"I dunno. Probably at least 11 months older than I will be whenever I don't feel I need to wear any! Good grief, aren't we the vainest old ladies ever?" I stuck my tongue out at my reflection in the mirror.

"No, Cardi. We're not vain. We're merely interested in maintaining aesthetics."

I harrumphed. "I must be aesthetically-challenged then. But I've always liked a challenge!"

Tuney gave me a grin and went back to applying her lipstick.

Most of our friends don't bother with anything more than

lipstick. But we Collins "girls" have maintained a bit of vanity into our mature years. *Or maybe I could just call it a bad habit,* I thought. We still wear foundation makeup, eyeliner, mascara and lipstick, color our hair (although some natural gray streaks are stubborn and won't take the color), and both of us wear contact lens, augmented with reading glasses most of the time.

I looked at myself critically in the mirror and heaved a sigh of resignation. "Is it really worth the effort to put on make-up?"

"I can take before and after pictures, and let you decide," Tuney offered sarcastically.

"Now that you've got your face made up! Gee, thanks – Not!" I turned my face sideways in the mirror. "I need something that really covers these wrinkles and sunspots," I complained.

"Try spackle," said Tuney sardonically.

I wrinkled my nose at her. "Or maybe hats with netting veils will come back in vogue again. That'd be easier."

"Heavy veils," said Tuney. She shook her head in dismay at the mirror. "I don't ever feel as old as I look in a mirror," she said plaintively. "Why is that?"

I thought for a second. "Our eyesight gets worse, or," I added, "we use cheap mirrors."

"Ah," Tuney brightened. "In other words, anything but actually us is the reason, right?"

"Sounds good to me," I replied. "Anyway, you always look beautiful, so qwitcherbitchin'!"

Once we were all done, the 2Bs2Ts decided to go back to the Greef General Store. Tuney and I debated whether to walk to the rose garden or cross the bridge to Vernon before we met Amy and everyone else at 5.

I'm so glad we chose the garden.

Chapter 23

The Sunken Garden

West of the ice cream shop was a large green area with a big gazebo. I wondered if it was built for band concerts long ago. Further on west, the park spread from the street down to the river. We walked on the grass rather than in the street toward the sunken rose gardens that had once been the former lock and dam. As we approached the start of the gardens, Tuney realized we might have to detour and go back to the road. A small, but very deep ravine separated the rose garden area from the other side of the park.

I trotted ahead to peer down the gulley. It started near the street and led straight down to the river. A tiny trickle of water oozed its way downhill, and weeds and grasses grew from the bottom up the steep sides, making it difficult, if not impossible, for anyone to climb down, up and out on the other side. As Tuney joined me, she pointed out what looked like a tunnel created by big honeysuckle bushes that were on either side of a mulch path, almost exactly opposite of where we stood.

I smiled, remembering the time Kris had built a living tunnel for the kids to play in. One spring he'd gotten chicken wire, some small lengths of rebar metal and some PVC pipe. It had taken him an entire day, but when he was finished, a chicken wire tunnel had stretched from one side of the garden catty-corner to the other side, with a few curves that served as "rooms" for the kids just for fun. The kids were so excited they crawled through the wire tunnel every day, even before anything was planted to grow around and up the wire. Kris had insisted that Sammi and Kyle help him plant seeds that would grow over the wire. They'd been young enough to eagerly want to help, especially when he told them that the plants would completely cover the framework and they could have a secret hiding place.

Tuney nudged me and pointed at the tunnel. "Isn't that neat?

I looked over and smiled. "I remember your kids wanting to come over to our house in the summertime because Uncle Kris would let them play in his garden tunnel!"

Tuney chuckled. "Last year, both Joey and Heidi had tunnels. Kind of neat to think Kris started a tradition that's being carried on. And Scott will probably start next year when his two are bigger.

I reached over and grabbed Tuney's hand. "C'mon, Widster. I want to walk through the tunnel and see the garden, so we'll have to hike back up to the street and then back down to those bushes." I tugged gently on Tuney's hand, and she smiled and followed me.

In a few minutes we were at the start of the tunnel, ready to enter. It was adult-sized with a canopy almost seven feet tall. The mulch path was wide enough for one person to walk through without ever being touched or scratched by the bushes. Someone had carefully pruned the interior, and Tuney thought it had to be someone who loved to walk through it. The wood was so thick.

Memories from childhood flooded my mind. Our home had been surrounded with hedge, but there were three honeysuckle bushes that had been planted in a triangle next to one corner of our lot. The bushes had seemed large to Tuney and me at the time because we'd been so small. But we had spent hours and hours playing underneath them. We soon considered that corner our 'fort.'

"Do you remember our fort?" I asked Tuney as we stood looking at the big arc of leaves.

"I was just thinking about that, too!" exclaimed Tuney. "We had to crawl through the bushes, and then there was a neat little space where we could both sit." She stepped into the tunnel, started to squat down, glanced up and saw my grimace of concern, then straightened up and spread her arms apart. "You get the picture." She grinned.

"I'm glad you remembered in time that your bones aren't 8 years old anymore," I said, laughing. "Remember Mom would bring out some cookies and lemonade, walk right to where we were hidden and then holler for us?"

"Ope!" said Tuney as she tugged at her capris and smoothed the knees. "I remember giggling and trying to be super quiet." She patted my arm. "She'd stand right there in front of where we were hiding for what seemed like an eternity…"

"But was probably only a minute," I interjected, nodding.

"…and then she'd say really loud, 'Well, I guess those two girls are gonna miss out on a treat. I'll just leave it here for the fairies to eat.'"

"And she'd set it down and go back inside," I finished. "We could see her, kind of, through the leaves, and she never looked back. Then we'd crawl out, grab the treat and pretend for hours that we were invisible, or fairies, or spies or something like that." I sighed, and we nodded and smiled at each other and the recollections of that precious time.

We started walking slowly through the tunnel, me in the lead. Tuney must have still been reminiscing because after a moment, I heard her chuckle and then say, "And we felt so sneaky thinking Mom didn't know where we were. It was only later that we realized she knew because she could see us. She knew everything!"

I stopped and turned around. "That's right! How old were we when we figured out she could see us in the bushes?"

Tuney shrugged. "I guess we knew deep down she'd at least seen us crawl in there," she said. Then added, "But we knew for sure when our kids did the same thing years later!" Her eyes twinkled at the recollection. "Remember? Both our families were at Mom and Dad's and suddenly we realized how quiet things were."

"Eww, quiet is bad when you're talking about kids," I nodded.

"I know. Especially because it was about the time Johnny Gosch went missing." Tuney shuddered, remembering the fear almost every parent experienced when a Des Moines Register newspaper boy disappeared while on his paper route. All that was ever found was his wagon containing some newspapers he'd yet to deliver.

I nodded solemnly. "That changed us. Our whole world was altered forever for that matter, wasn't it? The idea that you couldn't let your kids out of sight anymore or give them the freedom we'd had as kids was life-changing."

Tuney was thoughtful. "No kidding. That day at Mom's, I

was just starting to panic. I think we both were, and we sent the guys out to hunt for the kids. That's when we noticed Mom standing calmly looking out the kitchen window to the back yard. She turned and had a slight smile on her face. She reached into the cookie jar for a handful of cookies, had Dad get paper cups and plates, and asked me to get the pitcher of lemonade she always had on hand for the grandkids. That was her 'thing' I guess you'd call it." She smiled and rolled her eyes. "It suddenly dawned on us what she was doing, and I just felt so relieved. She told us to tell Tommy and Kris to come in, told Dad to help her carry out the 'fairy food,' and away they went out the back door."

I shook my head and laughed. "You and I stood at the window watching, and we could see movement in that corner of the yard. Dad always kept the bushes trimmed, but of course they were thicker and bigger by the time our kids played in there."

"Sure enough, I think it was your Kyle, wasn't it, who was the tallest of our five, and he popped his head up, saw Mom and Dad coming and ducked back down." Tuney was smiling.

"Mom and Dad did the ritual hollering all over the yard, then we could see Dad shrug and say something to Mom. They called a few more times as they got to the bushes, then they put down the food and drinks, and came in, grinning all the way." I stopped and grabbed Tuney's hand. "I'm so glad we have those memories of Mom and Dad!" Dad had died several years ago, and our Mom was in a care facility, suffering from dementia.

"We're definitely lucky!" said Tuney and we hugged each other tightly.

When we reached the end of the arbor, Tuney thought

about turning around and going back through it again. But a path that led down a slight incline beckoned, and she and I soon became entranced by the site that met our eyes. Limestone rock walls surrounded an area below the incline, creating a sunken garden. A rounded arch made of big stones formed the entrance. A sweet fragrance filled the air, coming from countless roses scattered throughout.

Against the garden walls were climbing roses. They were interspersed with rose bushes in different garden plots. The plots were designated by either small boxwood hedges, bricks or rocks. Some of the plots were square, some round, some with curves, but they were all filled with beautiful flowers that had been carefully tended by the hands belonging to the men and women of the local garden club.

In one corner a tiny bridge arced over an equally tiny pond. Tuney and I hurried over, curious to see if there were any fish in it. About a dozen koi fish lazily rose to the surface, their mouths pouting as they opened and shut them to kiss the water's surface in search of food.

Another section in the garden was designated the Butterfly Garden where Painted Lady, Cloudless Sulphur and Black Swallowtail butterflies flitted around patches of nasturtiums, catmint and dill. Tuney and I were soon busy snapping pictures of not only the Butterfly Garden, but other sections as well. A bed of purple echinacea – coneflowers – along with multiple colors in a bed of zinnias were flanked by metal park benches with ivy scrollwork on the back of the seats. A sundial stood on a flat stone that looked like it was granite, and I studied it diligently, taking pictures of all sides of the dial.

"One guess as to what you're buying as soon as we get home," said Tuney.

I looked up, smiled and said, "I love gardens and I've wanted a sundial forever!"

Tuney wandered around and soon called me to come look at a beautiful setting of flowering bushes with pink, coral and yellow snapdragons in front of them. Her exclamations of "Look at that beauty," and "I've never seen such color" could have been directed at either the flowers or the butterflies that could be seen.

"I'm glad we stayed outdoors, now. I'm so going to put in a garden like this!" I exclaimed. "I love the way everything's laid out."

"I wouldn't mind having one of the boys lay something out like this, too," said Tuney. "My yard's certainly big enough. Only I'd probably put some veggies in, and maybe a little wishing well instead of the pond." She walked back to the water and then summoned me to join her.

"Cardi, come give these poor fish a kiss. They're begging you for one," joked Tuney as the gold, reddish and white colored koi took turns swimming to the surface and then retreating to the cooler shadows underneath the bridge.

I blew the fish a kiss, then became concerned. "Are they hungry, do you think?" I asked. "I saw what looked like a gumball machine somewhere back by the park. But instead of gumballs, it looked like it had pellets in it and now I think that's probably fish food." I pointed off-handedly in the general direction the way we'd entered the park. "I'll go get some in a minute. But first, Tuney, come over and look at this little area of flowers. I want your opinion."

Tuney followed me to yet another corner of the garden. Tuney watched as I took pictures at different angles of a pretty little raised bed of flowers. I was excited.

"This is the icing on the cake of this trip! I've wanted a garden like this for years, and this is perfect!" I spread out my arms to encompass the entire sunken garden. "That's one thing I love about gardening. You can change how things look each year if you want! I'm going to see if some of the neighborhood boys want to earn some extra money to tear down that flower bed I've got near the river birch tree. I might even get someone to chop that birch down." I noticed Tuney's surprised look at that announcement. She knew I was proud of the landscaping in my yard.

"Oh, it's not that I don't like that tree, but it's growing too close to the garage and it sheds sticks and leaves like crazy."

"Cardi, you murderer!" said Tuney in mock horror. "You mean you'd actually kill John?"

I giggled. "Ha! Yup, ol' John Birch has done his time and I'm pretty sure I won't miss him. Maybe I'll buy a little 'Chris Pine.' I absolutely LOVE Chris in the Star Trek movies."

Tuney, Tommy, Kris and our entire families were used to my penchant to name things after real people, sometimes directly and sometimes with a little twist in the name. Once when we were teens, Tuney and I had been invited to spend a four-day weekend with our friend Kathy Donnelly at her family's vacation home at a lake in Minnesota. I had wandered down to the lake after I unpacked. Before the others were done, I came racing back to the cabin, telling them to hurry.

"Come on, everyone!" I yelled, jumping up and down. "Hank Aaron is down by the lake!"

Mr. Donnelly almost jumped up and down, too, so excited he was to hear one of his favorite athletes was nearby. He dashed out the door, shouting, "Where? Where, Cardi? Where is he?"

The others had quickly followed as I led them closer to the dock. Suddenly, I stopped and shushed everyone.

"There he is," I whispered excitedly, pointing at the end of the dock. They all looked.

A great blue heron, standing on one leg, turned its regal head to look at us, its crest raising slightly. When it saw humans, it immediately spread its wings and silently, effortlessly, flew off over the lake to a stand of trees along the shoreline on the other side.

"Goodbye, Hank Heron!" I called out, waving at the bird. I'd never seen such splendor in a bird. I smiled at everyone in ecstasy. "Wasn't he beautiful?"

Mr. Donnelly looked at me in disbelief and with more than a hint of disappointment. "Heron? Hank HERON? Cardi, I thought you said, 'Hank. Aaron!'" he sputtered. He gave me a disgusted look and glared at Mrs. Donnelly who had covered her mouth to hide the laughter that was bubbling out from between her fingers. With a final harrumph, he wheeled around on his heels, and walked as dignified as he could back to the cabin. Peals of laughter from everyone but me followed his every step. I remember just looking at him in puzzlement. Tuney and Kathy swore that as he passed them, he was muttering all sorts of things, but the only clear thing they could decipher was the word "damn."

Over the years there had been several dogs of mine named after favorite stars or characters: A pug named Pugsley Addams after the TV comedy show The Addams Family; rescue dogs Ralphie Barker and Scut Barkus in reverence to the 1980s movie "A Christmas Story" about a little boy named Ralphie Parker and his nemesis Scut Farkus; a kitten from someone's farm named Cat Ballou for the Jane Fonda movie of the same name, and an aquarium tropical catfish named Catfish Hunter. When the Des Moines Zoo had a Name-the-Baby contest for its new baby jaguar, my entry of "Mick" was no surprise to my friends. Tuney was even slightly disappointed I didn't win. Mick Jaguar was usurped in favor of the Spanish word for mighty – "Podorosa." I almost hate to admit that even inanimate objects were subjected to my names. I have a huge boulder in my front yard by the mailbox that I always refer to as Rock Hudson. Now, as I stood in this sunken garden, I could already picture a square-shaped flower garden in my backyard. I was mentally referring to it as "Madison Square."

Tuney smiled at me while I prattled on about what else I was going to change in order to recreate a smaller version of the sunken garden. It amazed her that I was so creative. She'd have me come over to paint a room or go shopping for new curtains or carpet. Kris occasionally had bankers from other cities over for meetings, and he often brought them home for supper. Inevitably, someone would ask me who decorated our home.

Tuney looked at me now, busily writing notes on some paper I'd found in my purse. "I wonder what Kris would say if he was here," Tuney said. "Ope! Cardi, I'm sorry!" The words were out of her mouth before she thought it might upset me. But I was nonplussed.

"It's just like I said yesterday morning, Tune," I said placidly. "This is one of the things that's not so bad about widowhood." I studied the notes I'd made about some of the flowers and materials, looked up at the garden sundial again, and then smiled at Tuney. "Besides getting what I want exactly, I'm going to put in a sundial where Kris died. Just for him. So that he knows I'll always be thinking of the time I had with him in the garden - and everywhere else."

Tuney's mouth dropped open, then closed quickly. She swallowed and smiled back at me. "I think he'd love that, Card," she said. Then with a wink, she added, "Especially since he doesn't have to pay for it!"

"Tuney! You cracked another joke!" I walked over and gave her a hug. "You're on a roll with your humor lately. We're both gonna be okay. You know that to be true, don't you?"

Tuney's smile left her face but her eyes retained the warmth they held for me. She nodded solemnly. "This trip, as short as it is, has helped me immensely. I know I've got a long way to go, but," she sighed and nodded, "yeah. I know. I'm definitely gonna be okay."

She started to reach over to hug me, but instead I held up my hand and high-fived her.

"Let's walk back to Mason House. I want to visit that caboose when the 2Bs2Ts are settled," said Tuney. "And we have to stop at Iron and Lace and get our packages!"

She and I walked back up the incline, turned around for one more look at the lovely sunken garden, and then set off down the street toward the shops and the haunted and hauntingly impressive bed and breakfast.

Chapter 24

2Bs2Ts And A Caboose

The bus was parked in front of Mason House, and about half of the passengers were climbing aboard to be taken to the other B&B about a half mile away. Amy waved at Tuney and ran over to her.

"How are you doing?" she asked anxiously. "I've been thinking about you and that ghost experience, and I feel so badly that I laughed and didn't try to help more."

Tuney laughed at her. "I'm doing amazingly great. I think I could go try to find George again! Maybe we could be friends," she said with a thumb's up. Amy looked relieved.

"Well, I'm so sorry that happened. I'm spiritual, and after seeing Al Capone, or whoever that guy was, I feel like these souls who are here without a body are just like anyone else. But I know I'm in a definite minority about that," Amy remarked.

Tuney gave her a quick hug and surprised both Amy and me with what she said next. "You know what? I agree with you totally. After all, we're all souls, aren't we? And there are three places souls are housed: Heaven, here on Earth inside a body, and here on Earth outside a body." Then, she quickly added: "I better make that FOUR places. I'm sure there are a few souls who are housed where it's plenty warm!" And she and Amy laughed. As another passenger hollered for Amy, she winked at Tuney, told us the suitcases we'd brought were in the Wash House Room, and she took off.

We walked on over to The Wash House. Tuney started to pull out her bathroom supplies but I called dibs on taking a shower first. While I was showering, Tuney plugged in her phone charger and laid down on one side of the bed. She hadn't planned to nap, but the next thing she knew, I was gently shaking her awake.

"Sorry, Tune, but I didn't want a repeat of what happened to us in the Dubuque hotel," I said. I was already dressed and had fresh makeup on. "Bonnie stopped over here a bit ago, and they're loving the caboose. They bought some wine and want us to come over and par-tay!" And I waggled my hips.

Tuney blinked, yawned, and rolled over to look at her phone to see what time it was. "Mmmmm! I didn't think I'd sleep, but I'm glad I did," she said as she sat up on the side of the bed. "I feel better now."

"Take a quick shower to get the sweat and dust off, and then we'll go," I urged. "I'll wait!"

"Okay, gimme five minutes," said Tuney as she grabbed a robe and hurried into the bathroom. It was a long five minutes, but in fifteen real-time minutes, we were rounding the corner of the annex to go to the caboose.

Every light was on inside, and that seemed to brighten up the yellow outside, even though the sun hadn't set yet. From the outside, it sounded like we were approaching a stadium: Music was blaring, there was high-pitched laughing, and voices in conversation were raised in order to be heard over the noise. I looked at Tuney, and Tuney cocked her head quizzically.

"I distinctly hear "Wild Thing" on the radio. They must be dancing! How many people did Chuck say this held?" she asked me.

"Four, but that was to sleep. I think they invited everyone who's staying at Mason House." I said. "I hope we're not the last! Should we run over to the general store and get some beer?"

Tuney paused. "Let's wait and see what's going on. We can always make a beer run later if we need to. I want to see who all is here!"

As we reached the end of the caboose where a few steps led to the door, two beautiful cats walked around the side. I bent over to pet the tortoiseshell one, and it purred and arched its back, so I could scratch it. The other cat had long gray hair and beautiful golden eyes. It sat down away from us to lick its fur and waited patiently for its companion to join it. The two cats then slunk into some bushes.

"Those are probably the official guards around here," I laughed as I watched them leave. "I think Chuck mentioned that they had a couple of pets."

"I think it was Joy. Not that it matters who said it. Hey! Hang on a sec," said Tuney, as she fumbled in her pocket for her phone. "I want to take a picture of the caboose."

It was awesome to think that a real caboose had been converted into a bedroom suite. It sported a sign that advertised it was an authentic 1952 rail car from Texas and was available for rent. I could hardly wait to see the inside. As Tuney and I climbed the three steps to enter one end of the caboose, we heard shrieks of laughter inside.

Tuney grinned at me and said, "I guess we know where to party tonight!" She knocked on the door, but none of the 2Bs2Ts heard. Tuney pushed the door open and she and I entered the remodeled caboose. At first appearance, it looked a bit like the interior of an RV. A narrow short hallway from the entrance led Tuney and me to a more opened area where we could see Belinda standing in front of a door that must have led to a bedroom. As we walked toward her, we passed through a galley-type kitchen with a small bathroom opposite of it.

Bonnie was standing in front of the bathroom, laughing and finally noticed Tuney and me.

"What in the world is going on?" I demanded. Bonnie cupped one ear with her hand, mouthed the word "What?" and then turned her head and swept her hands down and up a few times, ostensibly to order someone to turn the music lower.

"Where's everybody else?" asked Tuney when the volume decreased from deafening to pleasant. We both looked around, expecting to see wall-to-wall bus passengers. Tuney tried to look past Belinda into the bedroom.

"Well, I'm up here," came a muffled voice. Bonnie merely nodded because she started laughing and pointed upward.

Where the kitchen ended, there was a taller space with built-in metal stairs that were very steep and odd-shaped. There was no handrail until you got to the top, and that's where we spotted Tammy's legs sticking out from what looked like a hinged table near some leather seating.

"What are you doing?" Tuney asked, as she backed up to try to see the rest of Tammy's body. She still had her phone out and she started taking pictures. Amidst grunting, grumbling and several cuss words, Tammy was finally able to get her legs underneath her and slowly pivoted so she could look down on our astounded faces.

"Now that I've finally made it up here, I've been laughing so hard I need to pee!" Tammy said in mock consternation. That sent Bonnie into another shrieking fit, and soon Trudy and Belinda joined. Tuney and I stood there grinning, wondering what all the commotion was, but the laughter was contagious and soon we were giggling at poor Tammy.

"Someone help me down from here. Please," ordered Tammy as she faced the steep steps.

"You're going to have to turn back around, you ditz," laughed Trudy, who had been standing inside the doorway of the little bathroom directly behind Bonnie. Tammy looked aghast at her, heaved a big sigh, and muttered something the others didn't understand. She began backing up a bit, then tried to turn around.

"What did you say, Honey?" asked Belinda, who'd abandoned the bedroom to join the others. I began digging into my purse for my cell phone.

"I said I'd have been better off if I'd picked one of the haunted rooms!" said Tammy, huffily. We heard a grunt followed by a bump and a string of profanities.

"Oh, good grief," I blurted out. "Did that come from sweet little Tammy?" Her friends, instead of helping, were convulsed in laughter, and could only nod.

"Do you need some help?" asked Tuney sympathetically, and she put one foot up on a step.

"No," said Tammy, "but thank you. You're the only one who's offered some help and shown some sympathy." She peered over her shoulder at the others, and then winked, so Tuney and I knew she wasn't mad.

"Don't help her!" said Bonnie. "This is what she gets for being so stubborn and pig-headed. I tried to tell her she was too old to be climbing up there."

"You're the one who wanted to come up, too," retorted Tammy. "Besides," she added. "the smartest and bravest one should be the one to check out these things!" She managed to crawl up on one of the leather seats and from there grabbed the wooden table top that was hinged to the top, pushed it back to the wall and secured it there with a hook that was attached. The leg that propped the loose end of the table was also hinged and it laid flat against the table on the wall.

"There! Now at least I've got some room to try to get down." She used both hands to grab a side rail whose purpose seemed to be keeping anyone sitting on the leather seat from falling off the side to the floor below. Tammy's intent was to back down the ladder, but first she had to bend over so her head wouldn't hit the ceiling. She stuck one leg behind her, using it to search for a step on the ladder. She lost her balance, fell forward on the loft, and yelled "Son of a …oooh…motherless goat!"

Trudy cried out, "Motherless goat? Holy schnikeys!" and they all started laughing while Tuney tried steering Tammy's leg to the first step. I was snapping photos like crazy, but finally put my phone away. Being the tallest, I offered to help. I reached both arms up and planted my hands firmly on Tammy's rear end while Tuney ducked underneath me and grabbed Tammy's ankles to help guide her feet to each step. Finally, Tammy reached the floor and made a mad dash the few steps to the bathroom and slammed the door amidst gales of laughter from the rest of us. Bonnie motioned me and Tuney to take a seat on the banquette benches that were opposite the steps.

"She wasn't kidding about having to go to the bathroom, was she?" asked Tuney with delight.

I looked all around the caboose. "Wait a sec! Are you four the only ones here?" I asked.

"Yeah," said Bonnie, obviously surprised at the question. "Why?"

Tuney and I looked at each other and explained that judging by the lights and the noise, we thought every guest in Mason House was here.

Trudy was surprised. "Yikes! Were we that loud?"

Belinda was shaking her head. "Nope. Just us. But it would be fun, wouldn't it, to get more people in here!"

Trudy grimaced and looked out a window. "I'll keep guard in case Chuck comes over to kick us out," she said. "We'd better tone it down, though."

Tuney started skimming through the pictures she'd taken, I opened my photo gallery, and soon the five of us were laughing all over again. There was a photo of a foot, one of Tammy's rear end, pictures of the 2Bs and Trudy bent over laughing, and a lot more of parts of Tammy. She peeked out the bathroom door.

"Do I even want to ask what you're all laughing about?" Tammy said, grinning. She joined us, nudging me over so she could take a seat.

"What possessed you to even want to go up there?" I asked.

"It's Chuck's fault!" said Tuney! "He said there's a gorgeous view of the river from the cupola up there, and that if we didn't want to sleep together in the bedroom," and she pointed at the bedroom at the end of the hallway, "all I had to do was move the table and there was a fold-down twin-sized bed. I thought it'd be neat to sleep up there with the tree branches right above the windows and see the stars."

"Are you going back up there?" asked Tuney incredulously.

"Not on your life! I think it's dangerous up there, and what if you roll around in your sleep and fall to the floor? Someone could get killed. I don't want to end up the first ghost of the caboose!" Tammy looked up at the cupola and shuddered.

As we sat on the booth seats with a little table in between, Tuney started scooching around in her seat and finally leaned back in order to peek at the bottom of the table.

"What are you doing?" I asked her finally after watching her for a while.

"This reminds me of a cabin Tommy and I stayed in with the kids once," Tuney explained. She straightened up and raised an eyebrow at all four of the caboose's guests.

"Did Chuck specifically say that table upstairs? Or did he mean this one?" she asked pointedly

Tammy and Belinda looked blankly at her, while Bonnie's mouth formed an O and Trudy said, "Huh?"

Tuney started to giggle. "Get up from the seats, you nuts," she ordered. We all slid off and stood in the doorway of the bedroom while Tuney folded the table down, pulled some extensions out, then used the seat cushion back to make a nice soft twin-size bed.

"Oh, good heavens!" moaned Tammy. She buried her face in Trudy's shoulder. After a moment, she finally looked up and spotted me. "So help me, Cardi, I'd better not see a picture of my derriere on the ladder on Facebook!" She sat on the edge of her new bed. "I can't believe this!" She started laughing all over again, and soon all six of us were wiping tears of mirth from our faces.

"My turn to use the potty," yelled Belinda.

"Well, hurry," said Bonnie. "The tears are going to be

running down my legs soon!" We started laughing again at that thought, and I felt like I'd done a hundred stomach crunches, it hurt so badly from laughing. But in a good way.

"Does anyone have the time?" asked Bonnie when she came back after her turn in the bathroom. "I'm getting hungry again. Should we walk somewhere to get some food?"

"Well, we certainly can't drive, you fool," said Belinda drolly. "And the only place to eat is the ice cream shop. But they have sandwiches."

"Hope they're half as good as the fudge," murmured Tammy.

"We could get sandwiches to go and come back here," suggested Trudy.

"I kind of want to see the bridge, while it's still light out," said Tuney.

"Okay, Okay. I'm nominating me as boss," said Bonnie. "I move we all walk over to get sandwiches, and then eat them on the bridge! Who'll second the motion?'"

She looked eagerly at us. I bit my upper lip, Tuney cleared her throat, and the rest were silent. Bonnie rolled her eyes and grinned. "Hey! What? I'm the queen of compromise. I thought my suggestion covered all bases. I doubt we can order pizza. So you guys come up with an idea. I resign as boss."

"You can't resign because we didn't vote you in," noted Tammy. Bonnie made a face at her. Someone giggled, and Tammy grinned back at Bonnie.

"Your suggestion was good, Bon. Let's all walk over to the sandwich shop, eat there and then see if we're too full or it's too dark to walk off our food," suggested Tuney. "I can always go to the bridge in the morning. I don't think we leave until 8:30, is that right?"

Everyone agreed, so the six of us set off. I turned around

once to look at the caboose. Every light was still on, and I could still hear the music from the boom box that was part of the furnishings, although someone had turned it down lower than when we first arrived. *What a bunch of crazies,* I thought affectionately.

In just a few minutes, we were at the shop and decided to eat inside this time instead of on the porch. August in Iowa can be hot, and we are used to that. But hot August weather combined with a setting sun usually means mosquitoes, and no one wanted to risk getting bit.

We talked and laughed. The 2Bs2Ts recounted the shopping adventures they'd had while we Widsters had been in Mason House on the tour. Bonnie and Tammy had each bought a Nativity set at Iron and Lace, Belinda and Trudy had bought some paintings at another shop that featured artwork, and they'd each bought some Queen Anne's lace ornaments.

Tammy reminded us we'd be going to Cantril and Eldon tomorrow before the return trip to Des Moines. "And the huge Amish store will have tons of stuff you'll want to buy," she promised. "My friend drives down once a month just to stock up on stuff. Plus, American Gothic House in Eldon has a neat little gift shop."

"Gift shop," I cooed, perking up. I turned to Tuney with a smile. She gave me a warning look and rubbed her thumbs across her fingertips to remind me shopping costs money. "Spoilsport," I muttered.

"No, just being logical and commonsense. One of us has to," she said primly. "Between the two of us, we may not have any room in the car to get home with what we've bought already. And since I'm the one with the car, if we have too much to fit in, guess whose souvenirs would be dumped?" she warned.

"Whoa!" said Trudy. "Better be good, Cardi."

"That would be a miracle," Tuney said, amused. I nodded amiably. The rest of the evening we spent chattering about our families and friends back home, and by the time the shop closed at 9 p.m., we all felt as if we'd known each other forever. And I think we all felt a deeper kinship when Tuney thanked us for putting up with her meltdown on the bus.

"I can't even begin to explain how much I needed to get that off my chest – and I didn't even realize it. To have all of you willing to not only listen and offer comfort and support, but to not be offended and judgmental – well…" She paused and concentrated on what she wanted to say for a second. We all waited. "I guess what it means to me is that I feel, now, *included,* instead of *secluded.* You know?"

"Do you mean you felt left out of normal things with other people?" asked Belinda.

Tuney shook her head no, but wavered her hand and said, "Mmmmm, kind of, but not really. I was included in a lot of things. People were good to me. Maybe I can't describe it accurately."

Bonnie nodded vehemently. "I think I know exactly what you mean. There's a little voice inside us when we're hurting, and in my case, it kept reminding me that while people were helping me and truly sympathetic, I was still kind of the pariah. You know - the lady whose husband was the living dead. A loner because I couldn't describe the pain I was feeling. Maybe I secluded myself because I believed that's what people thought. Even after Ken died, I felt like instead of him being in limbo, now I was. And that voice was a constant reminder that nothing was the same and I was in it alone. Secluded is a great word to describe the feeling. It wasn't until I was able to start to get out and truly enjoy life again that I felt a part of the world. I was included again, because I was able to include the world. Is that it?" She looked at Tuney and patted her arm.

Tuney brightened. "Bingo! Especially your description of *included*. I've certainly *been* included in activities, like this bus trip with Cardi, for example. But I wasn't *feeling* included because I was too busy trying to figure out how to live without Tommy and keeping so much inside of me. It'll never be the same world." She paused and looked around at us and shrugged. "But then nothing remains the same, does it? So now I feel like your care and concern and love has me included." Tuney looked downward, suddenly embarrassed.

Tammy started to say something, but a big yawn caught up to her first. She covered her mouth, then said, "Well, I was going to invite you Widsters back to the caboose, but I guess I'm getting..." (another yawn interrupted her) "...too tired!"

Her yawns were contagious, so Tuney and I declined to go back to the caboose. Both of us were suddenly tired, and it was obvious the 2Bs2Ts were also ready to go to sleep. We strolled back to Mason House and said good night. Before she walked into our room, Tuney stood outside, looked up at the second story windows, and said softly, "Good night, George. Be a good boy and get some sleep so that everyone else can, too!" She caught me looking at her and quickly added, "I'm not sure now that was a ghost I felt. It might have been a muscle cramp. But just in case..."

"Muscle cramp?" I scoffed. "I've never seen anyone petrified of a muscle cramp. But, like you said, just in case..." and we walked inside to our room.

As soon as she hit the pillow, Tuney was asleep, despite the nap she'd taken. Me, on the other hand, while physically tired, felt wide awake as soon as I laid down. Dog gone it! I wondered if that was old age. It seemed to be happening more and more the older I got. I stared at the ceiling for a while thinking of everything that had happened in just two days.

I smiled in the darkness thinking how the trip had started off with the roadkill fiasco. Then the breakfast at the Amana Colonies, the hula hoop tree, Dubuque's little cable car elevator, the river museum and, of course, the ghost of Al Capone. I deliberated on whether I believe that had been a ghost. "Al" had looked totally flesh-and-blood alive, so maybe he was a guest dressed up, and the desk clerk didn't know about him. Oh, well, it would make for a fun story to tell our kids when we got home.

And then today! Had we only been gone from home two days? It seemed longer. The restaurant in Bonaparte, the cemetery, Tuney's run-in with "George the Ghost," shopping in Bentonsport and the lovely sunken garden had been interesting and fun to experience. And what a way to end the day with laughter and the friendship of our new besties, the 2Bs2Ts! I giggled at the thought of Tammy in the cupola, then decided if there was still one more day left, I'd better get some sleep.

Ten minutes later, I threw my side of the covers back. "Rats!" I muttered. I tossed and turned a bit more, then finally opened my phone's photo gallery. Some of the photos I'd taken earlier in the evening at the caboose made me chuckle softly. I sent them to each of the 2Bs2Ts. They'd given me their email addresses because we wanted to stay in touch with each other after the bus tour was over. Tuney and I hadn't laughed this hard for a long time, and I knew we'd benefitted from our new friendships with these other widows.

I turned to look at Tuney, fast asleep. She was so tired yesterday, and even this morning. But after that meltdown on the bus, she seemed to strengthen her emotions. I felt guilty that I hadn't realized she felt secluded, as she had put it.

Had I? I thought hard. I empathized with what Tuney'd said on the bus about wondering if there was a God. And truth be told, I think the time I yelled at God, I was even madder at the world than she had seemed on the bus. The difference was that I'd gone to my basement, thrown things, screamed, and cursed up a blue storm. Only I knew that. No one...but me and God. I guess that would qualify as being secluded, so why hadn't I known how Tuney felt?

I relived Kris's death and the months that followed, as best as I could remember. The shock had blurred a lot of things. When I'd start to feel alone or scared that first year, I'd just tell myself Kris was away at a meeting. As a vice president and then president of a bank, that happened a lot during our years together. Even though he'd retired, he'd stayed on the board and enjoyed having something to do when he couldn't garden or go fishing or hunting with the boys. Pretending he was gone only temporarily allowed me to include myself in family get togethers. I realized now that I hadn't bothered to dissect my feelings ever. I only wanted to quit crying, because crying did nothing but hurt and leave red marks on my cheeks, burned my eyes, and (heaven forgive my vanity) wreaked havoc with my mascara. I only wanted to think positive thoughts about life. And I'd done those. So why did it suddenly bother me when Bonnie and Tuney were talking about feeling secluded and included?

I frowned now as I recalled how many times after Kris's death someone would come up to me and tell me I was such a 'strong' woman. I always smiled and thanked them. Yes, I was strong. Strong, because I helped Tuney and Tommy out that entire first year of being alone after Kris died. Strong driving them to Iowa City. Strong picking up Tommy's prescriptions. Strong bringing food over to them. Strong sneaking into Tuney's home to run the vacuum or dust or wash up dishes. Strong taking care of Tuney's grandkids when their parents wanted to go see their dad in the hospital. I was included in my sister's life - in the physical, emotional and mental needs of Tuney and her family – *my* family. There were tons of things I'd done that didn't isolate me from the world. I was involved and included all by myself. No one had to take care of me - because I was strong. Strong as a bowl of jello.

I suddenly felt left out, a little isolated. *Why do I feel that way?* I puzzled. It certainly wasn't because no one liked me. I was having fun on this trip. I certainly was included in all the events we were sharing on this trip. I thought of the stories the 2Bs2Ts had shared about losing their husbands. Their feelings of love, loss and fear were told in various ways, but united us all. I hadn't told them much about Kris other than it was such a shock.

Maybe, I thought, *I had secluded my feelings.*

It was then I understood what Tuney and Bonnie were talking about. It wasn't physical inclusion. It was being able to release or share the raw emotions that we widows keep to ourselves. I raised myself up on my elbows and looked at Tuney, wanting to wake her up and tell her that I finally understood the fellowship, or inclusion, of being with others who understood the grief of specifically losing a husband. It was being a Widster.

I finally shut my phone off and lay still. Homesickness crept over me. I was homesick for Kris. I'd been half afraid that Chuck was wrong about the Wash Room House not being haunted, but now I prayed it was. Maybe Kris would appear, especially if one of Mason House's ghosts could contact him. Was that too much to ask? As I had almost every night since he died, I prayed to God and to Kris that I could at least dream about him. The last thing I remember thinking before I fell asleep was to wonder: *If a soul goes directly to heaven, does that mean it will never visit its living loved ones on Earth?*

Chapter 25

The Bridge

The sound of a door shutting loudly woke me up. My eyes flew open and I lay in bed for a moment, vaguely aware that I felt disappointed but wondering what had caused the noise. I sat up in bed. It was only Tuney, who opened the bathroom a crack and peered out tentatively to see if she'd awakened me. When she saw me, she opened the door wide.

"I'm so sorry, Cardi!" she apologized, rubbing her eyes and fluffing her hair. "I wasn't quite awake, I'm afraid, and I just barged right into the bathroom and slammed the door like I do when I'm home alone."

"Oh, that's okay," I yawned. "You go ahead and take your time. I'll use the bathroom after you."

I laid back down on the bed and stretched. The feeling of disappointment was starting to diminish, but it puzzled me, and I wondered why I felt that way. I flopped over on my side to grab my cell phone. For the millionth time I wished I could call my husband. As soon as I thought of Kris, I realized why I felt disappointed. *Oh, yeah, No dream. No Kris.* Just me alone again. Probably forever.

"Your turn!" called out Tuney as she left the bathroom. My day always started out with a wake-up shower and a shampoo. "Hey, I wonder how the 2Bs2Ts made out in the caboose last night. Wasn't that hilarious when…" She broke off her sentence as she saw my face.

"What's wrong?" she asked. "Do you feel okay?" She sat down on the bed next to me.

Kris always said I'd lose at cards because I could never put on a poker face. "Nothing."

Tuney rolled her eyes. "Every one of my children has given me that answer at one time or another, and it only means one thing: Something is bothering you. Now tell me what it is."

I sighed, sat up and gave her a little smile. "Nothing really. I think I've been on a high with all the laughter and everything that's so fun that my emotions can't take anymore and I've crashed."

Tuney looked skeptical and a little concerned. "We still have another full day of fun and frivolity, as they say," she said, trying to be light-hearted. "Can you take one more?"

"Of course. It's just…" I was listening to my voice, and it sounded almost teary. *Geez, girl, get hold of yourself. We had enough tears yesterday to last a year!*

"Just what, Cardi? Tell me, please."

I shook my head, scolded myself and then grimaced. "It's stupid, but I couldn't get to sleep last night until I started praying to dream about Kris. I was hoping maybe being this close to all this spirit or ghost stuff," and I waved my arms to encompass all of Mason House, "that maybe just once he'd visit me in a dream. I woke up this morning, and I felt kind of…empty, I think. You know?"

Tuney solemnly nodded yes. "I certainly do know. All too well."

We were both quiet for another moment. A small shaft of morning sunlight from the curtained window found a gap between the panels and suddenly hit me in the face. It was just what I needed. I blinked, then slapped my hands on my knees.

"I guess Mother Nature is strongly hinting that I shouldn't be wasting another beautiful day being a Debbie-downer, right?" I stood up, stretched once more, and smiled down at Tuney. "I think I'm going to take a quick wake-up shower."

"Good for you!" said Tuney. "It's only 6:15, and breakfast starts at 7 in the Inn. Hurry up and we can walk over to the bridge if you want. I bet there'll be so many stories at breakfast that we won't have time to walk over afterwards before the bus picks us up."

I hurried to shower and shave my legs, which made me grumble. "I don't know why I keep shaving my legs," I hollered through the shower curtain and bathroom door to Tuney. "It's not like anyone will care if my legs are stubbly."

Tuney poked her head in the door. "Well, I'll care unless you wear long slacks. But it's too hot for that, so if you're wearing your capris and you sit next to me, for Pete's sake, don't rub one of your legs against me. I'll get stubble burn!"

Old habits die hard, they say. In the shower, I scornfully looked at my razor, then dutifully began shaving. Pretty soon, I joined Tuney in the bedroom.

"Oh, good," said Tuney. "My turn again. I need to use the bathroom mirror to put my makeup on. I can't get close enough to this dresser mirror to see that well." She grabbed her makeup kit and walked in, leaving the door ajar to help get rid of the humidity from the shower. "I hate being nearsighted!"

I looked at myself in the mirror, then sighed and grabbed

my makeup bag. I raised my voice to talk to Tuney. "You know when I talked about being a widow wasn't so bad?"

Tuney, bending as close to the dresser mirror as she could to see to put on her makeup, grunted.

I took that as permission to keep talking. "Well, not shaving and not having to put on make-up anymore were a few of the things I was thinking about." I paused as I drew my lipstick around my mouth.

Tuney straightened up from the mirror to look over at the bathroom doorway. "Well, I have to say I agree with you about that. So why are we still shaving and *attempting* to make up our faces. It's getting harder and harder to line my eyes through all the creases!"

"We discussed that once already, remember? Aesthetics, my dear," came my complacent reply. "Some women age beautifully. Their eyebrows don't disappear, their lashes are naturally long, and they don't have all these age-spots on their faces like we fair-skinned Irish Collins's have! We have to look beautiful unnaturally."

Tuney turned one cheek and dabbed some more foundation on a brown spot that seemed to be more pronounced than the others. "You know, that sounds really pathetic, Card! And 'beautiful' is stretching it a bit, don't you think? I agree genetics is the cause for loss of eyebrows and thin lashes, but we made these stupid age-spots. I call them sun spots. If I could only turn back time! Think of all those years ago hanging out at the pool slathering iodine and baby oil all over. I wish someone had figured out what caused skin cancer and early aging before we'd done that!"

She walked out of the bathroom, blinking from putting her contact lenses in, stood next to me and looked in the mirror. She rubbed her chin thoughtfully, then stopped and with a gasp ran back to the bathroom.

"What's wrong?" I yelled.

"I forgot to shave my chin!"

I rolled my eyes. Looking into the mirror, I studied my reflection. I wondered how I'd look ten years from now and grimaced. *Hopefully, when we die and meet our loved ones, we'll look youthful again. I'd hate for Kris not to recognize me.*

It was only 6:35. Tuney quickly checked her emails to see if she had anything. Other than a few from the kids asking her how everything was going, there was one from Amy. She said that both B&Bs started serving breakfast at seven, so if we had our suitcases in front of our doors by 8:30, Mr. Smith would gather the luggage up, load them, and we'd be on the road to Cantril at nine. Tuney suggested we pack up now and then walk over to the bridge. We didn't have to eat at exactly seven, she told me.

She was glad when I seemed eager to walk. It was just across the street, and we were the only ones on it. It felt good to stroll through the cool morning air. It was the sort of morning that made you want to find a patch of soft grass and just lie down. I used to do that when I was a kid - a lot. I'd lie on my back to watch clouds, or on my stomach to watch bugs. *Wonder what people would say if I did that right now?* I thought. It would be nice to be young again, in the sun on the grass, feeling sheltered from life's troubles.

Tuney lifted her face to the sunshine. It wouldn't take long for the sun to beat down and heat things up. In the meantime, it was as if Mother Nature reveled in the quiet and calm of the early morning. I heard robins and meadowlarks singing. Red-wing blackbirds trilled among some cattails in a nearby pond. Whatever bit of disappointment I had not dreaming about Kris disappeared, and I felt invigorated now.

We crossed the street to the green area along the river bank and walked up a slight incline to the bridge. As we stepped onto the bridge, we could see that the banks on either side were flanked by different kinds of trees. A periodic break in the tree line revealed green grass, and I could see the area where the sunken rose garden was, as well as the fudge shop's porch, now empty in the early morning hours.

I Googled the Bentonsport Bridge and read aloud a few facts to Tuney.

"It's an early example of a pin-connected truss bridge. This one is large compared to a lot of other bridges, and is a long, five-span bridge. Each span contains eight panels."

Tuney looked at the bridge more closely. "What does it mean 'pin connected?'" she asked me.

I scanned my phone. "Not like a sewing pin, obviously. Uh, da-da-da-da, pin – oh! Bolts. That makes sense. A bolt connects things, right?" I scrolled through my phone some more. "Ah! Oh, here," and I started reading again. "It says a number of the pin bolts are square bolts. Square bolts were common, but not as pin bolts. Huh?" I looked up puzzled.

Tuney looked bored and just shrugged her shoulders.

I read silently for a few more seconds, but it was getting technical. "There's a lot more engineering or architectural terms I don't understand. But I guess the gist of it is, this is historical, they don't make bridges like this anymore, and it's a great place to walk and sit and contemplate life!"

"I could have told you that," said Tuney smugly. "Do you want to walk on over to Vernon?"

We leaned over the railing and stared down into the water. The river was low, and the current moved lazily.

"Not really," I murmured. "We shouldn't go too far from the Inn if we want to eat breakfast."

Tuney nodded her head in agreement and we kept staring at the water. From my vantage, I could make out light colored pieces of something in the water and wondered if they were the limestone rocks that were plentiful in parts of Iowa. By the riverbank, I saw rounded stones covered in green slimy-looking moss. A few fragments of rusty metal appeared to be near the shoreline, too, and I wondered if they had been pieces from one of the buildings that had once been near, parts from the bridge, or maybe even sections from an old boat.

"This is the Des Moines River?" I peered into the water to look for a fish. I asked more to start a conversation. I knew very well it was the Des Moines.

"Ope, you fool! Whaddaya think? Chuck was pointing it out through the room windows yesterday. Everything around here is Des Moines something or other," snorted Tuney.

"Well, I know we've seen a few Des Moines streets, but this isn't Des Moines county or anything. And the city of Des Moines is way north of here," I pointed out. Defensively. "I think it's kind of strange everything is named Des Moines."

"But the city was named for the river, and the river runs above, through and below it." Tuney said still staring mesmerized by the water's lazy current.

I knew that, too. But all I said was, "Mmmm."

Tuney stared at the water a while longer. It seemed to partially hypnotize us both by the sparkles the sun made on the water, and by the slow swirls and eddies that formed from unseen logs and rocks.

Finally Tuney shrugged. "Well," and she straightened up from the railing. "I wonder exactly what Des Moines means, don't you? I've sometimes thought about it, but never bothered to find out!"

"It's French. For *the moines,*" I quipped immediately, and Tuney burst out laughing.

"Ope! Aren't you getting clever in your old age, Widster!" said Tuney, prodding me in the shoulder.

"Actually," I admitted, "I bought a T-shirt from Raygun in Des Moines that said that."

Remembering our conversation about Idaho City T-shirt the other day, Tuney said, "You must really like Raygun."

"Well, surely you've been to it, haven't you?" Tuney shook her head no. "I love Raygun, It's in the East Village section of Des Moines. My favorite tee– and I wish I'd had it to wear in college – is *Iowa City – all our creativity went into the name!*"

"HA!" boomed Tuney. She and I turned to amble further over the bridge. "I need to get into Des Moines some time and visit that place. Do they have anything other than Des Moines and Iowa City sayings?"

"Oh, yes, they certainly do! Oh! Tuney!" I grinned. "You'd love this one shirt they have. You even said it a minute ago."

"Said it? What? What did I say?"

"Ope! You say 'Ope' all the time!"

Tuney twisted her mouth and looked puzzled. "I do? Ope? Really, do I say that often?"

I just looked at her and said simply, "Yup. Ope."

Tuney grinned quizzically. "Yikes, I didn't realize that. Well, you do, too. But is that all the shirt says – ope?"

"Nope," I said with a grin. "But the shirts are cute. They have the word 'ope' in big letters, then a definition and examples of when you'd use it."

"A definition? Really? Like what?" Tuney asked, knitting her brows with interest.

"Simple," I said. "It's kind of an 'oh' plus 'oops.' I think one example I remember is what you say when you're in the way: 'Ope. Sorry!'" I giggled. "You'd love the store. It's full of cool things. Mostly satirical and very clever!"

"Ope! I just got an idea! Guess what you can get me for Christmas, Widster? Size large, please," Tuney chortled.

I dug in my purse, and then mockingly said, "Ope! I'm gonna try to remember that. I forgot my pen!"

We neared the center of the bridge and moved to the railing again. From that vantage point, Tuney spotted a newer bridge to the west of this one. A car drove slowly over it. She looked down at the water again, and then suddenly chuckled.

"Remember the time we floated down the Raccoon River on inner tubes?" she asked as I took a few photos of the scenery.

My face split into a grin at the memory. "Oh, yeah! That was so much fun! How old were we? All I remember is getting the bottom of my swimsuit muddy and my front sunburned!"

Tuney laughed. "We were fourteen and fifteen, I think," she said. "And we thought we were so cool. I wore my new bikini." She looked down at her thighs and muffin top bulge under her shirt and grimaced.

I grabbed Tuney's arm. "Remember the boys who stood on the bridge out of town and were yelling at us to go topless?" I put my hand over my mouth at the thought. "And I think I yelled back at them."

Tuney remembered. That hot August day, before school started after Labor Day, we Collins girls and two other girl friends had taken inner tubes that our fathers had blown up for us, walked down below the river dam and laid on our backs across the tubes. I loved the feeling of the cool water from the river on my lower back and rear end. We could paddle with our hands to steer the tubes, but mostly we just floated lazily and slowly in a current that barely moved. We talked about boys, the teachers we did and didn't like, and the latest movie we all wanted to go see. We planned to go to a bend in the river where there was a sandbar. There was access to the road just about a mile south of town. Dad had promised to drop off our shoes, towels and coverups for us to walk back into town.

As we drifted toward the old railroad bridge, six high school boys appeared on the trestle and stood watching us. Naturally, we kept an eye on them, too, wary that the boys would spit on us or throw something at us. When we got closer, Tuney recognized that four of them were in her class, one was an older brother, and one was a class behind them in my grade. Tommy was one of the four, I remembered, but Tuney hadn't been interested in him then. Even if she had been, our parents wouldn't have allowed her to date. Not until she was sixteen was the rule.

"Was Tommy the one who started yelling at us to take our tops off?" I asked.

Tuney couldn't remember specifically if he had or hadn't. But she recalled that Tommy had joined in the rowdiness.

Tuney laughed out loud. "Cardi, you yelled something like "Only if you drop your shorts!"

"Oh, good grief," I screeched, turning to Tuney and slapping a hand against my forehead. "How could I have forgotten that?" I grabbed my head with both hands in mock dismay. "Ahh!"

"I remember that they ran across to the other side of the bridge and as we floated under them, they mooned us!" Tuney was animated as the memories came flooding back, but she quickly looked around her to make sure we weren't informing the public of our teen escapades.

We were laughing quietly at the memory. I started waving a hand. "Oh! Oh! Now I remember! It was the first time I saw …!" I couldn't complete my sentence. "First time I saw…" and I gurgled trying to hold in the laughter.

"Saw what? What? Say it, Cardi!" ordered Tuney through her giggles. Ever have one of those laughing fits where it's funnier to the spectators watching the one laughing than what it is she's laughing about?

I could feel that my face was red from not only from our hysterics, but embarrassment. "Wait!" I struggled to control myself and took a deep breath. I turned and looked at Tuney, closed my eyes, so her expression wouldn't make me laugh, and announced solemnly, "First time I saw their 'hoo-haws!'"

We both screeched out loud, and cackles, snickers, tears of laughter, and gasps for breath overpowered us. Tuney dug into her purse for tissues, found some and handed one to me.

Tuney looked helplessly around her. "Ope! Stop it, Cardi!" she murmured, as she wiped her face and tried to compose herself. "Why is this so funny now, after all these years?"

I put my hand on my cheeks, and groaned "My face hurts," which caused another outburst of laughter.

"Oh, my!" I sighed when the laughter had finally died down. I wiped my eyes with a tissue. It came away with black streaks. "I probably wasted my time on my makeup again!"

Tuney looked over at Mason House and saw a few people entering the front door for breakfast. "We should probably go, but first I want to know exactly what you mean by a hoo-haw," demanded Tuney, with a wicked gleam in her eye.

"Oh, come on, Tuney. You know!"

"Well, I bet you didn't really see anything other than their rear ends," said Tuney primly.

I straightened up, looked at my sister, and simpered. "You forgot I had a different vantage point than you. You three – was it Kathy, Sue, and Patty?... or maybe Annie was one, but whatever – you three were ahead of me and far enough past the bridge that you couldn't see straight up when the boys dropped their pants. I was just floating out from underneath the bridge and looked up when you guys screamed. I think I got partially blinded!"

Tuney snickered. I opened my eyes wide, took a deep breath and blew out my cheeks as I expelled the air. "So their...uh..."

"Genitalia?" supplied Tuney helpfully.

I reddened again as I pictured what had happened. "Yeah! Someone's hoo-haw was right next to one of the moons!"

We both burst out laughing again. "Good heavens," cried Tuney, when the laughter had subsided. "We're grandmothers! We shouldn't be talking and laughing like a bunch of junior high kids!"

"Why not?" I demanded. "And for the record, I like the name 'hoo-haws' better than 'genitalia!'"

Tuney groaned and rolled her eyes. "I can't believe my sweet Tommy was one of those naughty boys."

I nodded, then I slapped one hand over my heart and said, "But I swear to God, Tuney. I never saw his hoo-haw then. Or ever!" I grinned wickedly. "But I believe he had a cute little moon butt!"

"Cardi!" Tuney giggled again. "Jeepers! Weren't those boys ornery?" She and I stared at the river again and smiled softly as memories flooded our minds.

"Welp," I said turning toward Mason House. "Now I've worked up an appetite with all that laughing."

Tuney draped her arm over my shoulders and we started walking back. "You know you just added a "puh' sound to a word, don't you?"

"I did not, did I?"

"Yup! You said 'Welp!'"

"It's your fault."

"Nope."

"Ope, Tuney!"

And we giggled like little kids as we entered Mason House Inn for breakfast.

Chapter 26

Breakfast in Mason House

We followed the aromatic smells that wafted throughout the first floor and came to the big dining room. The 2Bs2Ts were already seated, and when we walked in, they called out greetings. Tuney grabbed a chair next to Belinda and I sat down next to Larry and Sue on the other side of the table. They'd roomed with Larry's cousin Roger and his wife Pat in the Wild Rose Room that was decorated with Lincoln memorabilia. Amy was seated at one end and another two couples who weren't with our group were also seated.

Joy was just serving a delicious breakfast to everyone. I felt my stomach rumble and was glad to see the portions were generous. Tuney asked Belinda how she and the others had slept.

"Like babies!" Belinda said triumphantly. "You'd think with all the laughing and talking that we'd be so wound up we wouldn't have slept. But I think my head hit the pillow and I was out."

Tammy was next to Belinda and leaned over to talk to Tuney. "It was probably all that wine, and then the walking we did, don't you think?"

Tuney grinned at Tammy. "And don't forget the mountain climbing you did in the caboose!"

Tammy laughed. "Wasn't that crazy? I'm so glad you knew where to find that other bed, or I'd probably still be stuck up there. Come to think of it, the calves of my legs are kind of sore!"

"Eat up, bus tour gang," said Amy good naturedly. "We'll head to Cantril, and then to Eldon. We'll eat lunch around one o'clock or so in Pella. I've got fruit and snacks on the bus if you can't wait 'til then to eat something. But by the looks of the food on these serving plates, I think you're all going to be full!"

Joy had filled the center of the big table with several huge platters and smaller plates. Lemon scones, butter and home-made rose hip jelly, a sausage and egg quiche, hash-browned potatoes, crispy fried bacon, homemade banana bread, a fruit compote with berries and coffee, tea or juice were laid before them.

"Please help yourselves," smiled Joy. "And don't hesitate to ask for seconds. I've got more servings in the kitchen." She turned around and exited the dining room.

The entire table moaned in appreciation, and soon conversation quieted while forks, knives and spoons clinked and clanked on the china plates. As people began to finish and sit back from the table, conversation picked up again.

Joy walked in to clear off the table and was met with a chorus of thank yous and given praise for the delicious breakfast. Sue asked Amy about other trips. Two people who weren't passengers of Amy's listened as she recounted some past tours. They asked her about future tours they were interested in. Chuck walked in and received a chorus of good mornings from everyone. He smiled and asked if everyone had a good night's sleep.

Tuney and I both answered yes, as did most of the others. Larry looked at his wife, then said to Chuck, "I have to be truthful. I'm a little disappointed that we DID have a peaceful night's sleep."

Chuck looked surprised. "Well, I don't normally hear that as a complaint. Why's that?"

Larry got poked in the ribs by his wife Sue. She said, "It's only him. I'm thankful for a nice and restful night's sleep."

Larry smiled. "Oh, I'm glad I slept, too. But I was kind of hoping to meet President Lincoln or some of the Civil War vets who may hang around here. I'm really into history."

Chuck laughed. "Our ethereal guests are the only ones we can't count on to keep a reservation! We never know when they'll make their presence known. Sometimes I think they get their days and nights mixed up and are active in the daytime, instead of when we normally expect to see or hear them – in the night." He excused himself to help Joy in the kitchen and then to go back out to the garden to pull weeds before it got hot.

I was sitting next to Larry and told him Tuney had encountered the child George. Larry looked across at Tuney with interest and asked her to tell him what happened. Tuney shrugged and attempted to make light of it. She explained what had happened, but then added,

"Now, I'm not so sure it was real. You know how sometimes you feel things, but it turns out it's a tag in your clothing, or just a muscle twitch, or even your imagination."

Larry arched his brows. "I don't know, Tuney. Sometimes the unexplained is just that – unexplainable."

Tuney pursed her lips. "Yeah, I get what you're saying, but… well, you know things get exaggerated. Maybe someone once thought they saw something, or heard something, or…"

She was interrupted by a large bang, like a slamming door, upstairs. Everyone at the table quit talking and looked at the ceiling.

"What was that?" whispered someone.

"Maybe Chuck?" someone else murmured hopefully.

Tuney was just about to suggest that someone's door might have blown shut when we all heard the unmistakable sounds of footsteps running above us. Tuney clutched Belinda, and I stared wide-eyed at the ceiling.

Larry looked at his cousin Roger, seated on the other side of Sue, and said, "Let's check it out!" The two men scrambled to push away from the table and Amy jumped up to follow them. Someone giggled nervously. Everyone else sat still at the table, some still looking up at the ceiling. We heard the sounds Amy, Larry and Roger made running up the stairs. Their footsteps were louder than the sounds we'd heard earlier, and we could follow the "hunters" as the three walked around the second-floor hallway and landing. Pretty soon, we heard a little yelp followed by laughing, and then the staircase steps started creaking as the three made their way back downstairs.

Amy came to the dining room first, closely followed by Larry and Roger. They were pelted with questions. Joy poked her head in the dining room to see what was going on. Amy explained we'd been startled by a loud noise, then looked at Larry, and said, "Do you want to tell everyone what happened?"

He grinned. "Well, I thought maybe I'd get to see President Lincoln after all. But we didn't see anything up there but one of the little cats."

"That wasn't a cat that slammed the door," stated Trudy. "I have cats and they do not go around slamming doors."

Roger and Larry chuckled. "I said we didn't SEE anything up there!"

Some of the ladies in the group uttered nervous laughs. Sue frowned at Larry.

"Well, c'mon. What happened up there? Tell us!" she demanded.

Amy nodded. "I'll tell you. There's nothing to be afraid of. You probably all heard us walking up the steps. Or actually running!" She turned to Larry and Roger. "You guys are in super terrific shape! I was panting when I got to the second floor!"

They just grinned and patted each other on the back. Roger's wife muttered, "Oh, brother! Don't egg them on. Rog will probably make me call him Stud-muffin or Superman or something crazy like that now!"

Everyone tittered, then Amy continued. "I tried all the doors, and they were all locked except the Wild Rose Room, which is where Roger, Pat, Larry and Sue stayed. And one of the windows in that room was open, so…"

"So, Sue, you were the last one out, and you forgot to lock the door," finished Larry. Sue just stared at her husband but didn't say anything.

Amy continued. "And as we were going to go back downstairs, here comes one of your little kittens, Joy! It bumped into me and I let out a yell because it startled me. It was scurrying around and around like kittens and cats do. You know, its little back was arched, and it would zig-zag around. I would have brought her down here, but I don't know where she disappeared to!" As she explained, she made motions with her hands to demonstrate the kitten's antics. Then she raised her hands upwards. "So that's that, gang! No ghosts. Larry's still bummed that he didn't get to meet the president, and I was kind of hoping for a sighting. But we had a wonderful time staying here." She turned to Joy. "Thank you so much for everything!"

Larry sat down in his seat between me and his wife, and I overheard Sue as she leaned next to her husband and whispered urgently,

"Larry! I never opened one of the windows. The AC was on all the time! And I locked the door on my way out. I even double-checked it by twisting the doorknob!"

Before I could totally grasp the meaning of Sue's statement, Joy thanked everyone for coming. "But I must mention this, Amy, and I hope it doesn't disturb anyone. We have two full-grown cats. They stay outdoors all the time."

Tuney nodded in agreement and whispered to Belinda. "We saw them outside the caboose last night."

Joy added, "If you saw a very small cat or kitten, and it was gray," she looked at Amy, who shook her head in acknowledgment, "then you saw Josephine."

"Oh, I saw her in one of the windows yesterday morning," I said quietly to Tuney, remembering when we'd stood outdoors admiring Mason House Inn's architecture.

"Oh, what a cute name. Josephine!" said a few of the ladies.

Joy smiled. "Yes. She's playful and harmless. She's been here for as long as I can remember."

Amy frowned at this and said, "Oh, I thought she was only a kitten."

"No. She's a ghost."

Chapter 27

Cantril

*M*r. Smith had loaded everyone's luggage and picked up the passengers from the other B&B, then driven over to Mason House to do the same there. By 9:05 a.m., the bus was on its way to the tiny town of Cantril, Iowa. The group was chatting about Bentonsport, and the Mason House guests were telling the others about their breakfast and the other worldly noises they'd heard during breakfast.

Tuney and I were talking to the 2Bs2Ts about Joy's pronouncement of Josephine, the ghost kitty. Tammy and Bonnie were arguing about whether animals could be ghosts. I told them about watching the *Long Island Medium* on television and how the star, Teresa Caputo, had mentioned animals as spirits.

"I never really thought of stuff like that before Kris died," I told them. "But the older I get, the more I realize how much more in the world there is to learn!"

"Or how much more superstitious we get when we get older," complained Bonnie.

I agreed. "I'll give you that. There are still times I'm walking on a sidewalk and I sidestep a crack!"

"So you won't break your mother's back?" asked Tammy. "Same here! And my mom's been gone for years!"

I then listened in on Trudy and Belinda's conversation with Tuney. They'd tried to talk to Sue afterwards but she was pretty shaken up about her room being unlocked.

"And then to realize her husband had seen a ghost, even if it was just a little kitty – well, she was really upset," said Belinda.

Tuney nodded in agreement. "Well, I won't admit it publicly to others, but I know I was with that George character. Whew! What a roller coaster this has been for me," she confessed. "First I didn't believe in ghosts. Then the episode with George happened, and I thought, 'well, why can't there be ghosts?' Then this morning I convinced myself it was all my imagination, and now after the Josephine episode and the slamming door – well, I think I'm just going to try not think about it anymore!" She settled back in her seat.

Belinda looked at her curiously. "Do you mind if I ask if you've ever wanted to see your husband again? I sure do. I was afraid of ghosts when I was little, and now if my Steve appeared before me right now, I'd be thrilled – and he's been gone for ten years!"

Tuney smiled sadly at her. "Ten years? I'm so sorry. I just made it through the first year and thought it was horrible, so I can't imagine ten whole years – or longer. But yeah, of course I'd give anything to see him again."

Belinda smiled back at her. "Both of you Widsters have a lot to go through yet. I can only promise you that the cliché about time healing all wounds is accurate. You'll never get over losing a loved one. But the pain dulls after a time. And the memories become more and more precious."

Tuney just nodded, not knowing quite what to say. She

turned to look out her window and then craned her neck to see something that was forward.

Amy grabbed her microphone and announced that we were now following a slow moving vehicle. It was a horse pulling a buggy. It was driven by a young Amish man dressed in blue and black with a straw hat covering his head. The buggy had a Slow-Moving Vehicle emblem on the back.

The buggy turned off the main highway, and the bus followed. Tuney and I had slid toward the aisle so we could look forward out the front window.

"Oh, boy. It figures we get behind a slow-moving vehicle. I hope Mr. Smith isn't in a big hurry," I said, fascinated by the buggy. It didn't have a top on it, so we could see just the back of the young man's head, his shoulders and the horse's head.

Just then, Mr. Smith put his turn signal on and carefully passed the buggy, giving it as wide a berth as possible. The noise from the bus didn't seem to bother either the driver or the horse. Amy announced that we would very likely see more horses and buggies.

"The town of Cantril," Amy announced, "is home to the Dutchman's Store, and that's where we'll be stopping soon. From the outside, you'll think it's as old as Greef's General Store in Bentonsport is, but actually it was started in 1985." She described the Dutchman's as a Mennonite-run-owned-and-operated general store that has a wide variety of goods and groceries at very affordable prices. "For you quilters and sewers, there are lots of fabrics. Bakers can buy flour, sugar and spices in bulk. There are canned items like pickled pigs' feet, pickled eggs, and just plain old homemade pickles!"

"Ewww!" I said, squinching my face up as I looked over at Tuney. "I think I've lived okay all these years without pickled pigs' feet!" Tuney grimaced, too, although several people were saying it had been years since they'd had something like that and wanted to buy some.

"I just want to caution you to remember it's August and hot, and unless you buy a cooler and dry ice, you might not want to buy any perishables here."

"Do they sell jerky?" asked one of the men.

"I think so – and something like that is okay. Just nothing that will spoil, please," warned Amy. She glanced over at Mr. Smith, and he nodded vigorously.

As the bus rolled into Cantril, I noticed it was slightly bigger than Bentonsport, but probably not as big as Bonaparte. We soon pulled up to the Dutchman's Store. The first thing I noticed was how busy the street was. Cars, horse-and-buggies, and another bus were parked on both sides, and enough people were walking in and out of the store, the doors appeared to be revolving (which they weren't).

The store's building was huge and, except for a small gas station on one end, was two blocks long and two blocks wide. When Mr. Smith stopped the bus and we debarked, I saw it was three buildings: a tall brick building stood in the middle with a wooden building on each side. A very long wooden front porch ran the entire length of all three buildings. A shake-shingle roof on the porch shaded customers from the heat and served as protection from snow and rain. Wooden railings were connected at each post and a variety of ferns and flowers in baskets swayed in the August breeze, held by hooks from the porch roof. On each building hung a huge white sign that proclaimed in Dutch-inspired font "Dutchman's Store."

As we entered the porch, I was amazed to see all the fresh

produce, flowers and garden tools that lined both sides from one end of the block to the other. I started to look at flowers, but Tuney talked me into going inside first. Big shopping carts were available as we entered the store, and rows upon rows filled with all sorts of bulk and canned foods plus more fresh vegetables and fruits greeted our senses.

"Oh, wow!" murmured one of the 2Bs2Ts. Tuney and Tammy grabbed a shopping cart each, while Bonnie picked up a little basket.

"Which aisle should we start on?" Bonnie turned to ask the others. She was met with surprised looks at her basket. She held it up, said, "No?" and when the others smirked and shook their heads no, she grinned and put it back. "I was going to try to curb my spending, but you know me too well, I guess," she sighed as she grabbed a shopping cart.

As the 2Bs2Ts scattered to various parts of the store, Tuney and I started down an aisle with baked goods. Tuney and I loved seeing Mennonite and Amish women in their plain long skirts or dresses. Their hair was tidily captured with a small white bonnet. It was such a contrast to see them shopping elbow to elbow next to women in shorts and tank tops. It was the same with the men. Some Amish men had beards, some Mennonites didn't, but they all wore straw hats and blue shirts, while black suspenders held up their black pants. Some groups were chatting with local farmers and tourists who were clad in T-shirts, shorts or blue jeans. Some of them wore baseball caps.

"Remember when Mom would wear a dress to go shopping?" Tuney whispered to me. "Seeing the Amish and Mennonites in their dresses makes me feel really underdressed."

"I know, I feel positively naked!" I said. Only I didn't

whisper. Two women in dresses overheard me and looked up, startled. I blushed, gave a quick smile, and turned on my heels back down the aisle.

"Oh, for heaven's sake," muttered Tuney as she tried to turn the big cart around to follow me. She gave up after realizing she might knock into the shelves, so she just pushed it resolutely down the end of the aisle. There, she saw another aisle with bulk flower, sugar and cornmeal. The prices were very reasonable, she told me later, so she put a couple of each in her cart. She also found large bottles of pure vanilla and then spices like cinnamon, garlic powder, cream of tartar and chili powder which she grabbed. In the next aisle, she found me holding three packages containing six dozen cookies total.

I looked relieved when I saw the cart and placed the cookies next to Tuney's spices. I stepped back and surveyed her cart.

"Ah, geez, Tune," I said, only very softly this time. "What are you going to do with all that stuff?" I picked up the 20-pound sack of flour. "When was the last time you baked something?"

Tuney looked hard at the groceries she'd bought, and I could tell from the look of dismay on her face that she realized it was too much. But she wasn't going to admit it. Sticking her chin out, she declared, "I'll share with the kids. And you, if you want."

I just raised an eyebrow. Tuney sighed. "And I could probably put the flour and sugar in the freezer, too, couldn't I?"

I just shrugged and said doubtfully, "I guess. It just seems like a ton of stuff for a person who told me two weeks ago about all the things she threw away when she found bugs in the spices and flour."

"Ope!" she said guiltily. Then resolutely she added, "Well, that's why I need more. I threw the other stuff away. And it's also because I hadn't really cooked much after Tommy," she said. "But I want to start doing that more...maybe." She pursed her lips remorsefully at the cart, then focused on my cookies. "But I guess I could ask you the same thing with all those cookies! You trying to gain some weight?"

I just blinked at Tuney and said drily, "Ha-ha." But I picked up one of the packages and looked at it doubtfully. "Too much?"

It was her turn to raise an eyebrow. I growled, grabbed two packages and walked back around the corner. I returned in a moment, pointed to Tuney's cart, and asked, "Do you need help putting these back?"

Tuney grinned. "It's such a bargain! But you're right. I'll put back everything but the chili powder and the vanilla." She and I returned the bulk items and then Tuney suggested we check out and wait outdoors for the others so we wouldn't be tempted further. Soon we were seated on a bench outside the store, contentedly watching customers walk in empty-handed and leave with enough food to stock – well, a grocery store.

Eventually, the 2Bs2Ts, all laden with bulk items, some toys, craft supplies and fabric, walked out of the store, spied us and sat down with us. They started to show their bargains to me and Tuney, but Bonnie saw the one little sack Tuney was holding.

"Hey! I thought you two were going to buy out the store," she said in surprise. "Did you decide maybe my basket was a better fit than your cart?" She grinned. "I'm glad I switched!"

I answered for Tuney. "She had the cart half-full..."

"I did not!"

"...and then I show up with a measly three little packages of cookies, and she decides I can't have them..."

"Would you quit exaggerating?"

"…so, we compromised, and I kept one pack of cookies and she kept a few spices!"

"*That* part is the truth!" said Tuney. "I think I was so thrilled at the amount you could get for those low prices, that I'm afraid my eyes were bigger than my pantry!"

"Ohhh," murmured the 2Bs2Ts with a touch of remorse as they looked critically at all their stuff.

"Shoot!" exclaimed Belinda. "I wish I'd been with you guys. What in the world am I going to do with ten pounds of cornmeal?" She looked in desperation at the others.

"Probably the same thing I'm going to do with all these peanuts in the shell," said Tammy sorrowfully as she held up a grocery sack full of salted peanuts.

Tuney chuckled. "Oh, I bet you could give those to your kids, Tammy. I know mine love peanuts."

Tammy thrust her bag toward Tuney, who drew back shaking her head. "Take it," Tammy urged. "My kids live far away, and I'll be darned if I spend a fortune on mailing peanuts to them. It'll negate the savings I thought I'd gotten!" She sat back with her bag, looking self-disgusted.

Bonnie and Trudy investigated their sacks. "Well, I at least got craft supplies for my grandkids when they come over, so I know they'll use them up. But I also got a huge tin of cocoa, too."

"And I bought fabric for quilts so that was a good buy," said Bonnie. "But I also bought a whole bushel basket of apples to make pies. And now I'm thinking I'll be lucky if I get one pie made!"

Just then Amy walked out and saw the glum looks on the faces of the Widsters and their friends.

I looked up. "Amy," I said reproachfully. "If you ever take a tour group here again, *warn* them not to get carried away with purchasing bulk items if they're single!"

Amy grinned. "I'm sorry! I should have done that because that's exactly what happened to me the first time I came here. What all'd you buy?" She sat down next to me as the ladies took turns showing her their purchases.

"Wow! And there's no one you can share with at home?" Amy asked.

"I guess I could find someone," said Belinda, doubtfully. Then she perked up. "Hey, you guys can have some! Will you please take some of my stuff?"

"How are you going to divide ten pounds of cornmeal?"

Belinda's face fell. "Didn't think of that. Maybe I should go in and buy some plastic baggies," she said.

"Don't," said Amy. "I have a ton of bags on board. Let me call Mr. Smith. He parked a block away and he can run up here with the bus, pick you guys up and then you can divide whatever purchases you want to. The rest of the busload has about 20 minutes left to shop before we load up and leave for Eldon."

Everyone cheered up at that, and soon Mr. Smith drove up, helped us board, then drove back around to a small parking lot a block south of the Dutchman's Store. Amy had lots of baggies and some plastic grocery bags Bonnie could use to divide the apples. The bulk items were soon divided into eighths, one for each Widster, 2Bs2Ts, Amy, and a pleasantly surprised Mr. Smith.

As I handed him a baggie with some of my cookies in it, I asked him a question. The others heard me ask and moved to the front of the bus to hear.

"You know, this whole trip, I now know most everybody by their first name," I began. Mr. Smith looked up and smiled. "But…"

"But you don't know mine," he said with a wink.

The ladies all giggled. I made a face and then said with an answering smile. "Right. Is it a secret, or do you just prefer to be called Mister Smith?" I asked politely.

He shook his head. "No, I don't mind a-tall telling you my name," he said.

I felt a twinge of guilt about not talking to him before now – almost at the end of our trip. But then again, that might have been because whenever he joined a group of passengers at an outing, he usually talked with the few men who were on board. I smiled apologetically at him.

"Do I detect a slight accent?" Tuney asked shyly. She'd come up behind me and sat down on the seat Amy used. He turned his eyes to hers, and they twinkled with delight.

"Yes, ma'am," he said. "And I thought I was pretty well rid of it. So you have a good ear."

"Accent? I didn't hear an accent," said Trudy.

"Well, I was born in Texas, grew up in Colorado."

"How'd you get to Iowa? And why?" giggled Trudy. "I love Colorado!"

He smiled at her. "Well, I ended up going to Viet Nam when I was 19," he began. Immediately, all our faces grew solemn, and a profusion of thanks to him for his service came in chorus. By the look on her face, I knew Tuney was thinking the same thing I was: We were proud to know quite a few of our high school friends who were veterans from that war. But we also knew several classmates who lost their lives.

He waved it away. "No need to thank me! But thank you all the same," he lifted his head high, and blinked a few times. He cleared his throat and continued, "My buddy and me, well he was from here in Iowa. We hadn't been in Nam too long before we got ambushed one day on patrol."

I had been standing, and now I sank into the seat behind Mr. Smith. He turned around to all of us ladies with a sad smile on his face.

Mr. Smith cleared his throat again, then quickly said, "My buddy, Joe, was killed. I finished out my tour, then just felt I had to go meet his family." Murmurs of sympathy came from the group.

"I don't want to appear hard-hearted, but I sometimes think there was a reason Joe was killed so that I would come to Iowa. You see, when I met Joe's family, his 18-year-old-sister Cindy, well, let's just say I managed not to get captured in Nam, but sure did in Iowa!"

Everybody loves a love story! We all smiled brightly as Tuney said, "Oh, Mr. Smith! You mean you met and married her?"

He beamed. "I sure did. We had three girls and spent 47 years together." He hesitated, then added, "She passed away a few years ago."

Tuney's smiled evaporated. "Oh, I'm so sorry," she murmured. I patted him on the shoulder, while the 2Bs2Ts all empathized with him. Again, he waved away our concerns. "No need. I have no regrets. I've heard so many sad stories from being a bus driver on trips where there are a lot of people who've experienced the loss of a loved one. It kinda helps me, you know?" He looked at us. "I know you're all widows, so you know what I went through, and I know what you went through, and yet here we are – all having a great time and enjoying each day of life. Right?" He smiled.

"Right!" some of us answered. Tuney was silent. I looked over at her with some concern, but when she looked at me, she smiled. Then we all remained quiet, not sure what to say, yet each thinking that we should since we were all survivors of a loved one's death.

Mr. Smith had looked down, then looked up at us again, and smiled. "I have to say that the back of my bus has never held such a bunch as you six with all your laughing and talking."

That broke the ice. We all burst into laughter. "And so, before everyone else returns from shopping, you" – and he pointed at me – "asked me a simple question, and here I've wasted all your time!"

Of course he hadn't wasted our time, but I spoke up. "That's right! I was beginning to think you're quite the Artful Dodger! What is your name?"

He laughed, and then said simply. "Stirt. Stirt Smith."

There was a moment of silence while some of the women cocked their heads trying to understand what he said. Tuney saw his eyes twinkle.

"Pardon me?" she asked. "Would you repeat your first name, please?"

"Stirt."

Tuney looked at him to see if he was kidding, but except for the twinkle in his eyes, his expression was serious.

"Stirt," she repeated.

"Yes, ma'am."

"Rhymes with …uh…skirt?"

"Or dirt."

"Oh!" Tuney had been going to say 'dirt,' but didn't want to sound rude. Now surprised, she fumbled around and finally said, "Well, that's certainly a unique name."

Stirt raised his eyebrows, then slowly shook his head no. "Actually, it's quite common, I believe."

Bonnie chimed in. "You mean, it's a family name?"

Trudy added, "Or do you mean it's common where you're from? I've never heard of it before!"

The others all nodded in agreement with Trudy.

I frowned, and then I thought I got it. "Would you mind spelling your first name?" I said with a grin.

"Not at all," he said respectfully. "S.T.E.W.A.R.T. Stirt."

Someone giggled because, apart from me, everyone else looked totally confused.

"You got us, Stirt," I laughed. "Is that the Texas pronunciation, or the Colorado one?"

He joined in the laughter. "It's actually neither. It's from my older brother when he was little. He couldn't for the life of him pronounce my name any other way than "Stirt." It just stuck, I guess."

There was a chorus of "awwws" from the ladies. The conversation then started to veer towards nicknames. Suddenly Stirt jumped up and said, "Gotta get back to work, ladies! Here comes the whole kit and caboodle!"

Tuney looked out the side window at what appeared to be a mass exodus from the front door of the Dutchman's Store. And it was all headed our way. Stirt exited the bus in order to open the undercarriage for everyone's packages. In about fifteen minutes, everyone and everything was loaded, and the bus took off for the last part of the tour. Tuney and I settled back in our seats. I was getting a little worn out, but I could hardly wait for the next stop on the itinerary. Who'd ever think little Iowa was the home of an internationally known icon?

Chapter 28

American Gothic

*A*my announced that the next stop was only half an hour away in the tiny little town of Eldon. It featured the house in one of the world's most recognized portraits, *American Gothic*. Tuney lazily wondered aloud why it was taking her 65 years to visit such a historic location.

"I remember the time when Tommy and I and the kids drove to visit his grandmother, Esther," she reminisced to me. "She'd fallen and broken her hip and had to move to a nursing home. It was the first time she'd ever been away from her six-bedroom century-old white farmhouse. While her short-term memory wasn't good, her long-term memory was very active. And during that visit, for some reason, Grandma Esther wanted to talk about Nan Wood, the sister of artist Grant Wood. Poor Nan was destined to be forever known as the plain woman in American Gothic.

"'You know I met Nan Wood once,' was the first thing out of Esther's mouth after Tommy hugged and kissed her."

Tuney smiled as she remembered how puzzled she and Tommy were when they looked at each other. "Tommy sat down next to Esther's bed and said, 'Who's Nan Wood, Grammy? Does she live here?'

"She looked hard at her grandson, and said 'Don't you know anything? She's the model in her brother Grant Woods' painting. You know! American Gothic. Good heavens, child. Didn't you learn anything at all in school?'

"Tommy had drawn back, laughing. But I was intensely interested in what Esther had just said. I moved closer to the bed and asked, 'Really, Grandma? How did you happen to meet her?' Esther shot a triumphant look at Tommy, then proceeded to tell us that she happened to be at the Cedar Rapids art gallery where a lot of Grant Woods' paintings are. 'She really is a beautiful woman, not long-necked and plain like her brother painted her,' she said. After that conversation, she visited with us just a little longer before she started to nod off. She passed away a month later, so I never got the chance to talk to her again about Nan Wood and her one-time brush with fame."

"And now you're riding a bus to see the actual house in that very famous painting," I said.

Tuney looked up at the sky. "I wonder if Tommy and his grandmother are watching me from heaven." Then she stared out her window. I didn't think she was asking a question, so I stayed silent. I moved closer to my window and peered out.

The Iowa terrain had shifted from patches of trees around corn or soybean fields to much more woodsy and hilly areas. Tiny towns were entered and passed through almost before we could blink. The little burgs seemed old and worn out without too much activity apparent. I noted that each town had a few things in common: The section of highway that ran through each was named Main Street; each had a library; one or two churches were evident; and still standing were several old Victorian houses that must have been elegant in their day. In one town, an old building that sported a neon sign advertising liquor was right next door to the local church. I wished I had had my camera ready to take that picture – it was such an incongruous setting.

The bus continued and soon we entered Eldon, the little town that housed the iconic farm house with the fancy window that artist Grant Wood made famous. Eldon was only a bit bigger than some of the other tiny towns we'd driven through. Signs to American Gothic pointed the way, and the bus dutifully followed them and turned up a narrow street.

"There it is!" I cried out, pointing out the window when I spotted the gabled roof of the famed white farmhouse.

A large, obviously newer, parking lot that looked as though it could hold over 100 vehicles was in front of a walkway. One path of the walkway led north to the painting's American Gothic house, while the other one led to a beautiful new building that was identified as the American Gothic Museum. Purple coneflowers, sedum, black-eyed Susan, other flowers and some small ornamental trees were featured in a huge garden to one side of the museum.

"Oh, the house looks smaller than it does in the painting, don't you think?" I said as I grabbed my purse and stood up eagerly in the aisle.

"What a nice surprise this is!" said Tuney in delight. "I thought we'd just be driving by the old farmhouse somewhere in the country. I can't believe all the years I've seen the Grant Wood painting of this house, and here it is in person, so to speak!"

"Where should we go first – house or museum?" I asked.

Amy answered my question when she announced that the first section of the bus could go up to the house. A museum curator would be on hand to give them a very special tour inside the house, which wasn't normally opened to the public. The second half of the bus was instructed to go inside the museum and would be called to the house after the first tour was done.

"And don't worry you won't have enough time for photos and browsing. There's lots to see, so we're here for an hour and a half. Then we'll head north, stop in Pella to eat and browse around, then home!" announced Amy. We all cheered and clapped. It kind of surprised me but I was glad to find out that I wasn't the only one ready to get home. *Maybe it's when you know you're going home, you just want to get there as fast as you can,* I thought.

There were a few moans and the 2Bs2Ts turned around to the Widsters. "I can't believe how fast this trip has been," said Belinda. "I'm going to hate to leave you two!"

My thoughts of how good it would be to veg out at home dissipated rapidly. Hearing one of our new friends say she'd miss us hit me hard Since I was standing behind her, I hugged Belinda. "Oh, we are, too! We definitely have to keep in touch." And I truly meant it. I turned to Tuney, and she quickly nodded with a sad pout on her face.

As soon as we exited the bus, we walked up to the museum. To the left of the entrance doors, a replica of the farmer and his daughter were caricaturized in a painted wood sculpture. The 2Bs2Ts went inside, but Tuney paused. Instead of entering the museum, she turned toward the sculpture.

"I say it's selfie time!" she said and trotted over to stand behind the sculpture with her head showing between the two figures. "C'mon, Cardi! We have to document this."

I dutifully followed her and ended up squatting in front of the statue with Tuney behind me. Tuney tried to take a selfie of the two of us with her phone, but finally gave up.

"Here. You have longer arms, Cardi. You try it." She gave her phone to me. After three more unsuccessful tries, we critiqued the photos.

I looked at the pictures and snorted in disgust, just as Bonnie stuck her head out the museum door to see where the Widsters were.

"Oh, good idea!" she said when she saw us by the statue. I opened my mouth to ask if she'd take our photo, but Bonnie pulled her head back in. In a moment, the 2Ts2Bs joined us.

"Let me take your picture, you two," Bonnie said. Tuney and I both said "phew!" at the same time.

"Then we'll take your group," I said. In a few minutes, we had individual photos taken, ones of each group, and then a final attempt of all six of us together. We laughed hysterically at how many times I, with the longest arms, had cut someone's head off, or left out someone on the side. Just when we were going to give up on the group selfie, another couple walked out the museum door and watched us for a minute.

"Would you mind taking a photo of my husband and me, please?" asked the lady. I started laughing and said, "I'd love to if you wouldn't mind taking a shot of us all! My long arms weren't near long enough to do a group selfie!" The other couple happily complied, and we got our first official group shot after all.

Entering the building, we were greeted by a staff member of the museum. She pointed out the room with most of the history, information, photos and statues of American Gothic. On the other side of the entrance vestibule was a gift shop and an open closet full of American Gothic costumes.

"America Gothic, as you can imagine, is the first most parodied piece of art in the United States, and the second most parodied work of art in the world." Tuney murmured to me that she never realized how popular it was in the world. I nodded, then held my finger to my lips so I could hear the curator. Tuney had to smile. It wasn't often I had to shush her up. "The first is the Mona Lisa. We have copies of some of the many parodies, from Sonny and Cher, which you may be young enough to remember (wink, wink) to The Property Brothers from HGTV. You are more than welcome to dress in costume and stand in front of the farmhouse," she told us. "One of our staff will be happy to take a picture of you. And then you can tour the house, if you'd like. We have volunteers who will tell you about the farmhouse, and how Grant Wood came to paint American Gothic."

I clapped my hands in delight. "I want to dress up for sure! This is awesome!" I bubbled. "Look at what we can look like, sis!" I pointed to a photo of tourists posed in costume in front of the house.

"Halloween has always been your favorite holiday, Cardi," said Tuney, as she glanced at the photos of others in costume.

I rolled my eyes at her. "Yours, too. Just not the scary parts, right?" and grinned back. "Let's hurry through the museum part, and then we can get our pictures, okay?"

Tunney smiled. "All right! But I'm not dressing like the farmer!"

Hurrying through the museum was not to be. We spent almost half an hour reading about Nan Wood, the artist's sister who was the model for the daughter, and about the other works of art from Wood that are in an art museum in Cedar Rapids, north of Eldon. As we wandered around the displays,

Tuney shared with the 2Bs2Ts the story of Tommy's grandmother and how thrilled she was to have met Nan Wood. Stories of how Grant Wood happened upon the farm house while visiting a friend who lived in Eldon were available to read. Pictures, statues, and newspaper articles filled the artifacts room. The different couples who lampooned the portrait delighted us, and we laughed at some that depicted the farm couple as Bonnie & Clyde, the Walking Dead, and rock stars. One of the parodies was of Iowa native turned star Tom Arnold and his then-wife, comedienne Roseanne Barr.

"I forgot Tom and Roseanne lived near here!" exclaimed Tuney.

I frowned, trying to remember something I'd read about them. "I think they started to build a home, but didn't, or else it got stopped in the middle of construction," I said. "It was in the '90s."

"I loved Tom in the movies, especially with Jamie Lee Curtis and Arnold Schwarzenegger – I forget what it's called, though – and I saw Roseanne open for an act at the Iowa State Fair once before she got really famous and was a TV star. She was so funny!" said Tuney. She took her camera and snapped a picture of their parody.

"You're nuts, Sis," I said. I started to look around and moved toward another aisle.

"I don't care. Next to John Wayne, who else besides Tom Arnold is a famous Hollywood movie star from Iowa?" demanded Tuney.

The 2Bs2Ts turned and started supplying names. The answers were rapid and punctuated with laughs as I Googled "movie stars from Iowa" to add more names.

"Donna Reed. Ashton Kutcher. Johnny Carson. Adam DeVine," began Tammy.

Bonnie interrupted. "Oh, yeah! And Ronald Reagan lived here for a while."

"Uh, Aquaman Jason Momoa and Superman Brandon Routh – both from Norwalk!" I read. "And there's Danai Gurira on Walking Dead. It's TV but I'm counting her as a star!"

"I almost forgot. Cardi, what about Bilbo Baggins – or was it Frodo in *The Lord of the Rings*? Does Google say?" asked Tuney.

I held my hand up. "It's Elijah Wood and he was Frodo," I said. I put my phone away. "You know that's quite a few from Iowa."

"Well, everyone in Hollywood has to come from someplace. Why not here? We've got talent!" asked Tammy. She paused to take another parody photo, this time of Madonna and Sean Penn.

Just then the curator walked in. She was smiling and said, "I'm sorry, but I overheard you listing famous actors. This is off the subject, but Iowa has famous musicians., too. Maybe you'd be interested in the Bix Beiderbecke Jazz Festival someday. It's usually in late July or early August. It's held only a couple of hours from here in Davenport."

"Oh, really? I love jazz," said Tuney to the woman. "And we were just up at Dubuque on this trip but not Davenport. So, we'll need to come back this way," she said. "There's been so much to see in just a few days that I can't believe it!"

"And we still have to see the house," I chipped in. "Plus, I want to get in costume and take our pictures in front of it."

The curator smiled and suggested that we would have time to do that before the house tour was done, if we could get dressed quickly. We talked to her about the museum, the town of Eldon, and then told her a bit about ourselves as we grabbed our costumes.

"For grown women, we're having as much fun playing dress-up as we did when we were little," declared Tuney. She got to be Nan and I was in the farmer's clothes.

"I know," I agreed. "But behave, or I'll stick my pitchfork in your fanny."

Tuney turned to the curator and said, "Please tell me that's fake." She took a step back from me in mock fear.

The curator smiled, but hesitated, then said, "We haven't had any accidents, intentional or not, yet. So please don't be the first!"

Once we'd put the costumes on over our own clothes, we pulled our cameras out again. The curator handed me a pair of rimless glasses, stood back, and gave us two thumbs up.

Another volunteer at the museum asked us to follow her. We walked outdoors on some pavement that led to the house. There another volunteer directed us to stand in a certain spot so that we were in the same position as the models in the American Gothic painting. She then took as many poses as Tuney and I wanted. We tried looking as somber as the models but ended up deleting those. Our American Gothic picture is all smiles!

"This was so much fun. I'm glad we're here, and if I haven't said it before, thanks for talking me into this trip," Tuney said to me as she checked her photo gallery while we walked into the museum to take off the costumes.

I just smiled. She had no idea how thrilled I was that she was with me.

Just then the half of our bus passengers who had toured the American Gothic house entered the museum. Amy announced that our group should head over to the house right away. As Tuney and I and the 2Bs2Ts walked over, a voice behind our group asked politely, "Do you funny ladies mind if I join you?" We all turned around.

"Stirt!" I cried. "Of course, you can join us!" He grinned, and cavalierly offered the two ladies who were bringing up the rear, Belinda and Trudy, one of his elbows each.

I immediately took a picture to capture the huge smiles on their faces. Belinda asked him if he'd gotten to get his picture taken in costume. He laughed.

"Yes, as a matter of fact, Amy and I posed together," he said. He stopped for a minute to take out his camera. We crowded around him as he showed us his and Amy's version of the farmer and daughter. Amy was wearing the coveralls and holding the pitchfork, and Stirt was in the dress looking solemnly to the side just as Nan Wood did when she modeled. It was hilarious, and we all burst out laughing.

"Hey, Stirt," said Bonnie. "You fit right in with us Widsters. I love your sense of humor!"

"But we can't call him a Widster," protested Tammy as we walked closer to the house.

"No," I said. "If he's in our group we have to call him something. But what?"

Tuney piped up. "How about the Widsters and Widbro?"

Stirt chuckled. "That's better than a wid-ther. That sounds like a lispy Widster!"

"Widther! I like that," laughed Tuney. "Reminds me of that little neighbor girl of mine. She was adorable. Her name was Lisa Susanne Smothers, remember, Cardi?"

I grinned because I knew where her story was heading. "I remember! She was a darling little girl."

"Why does *widther* remind you of a little girl?" asked Belinda curiously.

Tuney hastened to explain. "When they moved in to us next door, she'd evidently spotted my kids out playing. One Saturday this tiny little thing marched up on our porch when we were all home. She rang the doorbell, and when I answered, she said, "Hi! My name ith Litha Thuthan Thmotherth. Can I pleath play with thoth kith?' and she pointed at the boys and Heidi." Tuney laughed. "It was all I could do to hide my smile. She was so frickin' sweet. I think she was just four. But anyway, I told her yes, and then ran some cookies I'd baked for the newcomers over next door. I introduced myself to Lisa's mom and told her Lisa was in our yard playing. I was surprised when her mom looked a little concerned. She told me Lisa had been picked on for her speech and if the way she talked bothered my kids, to please send her home."

"Oh, poor thing," remarked Trudy. "Why didn't they get her some speech therapy?"

"Exactly," said Tuney. "I told Mrs. Smothers that I was a teacher and asked her if Lisa had ever had any speech therapy. Turns out they'd moved here from someplace in the West Virginia area, remote, I guess, from places that could provide extra help for anyone who needed it. But long story short, once they got settled, they did find a speech therapist, and by the time she was ending first grade, Lisa was pretty well over her lisp."

"Oh, good," said Stirt. "I know how hard it is on a kid to be made fun of."

We all looked at him questioningly. He pointed at his chest. "My name. Stirt Dirt. Or Dirty Stirty. I hated it. But once I learned to tell them I was Stewart, but that my brother always called me Stirt, then the kids were okay with it. And they'd call me Stirt without making fun of me just because they liked the sound of it better than Stewart."

"Well, Tuney, whatever became of little Lisa? She's probably in her upper thirties by now, isn't she?" I asked.

"She is. She's the same age as Heidi," answered Trudy. "And the neat part of the story is that she became a speech therapist. I think she's somewhere in Illinois – in a Chicago suburb, I believe."

Before we could talk anymore, the other passengers joined us on the porch. We all quieted down as the curator started talking about the American Gothic House. She told us it was built around 1882 and was owned by a Mr. Dibble. Hence, it had been known for years as the Dibble House. The design of the house, she said, was Carpenter Gothic, also known as Rural Gothic.

"I imagine you see this style everywhere and don't even realize it," said the curator, with a name tag that read Cheryl. "It's like Gothic architecture but uses all wood instead of stone."

She noticed some people frowning as they tried to picture her description. She hastily added. "Think of Notre Dame Cathedral in France, or Westminster Abbey in London. They're both great examples of Gothic Architecture." I could tell that explanation turned the lights on in a few heads, and Cheryl continued.

"Rural or Carpenter Gothic is something you see in homes and churches. But instead of all the stone used by European builders to build Notre Dame, the builders in America used wood because it was easier and cheaper. To jazz it up, the carpenters used pointed arches, steep rooflines and gables, arches on the windows and even towers. Usually you don't find all those elements in one home, but some fancier homes did use them all.

"In this home, Grant Wood was struck by how pretentious the Gothic window looked in this otherwise tiny little home. He happened to be attending an art exhibition by Edward Rowen. Another artist friend of Wood's who lived in Eldon named John Sharp drove Wood around the area. Wood had Sharp pull over so he could sketch the house. He later used his dentist Dr. B. H. McKeeby and his sister Nan as models for the farmer and his daughter."

"Daughter?" asked someone in the crowd. "I always thought it was the farmer and his wife."

Cheryl laughed. "I think more people think that than know it's meant to portray the dad and daughter. But since Nan Wood herself claimed she posed as the daughter, that's the story we stick with here."

She had us all step off the porch and back up to see the window. "There are actually two of these windows, this one up front, and an identical one in the back. The lace curtain in the front window is not the same as the curtain pictured in the painting. That's because that curtain was from Wood's imagination!"

We all oohed and aahed about that fact. Cheryl continued. "When we get inside, you'll be able to walk up the staircase that leads to the upper level. Please be very careful because the staircase is narrow. Try to imagine moving a bed or dresser upstairs. It would be super difficult! So, while the artist may have perceived these windows as 'pretentious,' they are very functional. They're hinged on the side. This allows people to move large furniture in and out through the windows much easier than it would be if they were plain windows that moved up and down with sashes, or even no windows at all. And while the historical society doesn't have exact proof, it's believed that Mr. Dibble ordered the windows out of a Sears and Roebuck catalog!"

Stirt commented to one of the other bus passengers loud enough for us to hear, "And sad to think that someday the curator will have to explain exactly what a Sears and Roebuck catalog is!"

"No kidding," came the even louder reply. Tammy giggled, and Cheryl, who'd also heard, ducked her head to hide a smile.

"Now if everyone will follow me into the house, the tour will continue." She led us through the front door.

Once inside, we found we were in the front room. It had a wooden floor, a front and a side window and was quite tiny, I thought. As we passed through an opening into an even smaller room that was the dining room, Cheryl had us turn to the left to the side room that served as the kitchen. It was updated, cheery, but also small. A door opened to a beautiful brick patio in the back. I could see an old-fashioned clothesline outside, too.

"Is there an outhouse here?" I asked Cheryl, wondering if the "original" was still intact.

"There used to be," she answered. "It was a farm and at that time, it was out in the country, so that was pretty much a given in the 19th century. But when they remodeled this area for the kitchen, look what they added!" Next to the opening that led to the dining was a door. She opened it with a flourish and said, "I think you could call this outhouse-size, but it's a thoroughly modern, tiny sliver of a bathroom." The 2Ts2Bs, Tuney and I crowded around for a peek. There was the smallest bathtub I'd ever seen. We all exclaimed over it. "Well, at least no one has to run outdoors anymore," grinned Cheryl.

After examining the kitchen and looking out the windows, we went back into the parlor or dining room. A window on the north side looked out to the back yard. A door was next to the window but appeared to be locked. To the east was another window. Cheryl walked toward a door near the east wall. To our surprise, she opened it and we saw the stairway.

"You're welcome to go upstairs," she announced, "but keep in mind that people in the 1880s must have been a lot smaller than we are today. You have to almost crawl up the stairs in order to keep from hitting your head on the stairwell ceiling." She demonstrated walking bent over, and we all laughed.

"Isn't that our normal way of walking?" teased Bonnie.

Cheryl laughed with us. "Well, if it wasn't before, it will be now. I'll stay down here to let groups of four go up and come down. There just isn't room on the stairway for one person to go up while one comes down." The 2Bs2Ts got in a line and slowly made their way up the steps. Tuney and I heard a thunk, followed by a cuss word, and knew Bonnie had made contact with the ceiling. We giggled.

"I can hear you laughing at me, Widsters," came a call from up the stairs.

"Are you okay?" I called back.

"Yes, but oh my goodness, it's even tinier up here than downstairs," came the reply.

"She's right," said Cheryl. "The stairway takes you to the back of the house. I think that room might have been used as a bedroom, but it wouldn't be comfortable with the slanted roofline. There's a tiny little closet there. When this house used to be rented out, it was usually to a single dweller who used that room as a closet and slept in the front bedroom. It's the front bedroom that has the famous window in it."

"Oh, wow! So, this isn't rented out anymore?" Tuney asked. "It would be fun to say you lived in American Gothic!"

"It'd be real fun if you did and had to call me to come extricate you from that little bathtub," I said sarcastically.

Cheryl laughed. "We only rent it for special events, now, like a conference or maybe a wedding reception," she explained. "I don't know if you ever heard of the pie lady," she continued, "but a young woman named Beth Howard rented this for four years. She's written books about pies, and she used to bake them to sell to tourists who came here. I think she was the last renter. When I spoke to her once, she had quite a few stories to tell about having to put up with tourists. They'd stop by at all hours of the night to pose in front of the house. The noise they made would wake her up if she slept with the window open. Sometimes during the day, they would march right inside her home if she hadn't locked her door."

"Oh, goodness," said Tuney, aghast at the thought of people being so rude. I gave her a look that she read correctly, and answered with a little grin: If there hadn't been this tour, she'd have been peering in every window and trying out the doors to see if she could get in. As I said before, we both loved old historic homes. Tuney especially loved being inside them.

Cheryl nodded. "But the worst part is that sometimes she found snakes and other creepy, crawly things that scared her."

"Ewww," Tuney and I both said in unison. "That would have been it for me!"

Cheryl was apologetic. "Me too. But the historical society didn't have much money at first, which is why we rented it out. Now with social media, I'm proud to say we get a lot of donations, have successful fundraisers, and lots of volunteers to be able to keep both the house and museum going so everyone can enjoy and be part of this iconic work of art."

We heard the steps creak, and soon Belinda, Bonnie, Trudy and Tammy exited the staircase.

"What did you think of it?" asked Cheryl.

"So tiny, but to look through the lace curtain and view that window from inside was amazing," said Trudy.

They urged Tuney and me to go upstairs, so along with another couple who weren't from our bus tour, we did. The staircase was cramped, but we made it without bumping our heads. At the top, we could look out the north Gothic window and see the beautiful lawn and trees in the backyard. Turning, we headed into the south front bedroom. The lace curtains that covered the window were sheer enough we could see out and watch some of our friends on the bus tour getting their pictures taken.

"Should we open this curtain and photo bomb them?" I suggested. I started to reach for the curtain, but Tuney grabbed my hand.

"Act your age, Widster," she warned, then smiled apologetically at the other couple who were eagerly watching me to see what I'd do.

"Ope! Sorry," I said to them. "Sometimes I feel more like six than sixty."

"You're older than that," argued Tuney.

"Not by much! You're older than me!" I retorted

I looked at the couple and saw them grinning. "Sorry again!" I said.

"Oh, don't be," the woman said hastily. "We've been on vacation without the kids. I was missing them, but you just reminded me how nice it's been without the squabbling." She smiled up at her husband, and they left us standing with our mouths open, staring at them as they headed back downstairs.

Tuney blinked first and looked at me. "Did she just …?" she asked quietly.

I looked at Tuney with my mouth still open. "Dis us? Geez. I don't know. I don't think she meant to, but wow! When someone young enough to be our child thinks we're squabbling, like little kids, that's…that's bad, isn't it?"

"Not to mention embarrassing!" said Tuney matter-of-factly. Then she pulled my hand. "Well, Brat, we'd better follow them. But we really didn't squabble that much, did we?"

I tried to think back to what I said, and then muttered, "You know, I think I take offense at what she said. We were just joking!"

Tuney snickered. "I agree, but c'mon, we gotta get outta here."

"Hang on one sec," I demanded. I scooted over to the window and saw that the young couple was walking toward the museum. The husband turned around to look back at the house. Impulsively, I stuck my hand near the window.

"Cardi, don't you dare…" Tuney started. Too late! I'd already flipped him the bird. It was only later on the bus, when someone several rows ahead of us was looking through photos she'd taken of American Gothic's exterior, that I discovered my finger had been caught on camera. Thank heaven they couldn't tell whose it was!

We saw Amy when we entered the museum through the gift shop and found out we still had about twenty minutes before the bus left.

"I want to buy some gifts while we're here!" I said eagerly. The gift shop was filled with American Gothic everywhere. Besides books about Grant Wood, his models, and Iowa history, there were artist's prints, shirts, socks and aprons. Baby bibs, book markers, tins filled with mints, Christmas ornaments, posters jewelry, pens and pencils were also available. All had either the words 'American Gothic' or the painting's picture featured. My enthusiasm quickly spread to Tuney, and soon we were picking up gifts for the grandchildren, a few friends and even the mailman, our doctor, dentist, and hairdresser.

Finally, Tuney declared that we'd better quit shopping to save some space in the car once we got back to Des Moines. She ordered me to check out and load up. Each of us had one large sack filled with American Gothic memorabilia. As we headed back to the bus to put our purchases away, I sighed.

"This was so much fun! But don't let me buy anything else this trip, okay?" I paused searching through my sack and looked ruefully at Tuney.

"You'd better be glad this is the last shopping stop," she replied, looking into her sack, too. "Make that *we'd* better be glad!"

"I know. I get carried away. But I figure if it's taken me over sixty years to make it here once, I probably won't be around in another sixty years, so I may as well buy up all the souvenirs I can." We started to laugh, and I added, "Plus that's another reason why widowhood might not be too bad. Would the guys have let us buy all these treasures?"

"Tommy'd have rolled his eyes so much, they probably would still be wobbling in his eye sockets," Tuney said solemnly, and then giggled. Then she added, "Well, unless there's a gift shop at the restaurant in Pella, I think we're done being able to shop."

"There are tons of stores in Pella," I warned. "Cute little boutiques with Dutch lace and wooden shoes, delicious bakeries, meat markets, antique shops, and…"

Tuney's groan interrupted me. "No, Cardi. I don't know how we'd get anything else on the bus, let alone into my car." She motioned with her sack toward our bus.

Stirt was waiting there for the tour passengers to return. He had the cargo hatch open, and I was surprised to see how much the other passengers had stowed there.

"Jeepers, Stirt," I said in dismay. "I had no idea we'd all done so much shopping. Where are the suitcases? Did you have to leave them behind?"

He laughed. "Nope! Got plenty of room." He took our sacks, tied name tags on each one, and set them carefully in the hatch.

"You're sure there's plenty of room? So we can shop in Pella if we want?" I asked hopefully.

Stirt grimaced in mock horror. "You may have to hitch a ride with someone else to get home, but I think we'll be okay. In the meantime, ladies, you're good to go!" We thanked him and climbed back on board. The 2Bs2Ts were already seated, and we spent time visiting and sharing each other's photos.

Amy was the last to board the bus. She quickly counted heads, and we headed north to Pella. Our itinerary was to have lunch, about an hour to walk around, and then back to the parking lot in Des Moines. The last leg of our journey was almost here.

Chapter 29

Pella Lunch

*A*n hour after we left Eldon, Stirt pulled the bus into the beautiful town of Pella and we parked along the town's center. Lunch was on the east side of the square at a meat market/restaurant, and we crowded in. Tuney and I found a big table on the second story floor so that the 2Bs2Ts could sit with us.

The realization that the trip was almost over sunk in. All six of us widowed friends sat at a table, talking about what we were going to do tomorrow when we didn't have an itinerary to follow.

"Laundry," supplied Tuney glumly. "After Tommy died, the first time I did laundry, I thought I would probably hardly ever do it again. I always did laundry at least once a week, and I still do, even though it's only me now. Turns out, I'm the one who went through clothes the most."

Bonnie looked amazed. "Oh, for heaven's sake. You know, I never thought about that, but that's the same thing for me. And it's been over ten years. Why is that, I wonder?"

"You mean why is it that it took you ten years to realize, or why is it we women have the most laundry?" teased Tammy.

That started a flurry of confessions and questions that would have embarrassed our husbands…Or not, come to think of it. We all shared examples of why women's laundry is greater than men's.

"Guys wear whatever they can find lying on the floor," Belinda contributed. "I figured that one out my first week of marriage!"

"It took me a while when I folded clothes to realize I had five pairs of my undies compared to only two of his," confessed Tammy. That drew comments of revulsion, but we all admitted to experiencing the same thing.

"It's because men, at least my husband, don't put their dirty clothes in the hamper!" exclaimed Trudy. She grinned and reminisced. "I'd find his socks under the living room chair, a bath towel still damp put back in with the dry towels in the linen closet, and sweaty T-shirts in the garage where he'd taken them off when he got hot working."

"What about winter clothes?" asked Belinda with a smirk. "I always had to ask Steve to put his stocking cap, gloves and coat in the laundry to wash, and he'd look at me like I was crazy!" She grimaced. "He never thought he could get sweaty while it was freezing outside. He must have lost his ability to detect odors because he never could smell the oil and gasoline on his coat and gloves from his snowblower."

Trudy nodded. "My Jack was always willing to help me with housework," she said drily. "But it drove me crazy when he'd just put an entire pile of dirty clothes in the washer instead of sorting them by colors and whites. I hate to sound like I'm complaining, but then he'd fold the laundry by just folding things in half! Technically, I supposed he *folded* the laundry, but not like how I do it. I lay a pair of socks together and then pull the cuffs down over to keep the pair together. The T-shirts I lay flat, fold the sleeves in on the side, and then fold that rectangle in half lengthwise. Then I fold it into thirds."

"I always fold clothes that way, but then I always rolled the undies and T-shirts so that I could see the colors more easily, especially when the kids were little," added Bonnie. "It made more room in the chest of drawers, too."

"Husbands must be why clichés were invented," I mused. "If you want something done right…"

"Do it yourself!" the rest chimed in together. We burst out laughing, and some of the other passengers, looked at us with grins, wondering what was so funny.

We'd finished our lunches by then. Amy walked by and stopped at our table to see how our meal was. She looked at her watch and told us we'd have an hour and a half to wander around Pella. The 2Bs2Ts hadn't been to Pella before, and it had been many years for me. Amy listed the many things we could do that were within several blocks of the bus: The klokkenspel around the corner, the Vermeer windmill, the opera house, the historical village featuring Wyatt Earp's childhood home, and the Scholte House gardens and museum.

"Or, if you haven't gotten enough to eat on this trip," our groans interrupted her and she chuckled, then went on, "stop at a bakery. And check out any of the cute little shops. There are lots of Dutch souvenirs you can buy if you want to."

We all looked at each other and grinned. "Well…" began Bonnie.

"Noooo!" some of us said, but as one, we all grabbed our purses and got up from the table.

We decided to split up because Tuney and I wanted to walk over to Scholte House to see the gardens. At least I did. Tuney just sighed. As we exited the restaurant, we spotted Larry and Sue across the street at the windmill-shaped visitor information center that was located on one corner of the park. We crossed over and joined them.

"How was your lunch?" I asked.

Larry patted his stomach. "Filling. Just like everything else has been on the trip. "

"I know," I groaned. "I don't think I'll eat any supper tonight when we get home."

Sue looked at Larry and smiled. "He just bought some dried beef, jerky and beef sticks. I think that's going to be his supper. I just want a salad!"

The volunteer at the center was friendly and she asked us if we had any questions. When our kids were young, Tuney and I had taken them together to Pella's Tulip Festival one day early in May. I remembered vividly that tulips were everywhere – in front of people's private homes, in planters around town, and in beds in this very park, as well as Scholte House gardens. Now that it was summer, I could see that here in the park the tulips had been replaced with petunias, sweet potato vines, begonias, marigolds, zinnias and other plants. The colors were as pretty as the tulip beds had been

"What happens after the Tulip Festival?" I asked. "Do you have to dig up all the spent tulips?"

She nodded. "We do! It's a labor of love, but it's so worth it! Our city parks department plants around 120,000 bulbs every fall in well over 200 flower beds. We also have pots and hanging flower baskets. The tulip bulbs come in many varieties, usually around 70 or so, and we plant a variety of early, mid and late blooming bulbs, especially since the weather can vary quite a bit. A week or two after the tulip festival ends, the last of the late bloomers are dying out, so we eventually replace the bulbs with."

She pointed to some of the gardens in the park. "We used over 28,000 annual flowers and plants to keep the town colorful into late summer. Not as many plans as the tulip bulbs, but I think it looks pretty."

"Oh, it certainly does!" I breathed. "I'm so glad you do all this. It's beautiful." I turned to Tuney. "Let's walk through the park and visit the Scholte gardens."

"Okay, okay. But I thought you wanted to redo your garden like the Bentonsport garden."

"Oh, I do," I assured her. "But I love all gardens, and maybe there's something at Scholte that I can incorporate with what inspired me at the sunken garden."

We wandered down the middle of the park that led north. Even though the park is in the center of the business district, it was serene and peaceful. Traffic, both pedestrian and auto, was light. Before we crossed the street to the Scholte House Gardens, there was a large water fountain with four tiers built on a round tower of bricks. The water from the tiers trickled down into a little moat encased by a larger circular wall built of bricks. An iron fence surrounded the interior of the brick wall.

"Oh, Cardi! I remember this fountain from when Tommy and I brought the kids when they were little to Pella once after the tulip festival was over. We threw pennies into the water!" exclaimed Tuney in delight.

I peered through the fence where a burbler moved the fountain's water in a lazy circle around its base. "Count inflation now. It looks like people are throwing dimes and quarters, too!"

Tuney peeked in and then frowned. "I don't remember this fence, though. I think I remember the kids wading in that moat, Joey came out with a fistful of coins, wanting to use them to make wishes. Tommy told him they'd already been used to make wishes on, so they weren't any good anymore!"

"And he bought that?" I said incredulously. "Joey's too smart for that!"

Tuney chuckled. "Tommy regretted telling him that because Joe threw all the coins back in and then demanded more money from Tommy because he had 'lots and lots and lots o'wishes to make, Daddy!' he said!"

Tuney smiled at the memory and rubbed her hand slowly up and down one of the bars of the fence as she wistfully continued. "And Heidi and Scott started running around the base of the fountain. They were splashing and screaming and just having tons of fun." Then she looked around and whispered to me, "Until a cop drove up, that is. He asked Tommy and me if those kids were ours, and Tommy told him maybe!"

"*Maybe?*" I threw back my head and laughed. Tommy had been the epitome of a law-abiding citizen, and I could just picture him realizing that his kids might be getting him in trouble. "What happened next?"

"The cop looked at Tommy and then started grinning. 'Well, *if* they are, please get them out of the water. The city council doesn't want anyone getting hurt and suing the city. And if they're not, I'll probably just stick 'em in my patrol car and take them to the park that has playground equipment they can burn off their energy!' Then he winked at Tommy, they shook hands and he left. While they were talking, I'd been trying to grab the kids and they were screaming and hollering, until they heard the policeman say he'd put them in his car, and that shut them up! I think that man must have been a father. Or else he just pitied us!" She shook her head at the memory and grinned.

"Well, if this fence means anything more than just aesthetics, then I'd say your kids weren't the only ones who waded here. You put water anywhere near where a kid can play in it, it's too much of a temptation."

"You're probably right. Plus, I think the coins thrown in are donated to a charity. I'm sure before the fence, plenty of people like Joey took out more coins than are put in, so it's probably a necessity."

We started to walk across the street, and Tuney turned back for another glance at the fountain. "Too bad, though. It made for a wonderful memory to see them having such fun!"

I barely heard her because I spied the neatest statue. There at the entrance to the Scholte Garden stood a beautiful bronze creation of a Dutchman standing by his bicycle to fill up his pipe. He wore a cap, had a scarf loosely tied around his neck, wore a jacket and loosely fitted trousers. One foot was planted firmly on the ground, while his other rested on one of the bike pedals. The bicycle was plain but with a basket on the front. The details of the sculpture were amazing, and I made Tuney take a picture of me standing next to the model.

The flowers were now gone, but the entrance past the statue featured magnolia and redbud trees as we entered the gardens. Unlike the sunken rose garden in Bentonsport, this one had pathways made of bricks. I liked how they meandered around each bed of flowers. In the spring, these plots would be filled with all sorts of tulips. In August, the shaded gardens next to the house were filled with sedum, daylilies, ferns, coralbells and hostas. In sunnier sections, there were lots of geraniums, each filled with one color. There were pink, salmon, bright red and white, and I told Tuney that I honestly couldn't pick which garden was the prettiest. Other flower beds held red, white and blue petunias, some sported dwarf sunflowers and sorghum, and others had blue delphinium and pink foxglove. I snapped pictures of them all, and at different angles.

Tuney watched me patiently, then asked me to take her picture standing next to another bronze statue. This one was a Dutch woman carrying a flower basket. A little girl shyly peeked around from behind the woman's legs. Both were wearing traditional Dutch bonnets and long dresses. A little boy was offering two tulips to the lady, who was smiling and reaching her free hand to take them. I took Tuney's picture, then had her take mine – this time crouched as low as my often-achy knees would bend and peeking from behind the woman's skirt.

Tuney dutifully took the photos, then dryly commented that we had about 45 minutes left. "If you're through posing, do you mind if we walk over to the bakery? I want to get some Dutch letters."

I didn't mind one bit, I told her, so we crossed the street back to the park, and this time walked to the south side of the central park square. It was no great feat to find a bakery – we just followed the delicious aromas.

"Criminey sakes," I said to Tuney as we entered one of the two bakeries on the block. "How is that I'm as conditioned as Pavlov's dog to drooling whenever I smell anything loaded with calories?" The bakery cases were full of every kind of baked good that I would describe as delectable. There were

sugar and almond cookies, decorated with colorful icing. There
were assorted bar cookies – and for some reason, my eyes
settled on the pecan pie bar immediately. There were different
breads, some frosted and some not, but smelling of apple and
cinnamon. There were cakes and homemade candies, and
Tuney's favorites: S-shaped Dutch letters, flaky and filled with
almond paste.

I stood for a minute, then surprising both myself and Tuney,
I told her I'd wait for her outdoors. *Maybe the temptation
wouldn't be so great if I had a brick wall between me and the
decadent baked goods,* I thought. Outside the store was a bench,
and I sat relaxed, watching curiously as people walked by. I
thought my little home town had the friendliest people in it,
but the folks here, half of whom were probably tourists, were
every bit as pleasant. *Come to think of it,* I thought, *I haven't
been any place that wasn't overly friendly on this trip.*

For a trip that I'd hoped would get Tuney's mind off Tommy
so she could quit grieving, I found it odd that it had made me
think more often of Kris than I had let myself do for a long
time. I saw a man across the street walking with a woman, and
he reminded me of my Kris. He was tall, had dark hair with
quite a bit of grey in it and was talking and smiling down at
the lady. A moment later, an elderly couple came walking past,
and they were both holding hands. I smiled as we made eye
contact, and the gentleman nodded back with a smile as his
wife waved at me with her free hand. A wave of regret that
Kris and I would never be that "elderly" together hit me, and
I felt those dreadful tears that had plagued me this trip start
to burn my eyes.

But by the time Tuney exited the store and joined me on
the bench, I'd blinked them away and was able to act like

nothing had happened. She opened one of three bags she bought.

"Whadja buy?" I asked, using one finger to open the top of the largest sack a little wider.

"One for you," she replied. She reached into the sack, pulled out a large S-shaped pastry and handed it to me. Then she pulled out another one and said, "And one for me!"

"Tuney! I don't need this," I protested. The pastry was grasped firmly in my hand, though.

She shrugged and reached over to take it back, but I drew away. "I said I don't *need* this, not that I won't eat it!" She just grinned.

After we had indelicately devoured the Dutch letters, we stood up. "Where to next?" I asked.

We decided to walk toward the klokkenspel. That meant passing one of Pella's several meat markets and another bakery. I hesitated when we reached it, then told Tuney to wait a minute. I walked out a few minutes later with an assortment of freshly made, melt-in-your-mouth delicious sugar cookies made with cream cheese, frosted with the best almond frosting I'd ever eaten.

"I just saw your will-power hightailing it out of town," said Tuney as I gave her a cookie.

"Shut up. You started it, so it's your fault. At least I tried to avoid temptation!" I bit into one of the cookies. "Mmmm! This is sinful, but heavenly, at the same time!"

Tuney grinned and we contentedly strolled on eastward across the street to the middle of the next block to the building that housed the klokkenspel.

The klokkenspel was amazing. A big clock faced the street. It was almost three o'clock – the time that the bells' four-foot mechanical characters representing Pella's history would perform. Beneath the clock was an entrance through some archways into a little courtyard. Beautiful murals were on the walls of buildings on either side, and there were several S-curved benches for people to sit and watch the show. At three o'clock, bells chimed the time, then began playing some music as the mannequin-like figures appeared directly below the clock behind a little glass rectangle. The dolls moved about performing a little story about the history of Pella. All the while the bells pealed their music. In ten minutes, the delightful show was over.

"Oh, that was so neat! I'm glad we saw it," said Tuney. "I took some pictures to show the little kids when I get home." She placed her phone back in her purse, looked at the tower clock and said, "Time for us to get back to the central park where the bus will be."

There were quite a few people from our tour near the klokkenspel. We joined them and made it back to the restaurant to cross over to the bus, right as Amy came out.

Stirt was at the bus, and I could see that the 2Bs2Ts had boarded already. Amy herded us across the street and counted heads as we climbed aboard. We settled down for one last quick ride on the tour.

Now that we were through with the tour, I just wanted to get back home as fast as possible. That is, until Belinda and Tammy turned around in their seats to talk to me.

"Cardi? We have to keep in touch," said Belinda. "You and Tuney have been so much fun, and I really loved meeting you two."

"Oh, Belinda! I'm gonna hate not seeing you guys any more. I know Tuney and I both had such a good time, and you four were the reason. Gosh, I feel like I've known you forever!"

I felt a little despondent thinking that I might not see them again. I'd been so eager to get home, see the kids and get started on my new garden that I hadn't stopped to think about my new friends not being around. I looked over at Tuney and saw she was at the edge of her seat, talking to Trudy and Bonnie, too.

"Well, we four were talking last night. We decided that since we had so much fun on this bus trip, we want to take another one with Amy. If we do, would you and Tuney want to go with us?" asked Tammy. "Please?" She reached between the two seats and grabbed my hand.

I brightened up immeasurably. "What a great idea! I'd love that!" I saw Tuney was nodding her head vigorously. Trudy and Bonnie had just asked her the same thing. She glanced over at me and we both gave a thumb's up. I turned back to Belinda and Tammy.

"Let's plan on it, definitely!" I scrounged around in my purse and handed an old envelope to Tammy. "Please write your phone numbers on here, would you?"

I was surprised when they both started laughing at me. "Girl, you need to get in the 21st century," Tammy chided me jokingly.

When I looked puzzled, Belinda handed me her phone and asked me for mine. "You have phone contacts on here that you've put down, right?"

Oh, duh! "Jeepers, I didn't even think of that. I'd put your emails on my phone." I pointed at my head. "Sorry, guys. I've dyed my hair blonde so many years, I think I've bleached my brain!" While they chuckled, I entered my phone number, email and address into Belinda's phone.

"This makes so much more sense," I sighed as we finished exchanging information. "I won't lose your information now that it's on my phone."

"Just don't lose your phone," warned Tammy, waving her phone at me. "I did once. Thought I'd die. I couldn't call anyone, didn't even know my own kids' phone numbers, and was scared someone would somehow steal information."

"What'd you do?" I asked wide-eyed, and I carefully put my phone in the zippered compartment of my purse.

"Fortunately, my son stopped by that night to check on me when he couldn't reach me. He took his phone out toward the car and dialed my number. It was in my car between the seats! It had probably fallen there when I carried in groceries. Now I have my kids, doctors, and emergency numbers written down..." She started rummaging through her purse. "Somewhere!" and Tammy cocked her head to think. Then she shrugged, giving up the search. "Oh, well. I just won't ever lose my phone again."

I grinned and glanced at Belinda who was making little crazy circles with her finger pointed at Tammy's head. I thought then how much I'd miss everyone and made a promise to myself that Tuney and I would at the very least make a road trip to their town to meet up with them in a few months.

The rest of the time on the trip back to Des Moines was spent re-hashing the trip. Bonnie admitted her favorite part of the trip had been the Dubuque casino.

"Because of BAABA?" I asked straight-faced.

She opened her mouth, shut it quickly and narrowed her eyes, while the rest of us giggled. "No, smarty-pants! Ha-ha!" She opened her purse and pulled a wad of cash out. "Because of this!" Trudy, Tammy and Belinda were surprised.

"Where'd you get that? How much? And when did you get it? " we asked her.

"Slots! One thousand dollars! And I snuck it in when I was with Cardi and Tuney! " She waved the bills around and fanned herself with them "That's why I was so excited to see BAABA. I thought they were ABBA and I was going to buy tickets with this," she said as she stuffed the money back into her wallet and zipped her purse shut tightly, "But now I'm going to use it on our next bus trip!"

"Woo-hoo!" I said. "And if we hit a casino the next time, I'm sticking to you like glue!"

"I've never won anything big in my life," she said delightedly. I couldn't help but feel thrilled for her. Tuney and the others were excited for her, too, and Trudy gave her a hug.

"I just can't believe you kept that a secret," said Trudy. "She's the biggest blabbermouth in the world, you know," she told me and Tuney.

"Oh, I am not!" Bonnie declared, but her eyes were twinkling. "And I did call my daughter and tell her. I had to tell someone!"

We kept on bantering back and forth with each other. Tuney got ribbed about George the ghost. In turn she teased Tammy about getting stuck in the caboose cupola. But before we could run out of things to say to each other, Amy stood up and announced that we'd arrived at the parking lot where we'd all left our cars.

"Ope!" I heard Tuney say. We stood up and hugged each of the 2Bs2Ts, gathered up our purses and grabbed a few shopping sacks from the overhead bins that we hadn't stored underneath the bus.

Amy helped people down off the bus while Stirt was unloading luggage and packages. Tuney and I, as we'd been when we started the trip, were the last ones. Amy grabbed me first, then Tuney, and gave us a big hug.

"All right, dear friends," she said. "Tell me the truth. Are you glad you took this trip? Am I going to have to keep harassing you to take another one?"

"I can't wait until the next trip, Amy!" I said fervently. "When's it going to be? Where's it going to be?"

She smiled. "I don't have the date confirmed yet, so I'll call you. But it's going to be somewhere special, and that's all I'm going to say."

Chapter 30

Home

Tuney looked at me, then looked up to the cloudless blue sky above. "Somewhere special…I've always wanted to go there," she murmured dreamily, then turned to look at me and Amy and grinned.

Amy and I grinned back and looked at each other. "*Blazing Saddles?*" Amy said, referring to the Mel Brooks' movie.

Tuney winked. "Kind of, I guess" she admitted. "Except it was 'nowhere special,' wasn't it?" I nodded. She, Tommy, Kris and I loved that movie and had watched it enough times we could recite practically every line.

"Well, I promise it will be special," said Amy.

Tuney gave her another hug and whispered something into her ear. Amy drew back and stared into Tuney's eyes. "I'm so very, very glad," Amy said softly back to my sister. She leaned in and kissed Tuney's cheek. "You two Widsters take care of each other. And watch out for road-kill on the way home!"

Tuney's eyes got big. "Oh, my lord!" she said, turning to me. One side of her lip. "I totally forgot about the skunk smell. Do you suppose it's gone by now?"

"Ope! I hope so! Otherwise we have a longer time to be with it than we had when we got here!" I wrinkled up my nose in distaste at the memory of the odor.

We got our packages from Stirt, but our arms were so full, he offered to wheel our luggage over to the car. Tuney fumbled for her keys and opened the door.

"I smell something, but it's not too bad," she said hesitantly.

"That's the stupid air freshener you bought, Tune," I said, sniffing lightly. I hadn't wanted to take a deep breath of the skunk if it was still perceptible.

Stirt leaned into the car to take a sniff and laughed. "I think you'll both make it home all right. You might smell a bit pine-y, but that's better than dead-skunk smell any day."

He stepped back and smiled at us. "Hey! And thanks for making the bus laugh, and for making me part of your conversation about losing a loved one," he said. "I wish you Widsters a safe journey home!"

Tuney and I both hugged him. "Same to you, Wid-Bro! Thanks for your help with our shopping bags and luggage." Tuney said. We said goodbye and watched as Stirt and Amy got on the bus.

We crammed suitcases in the rear and carefully arranged our purchases so that anything fragile was protected. We climbed into the front seats and Tuney turned the car on and the air conditioner up to full blast. She sat with her hand still on the key in the ignition, watching as Stirt and Amy pulled away from the parking lot and waiting for the car to cool.

"Tuney, is anything wrong?' I asked after we'd sat quietly for a few more minutes. The car was cooler and I was anxious to get home.

She stared ahead for a second, then turned to me with a smile on her face. "Not a thing. Or at least a lot less than there was before I took this trip. I was just reliving this trip again. Thanks, little sis!"

She backed out of her parking space and began our trip home. "This has been some journey – way more than I bargained for," she said. "I didn't know what to expect."

I was quiet, except to say "Hmmm," and nodded. Then I asked, "If I'm not being snoopy, what did you whisper to Amy?"

She grunted, then replied, "Remember I told Amy that quote about a journey? You know, "Travel far enough, you meet yourself?"

"Yeah. Did you?"

Tuney shrugged. "I told Amy I did. At least I think I met a different version of me.

"Did you like who you met?"

Tuney kept her eyes on the highway but raised her eyebrows. "Of course! C'mon! What's not to like?" She asked lightly.

"About you? Uh, let me count the ways," I teased back.

A few days ago, Tuney would probably have responded to my teasing in a snarky way instead of playfully.

"At first, there was plenty not to like, I admit. And you know I'm sorry for being so grumpy and … well, just plain bitchy." She reached a hand over to me and I squeezed it. She pulled it away only to make a turn. Then she glanced at me again.

"Especially after that rant on the bus, I realized I'm the only personality I have to wake up to, you know? And did I like being sad and irritable most of the time? No." She shook her head emphatically.

"So that quote you told Amy was kind of your mantra during the trip?" I asked, my curiosity piqued.

"Well, I didn't plan on saying it, that's for sure. I don't even know why that popped out of my mouth when I met Amy. But halfway through the trip, I thought maybe I was meeting – or at least *could* meet – a new Tuney." Then she sighed. "I know that sounds so corny!"

I looked straight ahead. "No, not corny at all. I know what you mean, Tune." I looked out my window, then glanced over at her. "We're not the same as we were before we lost Kris and Tommy. But at least we're starting to feel more like people again, instead of just a body full of painful and jumbled-up feelings."

"Yes! I think that's what I want to say!" She glanced at me. "I was a jumbled-up mess. "I'm sorry I wasn't there for you after Kris died."

"Don't be sorry! You and Tommy both were there for me! But you also needed to be there for Tommy."

"Yeah." She sighed and we both were quiet for quite a few minutes. Then Tuney cleared her throat. I was surprised that she wanted to talk so much. The ride home was certainly going to be different than the ride away.

"This trip…I think I needed to get away from home. I needed to make some new friends – friends who understand what I'm going through."

I almost asked what I was, but I kept quiet. I knew what she meant.

"And I needed to find out that I could function outside my comfort zone." She paused. "I haven't told anyone, not the kids or you, but after Tommy died, I'd lose lots of sleep being afraid of noises I'd hear in the night. Just usual creaks and maybe noises from bugs or animals outside. But I was nervous and scared." She paused and then stated with confidence. "Can you believe I met a ghost and I'm not curled up in a fetal position? Now I'm not afraid anymore. Of anything." She looked at me. "Are you?"

I didn't want to tell her that after over two years of praying and wishing, my greatest fear was that I would never dream of Kris; that I feared the pain it caused me every morning I woke up to realize he hadn't been in my mind; and scared that I was almost ready to give up. Instead, I looked at her, smiled, and nodded.

Tuney sighed. "This past year, I feel like I've died a thousand deaths. But I've made it through."

"I know. I'm proud of you." I paused. "I've made it through two now."

"Two years." Tuney sighed again. "Cardi, am I just on an emotional high, or will life really get better?" she asked wistfully.

I could be truthful and say I don't know.

"Yes. Yes, it will, Tuney."

She patted my knee, then said, "I believe you." Then she added, "You know, I'm serious about wanting to go on another bus trip. After all, you only live once!"

I caught my breath sharply, and Tuney looked quickly at me. "What?"

"Oh, nothing, really. It's just that I remembered something. Once, Kris took me to the James Bond movie *You Only Live Twice*. I said something afterwards about it being a good thing Bond could live twice when the rest of us could only live once." I looked over at Tuney and cocked my head slightly as I tried to remember exactly what Kris said. "He tousled my hair, and said, 'Wrong! You get to live every day. You only *die* once.' It didn't mean anything to me at the time. And I'd forgotten he'd ever said that until now."

I looked at Tuney and told her thanks for the reminder. She was staring straight ahead, absorbing what Kris had said to me.

"*Get* to live every day," she repeated. "Wow! If I'd heard that or even thought of it myself, maybe I wouldn't have had that tirade on the bus. I guess I was being selfish. Life is good, isn't it?" She looked at me, and in her eyes, I saw a little bit of steeliness. Or maybe it was tears glistening.

Then I realized the tears were mine.

****

We didn't talk much more after that. I don't know if it was because the three days' worth of walking, talking, laughing and learning were a little too compacted for our sixty-something-year-old brains. But when Tuney dropped me off at my house, I felt exhausted. She helped me carry my suitcases and shopping bags to the front porch. I invited her in, but Tuney said if she didn't get home now, she'd fall asleep standing up. We hugged goodbye and she told me she'd call me in the morning. After I got everything I'd bought dumped inside the front door, I took a shower and went to bed.

I sat on the edge of the bed and stared at Kris's picture that sits on my nightstand. Thinking about him, about life, and about death, I felt very small.

"It's over two years, Sweetheart," I said to him. I waited, listening for his voice to tell me he was proud of me, he loved me, he was okay – even just a hi. But there was only silence. I picked up his picture and kissed it. Turning off my nightstand light, I stretched out on my side of the bed, and stared at the ceiling.

I thought of the bus trip. Each day had passed quickly because we'd had a full itinerary. I decided instead of waiting each day for night to come in the hopes of seeing Kris, I was going to make my own itinerary each day to fill it up. That would be getting to live every day. Kris would be proud I finally understood what he'd said. I sighed and closed my eyes.

A second later, I felt the mattress jostle, and in my tiredness took it as Kris coming to bed. He always sat on the corner to take off his shoes and socks. The bouncing of the bed he caused always irritated me. I sat up to scold him before I realized that it couldn't be him.

But it was. It was my Kris! He stood up, smiled at me, and I cried out. "Oh, Kris! Is it really you?"

He didn't speak, but he nodded his head in affirmation and smiled at me. I saw the crinkles around his eyes that were the laugh lines I so loved. I threw off my covers to run over to him, and ...

I woke up. I was in bed with the covers around me. It was still dark, but I could see that dawn was beginning to break. For a moment I lay still, confused. I hadn't been asleep. Or had I? I closed my eyes again, scared that like so many other dreams, this would evaporate like morning mist when the sun hits it.

Yesterday morning when I'd awakened at the Wash House Room, I'd felt empty and pathetic that I couldn't dream of the man with whom I'd spent most of my life. Now this morning, half an hour later after waking up, the sight of him was still so vivid that my heart was singing. Whether it was a vision or a dream didn't matter. I had seen him. I had spoken to him. I felt peaceful. Contented. Thankful.

I picked up my phone to call Tuney. But before I did, I stared at Kris's picture, then leaned over and kissed it. Tears were streaming down my cheeks, but I was smiling.

Maybe I'd never dream of him again. But I knew he was okay. I knew I was going to okay. I knew his love for me hadn't died when his body had.

And I knew I had told Tuney the right thing – Life really will get better.